ALSO BY JANICE HADLOW

The Other Bennet Sister: A Novel

*A Royal Experiment: Love and Duty, Madness and Betrayal—
the Private Lives of King George III and Queen Charlotte*

Rules of the Heart

Rules of
the Heart

—⁓— A NOVEL

Janice
Hadlow

Henry Holt and Company

New York

Henry Holt and Company
Publishers since 1866
120 Broadway
New York, New York 10271
www.henryholt.com

Henry Holt® and Ⓗ® are registered trademarks of Macmillan Publishing Group, LLC.
EU Representative: Macmillan Publishers Ireland Ltd., 1st Floor, The Liffey Trust
Centre, 117–126 Sheriff Street Upper, Dublin 1, DO1 YC43

Library of Congress Cataloging-in-Publication Data

Names: Hadlow, Janice, author.
Title: Rules of the heart : a novel / Janice Hadlow.
Description: First U.S. edition. | New York : Henry Holt and Company, 2026.
Identifiers: LCCN 2025028502 | ISBN 9781250129468 (hardcover) |
ISBN 9781250129475 (ebook)
Subjects: LCGFT: Romance fiction | Historical fiction | Novels
Classification: LCC PR6108.A354 R85 2026 | DDC 823/.92—dc23/eng/20250617
LC record available at https://lccn.loc.gov/2025028502

Our books may be purchased in bulk for specialty retail/wholesale, literacy,
corporate/premium, educational, and subscription box use. Please
contact MacmillanSpecialMarkets@macmillan.com.

First U.S. Edition 2026

Designed by Gabriel Guma

Printed in the United States of America

10 9 8 7 6 5 4 3 2 1

To Claire, with love and thanks

Rules of the Heart

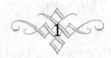

$\mathcal{D}$inner is over. The ladies have left the men at the table and moved into the drawing room. I stand at the door, looking for somewhere to sit. My usual place is taken—I see my old friend Lady Melbourne comfortably established in the chair both she and I know is considered mine. I nod politely, but don't attempt to join her. My spirits are too low to bear the sly cuts and thrusts of her conversation. Instead, I head for a small sofa near the fire—I'm always cold these days.

My head aches. The evening has been too loud, too long, and too crowded with people who don't interest me. I shan't stay much longer. Lord Holland, who's appointed himself my protector for this evening, has gone to find a drink to warm me a little; once I have finished it, I shall call for my carriage and go home.

I never really enjoy myself here anymore. Devonshire House is too full of memories for that; wherever I look, I feel the loss of my sister Georgiana, who presided here for so many years; now that she's gone, it seems to me a subdued and melancholy place, bereft of her sparkling presence. But for those who don't mourn her as I do, it clearly still possesses all its old exhilarating appeal.

As I wait, I notice two young girls edge into the room, clutching each other's arms in a flurry of smiles and excitement. I don't recognize them. They must have been placed a long way from me at the table. Someone's cousins, someone's nieces, the friends of friends of friends? Perhaps it's their first time here. Their behavior certainly suggests they're new to our ways, novices who haven't yet learned that it really isn't done to look about with such undisguised amazement.

Their eagerness to drink it all in makes them forget all discretion. They don't scruple to stare, absorbing every detail of their surroundings—the glittering room, all gold, glass, and candlelight, that shimmers with the promise of adventure. The taller of the two taps her fan nervously against her skirt. So this, then, is the heart of the fashionable world they've read so much about, the vortex of dissipation, as the newspapers once described it? It's clearly everything they've hoped it would be and more. Thrilled, they settle themselves on a pair of stiff chairs at the edge of the room, looking hungrily about them, waiting for something, anything to happen—and then their eager, searching glances come to rest upon me.

I see at once they know who I am, and, from the alteration in their expressions, that they've heard all the stories. I pick up the poker and stir the fire, attempting to appear unmoved, the picture of a sedate, respectable matron. The girls look a little disappointed—but then Lord Holland arrives with my warm wine. This is altogether more promising, and the girls lean forward in anticipation. They watch as he sits down beside me, a bit too close for my liking. His knee is almost touching mine. I move away. He edges a little nearer. I move away once more. He smiles, as if to say, "Well, I shall not insist," and offers me my drink—but as I reach for it, he takes my hand in his and attempts very gently to kiss it. I imagine the girls holding their breath as I pull away from him and calmly shake my head. He shrugs, unperturbed, and begins to chat away with his usual ease, as if nothing at all had happened. I turn away, exasperated—why do men behave like this?—and find myself looking directly into the fascinated gaze of the two young women.

I don't know why I immediately drop my eyes in shame. I've known Lord Holland all my life and never given him the slightest encouragement—it isn't my fault if he can't control himself—but I am the one who is subjected to the full force of their insolent curiosity. I suppose it's the price I pay for my past. A woman who's shown herself indifferent to the rules that govern respectable society must expect to experience a thousand such petty humiliations, especially if she's no longer young. I should be used to it by now; but there's something in the girls' shocked delight that cuts me to the quick. What a coup for them, on their first outing into high society, to have been thrown into the company of Harriet Bessborough, a woman of such dubious reputation! And how extraordinary to have seen her in action, as it were, brushing away the attentions of a man—a married man too—with as little concern as if she were swatting a fly.

I decide I shan't give them the satisfaction of knowing they have disconcerted me. Instead, I sit up a little straighter, and in doing so, catch sight of Lady Melbourne in my corner. I see now why she was so keen to hide away there. Her latest young suitor—he can't be more than twenty—has drawn a stool up to her chair and leans toward her, desperate for some proof of her notice. A look, a smile, a playful flick of her fan on his arm, anything will do. Oh, these desperate youthful acolytes! How painfully they crave any recognition from experienced women of the world. This young man would do anything for the privilege of being counted among Lady M's acknowledged admirers. She must be at least thirty years older than he, but isn't the least embarrassed by his earnest supplications. If those young girls had turned their inquiring gaze upon her, she wouldn't have quailed and looked away as I did, but would have returned it with such an imperious stare that they'd have gathered up their skirts and slunk off, afraid she might rise up and box their ears.

But then Lady Melbourne is exactly who they think she is, and quite unashamed to own it. I've known her since my very first entry into society, long enough to understand the qualifications she looks for in an attachment. I doubt this particular young man has much of a chance with her, as he is neither wealthy nor grand enough for her tastes. She's always chosen her lovers with a frank pragmatism—she's often told me it's just as easy to surrender to a rich man as to a poor one. It's said the Earl of Egremont paid Lord Coleraine £13,000 for the transfer of her favors, with Lady M herself taking a hefty cut from the fee; and certainly, both she and her family have done very well from her judicious bestowing of her affections. Promotions, sinecures, that invisible influence that smooths the progress of sons and enhances the prospects of daughters—her liaisons always come with some worldly advantage attached. None of them touches her very deeply, leaving barely a ripple on the smooth surface of her life. It's a matter of great pride to her that she is mistress of her emotions; she thinks much less of me for being, as she puts it, such a sad slave to mine. I have allowed my heart to rule my head throughout my life, and what, she asks, have I to show for it? Can I say I am more secure or more respected than she is? Can I even say I am happier?

Once I would have smiled at her arguments, telling myself she spoke as she did because she'd never known real love. I never disputed that I had chosen the harder path—a great passion is by its nature stormy and disruptive. It brings with it as much pain as pleasure, turns your life upside down, spins you this way and that until you hardly recognize yourself anymore. But for all this, I believed most fervently that the joys of a great love far outweighed its miseries—and that not to have experienced it was not to have truly lived. Yes, there was a price to be paid, but for most of my life I never begrudged it. Now I'm not so sure. When I compare her situation with my own, I wonder if she wasn't right all along. Increasingly, I find myself envying her sleek, unruffled satisfaction with her lot. Her indifference to the siren calls of love certainly seems to have protected her from everything I have suffered—and continue to suffer, to this day.

Perhaps I should have worked harder at toughening up my heart. God knows, I've had long enough to try. Men have been snapping at my heels since I was barely out of the schoolroom, and even now, when I am fifty-one years old, too fat for fashion, my beauty all gone, my children married, a grandmother twice over—with all that to dissuade them, still they won't leave me alone. Lord Holland is only one of four men who are currently trying their luck—two of the others are young enough to be my sons. I suppose the knowledge of my having had lovers in the past encourages them to think I might be persuaded to do so again; but five minutes in my company ought to be enough to show them the fallacy of that idea. Surely my dejection must be enough to convince even the least observant of them that I have nothing to offer them now.

It wasn't always so. I've always had a desperate hunger for affection, yearning for the chance to lose myself entirely in my feelings for another human being, to unite myself with a lover so completely that we would be as one, in body, heart, and mind. I have been searching for this consummation my whole life through—and for a while I believed I'd found it. When I least expected it, when I honestly believed it was too late, I met a man who lit up my life and touched my very soul. He triggered in me a passion so great that I instantly understood everything I had felt before was only a pale shadow of real love. In his arms, I found at last what I had sought for so long, and for seventeen years, I loved him more than life itself.

Under the power of that love, I gave up everything I once thought valuable—loyalty, honor, pride, and dignity, all domestic happiness, even my own self-respect. I did so gladly, in thrall to a passion I couldn't resist. It was both wonderful and terrible, leading me to the very brink of ruin, and the worst of it is that, even knowing what I do now, even after all the suffering I've endured, if he asked me to do it all again, I cannot be sure I'd refuse him.

I shiver a little at these painful recollections, and Lord Holland offers to find my shawl. Once he's gone, I sit silently with my thoughts. I used to meet my lover in this very room, waiting for him in the chair where Lady Melbourne now entertains her young friend. Sometimes we could risk only a few minutes together—we were always obliged to be so very careful—but he would contrive to brush my fingers with his, and I— Well, even now my heart leaps at the memory of his touch. I must put a stop to this. He is gone now, never to return; and all that is left to me is recollection and remorse. It's been over two years since the final blow fell, and I'm still reeling from it. I'd hoped time would ease the pain; but instead, it's only brought with it a different kind of suffering. All I think of now is what did it all mean? I used to tell him I would have gladly died to make him happy, and believed it too—but were his feelings ever as strong as mine for him? Were they ever as strong as mine for him? Once I thought so—but now, as I sit here alone, knowing I will never feel his touch again—I'm not sure what I believe about the strength of his love.

At this, I feel familiar tears well up threateningly in my eyes. I don't allow them to fall, but know I must take my leave if I'm not to embarrass myself. When Lord Holland returns, I say I'm tired and must go home. He's all concern and orders my carriage. When it's ready, he takes my hand, and this time I don't resist as he raises me from the sofa and leads me out of the room, his arm entwined in mine. He looks pleased, as if he's achieved some small but satisfying triumph. The two girls watch silently as we pass, delighted to have witnessed our little spectacle. They don't mean to be cruel, but they're young, and that makes them heartless. Never having suffered themselves, they're blind to what others are forced to endure.

Suddenly all my anger with them dissolves and is replaced by a kind of pity. They're so innocent, wide-eyed, and vulnerable. They have no idea at all of what lies waiting for them in the world. It occurs to me that one day, when I am long dead, they may be sitting somewhere, just as I was tonight, older and wiser, buffeted and beaten about by life and love, unable to meet the beady, disapproving eyes of their granddaughters. Then they'll understand. It isn't a kind thought, but it makes me smile, and I'm almost calm as I walk through the shining bright rooms and out into the darkness beyond.

I sit in my carriage alone, having finally persuaded Lord Holland that I did not require his company on my short journey home. I'm very melancholic—I've pulled my grief around me as one does an old shawl—it's unbecoming and uncomfortable, but I'm so used to it that I can't give it up. Soon I'm torturing myself in the old familiar way once more, poring over the same obsessions again and again. Was there a moment when I should have seen his affection drawing away from me, like the waves retreating from the shore, leaving me stranded and alone on the sands? How else to explain the particular way it all ended, the shock of the choice he made, which I, who thought I'd imagined every possible manner of our parting, never saw coming.

Only he could answer any of these questions, and I could never speak of such things to him now. The old connection between us, which I used to believe unbreakable, is quite altered. When we speak or correspond, we restrict ourselves to the careful language of friendship. I sense he's determined never to go beyond that, and I've tried to abide by his rules. If I did find the courage to ask what I long to know, I'm not sure I could trust him to tell the truth. Like most men, he's wary of examining the history of his affections. Now his feelings for me are mild and manageable, he doesn't care to admit they were once very different. I suspect he's consigned such memories to some part of his mind where they are firmly locked up, never to be considered except when briefly plucked out of their hiding place, greeted with a wry sigh, and given a little polish before being safely returned to their confinement once more.

No, there's really no chance I'd learn much about what he felt for me from the man he is now. It's his younger self I long to speak to, the person he was when he seemed to want me so much. I see him for a moment in my mind's eye as he was then—more beautiful than anyone I've ever known, perfection in human form—and my heart beats a little faster at the memory of his leaning in to kiss me. What would I ask, if I were to find myself in *that man's* presence once more? What questions would I pose, what evidence would I seek, to help me understand what our affair had really meant to him?

I know, of course, that this is impossible. No matter how much we long for it, we can't go backward; all we have to rely upon is our memories, uncertain and partial as they are. Then suddenly, out of nowhere, a thought strikes me. The man he used to be is indeed gone forever—but I still have something of him from that time, a testament of sorts to what he once thought and felt for me. I have his letters—over seventeen years of them, from the moment of our first meeting to the final breaking of the news I thought would kill me. We were often apart during the long years of our affair, and writing was our only means of maintaining the connection between us. We were obliged to take the greatest care of what we wrote, for discovery, the threat of which constantly loomed over us, would have ruined me—but despite the risk we were always candid, as frank and as open in what we said to each other on paper as we were in person.

Why hadn't I thought of this before? All those hundreds and hundreds of letters—surely they could illuminate the truth of what had passed between us? If I could find the courage to look upon them once more—then I should hear his voice as it used to be—hear him make once more the passionate declarations that had broken down my resistance, hear him tell me how much he was determined to possess me, body and soul, how happy I made him, how all he wanted was for the pair of us to be together as one. What should I think of them now, knowing as I do how matters ended? Perhaps I should see, with a clarity my grief currently denies me, how his sentiments shifted over the years, how our connection had changed, creaking and groaning under the weight of all the subterfuges and betrayals that are inevitable in a guilty affair like ours? And finally—if I could steel myself to read them all—after such a thorough unearthing of the past, I might reach some conclusions about the strength and meaning of his attachment to me.

I didn't imagine such an undertaking would bring me much comfort—there'd be too much remorse, too much regret involved to expect that. But if I couldn't hope for solace, I might gain some understanding of what I once was to him, which I think is all I can really hope for now. And if I proved myself capable of even that small step—well, could resignation to my fate be far behind? And really, that's all I long for now, the chance to heal, even a little, the wound of his loss, which pains me constantly through my empty days and keeps me awake through all my sleepless nights—any state of mind would be preferable to this.

I know very well that if I embark on this course it won't be achieved without pain—uncovering a past like mine is bound to bring in its wake as much misery as joy—but if, in the end, it leaves me at greater peace with myself—then, whatever it costs, it must be preferable to remaining as I am now.

Some of his letters, a very few, I burned on his instructions; but the rest I kept, locked into a large cedarwood box that is always in my possession. The only other person allowed charge of it is my maid Sally, who knows all my sad history and whom I would trust with my life.

She has the box at present, stowed away in some secret place. After we parted, I couldn't bear to open it—even a few scribbled lines in his dear familiar hand were enough to bring tears to my eyes. The thought of opening it once more frightens and excites me in pretty equal measure. But, as the carriage turns into Cavendish Square and arrives at our house, I've resolved in my mind to take the risk. The coachman reins in the horses, we draw to a halt, and Mr. Peterson, our butler and my dear Sally's husband, hands me out of the carriage, warning me to take care of that final step to the pavement. I hurry through the front door, stopping for moment in the hall to ask if my husband is at home. Once I learn he's out, I rush up the staircase to my bedroom. By the time I'm safely within, I'm already planning how I'll arrange everything. I'll begin tomorrow, I tell myself, before my determination wavers. There's nothing to be gained by delay.

In my bedroom, Sally is waiting. We don't say much to each other at first; she's been with me for so long—nearly thirty years—that our regular routines don't require much in the way of words. She helps me undress, sits me down, and begins to take down my hair. She came into my service when she was only fourteen, a bright-eyed Derbyshire girl, trained up at Chatsworth, where my sister quickly spotted her deft fingers and lively mind, and thought she might do well for me. I was only twenty-two myself when we first met, but was astute enough to recognize her value and hired her immediately. She's never left my side since. Together, she and John Peterson have run our household for what seems like forever. They had no children; I've never presumed to ask Sally her feelings on this, and she isn't the kind of person to volunteer her thoughts on the subject; but she has been like a second mother to my own three sons and daughter, all of whom love her almost as much as I do myself.

Only when she's removed the last pin do I tell her about my plan to read his letters. I don't hesitate to confide in her. She's stood loyally beside me through all the passionate highs and despairing lows of my long affair; there's virtually no secret she doesn't know, no truth I haven't entrusted to her. She's cared for me tirelessly through the worst times, dosing me with laudanum when sleep would not come, always at hand when I needed her most, supporting me when there was no one else to whom I could turn. She is far, far more to me than merely a servant—I count her as my friend, perhaps the most staunch and unswerving one I have. We have been through so much together that I truly believe she knows me better than anyone else on earth. For all these reasons, I value her judgment more highly than that of many people of my own station in life—and am a little disappointed to see, from her purse-lipped reflection in the dressing-table mirror, that she doesn't like the idea at all.

"You don't approve?"

"No, I do not."

She begins to brush my hair, long strokes, steady and sure; but I feel her mounting displeasure in the changing rhythm of her brushing, quicker and more impatient.

"I can't see what good it will do. It will only reawaken the most painful memories. Wouldn't it be better to leave it alone?"

"I agree it's a risk." I pick up a ribbon from the dressing table and wind it around my fingers. "But I truly believe it might bring me some some relief. Or resignation, if you like."

She puts down her brush. I see she is very unhappy.

"I'm afraid it will be too much for you—that you won't be able to endure it."

"Perhaps I'm stronger than you think?"

"I do most sincerely wish you'd leave it alone."

I turn to look at her. "Why? Are you afraid I won't like what I find? That I'll discover he never really loved me? That it all meant nothing?"

She pauses for a moment and puts down the brush. I know her feelings for him are not the warmest. She understood how happy he made me, what joy and excitement he brought me in the good times; but she saw for herself, at firsthand, the misery and despair into which the bad times plunged me; and these, I believe, have always weighed heavier than the joy in the forming of her cool opinion of him.

"That's not something I can answer. I can't say what he felt, only that I doubt you'll find what you're hoping for. I don't think a man can ever say when and why he stopped loving you, any more than he can tell you why he began in the first place. They don't give it enough thought for that. I fear you'll cause yourself a great deal of pain and have nothing to show for it at the end."

"So what would you have me do instead?"

"Why, the only thing you can do. Bear the pain as best you can until it starts to go away. It does in the end, so they say."

"I only wish that was true. The passing of time hasn't remotely dulled the pain of losing him, and it's done nothing to ease my grief for Georgiana. She's been dead for six years now, and I still regret her loss just as bitterly as I did on the day she died."

Sally sighs. She knows how deeply I miss my sister.

"And anyway," I continue, "I don't think I have it in me to be so patient, waiting for some promised solace that never arrives. And even if you're right, and I discover nothing in the letters to my liking—I can hardly be in a worse place than I am now."

"Well, if I can't make you think again, may I at least offer one final piece of advice?"

I nod, uncertainly.

"I don't want to make it about him alone." Her tone is both brisk and pressing, as if this is one point she's determined to land. "He already has enough power over you. If all you do is take the measure of *his* affections—worrying away at what he thought, at how he felt—you're only adding to his importance, giving *him* the last word."

I see she's agitated now. She picks up the brush, plays with it, shifting it from hand to hand.

"If you really want to achieve this understanding you talk of, this resignation you say is the purpose of it all—then you must put yourself in the picture as plainly as he. Your feelings in the matter—they're just as important as his. You'll never arrive at anything approaching the truth if you don't think them worthy of consideration. It's your story too, you know. Don't let the strength of his attachment—was it this, was it that—stand as the last word upon it. It's as much for you to say as it is for him."

I'm so moved I can't speak. I reach over and take her hand.

"I'm sorry," she says, "if I spoke too plain, but that's what I think."

Lying sleepless in bed later that night, I feel the truth of Sally's words. I must not forget I played my own vital part in our affair; and although it is the state of his heart that preoccupies me just now, I must be equally willing to explore the workings of my own. I mustn't shrink from asking myself what it all meant for me. What was it all for, this grand passion to which I gave myself up so eagerly? Was it worth everything I suffered? And now that it is over, how am I to think of it? With pride at those moments of transcendence? Or shame at the betrayals at which I connived?

I sometimes believe few people appreciate better than I do how opaque and mysterious are the wellsprings of love; if that sounds like boasting, let me be clear it is nothing of the kind. I'm not to be envied for this knowledge; it has been acquired through bitter experience. But I remain convinced that no attempt to understand the workings of the human heart is ever wasted—and in that spirit alone, I know it is impossible I should not tell Sally to have the box in readiness for me to begin. I should think of it as nothing less than a reckoning with my past—one that, God knows, is much overdue.

When I come back to my room the next morning after breakfast, the cedarwood box is waiting for me. I close the curtains, bolt the door, and open the box. Inside is bundle after bundle of letters, stacked carefully. Most are from him, and these I have arranged chronologically; some, I have even marked with numbers, for I am a methodical creature, in my housekeeping if not in other aspects of my life. I reach into the box and take out one or two close to the top. Here are letters, written in different hands, from the people closest to me—from my sister Georgiana, my brother, my dearest friends— all sharing this hiding place because, like his letters, they contain thoughts and confessions too private to be seen by anyone but me.

I pick out a note at random—and when I see it is from my sister, tears spring immediately into my eyes. I can't recall a time when I did not adore her, with an affection so profound that our mother used to laugh and say that if Georgiana asked me to jump into the lake, I would only beg to know how high I should leap and how far I was to swim. She was quite right—I was Georgiana's devoted disciple, in awe of her beauty, her wit, and her charm, and wanted nothing more from life than to be allowed to stand mutely at her side as she took possession of all our society could offer—wealth, position, power, and fame, all of which I considered no more than her due.

Before he came into my life, she was without doubt the person I loved best in the world. I wipe my eyes with my sleeve, like the little girl I once was, then kiss the letter gently and return it to the box. As I do so, I catch sight of something I don't recognize—a small envelope, still tightly sealed, with a single line of writing upon it. I extract it and draw it closer to my face—my sight, of which I was once so proud, is no longer what it was—and recognize my own handwriting, the ink much faded now. Angling it toward the light, I see it's no more than a terse inscription—"Naples, 1794." I feel something inside, but when I scrabble to open the envelope, I find it's been so tightly sealed that I'm obliged to fetch a knife and cut it. Inside is a small bunch of dried leaves, bound together in a plait of green ribbon. As I raise them to my face, for a moment I catch their scent—the spicy aroma of bay, thyme, basil, and others I can't make out, the strong unmistakable fragrance of the herbs and plants of the south. Their bouquet doesn't stay in the air for long—these dried remnants were cut a long time ago, and once they're released from their hiding place, their perfume soon dissipates. But it lasts just long enough to transport me back to the time and place where everything began—where my life was changed forever, where everything I thought I knew about myself dissolved before my eyes, where I began the journey that led me, with many twists and turns, to the place I am now. It takes me back, in short, to the moment of our first meeting, to my first encounter with the man who was the great love of my life.

Holding the little packet in my hand, I lay myself on my bed, moving slowly as if I've had some serious shock—and indeed, I do feel as though all the breath has gone out of me. I've heard it said that smell is the sense that, above all others, can summon up the most powerful memories—that there is something visceral, beyond rational thought, in its ability to return us to the past. And indeed, as I close my eyes, the little fragments of herbs clasped tightly in my hands, I feel the truth of this. The familiar furniture of my room, the everyday sounds of our house in the morning, the gray-clouded London weather beyond my window—all of them disappear, just as when the scenery is shifted at the theater to announce the next act, and suddenly I am somewhere else. I see clear blue skies, warm sunlight on green hills, a turquoise sea now and then in view, the whole country illuminated by that clarity of light only to be found in Italy.

For that is where my thoughts have taken me, far, far away from the low rainy damp of England. And I am myself changed just as thoroughly as the landscape. Nearly twenty years have dropped away from me. In my mind's eye, in this instant, as it has sprung so powerfully into my recollection, I'm thirty-three, bowling along in a carriage on the coastal road that skirts Naples, on my way to visit a friend of whom my husband disapproves. I understand his misgivings—Lady Webster is a formidable young woman of strong opinions, married to a man she hates, and whom she has every intention of divorcing as soon as she can. The fact that she was at that time carrying his baby made no difference at all to her determination to be free of him. She has no patience with conventional pieties, and, as a result, her enemies—of whom her bluntness has ensured she has a great number—say she has no morals at all. This wasn't entirely untrue, but nonetheless I like her. As is common with timid, uncertain natures like my own, I'm drawn to her strength and bravado. I am, in truth, no happier in my marriage than she was in hers; but she refuses to be the victim of her circumstances. Instead, she'd resolved to take control of her future, and I envy her courage, even as she sometimes frightens me a little.

When I arrived at her villa, she was very pleased to see me. We settled ourselves on an airy terrace, which overlooked the wooded valley that led down to the sea, basking in the fresh spring breezes and drinking the squeezed juice of the sweet little oranges picked from the trees below us, which are never to be had at home. We talked for a while of those subjects women tend to discuss when one of them is with child and no man is present; but Lady Webster soon tired of that.

"We must find some more suitable topic to discuss before my other visitor arrives. I've invited a gentleman to join us. He arrived here not long ago and was kind enough to sit and chat with me the other night, when everyone else at the assembly was dancing."

"That shows great consideration on his part."

"Yes, it disposed me to like him, and I did."

The brightness of the sun, the cheerful birdsong, the general air of pleasurable lassitude encouraged me to be playful.

"Perhaps he's a candidate to replace your current husband?" I inquired archly. "When the time is right, of course."

"Oh no," she replied calmly, not in the least resenting the question. "For one thing he's a second son, and I should dearly like a title, if it can be managed. It will take off the stain of divorce a little, you see. And, besides, he's far too proud a man to put himself under my direction—and I do want a man who won't mind being led a little."

She rubbed her back and let out a little sigh. I remembered only too well how it felt to be burdened as she was now. I pitied her, at the same time sincerely hoping I should never find myself in her condition again. Four children—and three of those sons—were enough to complete any family, in my opinion.

"I believe you'll like him, though. I wouldn't have asked him if I'd thought otherwise."

"May I know this gentleman's name?"

Lady Webster laughed. "I think it will be far more interesting if I don't tell you in advance. I'd like to see what you make of him— hear your impressions afterward, with no prior expectations fixed in your mind."

I frowned. This seemed a foolish conceit, and I protested I would be at a great disadvantage if I was to know nothing of this person I was shortly to meet.

"I assure you, he's quite respectable—it's just a little tease on my part. Consider how few pleasures I can enjoy in this sad state and indulge me a little."

What could I do but give in to her whim? But her insistent prohibition had exactly the effect she'd intended, of making me intensely curious about this anonymous stranger.

It was half an hour before he arrived, ushered toward us onto the terrace by Lady Webster's servant. I saw before me a tall, self-possessed young man in a loose pale coat, carrying a large straw hat. When he made his bow to us, it was done as gracefully as I have ever seen it performed, a single lithe movement, without fuss or awkwardness. Lady Webster smiled, clearly more than satisfied with her guest, gesturing languidly in my discretion.

"May I present to you, sir, Harriet, Countess of Bessborough?"

I inclined my head with a gracious smile. I noticed now that he was dark haired and broad shouldered, with an athlete's figure, and eyes of a startlingly bright blue.

"And Harriet," continued Lady Webster, eager to finish the formalities and reveal the name of her prize, "let me introduce you to Lord Granville Leveson-Gower."

He bowed once more, holding my glance for a fraction longer than I had expected.

"I apologize for appearing before you both as though I have been tramping the hills," he began, "but as that is indeed what I have been doing, I hope you'll forgive me. In this climate, morning really is the best time to walk, the earlier the better."

"Are you a great walker, then, sir?" I asked.

"Yes," he replied, "but only on my own terms. I like to go fast and I like to go alone. Then I can roam wherever I wish, as far and as freely as possible."

"Remind me never to offer myself up as your companion, then," Lady Webster observed tartly. "Even when not in my current condition, my idea of a good walk is a slow stroll around a flower garden. I should be quite the wrong partner for you."

He nodded, as if to convey he appreciated the truth of that remark, in both its immediate and more general application; and then entered upon a description of everything he'd encountered on his excursion—the dappled light breaking over the trees, the air so pure just before daybreak, the thrill of reaching a lofty vantage point in time to see the sun rising over the distant sea, all truly incomparable.

"And what about you, Lady Bessborough? Your friend has no wish to see them, but shouldn't you like to see such marvels for yourself?"

"Indeed I would—nothing moves me more than the beauties of nature—but, like Lady Webster, I fear arriving at them would be beyond my powers. I am not such a mountain goat as you seem to be, Lord Granville."

He smiled, fixing me once more in his intense blue gaze.

"Then perhaps I might ask how you amuse yourself down here on the ground, as I hear from Lady Webster you've been in Naples for some time."

"Well," I began, "the weather is charming, the people welcoming, and there's a great deal to see. The classical remains are particularly striking."

I sounded like a girl at her first ball, nervously mouthing the blandest social pleasantries. He, on the other hand, was completely at his ease.

"I'd very much like to hear which ruins you feel are most deserving of a visit. Do tell me something of those you particularly enjoyed."

The conversation that followed couldn't have been more commonplace, but I was distracted, uneasy in both body and mind, like a dog who senses thunder coming and prowls about warily without knowing why. Soon we were deep in conversation, debating the merits of Herculaneum over Pompeii, or Paestum. But all the time we were speaking, my thoughts were elsewhere. As discreetly as I could, I was drinking in every tiny detail of Lord Granville's appearance. His hair, which he wore tied back in a queue, was a rare true black, with the slight sheen of blue found in a swallow's feathers. The contrast between the inky darkness of the curls that framed his face, and those extraordinary eyes—would they best be described as azure or turquoise?—was like nothing I'd ever seen before. Clear skin, with a slight tinge of the sun from his morning walk, set off to great advantage a full red mouth. When I found myself wondering how it might feel to be kissed by those lips, I came to my senses. I was horrified at myself. What was I doing? How could I have been so bold as to assess a man in this way, feature by feature, as if he were a piece of art to be admired? To cover up the blush I felt rising into my face, I took a sip from my glass and turned toward Lady Webster, as if nothing could be of more interest than whatever she might say next.

"We English do indeed enjoy sightseeing," she observed, "but as you'll soon discover, it's far from our only occupation. It's often said—and with much justice, in my opinion—that the favorite pursuits of the English in Naples are gambling and gallantry."

"Both at the same time?" replied Lord Granville gravely. "That must require considerable application on everyone's part."

"As you don't believe me, I see I must appeal to Lady Bessborough to confirm the truth of what I say. Come, Harriet, is it not so?"

"Not in my case. I vowed that I should gamble no more. It's too seductive a vice for me, and I've promised myself I'd never surrender to it again. And I'm afraid I'm too old and too wise now to indulge in any kind of gallantry."

Lord Granville inclined his head politely.

"You must have many admirers who'd be sorry to hear you're so immovable on that point."

Once again, I feared I might blush; and before I could conjure up some appropriately dismissive retort, Lady Webster leaped in.

"As to gambling," she began in her archest tone, "I hear you are yourself no stranger to the tables, Lord Granville. That when you were in Paris not long ago you were a great frequenter of them, winning and losing considerable sums with the same apparent indifference."

"I admit I'm guilty as charged," he replied. "I've indulged far more than I should have done and won't quarrel with Lady Bessborough as to gambling's many perils. But surely"—and he turned that brilliant smile upon me once more—"a little gallantry is different: it does no one any real harm, providing it's no more than an innocent flirtation?"

"I'm not sure gallantry can ever be truly innocent," I said in my primmest tone. "Even if it begins as such, it rarely remains so. Flirtations are fraught with misunderstanding. I've come to believe that between men and women, the only truly innocent choice is friendship."

"Then I very much hope that I shall be permitted to become your friend."

"I'm sure we shall see a great deal of each other if you plan to stay for a while. The English here are a small circle, and we soon come to know each other very well."

He nodded; and after a few more pleasantries, declared he must leave us—he was engaged for a fencing lesson and must not be late. Lady Webster rose, insisting she must accompany him to the door, and despite his protestations, would not be denied. I watched him walk away, with the easy confident air of one who is used to being looked at. I sat for a few moments, gazing into the garden but seeing nothing, wondering why I was so disturbed by his presence. Then— suddenly—he was back, smiling at me once more.

"I forgot my hat."

He swept it from the chair where he had hung it, and leaned toward me.

"I should like to call on you sometime, if you have no objection."

I was taken aback by his directness; but I kept my voice steady. "Lord Bessborough and I will be pleased to receive you."

"So that you don't forget—I'd like to give you something as an aide-mémoire. I wish I had something better to offer—but all I have is this." He pulled from his coat pocket a small bunch of green sprigs—herbs and leaves, all with the fresh scent of the hills. "If I'd have known I was meeting you, I'd have tried to find some flowers."

He held out the little bundle; I hesitated for a moment—and then I took them.

He smiled that brilliant smile once more, bowed, and walked away. It was the plainest, smallest gift imaginable—but we both understood the significance of my accepting it. Had I really believed what I'd said about flirtations, I would never have done so. But instead, I placed it in the pocket of my gown, where Lady Webster should not see it.

A moment later, she was back in the room, delighted with both her guest and her little deception.

"So you see now why I wanted you to meet him without knowing in advance who he was?"

I confessed I did not.

"Oh, really. Lord Granville is generally believed to be the best-looking man in England. I thought if I named him, you would know what to expect, and I wanted to hear your opinion of him, entirely untainted by his reputation."

I wasn't sure what to say. I could hardly confess I thought him the most beautiful man I'd ever seen.

"Do you think him as handsome as most other ladies do?"

demanded Lady Webster. "They throw themselves at him in droves, by all accounts."

I protested I didn't think this was an entirely proper conversation for us to continue—in truth, I did not wish to be pressed any further on the impression he had left upon me. But Lady Webster was relentless, and eventually I capitulated.

"I agree he is very well-looking."

"He was quite a sensation when he first appeared in London. You've been so long out of England that it must have been after you left. He's only been in society for about a year, for before that, he was still at university."

I looked up, surprised.

"He's still very young, then?"

"He's twenty-one, if you count that as young."

Twenty-one. Twelve years younger than I. And I had taken such brazen pleasure in admiring him. I knew there were many women of my age who would have seen nothing wrong in enjoying such youthful beauty, who had happily taken younger lovers for themselves. But I had never counted myself among them. I'd always considered myself not much influenced by male good looks—it was wit and intelligence that drew my attention. So I was extremely shocked by the strength of the attraction I'd felt for Lord Granville. I'd never been so moved by the physical presence of a man, and certainly not by one so young. I was thoroughly unsettled and couldn't bear to be interrogated any further by Lady Webster. Thanking her for the introduction, I pleaded exhaustion and bid her a brisk goodbye.

When I arrived back at our villa, I found my husband admiring a purchase he'd made that morning. Lord Bessborough—or Lord B, as I've always called him—was an avid collector of art, particularly of the great Italian masters, and pleasure in his new acquisition had clearly put him into an extremely good mood. Over more than a decade of marriage, I'd learned to welcome and indulge the sunshine of his good temper whenever it appeared, and I readied myself to do so now. Smiling with pride, he beckoned me over to the table upon which his latest treasure was laid and gestured toward it admiringly.

"It's a drawing of the famous statue of Antinous—do you recall his story, Harriet? He was the young friend of the emperor Hadrian—his companion in the classical way, if you understand me."

I looked more closely—and saw a beautifully shaped head on broad shoulders, a strong, proud face, the severity of whose finely chiseled cheekbones and jaw contrasted with a full, soft mouth. His hair curled, in the Roman style, over his brow.

"You understand why I had to have it?" my husband said softly. "Something as beautiful as this?"

I looked again. The eyes were blind white marble, but I felt that in life they must have been blue—a deep, sapphire blue, ready to pierce the heart of anyone who looked at them for too long. For this perfect young man, who carried his beauty with such easy assurance, though dead for over a thousand years, was the very image of Granville Leveson-Gower, who had sat opposite me this morning on Lady Webster's sunlit terrace.

"It wasn't cheap," said my husband as he carefully returned the image to a soft leather envelope, "but can you see why I was so tempted? Why couldn't I resist?"

"Oh yes," I replied calmly. "No one could look upon beauty like this and not be tempted."

He smiled, pleased with my approval. Hot, tired, and desperate to rest, I longed for nothing so much as to lie down for a few hours in the coolness of my room. When I flung myself on my bed, I felt something pricking at my side—and pulled from my dress the little bunch of herbs Lord Granville had given me. I held it to my face for a moment, breathing in its perfume. I went to my drawer, pulled out a ribbon, and tied the leaves together before sealing them tight in the smallest envelope I could find. Then I took my pen and wrote upon it: "Naples, 1794." For I think I knew even then that this was a moment worth marking, that something of the greatest importance had begun.

⸰⸰⸰

*B*ack in the gray present, still holding the little envelope in my hand, I arise from my bed, wander toward the window, and gaze absently into the rainswept street below, trying to put myself into the head of the woman I was on that warm Naples morning. Certainly, I was no prim little innocent. I'd been raised in the heart of the fashionable world and was no stranger to its relaxed ways. I knew its rules, understood very well how its little games were to be played—indeed, I was the veteran of several ill-judged ventures into infidelity myself. I knew the risks and had seen for myself what happened to the woman who played her hand badly—the divorce or separation that followed the exposure of her transgression, the loss of her children, the life of exile and remorse. I couldn't then claim to be ignorant of what it would mean to respond to the mutual attraction I had sensed between me and Lord Granville.

I knew only too well what I should have done—thrown his wild bouquet out of the window, refused his request to visit me, allowed myself to see him only in public places, permitted nothing to pass between us but the occasional piquant flirtation, until he grew bored and found some other, more accommodating lady to please him.

I tried to hold myself to this excellent plan—but when I look back, I'm forced to confess that my attempts to do so were more than a little half-hearted. The truth was, I wanted to see him again. I wanted to know him better, to discover who he was, to find out if his character would turn out to be as appealing as his looks. I'd never have admitted it, not even to myself, but I rather hoped I hadn't mistaken the keenness of his interest in me. Not because I was looking for a serious affair; no, that wasn't at all what I sought.

A little flattering attention, especially from so striking and desirable a quarter—the sense that I was still worthy of admiration, that I might be desired by such a man—the knowledge, indeed, that someone thought me lovable—these were ideas that weakened my resolve to turn on my heel and see him no more.

I understand now that I was extremely lonely when we first met. With the exception of my children, I felt as if there was no one who cared for me as much as I did them. Mine has always been a very affectionate character; I am open and generous in conveying my emotions to others—too generous, some would say—and I long for them to be reciprocated with equal warmth. Yet somehow, they never were—or at least, that's how it felt to me. Even as a child, I yearned to be cherished and prized, but realized very early that my parents always felt more for my brilliant sister than they did for me. I never resented this, for who wouldn't prefer the extraordinary Georgiana to my undistinguished, unremarkable self?

Whether it was the openness of their preference, or merely a trick of my hungry, needful nature, the result was the same—I was always unsatisfied, always craving an affection that was somehow withheld. I can't remember a time when I didn't long most desperately, not just to offer up my own love to some deserving object, but to know my sentiments were entirely and ardently returned. That and that alone, I came to believe, would make me truly happy. Without it, I should always feel myself incomplete—there was a void within me, which nothing but a great passion, one in which my lover and I were equals in desire, would fully satisfy. When I met Lord Granville, I'd been seeking this emotional consummation for so long and been so often disappointed that I'd all but given up on ever finding it. I'd resigned myself to a half-life without it; so, I couldn't have been more vulnerable to the power of his attraction, even if at first I thought it would amount to little more than a pleasant distraction from my deep-seated disappointment. Where I came to know him better and recognized the depth of what we felt for each other, I became even more susceptible to the possibility he offered. The knowledge that this might be the last chance to achieve your greatest desire—to connect at last with the love of your life—contributes greatly to the strength of its appeal.

So I would never attempt to deny how strongly my own wishes and desires helped propel me into our affair. But in justice to myself, I should add that if I'd found the affection I hoped for in the place it was supposed to reside—within my marriage—then matters might have turned out very differently. I made a terrible mistake in the most important choice that faces a woman—that of choosing a spouse— and suffered for it, often severely, for more years than I care to recall.

I was born a Spencer, the daughter of an earl, into a family of wealth, property, and a great deal of privilege; so, inevitably, as my sister and I grew into our teens, there was much speculation about whom we would marry. Georgiana was often pursued, but it came as no surprise to me when she effortlessly hooked probably the biggest fish in the matrimonial sea—the young Duke of Devonshire, one of the very richest men in the country, with estates all over England and Ireland, including Chatsworth, a veritable palace in the Derbyshire hills, and Devonshire House, one of the grandest addresses in London. Our parents were delighted, as was I, for all this seemed no more than Georgiana's due—and, in 1774, when Georgiana was just seventeen, they were married.

It was quickly apparent to all who knew her best that the union was not a success. The Duke was chilly and distant, frustrated by my sister's failure to conceive a child, and much occupied with his mistresses. In the absence of a satisfying domestic life, Georgiana turned to a more public existence, devoting her considerable talents to establishing herself as the leader of the fashionable world. Her matchless sense of taste, her winning charm, and the seemingly inexhaustible resource of the Duke's money soon ensured her position as the unchallenged queen of society. She was a most effective political hostess too, devoted to the Whig cause, as all we Spencers were, which meant we distrusted the power of an overmighty king and wished to see the voice of the people better represented in Parliament. Politicians deferred to her, as did dandies, other duchesses—indeed anyone who longed for an invitation to her parties, who yearned to feel themselves at the heart of things, where everything might be decided, from the shape of a gown to the appointment of an undersecretary at the Naval Service.

Never before or since has anyone enjoyed such celebrity in so many and such varied spheres; but it did nothing to change the Duke's feelings for her. The joke ran that he was the only man in London not in love with the Duchess of Devonshire. Certainly, he made his indifference plain. Georgiana kept up a good front, as the saying goes, but I knew she was unhappy and, amid all her entertainments, dinners, and routs, often very lonely.

So when the opportunity arose for me to marry the Duke's cousin, Lord Bessborough, Georgiana was immediately excited by the idea. I understood her reasoning—in marrying Bessborough, I shouldn't be torn away from her company but could continue to remain at her side. If I'd accepted some other man, he might have carried me off who knows where, to his own family, and limited my access to Georgiana, insisting I spend my time with his own relations. I couldn't bear the thought of such a separation; and neither, as she made very clear, could Georgiana. So when Bessborough finally summoned up the courage to propose—for he was a diffident suitor—I calmly accepted. I did so without giving my decision much serious thought. My parents encouraged the match, and such reservations as I had—I was a giddy, vivacious creature in those days and wondered sometimes how I should get on with this silent, somber young man—I drove from my mind, for nothing mattered to me as much as securing my closeness to Georgiana. The truth of the matter is, I married my husband to please my sister and ensure we shouldn't be parted. It wasn't long before I realized what a terrible mistake I had made.

I can't say my expectations of married life were ever very high. I was nineteen when I married Lord B, but young as I was, I had few illusions. I never imagined there'd be anything like passion between us, and as for love, that seemed far too much to hope for. I would have been content with mild affection or simply companionship. I'd seen other marriages do well enough on such slender foundations, and hoped ours might be made to work as comfortably as theirs. I was soon disabused of that fantasy. Everyone told me Bessborough was a sensible, amiable man, who harbored a great warmth for me beneath his shyness; but if this were so, I saw no signs of it. My new husband didn't seem to care for me at all. He spoke to me brusquely when he did at all, and rebuffed all my attempts to involve myself in his life. He made it only too apparent he had no need of my company, preferring to spend all his time at Brooks's club, where he drank and gambled with a gloomy, single-minded intensity, running up enormous debts he could not afford to repay. At dawn, he would come home in the blackest of moods, looking for someone to blame for his folly other than himself, and it was then that his greatest defect was revealed to me: his terrifying, ungovernable temper.

This came as an appalling shock to me. The first time I saw him so angry, it made me shake with fear. I'd never seen a man behave like this; my father and brother rarely raised their voices to anyone, in my presence at least. I told myself it was an aberration, but I learned very quickly that was not the case. It happened time and time again, and anything was enough to set it off—a dish not to his liking at dinner, some untoward accident in the house—but whatever provoked his displeasure, I was always the one to bear the brunt of his fury. Everything that frustrated him, everything that turned out otherwise than he wished, every disappointment, every problem that came upon him—all, in his eyes, were my fault, and he did not hesitate to make me suffer for it.

I honestly believe his rage against me was utterly beyond his control, for he didn't confine himself to scolding me in private but began berating me in public as well. Once, at a grand assembly, his behavior to me was so insulting that the Duke of Devonshire's sister, a formidable person, reprimanded him in the strongest terms for his treatment of me. It did no good, of course; he was humiliated, and that made him even more hostile toward me.

I remember one night when his temper reached new and alarming heights, worse than I'd ever seen it before. He came home very late from Brooks's, barged into my room, white-faced and desperate, and shook me roughly awake.

"I've lost a great deal tonight, much more than I can pay. Get up. I need you to go and speak to your brother."

I was sleepy and stupid and didn't grasp at first what he meant.

"I don't understand. What can George do?"

"Lend me the money, of course. And if he won't oblige, then go and ask your sister. Or your mother. Or anyone, I don't care. I must get it from somewhere."

"I can't do that." I was still innocent enough to be horrified by the thought of begging from my relations. "I won't do it."

"Yes, you will. If I tell you, you will."

He took me by my wrist and pulled me roughly from my bed. He stood over me, and I could see the frustration in his eyes. He loomed above me, tall and threatening. I was genuinely afraid of him then.

"I will go tomorrow." My voice sounded small and fearful.

He let go of my arm, sighed, and moved away.

"Just get the money."

He turned and walked away. I crept back into bed, shivering with shock, hugging myself until I was calmer. In the morning, I did exactly as he'd asked. I went to my brother's house and explained my mission; with only an inquiring stare, he lent me as much money as he could. A bruise had appeared on my wrist, and I think George must have seen it, for while he did not comment at the time, he began to call upon me at home with no warning, as if to check upon my well-being.

Even now, I don't like to dwell upon those days. I was often very fearful of him, terrified of what he might resort to when in the grip of such fury. I was far from alone in finding myself treated harshly by my husband, and I'm aware other women have suffered far more than I did from the violence of their husband's tempers. But somehow, I'd never imagined myself in such a plight. I spoke of my situation to no one, not even Georgiana. I knew, I suppose, that I was not truly to blame for Lord B's unkind treatment of me. But while it lasted, I was most grievously ashamed of it. I came to understand later, when I was older and wiser, that if anyone deserved to feel guilt, it was he; but I suppose if a woman is told often enough she is responsible for her husband's bad conduct, that she drives him to behave as he does, eventually she comes to believe it.

Certainly, I brooded a great deal on what it was about me that seemed to bring out all my husband's worst faults, why he seemed to harbor in his heart such a powerful resentment toward me. I was very young then, without much knowledge of relations between men and women, and so it was some time before it occurred to me that there was one obvious reason for his bitterness—the fact that from the beginning, we were very ill suited to each other in bed.

The wedding night is often a great shock to girls who have been brought up to remain innocent of what is to come; and some never recover from the distress of discovering what is expected of them. A gentle, careful lover can do a great deal to soothe fears and ease matters along; but it is a fortunate young woman who meets with such a paragon when he is most required, and I was not so lucky. I did not find Lord Bessborough physically pleasing, and from the first time, I disliked the act extremely.

"It will get easier," he told me one night, after another doleful encounter. "I believe many women find it distasteful to begin with. But they come to like it in the end."

"How long will it take before that happens?"

"That's hardly a question for me. You should speak to your sister. She may have some advice for you."

This I did not do, for I knew Georgiana's marriage was no happier than my own, and I doubted she would have any wisdom to offer me. So I made up my mind to endure the duties of a wife with what stoicism I could, though I never pretended to enjoy them. Perhaps Lord B and I would have been happier if I'd been sophisticated enough to carry out such a deception, for nothing humiliates a man so much as the knowledge that he cannot please a woman. And it is but a short step from regretting his incapacity to blaming the woman for shrinking from him.

If this was my offense, then I am sorry for it; but it was entirely beyond my control. It was not my fault that I could not bear his touch. Even so, I believe I faithfully fulfilled my marital obligations toward him. Certainly, my dislike of our relations did nothing to curb Lord B's persistence in this respect. Our first son, John, was born just nine months into our marriage, with Frederick following quickly after. In just six years, I gave Lord B four healthy children, three of them sons, so he had no reason for complaint in that respect. I confess I would have been content if we had lived together as brother and sister thereafter, but he would never have agreed to that. He always wanted more from our intimate relations than I could give him. Now it is all so long ago, I find I feel a hint of pity for him, married to a woman incapable of disguising that she never wanted him in that way. But while it may help explain his cruelty to me in those early years of our marriage, I will never persuade myself it excuses him. There are many things for which I know I should ask Lord B's forgiveness, but this is not one of them.

When I understood my situation with Lord B, I attached myself even more closely to Georgiana, certain of finding in my sister all the kindness, warmth, and affection I could not expect from my husband. In the years that followed, I was rarely out of her company. Everywhere she went, I followed. If she was indeed the undisputed queen of society, I was her attendant handmaid, always at her side in whatever she undertook. When she famously outraged polite society by canvassing for the Whigs at the great Westminster election, descending from her carriage to mix among the rough-and-ready electors, I was a footstep behind her, shaking hands, and, if rumor was to be believed, kissing butchers in return for their votes. I was with her, too, in more decorous circumstances, clothed in whatever new style of dress or hair she had decided to launch into the world, her partner in executing the lavish spectacles she put on at Devonshire House. Even now that I'm old enough to know better, to look askance at the sheer waste of money, time, and health this thoughtless life involved, I still feel a tiny frisson of excitement when I recall those days. We were young, rich, and handsome—with the fashionable world prostrate at our feet. We did exactly as we wanted—our parties lasted from night into day, we slept and rose whenever we pleased, time had no meaning for us. We were equally indifferent to what we spent. Money meant nothing; it slipped through our hands like water; there was always more of it to be had or borrowed; what did it matter?

These were the wildest times in my life, and I threw myself into pleasure with the determined heedless abandon only deep inner unhappiness can provoke. And then, as if to compound my sins, I followed in the footsteps of so many other miserable women trapped in loveless unions—and embarked on a series of affairs.

Why did I do it? All the usual reasons, I suppose. Distraction; excitement; a desire, hardly admitted even to myself, for revenge on the husband who'd failed me. A hope, too, that perhaps in this man, or in the next, I might find my soulmate, whose true self would fit together with my own as perfectly as two pieces of the jigsaws with which I entertained my children.

My first liaison, with my cousin John Townshend, meant nothing really. It flared up brightly but briefly and was, in truth, little more than a dalliance. We were never, strictly speaking, lovers at all; I was happy when it was over, for he was a volatile and jealous man, who had begun to alarm me with his moods and fancies. The second, with the far more affable Charles Wyndham, lasted longer, until my brother came to hear of it and demanded I give him up. The third, however, was a far more serious business, and very nearly destroyed me.

This man was, in every sense, the worst possible choice I could have made: reckless, untrustworthy, disloyal, and an inveterate liar. I cannot plead ignorance of his character, for I knew very well who he was—and yet I blithely delivered myself into his hands. Why do women do these things, giving themselves to men they know are unworthy of them? In my own case, I think I'd concluded I didn't deserve anything better. I had largely escaped retribution for my earlier liaisons; there'd been rumors, and in Wyndham's case, even a mention of our affair in a newspaper. Thankfully, none appeared to have reached my husband's ears, although my brother knew all and extracted a promise from me that I should never enter such a connection again. I was profoundly grateful for my escape, but there was part of me, I think, which believed I still merited punishment. I have never put a very high value upon myself; and Lord B's constant and unremitting insistence upon my many failings had only strengthened my poor opinion of my worth. Well, if I had been looking for a nemesis, someone who would treat me as badly as I thought I deserved, I could not have chosen a better candidate.

His name was Richard Sheridan, and I'd known him for years. But then, everyone in England knew him. He was our most celebrated playwright and the greatest satirist of our age, but we had a closer connection to him than most admirers. My sister and her circle were the barely disguised subjects of his best-loved work, *The School for Scandal,* which was intended to skewer the pretensions of the rich and foolish; but it was done with so much cleverness that, rather than take offense, we all laughed and preened at the portraits of ourselves. In no time at all, Sheridan was mixing freely in the very society he had ridiculed. He was a great success. Boredom is the great curse of fashionable life, and Sheridan could always be relied upon to entertain the most jaded and exacting audience.

He was also a passionate believer in the Whig cause, which helped endear him to my sister; and soon he began to think of a career in politics. He was a great success at it, with his extraordinary gifts as a public speaker, his taste for drama and intrigue, and his deep understanding of human motives, good, bad, and mercenary. He was very ambitious, and for a time was talked of, not least by himself, as a possible successor to Mr. Fox, the leader of our party.

No one could have called him a handsome man. He was red-faced and portly, and when drunk, as was often the case, was disheveled in his dress. But none of this hindered his eager pursuit of women, or the surprising rate of success he claimed to have enjoyed. He told me once that he had had so many lovers he could not count them all. His poor wife suffered greatly from his amours. I regret extremely now that I added to her sorrows. I can only say that I was well repaid for my thoughtlessness.

For, as I was to discover to my cost, Sheridan was—like many men who present a comic face to the world—both cruel and selfish at heart. He was quite without scruple in the way he treated others, merciless in discarding those who stood in his way, whether political allies or unwanted mistresses. He was sentimental, and tears sprang easily to his eyes, but I think he was incapable of genuine feeling, caring only for himself.

So why, with so many counts against him, did I surrender myself to him? He was clever—and I've always been drawn to quick, agile minds. No one was more articulate—he used to say he could talk away his looks in ten minutes, and indeed that was the case for me. He was probably the wittiest man I ever met—most take themselves so seriously—and could always make me laugh. He was, as I soon realized, everything my husband was not—charming, too—and moreover, he really seemed to want me, which counted a great deal in his favor. He used to write me the most tender little notes—well, I see now how foolish I was to be swayed by them, but for a while, I was captivated. Sally, who was in my service by then, never liked him. I only wish I'd paid more attention to her censorious distaste, for in this, as in so many other matters, her judgment was far more acute than my own.

It's plain to me now that our liaison was bound to end badly. Sheridan had no idea of discretion, and I too was astonishingly careless. I had trodden very close to disaster with my earlier affairs, and, although somewhat blown upon, had escaped with my reputation just about intact. This should have urged caution upon me—did I really expect to be so lucky again? But instead, I was stupidly, thought-lessly reckless. I had convinced myself that Lord B, who'd given no sign he knew about my earlier transgressions, was either completely ignorant of my behavior or too indifferent to care what I did.

I soon discovered to my cost how wrong I was in both these assumptions. I returned home one evening from an assignation with Sheridan, to find my husband waiting for me in the drawing room. He was never in the house at this time—he was usually at Brooks's by now—and I understood immediately that something was horri-bly, terribly wrong. He gestured to the sofa.

"Sit down, Harriet, and don't make a scene. The servants are no doubt already aware something has happened. Let's not confirm their suspicions any further."

He was very cool and collected, which frightened me more than his habitual shouting and scolding. This was a different kind of anger. I understood there and then that he knew everything and was far from unconcerned at what I'd done. I shivered slightly, waiting for the blow to fall.

"I'm fully aware of what you've been doing and with whom. I have witnesses, and letters I've intercepted that prove it. I'm satis-fied I have quite enough evidence to divorce you. Be assured that is my intention. No—do not speak. There's nothing to say. My mind is quite made up."

He turned and left me. I sat there for a moment, too appalled to move, until finally, I found the strength to struggle upstairs to my room. There I found Sally. My face told her what had happened; she took me in her arms and held me tight, and I sobbed and sobbed until I had no more tears to cry. How could I have been so stupid, so selfish, so utterly and completely wrong?

The next few days were some of the most miserable in my life. I was consumed with remorse, as I thought of what was to come, the disgrace that would fall upon everyone for whom I cared—my mother, my brother, my sister—all would suffer the consequences of my conduct. But it was the fate of my children that cut me to the quick—they would be taken from me, and if Lord B was vengeful, I might never see them again. The mere prospect of such a separation was almost more than I could bear. I knew only too well my failings as a wife—but I'd always been a most tender mother. I'd fed all my babies at my own breast, refusing to put them out to nurse, and had been a constant presence in their young lives, guiding their first steps, listening to their earliest words, and teaching them their letters. William, my youngest, was barely two years old. If they were to be torn from me now, they would feel the separation as painfully as I would myself—and I should be to blame. I positively howled at this thought, almost deranged by the knowledge this was all my doing.

I was saved from all these horrors by a most unlikely rescuer. One morning, when I was at my lowest ebb, hopeless and despondent, the Duke of Devonshire called upon me. I was terrified he had come to berate me, delivering judgment from his lofty eminence as head of the family; and I bowed my head, ready to be arraigned once more for my sins. I could not speak, for guilt and shame; and as he has never had any small talk, we sat in silence for a minute before he spoke.

"I met Bessborough earlier today, who informed me of his intention to divorce you."

Speechless, all I could do was nod my assent.

"I told him this was not a measure I could agree to—that indeed, I am most strongly opposed to it,"

He tapped his fingers on his chair, his annoyance and impatience very clear.

"It would be a great embarrassment to the whole family. I should not like it myself, and none of our relations wishes to see our name mixed up in it. If Bessborough decides to proceed, he'll be obliged to do so alone, for we shan't support him."

I tried to speak—but the Duke held up his hand to stop me.

"I urged him to consider the feelings of his father. Does he really believe a frail old man well into his eighties would survive the noise and trouble of a divorce?" He paused for a moment. "I think he saw the strength of my argument."

I was so surprised I could barely struggle out my thanks. He nodded mildly, as if it was nothing at all. I would have thrown myself at his feet with gratitude, but knew there was nothing he would dislike more, so I allowed him to take his leave without subjecting him to any further unwelcome displays of affection.

Later that day, my husband summoned me into his presence. He stood at the window, staring blankly into the garden, his back to me. I slid onto the sofa as abjectly as I could, doing all in my power not to provoke him. When he turned toward me, his gaze was as icy as I had ever seen it. I could not meet it and immediately fixed my eyes upon the floor.

"I shan't inquire," he began, "how you persuaded the Duke to take your part in this matter. But he has made his wishes known, and I'm obliged to obey them. I am to be humiliated twice, it seems—cuckolded as a husband and, in this most painful, most mortifying moment, made to feel my inferiority to my more powerful cousin." He laughed. "It seems then you're to have things all your own way. I shan't divorce you—at least not for now. But when my father is dead and beyond any shame you can inflict on him, I may think again. And if I ever have the slightest suspicion of anything of this nature happening once more—I warn you now, Harriet, no power on earth will prevent me from commencing proceedings against you."

I sat in silence, still not daring to look at him.

"Nothing to say? Then let me tell you how we shall go forward. While we are still bound to each other, I shall expect you to behave toward me as a proper wife. I cannot stop the talk that's already whispered everywhere. But I'm determined not to add to it. We shall appear in each other's company occasionally, sometimes dine together—in short, play our parts in this farce of a marriage as best we can, until the gossips find some other victim to feed upon. And in the meantime, I shall consider what I wish to do. For your sake, as well as his own, you should be very solicitous of my father's health, for I cannot say now what I should do if he were to die; and at the same time, I advise you to do nothing whatsoever that might give me the least doubt about the fidelity of your conduct."

Once he was gone, the very picture of injured pride, I tried to compose myself as well as I could. I had thought of the Duke's intervention as a reprieve, but I saw now it was only a stay of execution.

I lived for the better part of a year under this sentence, never knowing if and when the axe might fall. I tried not to complain, even to myself, for I knew only too well how much this situation was to be preferred to the alternative. For a while, I withdrew from society, retreating to our country house at Roehampton, where I tried, as hard as I could, to turn myself into a better person. I spent as much time as I could with my children. John and Fred, my eldest sons, were both now at schools in London, so that I necessarily attended to them from a distance, but I wrote them the fondest letters and kept them supplied with all the treats boys like best, from boxes of oranges to regiments of tin soldiers. Their younger brother, William, was the most fragile of my little brood, what farmers call a poor doer, his propensity to catch every passing sickness a great anxiety to me. I always nursed him myself when he was ill, and once caught chicken pox from him, which, for a time, I thought would extinguish what remained of my good looks, although both of us finally recovered. My daughter, Caroline, was the hardest of all to manage; she was always a willful little girl, her unpredictable behavior the despair of her governesses, and a source of great exasperation to her correct and punctilious grandmother. But I kept her close to me, hoping to calm her waywardness by smothering her in affection. I will do him the credit to declare that Lord B was always kindness itself to her, and that she was probably always his favorite; indeed, I must add that, for all his coldness to me, he was a most loving and attentive father to all our children, lavishing on them a warmth he had never extended to me.

I did my utmost to take comfort in my little family, trying not to dwell on my uncertain future, but for all my efforts, I didn't always succeed. I spent hours at a time running over my many faults, excoriating myself as the wickedest and most abandoned creature alive, obsessing over my selfishness and stupidity. My state of mind was further depressed by Lord B's still expecting me to receive him in my bed. He might not yet have decided whether I should remain his wife, but while I did, he saw no reason why I should not perform all the duties of a married woman.

Under the weight of all these oppressions, my health began to falter. It started with fits of dizziness, and a feeling of fullness—I don't know how else to describe it—in my head. Then I couldn't get my breath. Finally, I fell into convulsions, which brought on a deep delirium, and I don't remember anything after that. When I awoke, I was horrified to find myself paralyzed along the entire left side of my body, unable to move my arm or leg.

I lingered in this state for a very long time, with no doctor able to say exactly what was wrong with me. In the absence of a diagnosis, terrible rumors circulated about the cause of my condition. Some said I had tried to take my own life; others alleged that Lord B had hurt me in some way or dosed me with medicines that had all but killed me. That such awful stories gained credence was proof of how badly we were known to live together; and I'm glad I didn't hear of them till much later, for they would only have made me more distressed than I was already. My own belief was that I had miscarried, at about four months, around the time my symptoms began. It was a more prosaic explanation, but no less fraught with danger. For a long time, I was so weak and so helpless that I honestly thought I would die.

But I was only thirty and stronger than I imagined. Against all expectations, I survived; but my recovery was long and slow. Months later I was still unable to walk, and obliged to be carried everywhere—but slowly, slowly, slowly, I began to feel the worst was over. And not just in my physical state, for I had begun to glimpse other changes in my situation, which encouraged me to believe my future might not be so bleak as I had feared.

It was the strangest thing, but after my illness, Lord B's behavior was quite altered toward me. Georgiana, who had nursed me faithfully through the worst of my illness, told me that when I seemed close to death, Lord B had been beside himself with anxiety and apprehension. Certainly, once I was conscious again, he showed me nothing but the greatest and most transparent concern. He was always at my bedside, patient, considerate, and even kind. I was wary at first, thinking this the product of momentary guilt, and didn't expect it to last. But I was quite wrong. Even as I got better, his old habits did not return. There was no more shouting, no more furious anger, and certainly no more of the rages that had threatened and frightened me so much over the years. Most importantly, there was no more talk of divorce.

Confined by my invalid existence, I had plenty of time to reflect upon what had caused this change in his manner. Perhaps the possibility of losing me had awakened something in him he had not known was there—pity, compassion, or just the habit of our being together. It occurred to me that he liked me better when I was weak and helpless, for then I posed no threat, was completely in his power, and could neither annoy nor humiliate him, as I had done before.

Both might be true, or neither. I had been married for ten years to this bitter, resentful man, but had no more idea what went on in his private mind than I did when I first stood beside him at the altar to make my vows. We were strangers to each other, really. After a while I decided it was useless to look for reasons, for I should never know the truth. Instead, I would accept what he appeared to be offering me—a truce, if you like, a cessation of hostilities—and be thankful that a huge weight of worry and desperation had been lifted from my shoulders as a result.

I cannot pretend that, from that time on, everything was perfect between us; but nor can I deny that our relations were much improved. I've often asked myself how different our lives might have been if he'd behaved with as much simple decency toward me when we were first married as he discovered in himself after my illness. I used to say that if that had been the case, he should never have had the slightest cause to complain of me. Now I'm not so sure. Even when he behaved well toward me, I confess it was never enough to make me truly love him. And that longing for love, that desire for completeness, was not to be assuaged by a few kind words and a little more warmth on his part.

But if love was beyond me, gratitude was not. I had betrayed him, and he'd given me another chance, hauling me back from the precipice on which I teetered; not many husbands would have done the same. For the rest of his life, I would always be in his debt. And if his forgiveness imposed a great obligation on me, his newfound consideration made it weigh all the more heavily. When he had treated me badly, I'd told myself he was giving me permission to betray him, for it was only what he deserved. But now, that slender justification was denied me. Taken together, his willingness to have me back and his fumbling attempts at improvement surely made it impossible for me to consider any further lapses in fidelity. And anyway, hadn't I seen and felt for myself the dreadful consequences that could result from such adventures? The remorse, the guilt, the fear? I had been spared not once, not twice, but three times from the full consequences of my actions. I should not tempt fate a fourth time. As I lay on my convalescent bed, I vowed I would never go wrong again. There would be no more ridiculous attempts to find love. That was all over for me. All I longed for now was a quiet life, with my children, my family, and my friends to fulfill me. That would be enough for me.

When I was finally well enough to travel, the doctors instructed me to take the waters at Bath. The Duke, in yet another act of kindness, rented us a house there, large enough to accommodate me, my sister, and my sister's friend Bess Foster. Under their care, I hoped I would slowly regain my strength, living in as retired a manner as possible, with nothing to think of but my recovery. I imagined all would be peace and quiet and calmness. I couldn't have been more wrong.

4

*A*t first, everything went well in Bath. I was always at my happiest in Georgiana's company, and Bess had been for many years her closest friend. By that time, if I'm candid, she was far, far more than that—but I'm not sure there's a name to describe exactly the complicated tangle of affections that united them. Their relations had begun, some years earlier, with a chance meeting between two unhappy women. My sister was at her lowest ebb—childless, marooned in a loveless marriage, desperately lonely. Bess's situation was even worse—separated from a husband she'd hated, never allowed to see her two young sons, living in extremely reduced circumstances. Misery, I suppose, called out to misery—Georgiana felt an immediate bond with a woman whose sufferings seemed so very like her own. Bess responded with equal strength of feeling, offering her all the sympathy and affection of which she felt deprived—and soon Georgiana was so deeply attached to her that she couldn't bear them to be parted. Bess was installed at Devonshire House, and there she remained. The Duke seemed perfectly happy with the situation—with good reason, as it turned out. It wasn't long before Georgiana discovered that the friend she considered her dearest companion had also become her husband's mistress.

Another woman might have insisted on Bess's instant dismissal from the household; but Georgiana decided she would rather share the Duke with Bess than face the prospect of life without her and acquiesced in the affair. They lived together in a ménage à trois for the rest of my sister's life. Even the birth of Bess's two children by the Duke did little to disturb their arrangements.

Understandably, Bess was very unpopular in the Duke's family and my own, both of whom thought her a scheming adventuress who'd always intended to snare the Duke and had wickedly deceived my sister to achieve her ends. I'm probably the only one who doesn't share this black picture of her character. God knows, I'm aware she's no saint. I've known her long enough to understand there's an element of calculation in almost everything she does, and I'm sure that when first my sister and then the Duke fell under her spell, she saw immediately where her interests lay. And yet for all that, strange as it might seem, her arrival in their lives was not without benefit to both Georgiana and her husband. Bess's soothing, placatory manner did much to improve the Duke's temper; at the same time, she calmed Georgiana's mind, providing her with the boundless indulgent affection she craved, thus making their married life far easier than before. My sister assured me so often that this was the case that I never attempted to quarrel with it. And I should say, I believe Bess herself was changed by their connection. The more she knew Georgiana, the more she came to appreciate the matchless generosity of my sister's heart, and whatever her motives might have been at the beginning of their friendship, Bess quickly grew to love her as deeply as she could love anyone.

I decided early on there was nothing to be gained in setting myself up as Bess's rival in a contest for Georgiana's affections. Instead, I worked hard to win her trust, and soon the three of us were staunch allies, pledged to support each other in all our difficulties. I tried not to regret that I was now required to share with another my sister's most intimate thoughts, which she'd once disclosed only to me. On the whole, I think I managed my misgivings pretty well; but for all my efforts, there were moments when I found my generosity challenged, as was the case when, after I'd been in Bath for a few months, Georgiana told me she had a terrible confession to make. She was pregnant—and the Duke was not the child's father.

At once, my heart leaped out to her. I was overwhelmed with emotions—shock, fear, an anxious apprehension for all this might mean—but my strongest sensation was the deepest, most profound pity for her state. I knew only too well how it felt to live in mortal fear of discovery, to spend every waking hour dreading exposure of your transgression—and my situation had been nowhere near as desperate as hers. Carrying another man's baby was a far greater danger to everything she held dear than an illicit affair. I went to her and took her in my arms while she cried and cried. Eventually, she composed herself enough to speak.

"Don't say anything. I know how stupid I've been. And the Duke was so pleased with me, after Hart was born."

Hart—or Lord Hartington, as he was formally known—was the Duke's long-awaited son and heir, to whom, after sixteen years of marriage, Georgiana had recently given birth. Her sad history of disappointed hopes had finally been broken by the arrival of two healthy daughters, which encouraged her to think that eventually a boy might follow—and when he did, no one was more triumphantly delighted than his father.

"He's still just a baby—barely eighteen months old—what if he's taken from me?"

She began to cry again; and at this, Bess slipped into the room and took my sister's hands in hers.

"Come, my love, this does no good, either to you or the child. I think you should lie down—see if you can sleep a little. I'll come up in a while to see how you are."

I saw Georgiana hesitate for a moment, but when Bess guided her to the door, she went silently to her bed without protest. As I watched her go, I felt a powerful pang of jealousy run through me. So Bess already knew—Georgiana had spoken to her before me. It was an unworthy thought to have in such a terrible moment. Usually, I told myself nothing meant more to more to me than Georgiana's well-being, that Bess was essential to her and that therefore I had no reason to complain. But I still recall the bitterness of my regret, on that long-ago morning, when I realized I had not been the first person in whom Georgiana confided, that Bess had indeed usurped the place in my sister's heart that was rightfully mine. This, however, was the worst possible time for such selfish considerations, and when Bess returned, I put all such thoughts out of my mind.

"I suppose it's Grey's child?"

Bess nodded and perched herself delicately upon the edge of a chair. She was—and indeed still is, so many years later—extremely beautiful, one of those small, slender women who look as if a strong breeze would blow them over, large-eyed and frail, as if in constant need of a strong male arm to support her. You would never guess from her appearance what a tough little creature she really is.

"Yes. I'm sorry to say it is. And he's behaved just as badly as you would have expected. He's trouble, I'm afraid."

We'd known Charles Grey for years. He was one of the many ambitious young men who hung about Devonshire House, a rising politician desperate to make his mark. He was seven years my sister's junior and had first approached her as a patron, asking for her advice and guidance. But soon he was pursuing her as a mistress, and it wasn't long before they were lovers. He was very handsome in those days, vehement, impulsive, and passionate. But neither Bess nor I liked him. His bad temper was already notorious, as was his selfishness, and he scornfully dismissed all Georgiana's pleas to behave more discreetly.

"We need to get her away," said Bess. "Find some quiet place where she can have the child in secret."

Soon we had a plan in mind. Georgiana would retreat to the country, to some obscure place where she should not be recognized. Cornwall, we thought, would serve. I would accompany her, my poor health cited as the reason for our trip. She should have the baby privately and then return. Bess, in the meantime, would try to manage Charles Grey.

It was a good stratagem, and when we put it to Georgiana, she immediately agreed to it. It wasn't long before we had everything needful in place—a house found and our travel arrangements made. But then, out of nowhere, all our clever schemes were blown apart. The Duke received an anonymous letter in London, telling him to go down to Bath and look at his wife. He arrived one morning unannounced, marching into the house before Georgiana had time to conceal her state, to discover Georgiana six months gone with child, carrying a baby he knew was not his own.

The hours that followed were agonizing. Huddled in her bedroom, Bess and I listened as the Duke abused my sister, shouting at the top of his voice while she cried and begged his forgiveness. Finally, he left with a great slamming of doors that made the whole house vibrate. When finally we came downstairs, we found Georgiana, her face blotched with tears, anxiously pacing about the room.

"I'm to go abroad," she said haltingly. "Cornwall isn't enough. It must be abroad."

"Did he say where?" I asked.

"No, just that it must be abroad. I'm to have the baby in some foreign place, and after that, he will decide if I'm ever to return."

"And what if you won't go?"

"Then he will divorce me, I'm sure of that."

She threw herself down on the sofa, a picture of misery and despair.

"And there's one further condition. You, Harriet, must come too. Your ill health is to be the excuse for all. Our story will be that your doctors have ordered you abroad and I have been so kind as to accompany you."

She threw her head in her hands and took a deep, shuddering breath before looking into my eyes as steadily as she could.

"Can you do it, do you think?"

I thought for a moment. If I agreed, I would be away from my family for at least six months, perhaps as long as nine. My children were still very young and would feel my absence terribly. I was in truth very far from well and not at all fitted for a long journey into some distant region. And what would Lord B say? Should I even be allowed to go? These were the thoughts that rushed into my head, and I suspected the reality of such a trip would be worse, in every respect, than anything my imagination had so far conjured up. But I knew before the words were out of my mouth that I had in me only one possible answer to Georgiana's plea.

"Wherever you go, I will go with you."

I wonder, if I'd known what lay before me—that I should be away, not for a matter of months but for nearly three long years—whether my answer would have been the same. I should like to think so, for I could not have borne disappointing my sister when she needed me the most. Once the decision was made, any hope of the retired and simple life I had envisaged for myself evaporated before my eyes. Georgiana's misfortune shook me out of England and sent me roaming across Europe, constantly moving from one place to another, living the rootless existence of the émigré. Eventually, it led me to that sunny morning on Lady Webster's terrace, where I found myself looking with far too much interest into the startlingly blue eyes of the man who was to turn my whole world upside down. Yes, it was my sister's pregnancy and the consequences resulting from it that brought me there; but that misfortune isn't enough to explain what happened next. Another woman might have basked in Granville's obvious admiration, and, while flattered by his notice, thought no more of it. I was not that woman. My previous liaisons, disappointing as they'd been, had—far from curing me of my enduring desire to find love—only stifled it for a while. Beneath the placid surface I presented to the world, imposed upon me by ill health and a deep sense of obligation to my husband, I still nurtured the hope that one day I might meet a man with whom I could share a deep and passionate connection. I tried to hide this secret far within me, hardly liking to admit it to myself; but it was there, nonetheless, like some deeply buried seed, waiting to be awoken. I was more ready, more susceptible than I knew on that fateful day when I first met Granville. I'd been waiting all my life to feel the way I did in his electrifying company; and it was this which led me to accept, even as I knew I shouldn't, that little bundle of fragrant leaves he smilingly held out to me on that fateful Naples morning.

*E*vents moved quickly after that. Once Georgiana, Bess, and I had agreed to the Duke's terms, we were left to manage the practicalities ourselves. The south of France was finally decided upon as the most suitable destination. I was obliged to persuade my husband to accompany us, as three women could not make such a trip alone. He was reluctant at first, but when I explained that I'd been instructed to seek a milder climate for my health, he finally acquiesced. We never told him the true reason for our journey, and I don't know how much he suspected. Georgiana was very careful to conceal her swelling figure from him in cloaks and shawls; and if those stratagems weren't enough to conceal the truth, perhaps Lord B simply decided not to acknowledge it, disappointed that the Duke had not taken him into his confidence. Grey, meanwhile, was furious at what he called Georgiana's betrayal in leaving him, adding to her misery with every enraged letter he sent. And then, amid our troubles, our mother arrived.

She'd heard my health had worsened, that I'd been advised to go away—and had hurried down to Bath to nurse me. She was appalled when she saw Georgiana's condition, and berated her soundly—but once she'd said her piece, she was determined to stand by her daughter and announced her intention to accompany us. So we were quite a little party when we finally left for France in the winter of 1791; there was Georgiana, Bess, and my mother—a few servants to look after us, including my intrepid Sally, who refused to be parted from me— plus me, Lord B, and our six-year-old daughter, Caroline, or Caro as we called her, who I thought would not do well without me. But I was obliged to leave my boys behind. Four-year-old William was sent to stay at his grandfather's house. John and Fred, aged eleven and nine, were already away at school and might stay with my brother on their holidays. I thought my heart would break when I kissed them good-bye. If I'd known how long we were to be parted, it would've cracked entirely in two.

We couldn't have chosen a worse time to travel through France. The Bastille had fallen only two years before, and the whole country was in a state of revolution, angry, restless, and increasingly danger-ous. We felt too uneasy in Paris to stay there for long, so we pushed southward. When we reached Marseilles, our party divided. My health required me to rest quietly for a while near the coast, while Georgiana and Bess made their way alone to Montpellier, where in some secluded retreat, my sister gave birth to her baby. It was a healthy little girl, whom she named Eliza. Georgiana was barely allowed to hold her before she was taken away and given to a fos-ter mother. (Later, the child was taken home to be brought up with Grey's parents in the far north of England.)

When we were reunited, Georgiana was pale and silent, her hag-gard looks betraying the guilt and remorse I knew she felt. For some weeks, I dared not speak at all to her of what she must have suf-fered in surrendering her child. Then one afternoon, as she sat, eyes closed, in the shady garden of our rented villa, I ventured what I thought were some words of consolation. I could only imagine how terrible it must have been, I murmured, but at least Eliza was alive and she herself had survived her ordeal.

"Survived?"

She opened her eyes and looked almost scornfully at me, as though my attempt at consolation was so ridiculous it barely deserved an answer.

"Well, I suppose I did survive, for here I am, sitting and talking to you. But when they took poor Eliza from me, something of myself was torn away too. I'll never be whole again. I'm only part of who I was before—a piece of a person, if you like, a poor imitation of my old self. The rest went with her—and there it will remain."

I know Georgiana had hoped that once Eliza was born and safely hidden with her grandparents, then perhaps the Duke would allow her to go home; she longed with every fiber of her being for the forgiving letter, permitting her to return; but though she looked for it daily, it never arrived. To add to our woes, the situation in France became more alarming by the day. We soon realized it was impossible for us to stay, and it was then we embarked on a truly wandering existence, attempting to outrun the political upheaval that was turning all of Europe upside down. We moved first to Switzerland—and spent several pleasant months there, until Lord B's father, who had long been in very frail health, summoned him home to attend to the ordering of his affairs. Lord B was very reluctant to leave us, but his father would not be denied. So it was that we were without his protection when events in France—the storming of the Tuileries in Paris and the subsequent imprisonment of the royal family—took a far more threatening turn. For Georgiana and me, who'd known the French king and queen well from our many visits to their court, this was very distressing news. But it also had an immediate impact on our safety, for in the ensuing unrest, French armies began to gather near the Swiss border. Lord B instructed us to leave for Italy, promising that he would meet us there as soon as he could. With only his steward and our few servants to accompany us, and obliged to travel in the depths of winter, we crossed the Alps, struggling through snow and in great fear of bandits, fleeing into Italy. Lord B finally joined us once more in Pisa. It was there we heard of the execution of Louis XVI—and shortly afterward, received the terrible news that Britain and France were now at war.

At every stage of our terrible journey, Georgiana never lost faith that at this place, or the next, she'd find a letter from the Duke awaiting her, but she was always disappointed. It was as if he'd totally forgotten her; and in the absence of any instructions from him, we decided to settle ourselves in Rome until his wishes were known. It was there, just when it seemed things could get no worse, that Lord B heard his father had died.

He was deeply affected, regretting that he hadn't been with him at the end. To his credit, he did not blame me, but I reproached myself, for it was solely at my behest he was absent when he was most needed. We were both extremely melancholy at being so far away from those who loved us. I was tormented terribly by my separation from my sons. I wrote each of them long and loving letters, I drew them little sketches of anything interesting we saw, and I sent them little presents, with no certainty of their ever arriving—but knew none of these trifles could be any substitute for my presence. I couldn't even promise them when I might return. I never seriously considered abandoning Georgiana, but I couldn't fail to be aware, as the months became a year, that both my children and my husband had paid a heavy price for my unswerving loyalty to my sister.

Although it was only two months since his arrival in Rome, Lord B decided that despite all the dangers involved in crossing Europe during wartime, he had no choice but to return home once more. As the eldest son, he'd inherited not only his father's earldom, but also the responsibility for sorting out his affairs.

I was surprised to discover how sorry I was to see him go. This must seem strange, given all that had passed between us, but while we were away, his behavior toward me had grown ever kinder and more considerate. Nothing was too much trouble for him—fetching shawls, hiring a docile pony to carry me into the country, and walking beside me into the green hills. His temper had mellowed to a degree I could hardly credit. Even my mother noticed it.

"It seems to me, Harriet, that you and Lord B live far better together than you have done for a long time."

"Yes, he's been very attentive to me since I've been ill."

I closed my eyes. This was not a conversation I wanted to have.

"I should put it more strongly than that," she continued. "From what I've seen, his recent behavior toward you has been"—she paused, searching for a word to convey the strength of her opinion—"exemplary."

"I'm grateful for his kindness."

"I know Lord B is not without his faults, but no husband is perfect."

I did not reply.

"And yours seems to be doing everything he can to conquer his failings."

Again, I said nothing.

"I wish to give you some advice. Harriet, please do me the honor of looking at me and attending to what I have to say."

Reluctantly I obeyed, opening my eyes and shifting in my chair to meet her determined gaze.

"It seems to me," she began, "that Lord B is trying his best to show you he's capable of being a better man than the one you married. All his little kindnesses, all his new attentions—these are his way of suggesting things might be different between you. You must see it. He's clearly inviting you to go forward on more affectionate terms than those you've lived upon before." She frowned and went on. "I tell you now, Harriet, Lord B is offering you a second chance—and for your own good, for his sake, and for the happiness of your family—I do beg you most sincerely to seize it while you can."

She leaned over and took my hand. "Your poor sister is a terrible example of what happens when husband and wife cannot agree. It's been painful enough to watch one daughter destroy herself. I don't think I could bear to see it happen again."

We sat in silence for a few minutes before she rose and swept away. I sighed. My mother didn't know the half of it. If she'd read the letters he sent me, if she'd seen for herself the warmth of the language in which he wrote, she would have argued her case even more forcefully.

I hadn't expected much in the way of correspondence, for I knew Lord B would have a mountain of business to deal with on his return. And indeed, the moment he arrived in London, all our many creditors pounced upon him, desperate to have their accounts paid at last from his long-awaited inheritance. Many of these debts were the results of his gambling; but others, I'm ashamed to say, were my fault, the consequences of all the ill-considered extravagances of my wild years, which I had for a long time struggled to put from my mind and had certainly never confessed to him.

When his letters began to arrive, I expected at the very least a harsh scolding now the magnitude of my foolishness was revealed; but instead, when I opened them, to my astonishment, there was nothing within but tenderness and affection. One letter I still recall. He wrote it late one night, after an exhausting day, harassed by lawyers, bankers, and bailiffs. He'd been shocked to discover how little money would be left for us after all the calls on his father's estate were settled. He was exhausted, miserable, disappointed, exactly the circumstances in which he would once have directed his frustrations at me; but instead, he told me, he'd discovered a great truth.

"I find what I have always thought, no happiness can be complete without you, whether I am in a hurry or a calm . . . something is always wanting, and that something, my heart tells me, is you."

I could hardly believe what I was reading. In the thirteen years we'd been married, Lord B had never once talked to me in the language of love. Now it seemed he could not stop. "I have no wish on earth," he declared, "but to make you comfortable and happy." On page after page, he poured out the strength of his feelings for me in the same plain and artless manner. I was profoundly moved by what he wrote. It touched me more than I can say that my silent, undemonstrative husband—once so hostile toward me—had searched so deeply within himself, overcoming years of resentment to confess with such simple warmth how much I now meant to him.

My mother was right—he was offering me an olive branch. Beneath every plaintive, loving expression I heard the same unspoken appeal—a plea to forget what had passed between us, to start again on a better footing, to try to live comfortably together as we had never done before.

What was I to make of his extraordinary change of heart? Could he really be trusted not to revert to his old ways, if I agreed to try again? I turned these thoughts over and over in my mind, none more than the question that had puzzled me from the moment those loving letters had begun to arrive—how to explain his transformation from sullen husband to tender suitor. What was it that had provoked this entirely unexpected outburst of fondness?

It was a while before I thought I understood. I'd seen the first inklings of a change of heart before we left England. Pity for me in the worst days of my sickness had begun it, combined, perhaps, with remorse for his previous unkindness to me—both had played their part in warming his affections. Now I was certain my utter dependence on him—for I was still very ill—was a great aphrodisiac to him. If that sounds too cruel, let me put it another way—my poor health and the very retired manner in which we lived while on our travels, with our acquaintances so few and our pleasures all domestic—in these confined and restricted circumstances, where I had neither the energy nor the opportunity to defy him, I gradually became the wife Lord B had always wanted.

In the remoter parts of France, in Switzerland, in Rome too, even if we had wished for it, there was no high society for my sister and me to conquer, nowhere for us to dazzle and draw all eyes upon us. Nor were there any grand dinners of the sort Lord B hated, no clever conversations in which he knew he did not shine, no other men to compete with, who were more handsome, more charming, more assured in every possible way than he would ever be—in short, no rivals to expose his deficiencies.

Instead, there was only us; and for the first time since we were married, I believe he felt quite sure of me. With no outside distractions and with my own spirits craving nothing but quiet, he could at last be certain of my undivided attention. He had me completely and utterly to himself; and this, he discovered, was very agreeable. In my reduced and solitary state, I was his to command—and then and only then did I become the woman he thought he could love.

Once I grasped this truth, I understood very clearly exactly what Lord B would require of me if we were to reconcile as he wished. To keep his newfound affection alive, I would be obliged to continue forever just as we lived now—a very solitary existence, with no temptations to draw me away from him.

It does not sound so much for a husband to ask of his wife; and if his temper continued so improved, and his feelings continued so kind toward me—why, I asked myself, should I not agree to it? My mother was right. With a little encouragement from me, we might go on tolerably well together. And think what I should gain in return. I should never feel again the terror and shame that had convulsed me upon his discovery of my affair with Sheridan. Surely I had no desire to live through that agony again? It would be a quiet life without much incident, but secure and comfortable. My own reputation would be safe; the peace and happiness of my children would be assured; my family need never be ashamed of me again.

These were such powerful considerations in favor of accepting Lord B's implied offer of rapprochement—why then did I not seize upon it as quickly and as thankfully as I could? I knew only too well what held me back. My feelings for Lord B had not altered in the same way as his had for me.

That's not to say they hadn't changed at all. I was deeply affected by the knowledge that he cared for me, and indeed, felt better disposed to him than I had ever done before. I saw that he was lonely; and sometimes I even pitied him for it. I understood too, that in his own faltering way, he was trying to make amends. Above all, I was profoundly, abjectly grateful that he had, it seemed, completely abandoned the idea of divorcing me. His willingness to wipe away my transgression with Sheridan, his preparedness to begin again with the slate quite clean—for this alone I owed him an immense debt of gratitude that could never really be repaid, putting me under obligation to him for the rest of my life. All this was true, but none of it was enough to make me love him.

And if that was the case, I doubted I could ever offer him what he really wanted. For then I should have to abandon any hope of discovering true love for myself, and hard as I tried to convince myself this was a right and necessary surrender, a stubborn, selfish desire reared up within me, a refusal to accept what I knew could only ever be second best.

The battle between these warring parts of my nature continued unchecked until I was exhausted by my own arguments. But whenever a letter arrived from Lord B, filled with loving assurances, I only grew ever more uncertain how I should behave to him when he returned. My rational mind understood exactly what I should do—follow my mother's advice and reconcile as well as I could with a husband who so obviously wished it. But as the weeks passed into months, I was still no nearer forcing my heart to accept what my head dictated.

6

e'd traveled south to winter in Naples after Lord B went home, partly in the hope of improving my health, for I still suffered with a pain in my side. The climate there is quite as hot as a London summer, and I soon began to feel the benefit of it. By the time spring arrived, I was so much improved I was accustomed to drinking my breakfast coffee in our garden, enjoying the warmth of the air. I was seated there one morning when my sister came running down the steps toward me. I saw at once that something had happened—she was still in her nightgown, and her hair hung down her back in a thick red-gold braid. When she reached me, she was breathless with excitement. "Oh, Harriet, Harriet, look—look what's arrived—he's written at last!"

She held out before me a single sheet of paper. I saw immediately it was the long-awaited letter from the Duke.

"Listen—this is what he says—he believes it's time for me to return—that I'm to make haste to do so—that he looks forward to hearing from me when I've made the necessary arrangements."

No man could ever have delivered such transcendent happiness, such deep and heartfelt joy, in so few words. Georgiana clasped the letter tightly to her breast, and I saw that her hands were shaking.

"There's more, but that's the most important part."

I couldn't speak. The first thought in my mind was that I should see my boys again. I began calculating how quickly we could make the journey, how fast we could get to Calais, or perhaps there was some better way, some quicker, safer route. I could already see myself embracing them, kissing them over and over again. Georgiana sank to the ground beside my chair and put her arms around me.

"We can go home," she said softly; and both of us began to cry.

⸎

We wasted not a second before setting out, each of us almost mad with joy at the prospect of our return. I made it only as far as Rome before all my dreams were shattered. My health took a severe turn for the worse; all the improvement I'd seen in Naples evaporated; soon I was coughing incessantly and even spitting blood. I suspect it was my mother who made sure my husband heard of it. Whoever was responsible, the consequences were immediate. I had a letter from Lord B telling me he'd heard of Georgiana's summons home and knew I would be eager to accompany her. But he was sorry to tell me he'd sought medical advice about whether I should travel in my poor state of health, and every doctor he'd consulted had advised most strongly against it. They all recommended I remain in Italy until the following spring to avoid the cold and damp of an English winter. He knew how unhappy this would make me, but his instructions were not to be disobeyed. I was on no account to set out with my sister, but to wait for his return, which would be as soon as his affairs allowed. He hoped to bring with him our youngest son, William—perhaps that would lift my spirits a little? Until then, I was to remain in Rome with Caro and my mother. Once he was back, we should travel to some mild and sunny place where I could convalesce. He suggested Naples, which had suited me so well before. Perhaps I could look out for a suitable house there? He understood

I would be disappointed, but hoped I saw he was acting for my own good.

Disappointment was far too weak a term for the deep despondency with which I greeted this news. Had I been strong enough, I might have defied him—but I knew it was hopeless: my mother would have ensured my obedience, and I was too ill to do anything but submit. I was utterly desolate—to have the prospect of home dangled before me and then snatched away so cruelly was almost more than I could bear. It might be another year before I was in England again—another year spent away from my boys. It was a consolation to learn that I might see William once more—but what of Frederick and John? They must surely have forgotten me by now. It had been some eighteen months since I last saw them; what did they look like? Who had they become while I was away? Would they even know me when I was eventually allowed home? I was inconsolable and lay in bed day after day, for I could see no point in getting up.

For hours at a time, Georgiana sat by my side, saying little but occasionally taking my hand in hers. On the third day, she finally found the courage to raise the subject I knew she'd been longing to discuss.

"I'm so sorry, Harriet. I always thought we'd go home together."

I nodded. I too had imagined it that way: two sisters, inseparable, ending our exile as we had begun it, together.

"You do understand I must go? That I can't wait for you?"

She hurried on—keen, I think, to get out the words she had been rehearsing.

"If I delay, the Duke might change his mind. I can't take that risk. Now that he's summoned me, I must leave."

"Yes," I said, "I see that."

"And I hesitate to say it, given what you must be feeling now, but the children—I can't resist the chance to get back to them. Hart was so tiny when we left—not much more than a baby. And Eliza—if I was home, I might get news of her." She sighed. "I feel I'm betraying you in leaving—but I have no choice."

"Bess will go with you, I suppose?"

"Yes," she replied, "but it should have been you. I know it should have been you."

She cried; I squeezed her hand.

"I understand. There's nothing you can do. He's sent for you, and you must go."

I managed a weak smile, enough to offer her a little reassurance. When finally she left my room, I noticed a new spring in her step, an eagerness in her whole person she could not suppress. It was plain she couldn't wait to leave.

———

*T*he following day, I got up, dry-eyed and resigned. I busied myself as much as I could in my weak state, with a thousand small tasks, which occupied me without for a moment distracting me from my misery. On the morning Georgiana and Bess left, we all wept. My sister held me in her arms as if our lives depended upon it, declaring through her tears that she would visit my boys the moment she arrived, that she should be a second mother to them until I was in my rightful place again. I cried when she clambered into the carriage that was to carry her and Bess away, and watched it until it disappeared from sight.

I understood entirely Georgiana's reasons for leaving without me; but I knew that if I'd been in her place, I couldn't have done the same. When she'd sought my help in her hour of need, I had instantly put her first. I hadn't hesitated, but had abandoned my children, left my home, and risked my health to follow her into an exile that sometimes seemed as if it would never end. There had been times when the miseries of our situation pressed very hard upon me; but I never wished

I'd acted otherwise. I had done for her what I now understood she had not been able to do for me; and both of us knew it. It was a melancholy conclusion. My sister's departure told me everything I needed to know about the limits of her affection. I had always suspected, I suppose, that I loved her more than she did me; now I knew it for certain. It was this realization that finally persuaded me to look more kindly on Lord B's overtures. He at least seemed to want my love.

By the time we left Rome, I had decided to accept what he offered me with as grateful a heart as I could muster. I would do everything in my power to be the wife Lord B wanted. I found us a house in Naples, as he'd asked, and set about making all the arrangements for him to meet us there. When he arrived, he'd find me as affectionate and welcoming as he could wish. We'd surely find a way to be tolerably happy together. Yes, of course I could; if I set my mind to it, I could do it. In Naples, we'd could start anew. Everything would be better in Naples.

A month later, when Lord B's carriage pulled up outside our Naples villa, it was my youngest son I most longed to see. I hadn't seen William for so long—in my mind he was still a toddler, but it was a sturdy little boy who came running toward me, shouting, "Mama! Mama!" I took him into my arms and covered his face with eager kisses, until he had had enough.

"Where is Caro? Can I see her? I bet I'm taller than her. She won't be able to push me over now, will she, Papa?"

"No," answered Lord B fondly. "She'll be obliged to stick to teasing. She's very good at that."

My husband approached me with a tentative smile, seemingly waiting for some sign from me. I took his hand, and he kissed my cheek. Neither of us made any grand gesture, though we stood a little closer to each other than was usual. That was enough, I felt, to convey my intentions.

Then Caro came shrieking out of the house and ran to her father, hugging him until William ran to join her, so that all three were soon noisily entwined together. I watched from a little way off, thinking how easily all this might have been taken from me and how wretched

I should have been to lose my beautiful children. It was only through Lord B's forbearance that I was here at all. If anything had been wanting to stiffen my resolve to be the wife he deserved, surely this sight was enough to do it.

So I determined to try my best; and the beauty of our surroundings helped, for even in December, Naples was an agreeable place to be, conducive to healing both body and mind. As promised, the climate alone had an immediately beneficial effect on my health, as did the freshness of the air. I coughed less. I stopped spitting blood. I could walk about a little. I was even equal to short strolls wandering the quiet hills of the countryside, arm in arm with Lord B. When we tired of woodland paths, there were the celebrated sights of Pompeii and Vesuvius to explore or drives to be taken along the cost. The whole place felt joyful and alive, and little by little, I began to feel the same. Soon I was in better spirits than I had enjoyed since Georgiana and I left England.

My recovery also owed something to the delicious food—I never expected to eat an octopus with so much relish—but I believe the lively sociability of Naples contributed most to my steady improvement. It was a long time since I'd been among smart people and lavish entertainments, and Naples offered great numbers of both. Many of us foreigners were established there. The English community was presided over by the British envoy Sir William Hamilton, already known to us through my mother, who was a great admirer of his classical scholarship. I quickly saw that she thought rather less well of Sir William's new wife, Emma. In her youth, Lady Hamilton had been kept by a succession of rich men—Lord B told me she'd famously once danced naked on a dining table before a most appreciative male audience. Now she was far more decorous in her habits, although she sometimes appeared at her husband's parties to perform what she called her "attitudes"—silent, unmoving poses that mimicked antique statues, clad in flimsy draperies which left very little to the imagination.

That was the Naples I came to love—a handsome, easygoing town, with an air of perpetual holiday about it, in which all the stricter social rules were relaxed. Everything was simpler there, including making friends. Acquaintances who at home might have taken an age to mature into anything closer there soon became one's most intimate companions.

It was thus I came to know Lady Webster so well. She'd been traveling on the Continent, and our paths had crossed a few times before; but in Naples she quickly became one of my closest confidantes. She was unhappily married to a husband she loathed, and when I first met her was heavily pregnant with his child. My delicate health meant I tired as easily as she did, so we spent many a drowsy afternoon resting together and, as women will in such circumstances, relating our marital woes to each other.

Lady Webster always made me think of an eagle or some other merciless bird of prey. She was very striking in her person, with a piercing, intelligent stare, an iron will, and a very sharp tongue. She reminded me sometimes of Lady Melbourne, though she was much younger. Still only in her twenties, she possessed the effortlessly commanding manner of an imperious dowager. She was perhaps the most selfish woman I've ever met, and quite open about her desire to have her own way in everything that mattered. Her pitiless disdain was curiously attractive to a certain kind of young man, and she had gathered around herself a little coterie of devoted admirers who were quite besotted with her, despite the impatience and irritation with which she often received their attentions.

"You're very cruel to them," I once remarked after she had delivered a particularly crushing rebuke to one of her followers.

"Nonsense," she replied. "And anyway, they like it. They're so used to being treated as if they were lords of creation, they can't quite believe it when one of us strikes a different tone."

She rubbed her stomach thoughtfully.

"The truth is," she continued, turning her haughty glance back to me, "I'm trying to cultivate the habit of authority. I'm readying myself for a different kind of life."

"Do you intend to take the veil?" I asked lightly. "You'd make an excellent abbess, ruling over the poor nuns with a rod of iron. William is desperate to visit a convent. Apparently, boys aren't allowed in after they're eight years old, so he asks me night and day to take him to one. Perhaps you could arrange it?"

Lady Webster ignored me. She never acknowledged a joke unless she herself had made it.

"I tell you what it is," she said, beckoning me closer. "I've resolved never again to be under a man's control, especially not a fool like Webster. I'm determined to find myself another husband. He must be sufficiently rich and powerful to give me the kind of life I like and clever enough that I can respect him; but of such a pliant temperament that he will have no objection to being mastered by me in every significant aspect of our lives."

I laughed out loud at this. "Where on earth would you meet a man like that? I'm sure I've never met such a creature."

"No, I don't suppose you have. But have you been looking? I doubt it. We women are taught from the cradle that it's the man's place to lead. A man who doesn't share the general taste of his sex for domination is unlikely to be admired for it; indeed, he may find himself considered not quite a man at all, by both his male and female acquaintances. For that reason alone, a man who prefers to put himself under the governorship of a woman is hardly likely to advertise it. But that doesn't mean they don't exist. I am persuaded they do, and furthermore, I am absolutely determined to find one."

"And if you succeed, what then? How will it be possible for you to marry him?"

"I shall insist we run away together, and then Webster will be obliged to divorce me."

"But what about your children? There are two of them, I believe. And this baby here? If you're the guilty party, they'll all be taken away from you."

"Yes, I know—and am sorry for it." Her face clouded for a moment. "But as things are, I'm really much too angry to be a good mother. They will be far better off without me. If we must part, so be it."

My shock must have been apparent, for she sighed and turned away.

"I see you don't approve. I admit it doesn't sound very well, when spelled out so plainly. But I suppose we must each find our own answers to alleviating the misery of the married state."

Yes, I thought, I understood as well as anyone how it felt to be inescapably tied to a man I could not love and how profoundly an unhappy wife might long to change her situation—but the idea of abandoning her children—and the ease with which Lady Webster justified it—horrified me, and I could think of nothing to say. I think both of us were relieved when a servant threw open the door and announced that Lord B had arrived to fetch me. Lady Webster clapped her hands.

"And here, exactly on cue, is your own partner in joy."

My husband looked uncomfortable as he entered the room. He disliked Lady Webster extremely, but if she sensed this, she gave no sign of it.

"Take excellent care of your wife, Lord Bessborough, and pray bring her back to me very quickly. What a pleasure it is to have an intelligent companion to converse with. Fools are so fatiguing, don't you agree?"

She took my hand in hers and patted it affectionately. "Come again soon. Shall we say Friday? I'm very bored. The sixth month is the worst, I think. Too large to move and yet still so long to go." She smiled graciously at Lord B, who made her a correct little bow, took my arm, and led me slowly away.

"Oh and don't forget, dearest Lady B," she cried, just before we reached the door, "if you should hear of anyone answering the description I gave you, do let me know at your earliest convenience, for it is a situation I'm very eager to fill."

Once we were settled in the carriage, I saw Lord B wasn't pleased. It had been a long time since I'd seen this once familiar expression of displeasure, but I'd noticed it had returned somewhat since we had established ourselves in Naples. I knew the fault was mine. I had honestly tried to satisfy myself with a retired life, venturing out only among those people with whom Lord B was comfortable; but as my health slowly improved, I'd begun to yearn for a little more. I very much enjoyed Neapolitan society. I liked finding myself once more among lively, entertaining people. I had tried to disguise my enthusiasm, for I knew my husband did not share it; but I had not succeeded. He saw only too clearly my growing appetite for the enjoyments Naples offered and couldn't conceal his disappointment. Lady Webster, in particular, represented everything he disliked about a world that he did not miss at all.

"I cannot think that Lady Webster is a very good friend for you."

"What do you object to in her?"

"She seems a cold, calculating sort of woman. Insincere. Unscrupulous, too, I imagine."

I could not entirely disagree but felt obliged to say something in her favor.

"She's very young and very miserable. I think she sometimes pretends to be more heartless than she really is."

I honestly thought this was unlikely but hoped it might be true.

He turned toward me, his look softer now.

"You always try to see the best in everyone, even when they don't deserve it."

I smiled, pleased to have smoothed away his irritation. He took my hand and kissed it.

"Shall we take the carriage out tonight? We might see Vesuvius on fire if we're lucky. The flames are said to be quite extraordinary in the darkness."

My heart sank. "Any other night, I should love to see it. But perhaps you've forgotten, we have a small party at home tonight. A little music, some cards, a light supper."

His face fell. "Who's coming?"

I swallowed hard. I saw where this was leading. "The Palmerstons. Lord Grandison. Sir William may look in later, perhaps with Emma."

"And what about Beauclerk? Is he invited?"

Charles Beauclerk was a young man who fancied himself in love with me and hung about our house hoping to attract my attention. He was said to be witty; but as he was paralyzed by shyness in my presence, I never saw any evidence of it. His admiration was mute, but determined, and Lord B disliked him very much indeed.

"He heard me telling Caro about it and asked if he could come too. I hadn't the heart to refuse him."

Lord B removed his hand from mine and stared into the street. I cursed my own stupidity. Why hadn't I told Beauclerk he wasn't welcome? I knew how Lord B would take it, and yet I'd replied, "Yes, come around nine; we'll be glad to see you." Why had I done it? Boredom? A childish desire to know myself still admired? A perversity of character that made me restless and discontented, incapable of doing what I knew was right? I sighed inwardly. There was no more talk of Vesuvius; we drove the rest of the way home without another word.

A few days later, in defiance of Lord B's disapproval, I went to visit Lady Webster again. And there, on her terrace, I encountered Lord Granville Leveson-Gower for the first time. Everything changed after that. Of course, in the days that followed, I tried to persuade myself that wasn't so, that nothing of any significance had really happened. It was true I'd been charmed by him; that much, I could admit. Nor did I deny the strength of the attraction I'd felt for him, or that I'd thought of him afterward far more than I should have done, calling to mind the beauty of the contrast between the blue of his eyes and the black of his hair.

But all this, I told myself, could be conquered. Patience and the imposition of a little self-control would soon see it off. It was probably as well for me that I couldn't foresee the true consequences that were to follow from that fateful meeting with Lord Granville—that they'd detonate all my good intentions to reconcile with my husband and lead me into a life of passion and joy, of betrayal and deception, such as even I, with all my romantic notions about love, had barely imagined possible in those distant, innocent days.

I really tried my best to put some salutary distance between Lord Granville and myself for a while, but in a circle as tightly knit as that of the English in Naples, that proved quite impossible. For all my efforts to avoid him, I often found myself in his company. He was traveling with three friends—Lords Morpeth, Boringdon, and Holland—all personable, well-connected young men, who could be relied upon to give a good account of themselves at card parties, dances, and suppers. Naturally, they were invited everywhere—and soon it became quite usual to discover one of them sitting beside me at some dinner or assembly. I was always relaxed and easy with his friends; but with Lord Granville himself, I was always a little on edge.

He had an intensity of manner which made me acutely aware of his proximity. His behavior was always perfectly correct—he was the very model of politeness—but he had a way of looking at me, never vulgar nor ogling, just fixing me sometimes with that clear blue gaze, which I found both exciting and disturbing. I wish I could say his attentions were unwelcome—how much easier my life would have been if that had been so—but really, I was flattered by them.

After so many exhausting years, after so much sickness and suffering, it was glorious to be admired by so handsome a man. It was as if, after a long gray winter, the sun had come out, inviting me to turn up my face and bask in its warmth.

I wonder, if I'd been ten years younger and as heedless as I was then, whether I would have actively encouraged him. But I was older now, and wary. I couldn't afford any more scrapes. Lord B had been astonishingly forgiving of my previous transgressions; I couldn't expect him to be so indulgent again. And anyway, I reasoned, it would be a great mistake to misunderstand the nature of Lord G's interest—surely all he intended was a little gallantry, a mild flirtation to pass the time until some more suitable—and much younger—lady appeared, to whom he would swiftly transfer his interest, my momentary appeal quite forgotten. Really, it all amounted to nothing. I had almost convinced myself of the truth of this—only for Lady Webster to shatter my comforting illusion.

We were driving down the highway that runs alongside the Bay of Naples. It was one of my favorite outings—the view was stupendous, the sea turquoise before us, with the scent of citrus and salt on its breeze. I should have liked to enjoy so much beauty quietly, but Lady Webster has never met a silence she did not hurry to fill and hadn't stopped talking since we left her house. Her subject was Lord Holland, one of Lord G's companions, whom she had taken up with great enthusiasm.

"He really is quite delightful, very well-read, his conversation intelligent, his mind properly informed on all matters of importance."

"He's a very decent young man," I replied, "with many excellent parts, if he can be persuaded to exercise them a little more."

He was Mr. Fox's nephew, and I'd known him since he was a child. His family connections meant he was already spoken of in some quarters as Mr. Fox's political heir. I wasn't so sure. He was clever and affable. But in my view, he lacked the steeliness of character necessary in a leader.

"With the right encouragement, I'm sure that could be resolved."

Then suddenly it dawned on me—and I understood Lady Webster's interest in this plain and rather callow young man.

"Are you telling me that you're seriously considering Lord Holland as a candidate for becoming your second husband?"

"Certainly," she replied. "He's everything I want in a man. Intelligent, but malleable. Hardly any bad habits, and those mostly the product of youth. Maturity will cure most of them, and I shall root out the rest. No objection to being led, but not a fool." Her face darkened. "I will never again be yoked to a fool."

"Well, I see the advantages for you. But what about his political career? Your being divorced will be a great hindrance to him. You'll never be presented at court, and many grand ladies will never visit you."

Lady Webster laughed.

"That will be their loss. Plenty of others will come—including you, I hope?" Skewered by her glare, I nodded meekly.

"And what does Lord Holland say? Is he aware of his fate?"

"I think he sees in which direction matters are tending. Of course, nothing can really be done until I'm delivered."

She leaned back in her seat, clasped her hands above her stomach, and smiled.

"Once that's over, I shall take him as my lover, we'll run away together, Webster will divorce me, and Holland will do the decent thing, and I shall become his wife."

"You seem to have everything in hand."

"I like him very much and think we'd go on very well together. Although he'll never be as well-looking as your Lord Granville, he has many other qualities to recommend him."

"*My* Lord Granville? What do you mean?"

"Your newest disciple. He follows you wherever you go and stares at you, hoping to melt your heart. Don't say you haven't noticed?"

"I assure you, you're quite mistaken."

"Am I? Well, Lord Holland tells me poor Beauclerk is desolate, thinks he has no chance at all with such an opponent in the field."

"I have no idea of myself as a bone to be fought over," I declared. "Beauclerk is a young man with a silly fancy, and if Lord Granville is indeed behaving as you say, he is in the same case. Neither of them is much more than a boy."

Lady Webster was unabashed.

"Lord Holland is exactly of an age with Lord Granville, and I can assure you, he is not a boy. Surely no man of twenty-one can be considered as such, unless he is of a singularly unenterprising character. Which is certainly not true of Lord Granville. Lord Holland tells me he's already had a liaison with a Mrs. St. John before they left England. And rumor has it that when he was in Paris, his own sister-in-law fell in love with him."

"That doesn't mean her feelings were reciprocated. He may have done everything in his power to discourage her."

"Gossip says otherwise." She reached for a cushion and placed it carefully in the small of her back. "Both these ladies were older than he. About your own age, in fact."

I did not like the direction of this conversation and had no desire to pursue it further.

"I don't think it reflects well on us to talk scandal when we know nothing of the people involved," I said primly.

"Perhaps it was nothing but idle calumny. But it's easy to see how these stories begin. When such a handsome man pays you serious attention, the question of surrender is always on your mind. 'Shall I or shan't I?' And after a while, everyone will think you have, even if you haven't."

With some effort, she heaved herself up into a more comfortable position.

"I'm so glad Lord Holland's looks are nothing extraordinary. Plainness is such a great encouragement to fidelity, don't you agree?"

"That may be true for women. I haven't observed it to make much difference to men's behavior, but perhaps your Lord Holland will be different in that respect."

"Oh, I shall make sure of that."

Yes, I thought, poor Lord Holland, he won't be allowed to blow his nose without her permission. I wasn't sure I should care for a man with so little pride in himself. Lady Webster saw I was not to be drawn on Lord Granville, and soon we were back on a different topic of conversation. For the rest of our outing, she talked of nothing but the man she intended to make her second husband, even as the baby of her current spouse kicked vigorously within her at every bump in the road.

Most people, I'm sure, would consider Lady Webster and her schemes very wicked indeed, and even I was somewhat taken aback by the brazenness with which she talked of them; but I couldn't wholly condemn her. Married very young and unwillingly to a much older man she disliked, what else was she to do? Bitter, disappointed wives are compelled to resort to deceit, betrayal, and lies, or how else can they get what they want? Men leave us no choice. All the power is in their hands. We women are left with nothing but petty ruses that humiliate us, even when they deliver the occasional victory. Really, what a world we have made of it. My leg ached. I thought I should have a bath once I was home.

———— ∞ ————

J felt much better once I was up to my neck in warm water. The bath took an age to fill and gave the servants a great deal of work, so it was an indulgence I rarely allowed myself. Sally sat waiting beside me, cotton wrap on her lap, but I wasn't ready to get out yet. I closed my eyes, and my thoughts wandered back to a subject from which, these days, they rarely strayed.

"Sally," I asked drowsily, "what do you think of Lord Granville?"

"He's very handsome."

"Yes—but beyond that. What kind of man does he seem to you?"

"I've hardly been in his company, so I can't really say."

I opened my eyes, alert now. I saw she was uncomfortable, but I persevered.

"You've seen him when we're out and about, when he comes to talk to me. Surely that's enough to have formed some impression?"

"He seems a very proud gentleman. Very certain of himself."

"There's nothing wrong with pride, if you have qualities that merit it."

"Well, I can't speak to that—but I think when a man looks as he does, it must have some effect on his character."

"And what do you think that effect has been on him?"

"I expect he's used to getting what he wants. I doubt he's often been disappointed. And if he did meet with any setback, it would only make him try all the harder to surmount it. His pride wouldn't let him do otherwise."

"You've clearly made quite a study of him," I replied, in what I hoped was a playful tone. "For someone we hardly know."

She refused to return my smile, determined to be serious.

"People get to know each other very quickly here. The usual rules don't seem to apply. Everything happens very fast."

I laughed. "You're quite right—we're obliged to find each other likable."

"It's plain Lord Granville finds you more than likable. Anyone can see it."

I'm ashamed to say I didn't dislike this idea, although I tried not to show it.

"He likes women's company, that's all. I'm not sure it's mine especially."

"I don't see him spending as much time with any other lady."

"You've given this some thought, haven't you?"

"I felt I had to, once I'd noticed his preference for you—his very marked preference. If I'm honest, it worries me."

"Why should it do that?"

"Because I want to see you happy—not distressed and troubled like before."

I didn't reply, but Sally was not to be deflected.

"Seeing Lord Granville making up to you brought it all back to me. Those terrible times with Mr. Sheridan." She took a deep breath. "And it made me ask the same question you've just asked me. What kind of man is he?"

"And what did you conclude?"

"I think he's dangerous. Very beautiful, very sure of himself, not used to being thwarted. If I was obliged to choose one word to describe him, that's what I'd say—dangerous."

Suddenly the water felt cold. Silently I held out my hand—Sally took it, helped me into my wrap, and hurried off to get me a drink. Well, I had asked, and she had answered. I had always encouraged her to speak frankly to me, so I could hardly complain when she was candid. We both knew her words were intended as a warning. It was up to me to decide if I would heed them.

9

A few nights later, Lord B and I were engaged to join an evening of entertainments with the Hamiltons.

Their events were always well attended, and this was no exception. My husband wasted no time escaping the crush of people, leaving me to fend for myself. I was standing in the hall for a moment, shrinking at the clamor and noise coming from the public rooms, when I felt a touch on my arm. It was Lady Webster, looking larger than ever.

"Good luck in there," she cried, "it's packed with people, a positive rout—far too much for me and my burden, so both of us are going home."

"Perhaps I should do the same. I've completely lost any taste for crowds."

"Your poor lovesick swain is in there somewhere. Have you decided yet whether to be kind to him or not?"

"I've no intention of indulging in that sort of kindness," I retorted, "with Lord Granville or anyone else."

She laughed. "Really? Then it will cause you no pain at all to learn that he won't be with us for much longer. Holland tells me his father has ordered him home. Duty calls, apparently. But not, you'll be glad to hear, to serve in the regular army. His mother would never have stood for that. He's to join a regiment of volunteers at Plymouth, guarding the docks against the wicked French."

"But he's only just arrived!" I was too surprised to disguise my shock. Lady Webster raised a knowing eyebrow.

"He takes the same view, apparently. Holland thinks he may delay his departure for a while but not for very long. Duty calls, apparently. You may not have much time to decide if you will or if you won't . . ."

She kissed my cheek with a very arch air and went to find her carriage. Lord B had still not reappeared, so I walked back to the great front door and stood there for a few minutes, breathing in the warm, jasmine-scented darkness. This was good news, I told myself: I couldn't be tempted if he wasn't here. Thus spoke my conscience—but my heart whispered, "Ah, but won't you miss him when he's gone, those eyes, that mouth." I refused to allow such thoughts. No, it was all for the best. Fate had intervened to protect me from my own weakness. There could be no other response but relief.

I took a deep breath and plunged back into the palazzo's great drawing room. I went in search of Lord B, but the press of people was so great I made but slow progress. I was forced to a halt next to an elderly couple of our acquaintance, who seized upon the opportunity to discuss in detail our respective states of health; but soon, the noise about us was so great that I could no longer hear the lady's account of the remarkable improvement in her symptoms since taking the waters at Bagni di Lucca. Her whispers were overwhelmed by the volume of argument coming from a group of young men, each convinced the best way to carry his point was to shout more loudly than his opponent.

"Youth, strong Italian wine, and politics," mused her husband, smiling. "Let us hope it won't come to blows."

I turned to look. There were Lords Morpeth and Boringdon, Lord Granville's friends, clustered together with a few other young men I didn't know. They all had the excited look of those watching some great contest, whose outcome was not yet certain, but which promised a good deal of entertainment before it was done. In the midst of the little circle stood Lord Holland, clearly one of the chief adversaries, looking a little defensive in his posture, but determined nonetheless to stand his ground. Opposite him was Lord Granville, his whole demeanor suggesting his scornful rejection of everything Lord Holland had just said. Despite their friendship, their political views could not have been more different, as Lord Granville was clearly ready and eager to demonstrate.

"Come, Holland," he cried, flushed with excitement, "you must admit the truth of it—the Revolution has done for you Whigs and utterly finished Mr. Fox. He doesn't understand it—and refuses to appreciate the danger it poses, not just to France, but to all Europe. He has nothing to offer but platitudes unequal to the situation in which we find ourselves. I'm sorry to say it, as you are his nephew— but Mr. Fox is yesterday's man—and for as long as he remains at the head of his party, he is a danger to us all."

The young men around him cheered or jeered, according to their party sympathies. Lord Holland leaped to his uncle's defense, declaring he would rather pledge himself any day to Mr. Fox's ideals than to the warmongering tyranny of Lord Granville's favorite, Mr. Pitt; he gave as good as he got, as the saying has it, and the argument rolled on, to the obvious pleasure of all concerned.

"No doubt they're practicing for when they take their seats in the House," observed my companion. "I suppose it's rather like boxing— the more you do it, the better you get."

I smiled, nodded, and excused myself, pushing through the other guests as forcefully as I could. I would not stay to hear any more. I couldn't trust myself to stay silent, and nothing would be gained by any intervention of mine.

God knows, such arguments were not uncommon in the difficult times in which we found ourselves. The revolution in France had at first seemed to promise the end of a system of government that elevated the power of the King, while stifling the voices of his people. Good Whigs like me hoped it might usher in something more like our own politics, which, imperfect as they were, placed the liberty of the people firmly at its heart. But events in France had moved swiftly beyond any such moderate ambitions, replacing them with an entirely new set of ideas, declaring the monarchy abolished, the church reformed, and all the old social distinctions eliminated. The Terror that followed had been pursued with a murderous zeal that was horrifying to witness. Old friends of Georgiana's and mine had died horrible deaths as a result of these persecutions. This was not what we'd hoped for in 1789. And now, we were fighting a war that was not going at all as had been expected, in which French armies seemed unstoppable, winning victory after victory across Europe.

In these circumstances, it was hardly surprising that the main, indeed the only political question of the hour was how Britain should respond. Lord Granville came from a staunchly Tory family, loyal supporters of Mr. Pitt's government, for whom there was only one possible answer: a more active prosecution of hostilities abroad, together with the suppression of any ideas at home that might encourage discontented Britons to follow in the footsteps of their revolutionary counterparts in France.

We Whigs found ourselves in a far more difficult place. For all our misgivings about the ferocity of the revolutionary regime, it was uncomfortable for us to ally ourselves with those, both at home and abroad, who seemed inclined to use the panic induced by French successes to reverse all the gains in British liberty that had been achieved at such cost over many centuries. And yet—as the French occupied more and more of Europe and showed themselves ever more ferocious in eliminating opposition to the revolutionary cause, could we really afford to retain our scruples? Mr. Fox, the leader of our party, sought a negotiated peace, arguing that it was the intransigence of France's enemies that had provoked her aggression; but his was an increasingly isolated voice, overwhelmed by the shouts of his opponents.

I was only too used to hearing Mr. Fox criticized, often very viciously; but there was something in Lord Granville's attack upon him that drove me close to fury. I was enraged by the crowing delight he appeared to take in his difficulties, astonished by his presumption in so rudely dismissing such a great man.

I confess a personal interest here, for Mr. Fox had been the object of my sister's and my love and admiration since we were girls. We were brought up to admire his principles, and firmly believed no one in our lifetimes had done so much to forward the cause of liberty and truth. Such was his character as a public man; but I had known him intimately all my life and knew that in private, he was the kindest and most generous of men, with a nobility of spirit I had never seen equaled.

To hear him belittled in this way by Lord Granville—an untried, inexperienced young nobody, who'd never fought an election nor set foot in the Commons, who had no appreciation of the complexities of political life, who could never expect to equal the goodness and grandeur of the man he ridiculed—was it any surprise I was angry?

It was only once I'd adequately rehearsed to myself all the displeasure I felt so strongly that I looked about and saw where my distracted, indignant steps had led me. I was at the farthest end of the salon, near a large arched alcove where I knew Sir William Hamilton had set up a very fine chessboard. We'd played there together on many quiet afternoons. People are often surprised to discover I'm fond of the game, and even more taken aback when I beat them at it, because, I suppose, they don't consider me a particularly calculating or, indeed, a very rational being.

I sat down at the board, took a deep breath to further calm my temper, and noticed that a game had been abandoned in mid-contest, the pieces left in place. I studied them idly at first, but my curiosity was roused, and I began turning over in my mind how the white player might gain the upper hand. Soon I was so engrossed that I did not notice Lord Granville's arrival until he slid into the chair opposite me.

"I've been looking for you to pay my respects—I thought I saw you come in, but later, you were nowhere to be seen."

"Good evening, Lord Granville." I offered him a chilly smile. "In fact, we were not far away from each other a little earlier. You were talking to your friends. I might have lingered, but when I heard the subject of your conversation I did not choose to stay."

"Ah." He frowned. He knew immediately what I meant. "I know you're a great admirer of Mr. Fox. Those words weren't intended for you to hear."

"No one should have heard them, Lord Granville, because they should not have been said. They were disrespectful in the highest degree. Whatever your differences in politics, it's unforgivable to talk in such a low way about a man who, if he cannot command your support, nevertheless deserves the courtesy of your respect. It was badly done, Lord Granville."

I spoke so severely that I shouldn't have been surprised if he'd walked away. Instead, he replied in an even, thoughtful tone.

"I am truly sorry if I offended you and admit my language was not well chosen. I apologize for that. But—I cannot deny that I disagree very strongly with Mr. Fox's position on the war with France, and indeed with almost everything else he says."

I sat back in my chair, arms crossed, ready now for a fight. "So you're one of Mr. Pitt's little band of true believers."

He inclined his head, determined not to be provoked. "I believe the Revolution poses a threat such as we have never seen before, and that it cannot be defeated except by adopting extraordinary measures—which your Mr. Fox is utterly unwilling to consider."

"If by that you mean war abroad and repression at home—then I believe Mr. Fox is right to oppose them. What use is victory, if by achieving it we lose those freedoms which we fought so hard to secure?"

"I fear you don't understand. These revolutionaries intend to turn the world upside down. And if the poor rise up at home, as they've done in France, you should be under no illusion how you'll be treated—Whig or Tory, it will all be one to them. You'll be as much the enemy as I. There will be no more Lady Bessborough then, but plain Mrs. Ponsonby—Citizeness Ponsonby, even. Your lands will be taken from you, and you'll be obliged to beg for your bread."

He was angry and I was pleased, glad to have ruffled that imperturbable self-possession of his.

"Bravo, sir, a speech entirely worthy of your cause, intended to create fear and suspicion among all who hear it. You think the prospect of a guillotine in Piccadilly should be enough to make me abandon every principle I hold dear. I cannot say honestly if I should be brave enough to die for my beliefs—but I refuse to be frightened out of them by such false comparisons. I have lived in France—which I believe you have not—and know their government pressed upon the people harder than our own does in England. I don't believe my countrymen would behave as the French have done. You Tories make so much of John Bull's virtues and yet seem incapable of trusting him to exercise them."

"A pretty argument, but not all in your party would agree with it. Several of your Whig friends are already in conversation with Mr. Pitt with a view to joining his government. Including your own brother, I hear."

That was a cruel stroke, but possibly true. My sister had written to tell me George had been debating whether circumstances obliged him to shift his alliance, but neither of us thought he would take so momentous a step. I refused to give Lord Granville the pleasure of seeing I was in any way discomposed.

"Everyone must make their own choices as they see fit. For myself, I refuse to allow fear or self-interest to justify the abandonment of all efforts which tend toward the betterment and happiness of our fellow creatures."

"I suppose, then, you're as much in favor of the abolition of slavery abroad, as reform at home?"

"I cannot support one without believing in the other. I imagine it is not a cause dear to your heart?"

"I don't think the time is right to embark upon it. Our situation is so fraught with danger that it cannot be considered now."

"And yet when times were quiet, it was said, 'Why should we disturb our peace with a subject on which opinion is violently divided?'"

"A moment may arrive when it will be right to act, but not when matters of such urgency press upon us."

"I don't know what can be considered more pressing than the righting of such a terrible wrong, which, as our own countrymen are the chief practitioners, it lies in our own hands to correct. Only a person with no sense of common humanity could wish to see such a measure delayed."

"By which I am to suppose you mean me?"

"Not just you, for sadly there are many others who make the same defense of such an abominable practice. But if you wish to assume a personal application, only you can discern the justice of it."

I was angry now. I fixed my eyes on the chessboard, to avoid having to look at him. I think he was equally put out, for we did not speak for what seemed an age.

"Well," he said finally, "neither of us can say that we don't understand what the other one believes. If we are not to part in anger," he continued, in a more conciliating tone, "perhaps we should occupy ourselves with something other than politics for a while? Finding you here suggests you play chess. Shall we have a game?"

It was a few seconds before I favored him with a reply—a slight, disdainful nod—and obediently, he laid out the pieces.

To those who don't play, it may seem strange that a game of chess can reflect one's mood. But it appeared to me as though all our moves were merely a continuation of our argument by other means. Sharp little feints, deceptive sacrifices, assertive attempts to land a knockout blow. It was an ill-mannered contest and ended as most games do when the players are in a passion.

"I believe that is stalemate, Lord Granville."

He stared at the board, then looked up at me. "I think neither of us was playing at our best. I should like a chance to show you my true capabilities. What do you say to a rematch?"

"I'll think about it."

"Of course. I'll await the favor of your answer."

I nodded coolly, stood up, and took my leave. Eventually, I found Lord B at the card table and sat beside him until he was too tired to play anymore, and we went home. My husband went to bed, but I stayed for some time on the terrace, watching the great yellow moon rise in the black star-speckled sky, turning over the events of the evening in my mind. Our argumentative encounter had demonstrated, in the strongest possible terms, that Lord Granville and I had not a single idea in common, that we couldn't be further apart on every belief I held most dear. At the same time, I'd glimpsed in him a haughtiness I much disliked, a sense of his own importance that would not be easily cowed. Not a man used to being thwarted, as Sally had remarked.

If I'd been sensible, these observations should have been enough to persuade me never to see him again. But when I considered that prospect, I didn't like it at all. The truth was, I had rather enjoyed our dispute—Lord Granville had at least respected my views enough to do me the honor of properly disputing them. I could never have had such a conversation with Lord B, who disliked extremely any form of abstract discussion. I sighed. Why should I deprive myself of the pleasure of such debates, especially when the author of them was to be gone in a very short time? And anyway, surely the great differences between us were in fact a form of protection against my becoming further involved with him, for how could I ever become seriously attached to a man who held such opinions? Such is the sophistry of a woman seeking to justify the hidden wishes of her heart. Any deeper involvement, I told myself, was out of the question. But I could quite safely enjoy the pleasure of his friendship.

The Italians have a name for what I had in mind—a male companion who entertains and attends to a lady without expecting any more intimate favors is known as her cavaliere servente. That was what I thought Lord Granville might be to me during the month or so he'd remain in Naples: a harmless but entertaining little diversion that I could easily manage. And then he would leave, and I'd have a charming memory to cherish in later years. By the time I went to bed, I had everything decided. I saw Lord Granville and myself indulging in a little bantering conversation in the sunshine, laughing and trading witticisms until he went home. Well—there's no fool like an old fool, as the proverb has it. Looking back, I wasn't so old— thirty-three that year, I think—but rarely has there been a bigger fool than I was, that bright, moonlit night.

The next few weeks were some of the happiest in my life. We did nothing but entertain ourselves—a little sightseeing, visits to the great palace at Capodimonte, the remains of Virgil's tomb, to Pompeii again and again, for it was always our favorite of all the great ruins. Once we even rode upon mules up to the very crater of Vesuvius, a sight to inspire both awe and terror—I still have in my possession a piece of lava which I gathered from the volcano's hot ground. Less demanding were the delightful picnics laid out for us in flower-filled gardens, accompanied by the most enticing food and the most delicate, perfumed wines. Sometimes we'd walk through groves of citrus trees just for the pleasure of plucking a ripe fruit direct from the tree. When I recall it now, I sometimes think Naples was as close to an earthly paradise as any other place I have visited in my life.

Whenever we were together—which was often, as he did all he could to ensure he was included in all our activities—Lord Granville took every possible opportunity to sit by my side and entertain me, recounting amusing stories while always hinting at the regret he felt in leaving a place whose attractions grew upon him more and more each day. I deflected all his flirtations with a ready smile and a light laugh. Lord B seemed oblivious to his attentions to me. It was poor Mr. Beauclerk, still trailing imploringly in my wake, who occupied all my husband's thoughts and contributed to his increasingly frustrated mood. As I grew happier, Lord B's mood darkened. But I was so absorbed in my own diversions that I didn't pay it much heed. I thought my innocence was sufficient defense against any suspicions he might harbor. I'd done nothing wrong, and I had no plans to do wrong. He had no reason for concern.

Lady Webster, however, was more perceptive.

"So you've decided to be kind to Lord Granville?" she asked me one warm afternoon, as we sat alone in a green glade.

"Not in the way you mean. He's a charming companion, but no more than that."

"I wonder if that's what he thinks. He looks at you as though he'd like to gobble you up."

"I believe he understands how matters stand."

"If you say so."

Her knowing expression provoked me; and it was this that determined me to speak plainly to Lord Granville about our situation. I couldn't bear him to think I was encouraging him to expect favors I did not intend to grant. It was a few days before we found ourselves alone, sitting on a terrace while my husband talked to Sir William Hamilton inside. I knew I must be direct so there was no possibility of his mistaking my meaning.

"I have something important to say, Lord Granville, and hope you will attend seriously to me."

"I can't think of any occasion when I've failed to do so. I hang on your every word."

"It must be obvious how very much I enjoy your company," I began, my voice very steady. "But you shouldn't be under any illusion as to the nature of my feelings. I've much enjoyed becoming your friend over these last few weeks. But you must understand:

friendship is all I have to offer. Nothing more can ever exist between us. Not now or at any time in the future."

"I'm glad to have your friendship," he replied, "but I can't pretend it will satisfy me. You must have observed that my feelings for you go far beyond what is usually the case between friends." He leaned toward me. "I am powerfully drawn to you—very strongly attracted—do you not feel it too?"

I shivered a little at his directness—then took a deep breath and drew away.

"My circumstances do not allow it. You must see that."

"It seems very unfair that two people, who feel as I believe we do, cannot gratify those feelings. That's the very point of being alive, is it not?"

I heard Lord B laugh at some remark of Sir William's. I could hardly believe another man was making love to me so close to where my husband sat. I felt a definite impulse of excitement—but refused to give in to it. I remembered where my duty lay and summoned up all my resolve.

"I'll pretend you didn't say that. I repeat, sir, I have nothing to offer you but friendship. If you can accept that, I will continue to see you. If not, I'm afraid all intercourse must cease between us. Those are my conditions."

"As I cannot bear to be denied your company, I'm obliged to comply. But you must understand that isn't what I want."

"You must swear to it—that my friendship will be enough for you."

"I'm afraid I would perjure myself."

"What you want you cannot have. If you do not swear, I will never speak to you again."

"Then I have no choice. I swear it. But an oath reluctantly sworn can never be truly binding. The mind might be willing, but the heart protests."

"Really, Lord Granville, you've sworn and must abide by your vow. That's all. Now you may fetch me some more wine, if you will."

Only later did the full implications of our conversation become plain. Yes, I'd been frank about what I could offer, but he'd been equally candid in declaring it was not enough. I could no longer tell myself I was ignorant of his desires. This was another moment when I might have put an end to things. Instead, I told myself I had drawn a line that was never to be crossed. This was the first time I deceived myself in this way, but it was not to be the last.

The days went by so quickly that it seemed no time at all before Lord Granville's departure was upon us. I didn't allow myself to brood upon his going, lest I reveal how much I would miss him. I felt this all the more because his behavior was then everything I could have wished, amiable but never importunate. He'd evidently taken my words to heart—we chatted and laughed, and everything was so easy and natural between us that I let down my guard. When he came to see me to make his final goodbyes, I was moved to tell him how much I would miss him. At this he seized my hand and kissed it.

"Let me write to you. I must write to you."

"I hardly think that would be right."

"Please let me write. I cannot bear it if you say no."

I should have refused—every rational fiber of my being cried out to me to deny him. Instead, I nodded. That was enough for him—he didn't wait for me to change my mind, and without attempting another kiss, he bowed and quickly walked away.

I watched him go, dazed by the touch of his lips on my hand. This was not what I'd intended. His departure was supposed to have put an end to our relations—consigned him to my memory as a pleasurable flirtation that would have made me smile when I thought of it back in gray, wet London. But in that fatal moment—the kiss had done it—my discipline had wavered. I'd opened the door of opportunity just a crack—but enough to keep his hopes fully alive.

I was furious with myself. How could I have been so stupid? But then I took a few deep breaths and began to think more calmly. There was nothing to fear in the exchange of a few letters. It was up to me to set the tone of our correspondence, and I could make sure there was no harm in it. A little light badinage, nothing more. I was more than equal to managing a few overheated letters from an intense, self-important young man who thought himself irresistible.

This was the second time I'd persuaded myself I was in control of what passed between us; and, as things turned out, the second time my confidence in myself was quite mistaken. My own feelings, it transpired, were no more to be trusted than his.

11

A month later, his letters began to arrive. I admit I was delighted to get them, far more excited than I should have been. Much as I'd tried to push him from my mind, telling myself the pleasant interlude I'd permitted us was over, it had proved quite impossible to forget him. My hand trembled a little as I opened the first one. I saw immediately he was far from happy. His situation at Plymouth was not much to his liking. Military life didn't suit him, certainly not when it was as dull and undemanding as his own duties were at present. He had little in common with his fellow officers and regretted extremely the loss of the easy society we'd all enjoyed at Naples. What was I doing? Whom did I see? Here a note of jealousy crept in. Was Beauclerk still making up to me? He missed me very much, far more, he was sure, than I missed him. Had I any comfort to offer him, any kindness to bestow?

I can't say I wasn't secretly flattered by his imploring tone. I was pleased he hadn't forgotten me, and indeed, more than a little thrilled by his importunate words. But I knew better than to let him know that. Instead, I replied in my archest manner, saying that although he was much missed, we went on as best we could without him; and as to Beauclerk, I was surrounded by so many amiable young men, it was hard to know which I preferred. I was as light and brittle as I knew how, hoping, I suppose, to quash his ardor with my breezy playfulness. It was all to no effect. His next letters were even more urgent and demanding, repeating again and again what he'd told me on our terrace, that his feelings for me were of the strongest possible nature and had only increased in their intensity since we'd been parted. I confess I wasn't entirely indifferent to the palpable desire I sensed in him; but I knew what I had to do and wrote back sternly repeating what I'd said to him before, that I hoped I was become too old and too wise ever again to involve myself in anything other than friendship. That was all he could expect from me; and the sooner he resigned himself to that, the happier he would be. Surely there were enough pretty young women, even in Plymouth, to whom he could transfer his attentions?

Eventually, I assured myself, if I persisted in my dismissals, Lord Granville would grow tired of such a fruitless pursuit and leave me alone. I understood, however, that any such success depended on my own attitude as much as his. I knew my own weakness; I was only too aware I was not as indifferent to him as I sought to pretend. Did I have the discipline, the power of will to sustain my "touch-me-not" demeanor? I hoped so; and at any rate, he was far away and likely to remain so. Distance should assist where my self-control faltered. I was safe; in every possible way, I was safe and had every intention of remaining so.

Then one morning, as Lord B and I were eating breakfast, a servant brought him a letter. He read it in silence and looked up with a smile.

"It's from Dr. Warren. I wrote to him a while ago, informing him of the considerable improvements I'd seen in your health."

My heart was in my mouth. I thought I could guess what was coming but was too afraid to let the idea form, too terrified of tempting fate.

"I'm sure you'll be pleased to hear," continued Lord B, "that, in his opinion, you're now ready to make the journey back to England."

He folded the letter and placed it carefully beside his plate.

"I think it is time for us to go home."

Before I knew what I did, I rushed to Lord B, threw my arms around him, and wept on his shoulder. I had no words. I should see my boys—after so long, I should see them and hold them and kiss them. His arm crept around me, hesitantly at first; and for a few rare minutes, I felt comfortable in his embrace. Then the moment passed. We disentangled ourselves, a little embarrassed by our brief intimacy. Wiping my eyes, I returned to my seat. He called for more coffee and began to mull over the route that might get us most safely to England. It wouldn't be an easy journey, he warned me. The state of the countries through which we'd be obliged to pass couldn't be predicted. The whole of Europe was up in arms, and it was impossible to say what dangers we might encounter on our travels. He hoped I was prepared. I nodded but wasn't really listening. All I could think was that I should see my boys again.

Our journey was in every respect just as fraught with difficulty as Lord B had predicted. We left Italy in May 1794 and didn't arrive home until the end of August. We crossed from Italy into Switzerland and then into Germany. As it was impossible to cross the Channel from a French port, Lord B's intention was to embark from the Low Countries, taking a ship for Harwich. It seemed as though every road we took was crowded with the sad human victims of the conflict erupting all around us—poor people with nothing but what they could carry fleeing the consequences of some past battle, soldiers trudging in long, exhausted lines, all the chaotic and harrowing evidence of the suffering that war brings in its wake. For much of the time I was very frightened, though I did my best to hide it for William's and Caro's sake. My husband deserves much credit for shepherding us with such care through so many horrors, finding places for us to eat and sleep, and swiftly coming up with new plans when changing circumstances rendered our previous ones impossible.

I expressed as often as I could my heartfelt gratitude and admiration for all he'd done for us; but, shut up together as we were, hour after hour, day after day, week after week, it was impossible for me to ignore his increasingly somber mood. He hadn't been happy for some time—not since the moment we'd been properly embraced by the lively society of Naples. For me, it had been the greatest pleasure to find myself again among the kind of people whose company I most enjoyed. For him, the experience was very different, reminding him of his shortcomings, exacerbating his jealousies, bringing on once more all the disappointments and bitterness of old.

In my heart I knew this was the case, but I'd preferred not to think of it. Now, I was obliged to take notice. Sometimes in the carriage, I caught him looking at me, as if trying to make out a puzzle that eluded him. I couldn't meet his gaze—I was too afraid of the conversation it might provoke. And in truth, another more powerful obsession pushed every other consideration from my heart—I should very soon see my boys again. I should hold John and Fred in my arms and kiss their dear heads. We'd been away for nearly three years. Would I even recognize them? Would they know me? Brooding on these questions left no room in my thoughts to worry about Lord B's state of mind.

When we finally arrived at the Dutch coast, I thought myself only days from the reunion I so craved; but we could get no ship to take us, and when we did, the winds were unfavorable. It was three long weeks before we were at last safe aboard the ship that was to carry us to England. The extremity of my agitation can only be imagined. When the blurred outline of Harwich emerged from the gray dawn mist, I thought I might weep. I don't remember anything of our actual arrival—all I recall is hurrying as fast as my stiff legs would allow, over the cobbles to the carriage waiting for us. Georgiana had promised she would be there to meet me, whenever I might arrive. And now, here she was, a tall figure running toward me, and then I was in my sister's arms again, both of us crying, transported with the pleasure of being united once more.

"John and Fred are waiting for you in London. Shall you stay here overnight or go on now?"

"Oh, we must go now. I can't wait to see them. Do let us go now."

Georgiana insisted Lord B and I take her carriage, that she and the rest of our party would come on tomorrow. It wasn't until we were finally on the road to London that I plucked up the courage to ask my husband why he seemed so low.

"We're about to see John and Fred again. Isn't that enough to raise your spirits?"

"I love our children, Harriet, and you know how I've hated being parted from them."

"Then why aren't you happier? We're home at last. Isn't this what we've wanted for so long?"

"I know it's what you've wanted. For myself, I'm no longer so sure."

"I don't understand—why would you possibly want to stay away?"

"Because there were times—when we began upon our travels, when I was in London and writing to you, when I first came back to Naples—there were times then when I honestly believed matters were better between us. I allowed myself to think we were happy together, in a way we never were at home. I liked that. I didn't want to go back to where we were before—but I'm afraid that's exactly what will happen. It'd already started in Naples toward the end. Back in London it will be worse. In a few months, the old life will have engulfed us once more—and we'll never be happy again."

I had never heard him speak with such feeling. I know what I should have done—leaned my head on his shoulder, told him no, that would never happen, that I too wished for a fresh start and would do all in my power to bring it about. But it was too much. I couldn't do it. Too much had passed between us for that. I took his hand in mine—but it was not enough—it was a moment too late—and after a few seconds, he withdrew it. We did not talk of this again.

A week after our arrival, we threw open the doors of Cavendish Square and invited everyone we knew to join us in celebrating our return. The house was packed with people, children running to and fro, guests crowded into every room, some truly happy to see us once more, others simply curious, anxious for any snippet of gossip they could carry away with them about how we looked and what we'd said.

I'd been surrounded by this noisy chaos for about an hour when I saw what I thought was a familiar figure enter the room. At first, I didn't believe my eyes—surely it couldn't be he. He was two hundred miles away, marooned down in Plymouth. But there was no mistaking that tall, arresting presence: it was indeed Lord Granville. I caught my breath as our glances locked. I was struck all over again by his extraordinary beauty; every other man in the room seemed diminished in comparison. It took him perhaps a minute to fight his way through the crowd to my side, by which time I'd composed myself enough to suppress anything that revealed how unsettled I was to see him again.

He was equally guarded, studiously correct as he made his bow and presented his compliments.

"I'm delighted, Lady Bessborough, to see you returned safely to London after what must've been an extremely trying and difficult journey. I hope you're quite recovered from it?"

"Thank you, sir, I'm quite well, and extremely happy to be home once more. But I'm surprised to see you here—I thought you were with your regiment?"

"Indeed I am and must return there tomorrow. But I have a message for you from an old friend in Naples that they asked me most particularly to deliver. May I beg the privilege of communicating it to you privately? If these ladies will excuse us for a moment?"

The twittering circle of cousins and cousins of cousins politely withdrew, no doubt to discuss this interesting young man elsewhere. I turned to him with my most charmingly neutral smile, but saw he had no intention of adopting an equally diffident manner. He loomed over me, urgent and determined.

"I came up as soon as I heard you'd arrived. I must see you. I have a great deal to say."

"I'll be very happy to see you, if you come as a friend, and promise not to repeat some of the things you said in your letters. I've made my position in that respect very clear."

"Yes, yes, I've read every word, over and over and over again—but I cannot accept it. I must talk to you. There must be somewhere we can go?"

He spoke very low, but the intensity of his manner must have suggested to anyone watching that our conversation was much more than light social chitchat. I began to be alarmed.

"Really, Lord Granville, you see how I'm situated here. It's quite impossible I should disappear with you. Whatever are you thinking?"

"I'm thinking," he replied steadily, "that I must see you. I'm thinking, as I do every minute of the day, of you. Of no one but you. Only and always you."

My head swam with pleasure, and for a moment I allowed myself to imagine doing exactly as he asked. But my weakness lasted no more than a heartbeat. I knew I had to break the mood, before we both lost our heads.

"I see I must send a little fire engine to put you out," I whispered in my most sweetly measured tones, "or your passion will totally consume you, which really wouldn't do at all."

He drew away, shocked—the last response he'd expected from me was mockery. I drew myself up, the dignified hostess once more, and delivered a dismissing nod, cool enough, I hoped, to quash the suspicions of all those who'd been idly watching us.

"It was exceedingly kind of you, Lord Granville, to pass on that message. Please stay and enjoy our party for as long as your duties allow. But you'll excuse me now if I attend to my other guests."

He stood looking at me for a few seconds, disbelief, hurt, and disappointment passing over his face. In his curt bow, I thought I also caught a hint of anger. I doubt he was accustomed to such blunt treatment. I turned toward a little knot of eager ladies; and the next time I looked up to scan the room, he was gone.

I heard nothing from him for weeks. I wasn't surprised. I'd wounded his pride, and I was sure that down in Plymouth, brooding over my snub, he'd sworn not to write again. But if he was indignant, so was I, and no more inclined than he to renew our correspondence. His inconsiderate behavior could so easily have exposed me to the petty speculations of those gossips who've always believed the worst of me; and if Lord B had heard of it, it would only have worsened his current unsettled frame of mind. For all these reasons, I decided I should not be the first to pick up a pen; so for a while there was a stalemate between us as complete as any to be found on a chessboard.

But even as I congratulated myself on my restraint, I was aware of other very different feelings within me. I knew how thrilled I'd been when he told me he thought of me every minute of the day—yes, I'd sent him away when he spoke those words, though now I longed to hear him repeat them again and again. But I held fast—I persevered in my silence—and eventually he was the one who capitulated and reignited our correspondence. I'd like to say he was chastened by my withdrawal, and henceforth meekly obeyed the rules I'd set for our future relations; but nothing could be further from the truth.

On the contrary, he expressed his desire for me even more ardently, declaring with even greater force that he could never be satisfied with mere friendship; his feelings were too strong for such a lukewarm return. Again and again, I told him he could expect nothing else from me; again and again, he demanded more. Eventually I took it upon myself to lecture him, adopting the gently condescending tone I felt appropriate for a woman of my worldly experience. His youth was largely to blame for his current infatuation. Such heartfelt passions were not at all uncommon in men of his age. They burned very brightly and, for a while, made the object of their affections appear as perfection itself. But this was all an illusion. Once the obsession was over, reality returned, and the dazed young man saw his *innamorata* once more as she really was. And in my case, as I steeled myself to remind him, that was a woman no longer young, whom he should regard more as a mother than a lover.

If I'd hoped to shock him into obedience, to dull the strength of his desire by waving my age before him like some great red flag—it made no difference at all.

Nothing, it seemed, could douse his passion. In letter after letter, he continued to argue and plead, deaf to my reasoning, impervious to my complaints, indifferent to my pleas that friendship was, and would always be, the only gift I had to offer him. This is what men are like when they are set upon victory. There's no compromising with them. They will have everything they want and will settle for nothing less. While the battle between the two of you rages, they declare themselves your abject slave; but once you submit, they turn into a tyrant, gleeful at having you in their power. I knew this well enough, and had I acted upon it, I should have stopped writing letters that made so little difference to Lord Granville's feelings for me; but I was too weak for that. Whenever I failed to reply with enough speed, he begged to hear from me; and I never had the discipline to refuse.

13

We'd been back in England a little more than three months, and already my health had deteriorated. Without the fresh air and warm climate of Naples, all my old complaints crept up on me once more. My persistent cough returned, along with the pain in my side. When I started to spit blood again, Dr. Warren decreed I must not spend the winter in the fogs and damp of London, and suggested I travel to Devonshire, whose mild coastal breezes he thought would suit me. Lord B found us a house in the seaside town of Teignmouth, and there we duly went.

It was a genteel little place, built around a beautiful bay and surrounded by many lovely prospects. I invited a friend to join me there to keep me company while Lord B, who dearly loved to draw, went out with his sketchbook onto the cliffs. Lady Anne Hatton, whom I'd met during our stay in Naples, was a sprightly young widow who'd taken cheerful advantage of her husbandless state on her travels. She was a charming and irrepressible flirt whose liveliness was an excellent cordial for an invalid like me. We were linked by other ties too; she was currently involved in an affair with Lord Morpeth, Lord Granville's great friend. She was ten years older than her lover and liked to think we had much in common, both mature women of the world pursued by younger men.

She had no doubt I would eventually surrender to Lord Granville and gladly played any part she could to bring that likelihood to pass. Closeted as we were in such a small lodging, it would have been impossible for me to receive his letters without their being noticed by my husband; so she willingly took upon herself the role of go-between, retrieving them from the post office where they arrived in her name. I hated the air of deceit, but I had no choice but to accept her eager kindness. Her knowing smiles as she handed over his correspondence made me very uncomfortable. I repeatedly told her, as vehemently as I could, that, on my side at least, our connection was quite innocent; but it was plain she didn't believe me. Certainly, she did nothing to dissuade me from following in her own footsteps.

She thought it a great stroke of luck that Teignmouth was only forty miles from Plymouth, where Lord Granville was stationed, and often hinted at the ease with which a meeting might be arranged. I wasn't sure I agreed with her, for I was a little afraid of another encounter, and thought there was some security in our staying apart; but I suppose our proximity made it inevitable, especially as Lord Granville's other great friend Lord Boringdon had his country house at Saltram, only a brief ride away from Plymouth. Lord Granville was frequently his guest, escaping from the regimental life he so disliked, and often suggested he and Boringdon might ride over to spend the day with us. I suspected Lady Anne had encouraged him in this idea, and when I hesitated to agree, she took matters into her own hands and raised it herself one evening as we sat with Lord B.

To my surprise, Lord B raised no objections to their coming—there were few enough people to talk to at Teignmouth at this time of year, so perhaps even he craved a little company—soon enough, the two young men arrived, and a most enjoyable day was had by us all. I'd been very nervous at first, for I greatly feared a repetition of the scene at Cavendish Square, but in fact Lord Granville's conduct was exactly what I could have wished—at least until the point of saying his goodbyes. Then, and only then, he found a moment to speak with me alone.

"There, you see, I do know how to behave. You can trust me, you know. In that and in so much else."

It took from my original pleasure, that the perfection of his demeanor had been so studied—I should have much preferred it to have been the product of a calmer, less heated obsession with myself—but I was gratified nonetheless.

So when, some days later, a note arrived from Lord Boring-don inviting my husband, Lady Anne, and me to spend a few days among his friends at Saltram—it should be quite a reminder of our old Naples times, for Lords Morpeth and Granville were both to be there—I thought it might be possible for us to accept it without too much risk.

When Lord B asked me if I wished to accept Boringdon's invitation, I answered calmly that I thought it would make a delightful expedition.

14

We were an intimate party at Saltram. Lord Boringdon was an excellent host, and soon we were all at our ease. I was intrigued to see how Lord Granville behaved among such old friends—he, Boringdon, and Morpeth had attended university together, as was evident in their manner to one another. Their conversation was full of shared jokes and plainly indicated their conviction of superiority to anyone unlucky enough not to be part of their tight, charmed circle. They had a highly developed sense of their own importance and made it very clear that they couldn't wait to edge aside an older generation who had made such a mess of the world and yet somehow failed to understand their day was done.

I've made them sound obnoxious, but really, their faults were nothing more than the irrepressible eagerness of youth. I thought them all very attractive. Their energy excited me, their mercilessness— another trait of youth—made me laugh, and their vigor and exuberance were to me a joy to behold.

But while their company was exhilarating, it also made me feel the full weight of my own extra years. Among them, I felt old. I was the mother of four children, a discontented wife of some fifteen years' standing, a battle-scarred veteran of several unhappy affairs, my health fragile, my confidence, such as it had ever been, in tatters—what did I have that any of these immaculately tailored young gods could possibly want? And how was it possible that the most beautiful, the most perfect of them all insisted he desired me?

One night at dinner I allowed my gaze to wander around the table, looking at them one by one, taking in their unlined faces, their animated laughter, the expectant optimism of their bearing. When I reached Lord Granville, he was staring straight back at me, looking, in the candlelight, to even greater advantage than usual. Immediately, I dropped my eyes and took too large a sip from my wineglass, blushing and asking myself, what could he possibly see there to admire?

When I awoke the next morning, I felt the effects of that wine. I was dull and stupid, with an aching head—I longed for nothing so much as clear air and the feel of a breeze on my face. It was early springtime, when pale blue skies are chased away by sudden showers, and everything underfoot has a fresh green sharpness about it. I decided that, a little later, when everyone was about their business, I might walk through the park to the edge of the woods. There was a great show of bluebells there, of which Lord Boringdon was proud; he'd said last night they were just now in bloom and particularly fine this year. That, I thought, should be my destination. I wanted no company, so I slipped out quietly and soon came upon a glade thickly carpeted with the celebrated flowers. I'd been there for no more than ten minutes, taking in their perfect, innocent scent, when I heard footsteps behind me. I knew who it was even before I turned around.

"Lord Granville," I said, as if we were in a London drawing room. I couldn't help noticing the bluebells were the same color as his eyes.

He stared for a moment, studying me intently.

"You remind me," he murmured in a low voice, "of the paintings

I saw in Italy. You look like a saint with her feet among flowers. Or Botticelli's Venus, but set against bluebells rather than waves."

"Although as I recall," I ventured, "that lady was not equipped, as I am, with a stout pair of boots and a sensible coat."

He smiled. "No, indeed she was not. But even in your boots, you look like a goddess."

I swallowed hard. If I did not take care, I should soon be mesmerized beyond retreat.

"You mustn't talk to me in that way, Lord Granville. I've told you many times that all I can offer you is friendship, but you've made it clear that is not enough for you." I took a breath. He stood silent for a moment, his expression unreadable.

"No, it isn't enough."

"I've said it before and I'll say it again. The strength of your feelings has clouded your judgment. You think you want me—but the woman you long for is an invention of your own devising, a fantasy. I urge you, in the strongest possible terms, to open your eyes and see me as I really am."

"But isn't that what I'm doing now? Seeing you as you really are? A Venus among the bluebells?"

If he'd hoped a playful reply would summon up a smile from me, he couldn't have been more wrong. I was exasperated, anxious, disconcerted—and my words came tumbling out of me, in a passionate tirade of frustration.

"Lord Granville, I am not some fresh young Venus, but a woman twelve years older than yourself, who bears upon her face and figure all the marks that experience has left upon her. This you refuse to see. Instead, you've conjured up in your imagination a pretty picture, no doubt delightful. But it isn't the real Harriet Bessborough you're pursuing, the woman who stands before you now—no, it's some phantom of your own creation."

I was angry now and began to pace about, crushing the flowers thoughtlessly beneath my feet.

"This is bad enough for you, since it prevents your getting acquainted with some delightful young thing of your own age, twenty times more deserving of your love, more able to return it, indeed, more suited to you in every way."

I knew my feelings had got the better of me, but I could not stop.

"But it's far, far worse for me. If I let down my defenses, I know how this must end. The day will come when you'll open your eyes and see the sad reality of who I really am—and then you'll ask yourself how you were so deceived—liking will become hatred—you'll despise me—and oh—I don't think I could bear it."

I was sobbing now, quite beside myself.

"I couldn't stand to be blamed by you for something I cannot change. You may say the difference in age between us is nothing now, but how will you feel when you're thirty-five and I am nearly fifty? Will I still seem like a Venus among the bluebells then?"

I covered my face with my hands, so that I didn't see him walk toward me but only felt him take me in his arms. I should have struggled, should have pulled myself away—but I did neither. He would have kissed me, but I would not allow it—though I did permit myself to rest my head against his breast, telling myself I should take refuge there only until I was more composed.

"I think of no one but you," he said softly. "You are all I want. Nothing you've said makes the slightest difference to what I feel."

"But you can't deny the truth of it," I cried, feeling my tears wet against his coat. "The difference in our ages is already marked enough, and must become more so as we grow older."

"I'm flattered that, when you look forward, I continue to occupy so large a place in your future." He smiled down at me, but I was angry and pulled away from him.

"This is no joke to me, Lord Granville—do me the honor of speaking to me seriously, or don't speak to me at all. What have I to offer you? Can you really answer that?"

He held out his hand, but I wouldn't take it.

"Very well—if you wish me to explain why I feel as I do, let me try to oblige. Your age does not concern me in the least. I find you very beautiful."

I dropped my eyes, as the warmth of a blush crept over me.

"But your looks are only the beginning. I like it that you've lived in the world and understand its ways. I know there are men who'd prefer a silent young innocent, but that would never do for me. I like a woman who's seen something of life and has something to say about it. I like a woman with a mind."

"That makes you very unusual."

"I was brought up the only boy among a clutch of clever sisters, and my mother is nobody's fool—so I suppose I learned very early to appreciate the virtues of sharp and penetrating female minds. You have your own opinions and aren't afraid to express them, as I discovered to my cost when I dared to criticize Mr. Fox. And even when we don't agree—which I know we do not, on many significant points—you never bore me. And you know me well enough by now to know how very much I hate being bored."

Warming to his theme, he began to pace up and down among the carpet of blue flowers.

"I like it, too, that you aren't afraid to laugh. Most women are as solemn as owls—they never laugh, or at least not in front of men; perhaps they think it unbecoming. But when I think of you, I think of your laughter—and of your smile, which, in case you do not know it, is singularly warm and beguiling. Just like you, in fact."

He stopped and stood quite still for a moment, considering.

"And finally—though I know you may find this indelicate—there is one other quality in you that attracts me very deeply. You are, I believe, a woman of strong feelings, physically as well as emotionally, though I'm not sure you know it yet. Nothing is so intoxicating to me than that I should be the one who awakens that passionate nature and goes on to satisfy it. Nothing would make me happier."

I could hardly believe my ears. I had never been more amazed in my life.

"That is the most extraordinary language a man has ever used to me. What can you be thinking?"

"I'm sorry if I've shocked you. But I thought some frankness was necessary if I were to persuade you I don't care about your age. What are the few years that stand between us, when weighed against everything else I've described?"

He strode toward me and took my hand.

"And really—do I honestly strike you as a man who doesn't know his own mind?"

He bent his head again to kiss me. His nearness was intoxicating. It took all my strength of purpose not to raise my face to his, but from somewhere I found the power to pull away.

"I'm going back now," I said, my voice unsteady. "Don't follow me. Wait a little and take some other way. We cannot be seen together."

I left him there, standing among the bluebells. I did not look back. As I walked to the house, by the most wet and roundabout path, I beat my fist into my hand. I had tried to show him the foolishness of his desire, to make him see the impossibility of taking matters further between us. But instead, in allowing him to speak to me with such freedom, I'd only given him even greater reason to hope. And what had I been thinking, to allow him to hold me as he did—it was a liberty I should never have permitted. Yet the shameful truth was—I'd enjoyed it. I'd enjoyed it very much. No wonder he'd felt himself entitled to refer to my passionate nature. I stood still for a minute and put my head into my hands. I was so ashamed. Nothing had gone as I intended. Under no circumstances could it ever happen again, and not just for the avoidance of further embarrassment. I wasn't sure I should have the willpower to extricate myself from his embrace a second time.

15

When I reached the house, I went straight upstairs to my room and rang for Sally. I needed her help, for my boots were sodden and the hems of my dress and coat stained with mud.

"Wherever did you go to get into such a state?"

I stood silently in my shift as she examined my clothes, purse-lipped.

"The dress will have to be washed, if it can be arranged. And the coat thoroughly brushed once the mud is dry."

"Let's not trouble the people here with washing. We'll be back in Teignmouth the day after tomorrow."

I was loath to call any attention either to myself or my where-abouts. Sally peered more closely at the dress.

"The longer it's left," Sally replied evenly, "the more likely it is to stain."

"I'd rather we did as I said."

She looked up as though she wanted to ask another question; but then she thought better of it.

"As you wish." She took the dress over her arm, holding the muddy hem away from her. "But I can give the coat a brush myself.

And let's put your boots somewhere private to dry. Where they won't call attention to their state."

Our eyes met. We understood each perfectly. "Of course," I replied in my brightest tone.

When I went downstairs a little later, I found my husband, Lady Anne, and Lord Morpeth playing a desultory game of cards.

"Thank God you're here," declared Lady Anne. "Now I might get a bit of conversation. Neither of these gentlemen"—she gestured to Lord B and her lover—"has a single word to say for himself."

"We've been attending to the game," murmured Lord Morpeth, "which might have been more entertaining if you'd done the same."

"Tell me all," demanded Lady Anne, paying him no attention. "Where have you been, who have you seen, what have you done?"

I expected to be asked to account for my movements, and knew that a partial truth is always recommended as being far more effective than a complete lie, for anyone set upon deception.

"I walked out to see the famous bluebells. Lord Boringdon had sung their praises with such enthusiasm that I wanted to find out if they were truly as remarkable as he said."

"And were they?" asked Lady Anne eagerly.

"I've never seen any to compare with them." I smiled. "You must go and look for yourself."

"There, Morpeth," said Lady Anne, playfully, "you can take me to see them."

"As long as it doesn't rain," he replied, gloomily picking up his cards once more. "Remind me, Bessborough, what are trumps?"

I allowed myself to breathe more easily. There had been no untoward questions, no awkward silences—I put myself out to be sociable, and soon we were talking with enough animation to satisfy even Lady Anne. So later that evening, when we all went in to dinner, I let down my guard somewhat. All was going admirably until Lord

Boringdon, who had drunk a great deal, leaned toward Lord Granville and addressed him in a loud, bantering tone.

"So I hear from my gardener that you were down among my bluebells this afternoon. I told him he must be mistaken, for I've never known you to take the slightest interest in anything in the horticultural line. But he would have it that it was you."

"I made an exception for them," Lord Granville replied smoothly. "You've talked of your bluebells every spring for as long as I've known you. It was impossible I shouldn't seek them out."

"And did they live up to their reputation?"

"Indeed they did. You can rest assured they are quite as fine as you say they are."

Preening with delight at the praise of his flowers, Lord Boringdon went on to explain that their exceptional beauty was entirely owing to their being of the right English kind. Too many people nowadays planted the Spanish variety, which had neither the color nor the perfume of *Hyacinthoides non-scripta*.

Warming to his subject, he told us more than anyone could possibly wish to know about the common bluebell and its many fascinating properties. Meanwhile, I fixed my gaze on my plate, determined that no one should see my expression. Had anyone else noticed the dangerous coincidence? When I steeled myself to look up, I was relieved to see Lord B was working his way steadily through his sirloin, with no indication of displeasure. Morpeth and Granville sat in silence as Lord Boringdon's dissertation drew to a close, paying me no attention. Only Lady Anne caught my eye, communicating with the merest hint of a frown that she at least was aware of the gaffe.

I excused myself early and went straight to bed. The following day our little party broke up and we all set off for home. As we readied ourselves to leave, I found myself alone with Lord Granville for the first time since our rendezvous in the wood. I was in the hall, putting on my gloves. Lady Anne and Lord B were already in our carriage, while the servants were making everything fast and secure. Lord Granville approached me, but I drew back, afraid of being seen.

"Promise me you'll write."

I held out to him the fingertips of my gloved hands in the most formal manner.

"I wish you a safe journey back to Plymouth, Lord Granville."

He took my hand and bowed.

"Say you'll write. I must hear from you."

I did not reply but merely inclined my head and walked briskly out to our carriage. Lady Anne talked all the way back to Teignmouth. Lord B said little, although that was nothing new. I chattered away myself, but by the time we were home, my husband's silence had begun to wear upon me. In the week that followed, I felt as though a great black cloud had settled above us; the whole house seemed consumed by gloom and foreboding. I could barely contain my own anxiety. Was it possible Lord B had heard something about what happened in the bluebell wood? Could a servant have seen us? Or had I been mistaken in thinking he hadn't noticed Lord Boringdon's unfortunate words?

It was impossible to tell from his manner exactly what had displeased him, for he barely spoke to me, and when he did, he was curt and formal, his former warmth entirely evaporated. I was sure it must be something serious; and when, out of the blue, he announced his intention to spend a short time in London, offering no reason for his sudden departure, I knew it was bad. He didn't say goodbye when he left. I was certain now some terrible storm was about to break over me; and a little while later, it did.

I received from my husband a coldly furious note, telling me that as a result of misgivings implanted in his mind by several occurrences at Saltram, he had taken into his own hands several of Lord Granville's letters addressed to me. He would not say anything further in writing but, in light of what he'd read, would expect an explanation for my conduct on his return.

16

*I*t was three days before Lord B was expected back, plenty of time to work myself into a pitch of anxiety and despair. What could Lord Granville's letters have contained? Nothing good, I was sure—at the very least, more loving avowals, more passionate declarations that the friendship I offered would never be enough. I forced myself to think rationally. If that was all there was, I might yet be safe, for his much-repeated frustrations clearly implied my refusal of all his overtures. God forbid, however, he had made any mention of our tryst among the bluebells. If he mentioned that, I should be hard put to explain it.

When I heard my husband's carriage pull up outside the house, I thought I might be sick; but I was determined to show no sign of it. Lord B strode into the little drawing room, dusty from the road, tired, and plainly very angry. He waved away my offer to call for a cooling drink and sat down heavily, throwing his hat on the floor and wiping his brow.

"Let us go straight to the point. We have been here before, so none of what I have to say will much surprise you."

I held up my head. If he expected me to plead and beg, he would be disappointed. I'd determined to stand firm and admit nothing at all.

"On the contrary, I'm quite taken aback, for I have no idea what I am accused of. You tell me you have in your possession letters from Lord Granville to me—they could have only been acquired by some underhand means. That you should stoop so low . . . Is that really the way one gentleman behaves to another?"

"Indeed it is, when that gentleman believes the other is making love to his wife. And if you had nothing to hide, why did you write to him via Lady Anne? That isn't the act of an innocent woman."

"Perhaps I wished to avoid an inquisition of exactly this nature."

He laughed. "The best way to have prevented that was not to have involved yourself in an illicit correspondence with another man."

He stared at me, waiting for an answer, but I made no reply.

"There was something strange about your behavior toward him at Saltram. I can't say exactly what it was—but I caught knowing looks among the others on occasion, especially Morpeth and Lady Anne. Something was going on, or so it seemed to me. And I'm sorry to tell you that what I found in those letters confirmed my very worst suspicions."

"Which are what, exactly? Can you tell me exactly what it is you suspect?"

He stood up, furious now, and began to pace about the room.

"Good God, Harriet, what do you think I mean? That you receive him in your bed—that he is your lover."

I knew that I must not waver, must remain completely calm.

"He is not my lover."

He shook his head in disbelief. "I am not a fool, you know. You treat me as one, but I see more than you think."

He paused his pacing and stood before the fireplace, struggling to control his anger.

"This is what will happen," he continued, speaking very deliberately. "You will tell him your correspondence is at an end. You will never meet again privately, and if your paths cross in public, you will acknowledge him briefly and move on. In short, all intercourse of any kind between you—of any kind—is to cease immediately."

He took a deep breath, and stood before me, now quite still.

"You must promise me you will obey these rules. If you cannot do so, I shall insist upon a separation. And this time, I won't be bullied or persuaded out of it. I mean it, Harriet, by God I do."

He turned and threw himself back into the chair, his face contorted with bitterness and humiliation. If he'd been alone, I think he might have cried. Pity stirred in me; and guilt too, for it was a terrible thing to see a man in such distress. I sat down beside him.

"These things you accuse me of—they aren't true. It isn't what you think."

He raised his eyes to the ceiling as if he could not bear to look at me.

"I know Lord Granville likes to write in the language of love— but it means nothing. A young man develops a passion for an older woman and convinces himself he's in love; and then nothing will do but he must confess his feelings to her, over and over again, in the hope that she'll listen to his entreaties. I imagine that is what you've read?"

No response.

"I can't deny there's a great deal of supplication in his letters. But you must also have seen there's no evidence at all that those desires have been gratified. Because they have not. None of the favors he clamors for have been granted. Not one."

Lord B still would not meet my eye, but he did not shout me down.

"I know I should never have allowed him to write to me as he's done, but the truth is, I didn't take him seriously. These youthful passions don't last. In a few months, it will have blown itself out. I admit I should have stopped it, and when I did not, I suppose he was encouraged to continue. But that, I assure you, is the limit of my guilt. There is nothing more between us and there never will be. I beg you to believe that."

Finally, Lord B turned to look at me.

"Is he your lover?"

"He is not."

"Has he kissed you? Touched you? Has anything of a physical nature happened between you?"

I hung my head. How terrible must my behavior have been, that my husband could so coolly ask me such a question.

"I deserve your suspicion. I know I've been guilty before—I'm only too aware of it—but on this occasion, I swear I am innocent."

I saw he was wavering, that he wanted to believe what I said.

"I've learned my lesson. All I have to offer anyone is friendship. And once Lord Granville accepts this, he'll find someone else to pursue. Then there would be nothing objectionable in my seeing him occasionally. You might even allow me to write to him now and then. I would take this as a sign that I am worthy of your trust—and believe me, I would never give you cause to regret it. I will abide by any rule you care to make and ensure he does so too."

His expression was stony. Then, suddenly, he put his head in his hands.

"When we were on our travels, there were times when I thought we were happy, when I allowed myself to hope we might live more affectionately together. But all the way home I feared that moment was over. And unhappily for me, I was right, for here we are, Harriet, just as I feared."

I was extremely moved by his frankness. I saw what it cost him to open his heart. I only wished I could respond in kind, to assure him my feelings for him were equal to his for me. But much as I longed to, I couldn't do it. There was a time when I might have loved the man he had become—but the memory of the man he had been—and everything I had suffered at his hands—I could not erase from my mind. There were many things I could feel for my husband—gratitude, sympathy, guilt, regret even—but I could never love him. It was too late for that.

"I won't betray you." It was all I could find to say at that moment. "If you trust me, I shan't let you down."

It seemed a long time before he replied. "I shall consider it."

He rose and left the room, and I did not see him again until the following morning, when he joined me at the breakfast table. He took a roll in his hand and tapped it absently against a plate.

"I have thought long and hard about our conversation and have decided I may have been too hasty in my conclusions."

My heart leaped in hope; but outwardly, I remained calm.

"I accept your explanation of your relations with Lord Granville. I cannot pretend to like it, but I accept there is nothing adulterous in it. For that reason, I shall not forbid you to see him."

He reached for the pot and poured himself some coffee. I knew it must be cold, but dared not call for fresh to be made.

"But I attach certain conditions. You are not to meet in private. In public, I shall expect you to behave in such a way as will provoke not the slightest suspicion. I shan't forbid you to correspond. There seems little point, for I'm sure you'd find the means to defy a ban if you wished it. But I must insist upon the same degree of restraint in your letters as in your behavior. If matters between you are truly as you say, this should not be difficult to achieve. And remember—if I've obtained his letters once, I can do so again. Perhaps that will help to keep you honest."

He sat back in his chair and stared levelly at me.

"Above all—I do not wish to be embarrassed any further. I have offered you affection and the chance of starting anew—which you don't seem inclined to accept."

I tried to interrupt, but he held up his hand to prevent me.

"Please—there's nothing more to be said about that. I understand how things stand and won't press you further. But I will not be made to look like a fool. Do you understand me?"

"I do."

"I have one last thing to add. You've asked for my trust—and I've given it to you. Few men would have been so indulgent. But Harriet—if I find my generosity was ill placed—if I discover I've been betrayed—I won't hesitate to take any action I judge right to find out the truth. I feel you should know this."

"There will be no need for that. No one knows better than I do the extent of your forgiveness. I can only say in return that you'll never have cause to regret your decision. I promise that most faithfully."

When I spoke these words, I really believed them. I honestly thought I could manage everything—keep Lord Granville close to me, enjoy his attentions, indulge the frisson of feeling he aroused in me, but without ever surrendering myself utterly to him. I believed I was strong enough not to be tempted further. Besides, I had made a solemn promise to my husband, and the consequences of breaking it—a humiliating separation with all the disgrace that suggested, and perhaps even the loss of my children—were surely sufficient to keep me on the narrow path of fidelity.

God, what an idiot I was—how very little I knew myself or what I was capable of.

17

I'd imagined Lord Granville would approve of how I'd managed things, but I couldn't have been more mistaken. He was
extremely unhappy with the terms I'd agreed to, complaining I valued obedience to Lord B over my feelings for him. When I told him it
was hardly surprising I should respect my husband's wishes in such
a matter—especially when he considered the generosity Lord B had
shown toward me—he had nothing to say, except that he was sorry
our meetings, chance and infrequent as they were, appeared to matter so little to me. He liked it even less when I suggested that perhaps
the shock of coming so close to disaster had been a salutary one, for
now he must accept that he could no longer ask me to return feelings
I could never entertain for him. When he accused me of intending to
give him up, I replied that there was no question of my abandoning
my friendship for him—but this must make him understand that
despite my recent weakness, this was all he could ever expect.

I didn't imagine this would do much to console him and indeed
it did not. He resented very much his being confined down at Plymouth. He disliked the military life extremely. In the absence of any
immediate prospect of a French invasion, there was really very little

for him and his corps of volunteers to do, and with nothing to fill his days, he was bored and unhappy. He missed me, he missed his friends, and he missed London, finding provincial society dull and uninspiring.

For myself, I didn't entirely mind his being forcibly separated from the temptations of the fashionable world—and not least, from me. I hoped that time spent away from my company might cool his emotions somewhat, making it easier for me to keep the promise of fidelity I'd made to Lord B. I should be so much safer, so much less vulnerable to my own frailty, once he'd ceased to pursue me.

I thought, too, that Lord Granville's banishment from London—for that was how he described it—might also prevent him from indulging to excess another forbidden passion—that of gambling. Although he'd hinted, back in Naples, at his liking for the tables, I'd been horrified to discover the degree to which he'd fallen under their spell.

I knew from my own painful experience, as well as that of my husband, my sister, and so many of my friends, that the urge to gamble, once surrendered to, soon becomes irresistible, and ends in nothing but misery and a mountain of debt. Needless to say, Lord Granville paid no attention to my pleas and warnings not to involve himself further in its toils; and when I proposed he consider his time in Plymouth as an opportunity to cure himself of his addiction, he took it very ill, thinking it a poor argument to justify his exile. I didn't understand, he complained, how isolated he was. He hated finding himself confined solely to male society—had I any idea, he asked, how limited, tedious, and utterly predictable men's conversation was, without the presence of some lively women to inspire and animate it? I thought it unlikely he had entirely deprived himself of female companionship, of some kind or another, but preferred not to inquire too closely.

All these discontents were powerfully real to him, and I did my best to understand; but there were times when I was frustrated by his willful blindness to the difficulties of my situation. He had no idea of the tortuous path I was attempting to navigate. Since my confrontation with Lord B, I'd felt myself under constant scrutiny. He was always watching me now. And if my husband, never the most astute observer, had noticed something untoward between myself and Lord Granville, might not others have seen it too? I was horrified when the Duke of Bedford, one of my oldest and dearest friends, hinted that Lord Granville's obvious attentions to me had already provoked comment, and I'd do well to ensure they attracted no further speculation. He wouldn't tell me who these eagle-eyed persons were; and I wound myself into anxious knots trying to guess their identities.

My first concern was that my mother might know; but no, I thought, if she had any suspicions, she'd have instantly confronted me with them. What about Georgiana? Could she have observed something? I hadn't discussed Lord Granville with her at all. I'd held back from confiding in her, as I had always done with my previous entanglements. I'd sometimes longed to open my heart to her, to feel the relief of admitting all that had passed between us; but something had always held me back. I think I feared that merely describing my situation with Lord Granville would somehow give it more substance, make it more real; moreover, it couldn't fail to expose my own ambivalent feelings for him, of which, for all my attempts to deny them, I was increasingly ashamed.

But though I hadn't spoken, others might have done so. Bess Foster, with her unerring eye for an irregular connection—perhaps she had noticed something? Lady Webster, who'd been there at the beginning of it all, was still abroad; but she knew Bess and my sister very well. Might she have written with some teasing allusion to Lord Granville's attraction to me? All such conjectures filled me with apprehension. Once begun upon, there was really no end to them, and I was soon reduced to a state of constant, apprehensive anxiety.

Although I missed Lord Granville very much, I worked hard

to convince myself that our separation was for the best; and I had almost succeeded in doing so when he wrote to tell me that after so many unsuccessful applications, he'd finally been granted leave from his regiment and would be returning to London immediately. I'm sorry to say that for all my good intentions my heart leaped at the prospect of seeing him again. I told myself I'd be very careful, that I'd take pains to ensure there could be no repetition of what happened at Saltram. We would never be alone together but would meet only in company, when the number of people around us would help me keep the promise I'd made to Lord B. So when my sister threw a great dinner at Devonshire House—and told me she'd invited Lord Granville—this seemed exactly the right place for our first encounter after so many months of separation.

Georgiana had mentioned his name to me when drawing up her guest list for the evening. Since our brother George—to the regret of us both—had, alongside many other moderate Whigs, joined Mr. Pitt's government, she'd thought it politic to include some Tories among her guests.

"What about Lord Granville? Might he do? He's a Pittite of the deepest hue—but very handsome, as I recall, which might take off somewhat the annoyance of his politics. I hear he's good company— Lord Holland says he's really quite amusing when he exerts himself, though inclined to be haughty. You knew him in Naples. I think?"

Her pen was poised above her list of invitees; her expression was bland, impossible to read. I met her look with an equally impenetrable smile.

"I think you could ask him. I believe he'd give a good account of himself. He's a very sociable being."

"You've seen him a little since your return, I believe?"

"Yes, a few times in London and then down in Devonshire. He and his friends were much in our circle in Naples, and we all grew to know each other very well."

She gazed at me expectantly; but when I said no more, she turned back to her list and added his name at the bottom.

I was standing at the far side of the great drawing room when Lord Granville arrived. As was always the case, the mere look of him took my breath away. He gazed around the room, searching, I hoped, for me—and when we caught each other's eye, I favored him with a brief nod, the barest possible acknowledgment of his presence. In return, he, too, inclined his head, but he didn't approach me, for which I was both glad and sorry—pleased at his discretion, disappointed that I should be required to remain at such a distance from him.

We were seated a long way apart at dinner, which made any conversation between us impossible. It seemed an eternity before the meal was over, and we ladies rose from our places, leaving the gentlemen to their port. I didn't immediately follow the twittering female throng that made its way back to the drawing room. I was too unsettled and restless to sit calmly among them; I needed to find some quiet place to compose myself first. I knew that in the next-door salon there was a retired seat before one of the great windows, where I might perch for a moment and find some relief. I had been settled there for perhaps five minutes when Lord Granville appeared before me.

"Good God, Lord Granville, however did you find me?"

"I excused myself from the port. I've heard enough dirty stories at Plymouth to last me a lifetime. I'd intended to join the ladies, but my path crossed with Bess Foster's. She mentioned she'd seen you head in this direction."

My heart missed a beat.

"She knows about us, then?"

"So what if she does? She's hardly in a position to throw stones. And anyway, what is there to know? As you so often say, we're merely good friends."

"In my experience, most friends are content to remain in that state, and do not press constantly for a more intimate connection."

He smiled and sat down. Not too close, but close enough.

"Is this a sufficient distance for a friend to observe?"

"It would be better if you weren't here at all."

"I hope you don't really think that. I've been thinking of you all day, imagining sitting near to you, imagining doing this—"

He took my hand and raised it to his lips. Before he could kiss it, I pulled it away.

"You must stop all this, Lord Granville." I was angry now. "I'm not the woman you think I am. I have no interest at all in some intimate little dalliance with you. I'm beyond all that. But if you're truly looking for something more, then perhaps you should be aware of what you hope for."

"I'm not sure I understand."

"Then let me explain. If you persist in urging me toward an affair, you must know that if I were to take such a step, it would never be for me some small and passing fancy. If I ever find the love I've longed for all my life, it will consume me, heart and soul. Once I give myself, I give my all—it's not in my nature to settle for half measures. You should understand this, Lord Granville; you should know what manner of woman you are involving yourself with, so you cannot say later you weren't warned. And if you don't like what you've heard, now is the time to withdraw."

I barely recognized myself. I'd never spoken so plainly before, never revealed so much of my secret self to another with such candor. I was afraid he might laugh. But instead, he moved closer to me.

"Your passion doesn't scare me. I told you before that I felt it in you. And now you've confirmed it, I'm drawn toward you even more powerfully."

At that he took my face in his hands and kissed me. This time I did not resist. The pleasure I felt when his lips touched mine was so intense I could hardly believe it. I gave up everything to the sensation of the moment, and cannot say how long it lasted, only that I wished it would never stop.

Finally, I detached myself from his arms, stood up, smoothed down my hair, and walked away from him without a word. What could I possibly have said? At Saltram, we'd gone from talking to touching; now we'd advanced from touching to a kiss. No wonder he paid no attention to my protestations and warnings. My words gave out one message, my actions quite another.

When I entered the drawing room, both my sister and Bess looked up at me quizzically, as if they hoped me to acknowledge, by some tiny hint in my expression, what I thought they suspected; but I offered no more than a polite smile and my apologies for arriving among them so late.

18

While Lord Granville remained in London, I took care to behave with as much studied propriety as I could whenever we were in company together. I only wish he'd been half as careful in his conduct toward me. He seemed to think what had passed between us entitled him to act with even more marked attention, coming up boldly to me at parties, sitting beside me at cards. I was in a constant fever of anxiety that it would eventually be remarked upon; and eventually, exactly as I had feared, it was.

Lady Melbourne has been one of my closest friends since my very first entry into society, when she steered me safely through many of the reefs and squalls that plagued my younger years. She kept me afloat when I believed my early transgressions had scuppered me forever, forcing me to hold up my head and bravely outface the disapproval of those who would otherwise have happily condemned me to social exile and ruin. Being quite fearless herself, she respects nothing so much as courage in others and has often harangued me for what she calls my tragic, drooping airs. I think I've always been a little afraid of her. She's certainly not the kind of woman you'd willingly provoke; she's imperious, in both her manner and person, tall and stately, with a proud embonpoint and a merciless stare. She can indeed be cruel, and I've often been the victim of her sharp and pointed remarks; but for all that, I know her flinty heart is sometimes capable of genuine feeling. She prides herself, however, on her bluntness, never shrinking from that which others might hesitate to name. So I suppose I shouldn't have been surprised it was she who was the first to warn me, in the most unambiguous fashion, of the risks to which I was exposing myself by allowing Granville to behave as he did.

She approached me during the interval of a concert during which Lord Granville had barely taken his eyes off me.

"I shall speak clearly," she said, lowering herself into a little gold chair, "as too much has passed between us over the years for us to tiptoe around these matters like silly young girls."

I knew only too well what was coming and shrank into my own seat, dreading what she was about to say.

"You must get that young man under control." She tapped my arm impatiently with her fan. "Bessborough is hardly the sharpest knife in the drawer, but even he will notice something soon. Are you his lover yet?"

"I am not." If anyone else had put such a question to me, I should have been shocked, but nothing Lady Melbourne said could surprise me.

"In that case," she continued, "my advice to you is to make up your mind whether you intend to make him the happiest of men or not. Either give in or send him on his way. Uncertainty makes men dangerous. They flail about and make scenes. And you can't afford that."

"Yes," I answered as calmly as I could. "I take your point."

"Well, that's my advice. Do with it what you will. But don't let matters go on as they are. Vacillation is the worst thing in these situations. No good will come of it."

She snapped her fan shut, rose up from her chair, and sailed off into the throng, like some majestic man-of-war in full sail, parting the crowds in her wake. She was right. I must either put a stop to things, or—or what exactly? I preferred not to let the words form in my mind, though I knew well enough what they were. I must turn Lord Granville away in such a manner that there could be no room for doubt—or become his lover. Which was it to be?

Lord Granville himself had clearly concluded that since our kiss, the odds of my surrendering had moved in his favor. I'm not sure, even now, of the degree to which what happened next was a conscious effort on his part to bring me even closer toward that end; but I cannot deny it played its part in wearing down my resistance.

I'd often told Lord Granville how much I valued candor and frankness in a lover, how firmly I believed that affection cannot thrive where there is deceit. I very much hoped, I told him, that any man who professed to care for me should not attempt to hide any of his previous or current romantic entanglements. I promised neither to judge nor to be jealous, insisting I valued honesty over all other considerations. Lord Granville generally received these pronouncements in silence, which didn't surprise me, as it's asking a great deal of a man to admit his other connections to a woman he hopes will look kindly on him. I supposed he would be too proud ever to make any such confession to me; but to my great surprise, I was wrong.

One afternoon I received a note from him asking to meet me in Green Park, for he had something he very much wished to tell me. He suggested he'd engage a cab, and together, we'd drive around for a while, so that we could converse without the danger of being seen. Such was the urgency of his tone that I reluctantly agreed.

When we were settled, with the blinds half down, he began.

"I've something to say, which I should have mentioned before now. I've considered everything you've said about the importance of honesty between those who profess feelings for one another"—he drew a deep breath—"and I admit I haven't been as open about my circumstances as you would have liked." He sighed. "I should have told you that, for some time since I've been at Plymouth, I have had a lady under my protection."

He paused, and when I offered no reply, he sighed again and went on.

"A little while ago, she gave birth to a child. A little boy. My son."

I made no comment.

"It is all finished now. Our connection is quite over, I promise you."

"And the lady?" I asked. "What became of her? And her child?"

"I did everything that was decent. I settled as generous a provision on her as my means would permit. I support the child and will always do so. The lady herself has an allowance, as well as a nurse and a respectable little house. Neither of them will be left in want, I can assure you."

"I'm glad to hear it. I hate that cruelty in men which enables them to dismiss a mistress as if she were a piece of old luggage they have no further use for."

"Do you really think I'm capable of acting so dishonorably?"

"I should hope not. But men are often harsh in these matters. And it's always the women who suffer."

I thought of my sister's Eliza, whose father barely acknowledged her. And of Georgiana's guilty, hopeless longing for a daughter she was never allowed to see. Bereft and wounded women, children without a place in the world. Tears sprang to my eyes.

"I can't help but feel sorry for her, the poor lady."

"You understand I did it for you? That I could not continue, feeling as I do?"

At this, I closed my eyes.

"How cruel love is," I whispered, "that the happiness of one is so often built on the wretchedness of another."

"Perhaps I shouldn't have told you. I only spoke because I thought you wished it."

"I'm grateful for your honesty. It means a great deal to me."

In silence, we made a final circuit around the park. Both of us, I think, were melancholy. But what more was there to be said? He wasn't the first young man to get into such a scrape, and he wouldn't be the last. What mattered was how he'd dealt with the consequences. He'd behaved in every way as decently as could be expected, and I believed him when he swore he'd continue to do so. Well, I'd asked him to be honest, and I couldn't complain if he'd obeyed me.

It was only much later, when my pity for his Plymouth lady ebbed away somewhat, that I allowed myself to consider the wider significance of what he'd told me. He'd given up his lover for me. I wish I could say it made no difference to my feelings for him, but that wasn't true. The knowledge of his sacrifice—for it was clear that was how he regarded it—drew me closer and closer to him, and despite myself, I sensed my resistance weakening.

19

J don't know what would have happened if I had seen much more of Lord Granville immediately after his confession, but fate intervened to prevent my finding out. My sister was suddenly taken ill with symptoms so alarming that I honestly thought she might die—and as long as she continued in such a perilous state, there was no room in my thoughts for anyone but her.

It came on very suddenly. She'd been troubled for some time with headaches and a pain in her eye. Then one night she went to bed feeling unwell and awoke to find that eye swollen to the size of an apricot. Appalled, the Duke summoned the best oculists in London, who pronounced it the result of an inflammation. Georgiana was terrified. Soon her poor eye stood right out of her head and was terribly ulcerated at the top. It seemed she would go blind if the horrible process could not be reversed, but none of the surgeons knew how this might be achieved.

I flew at once to Devonshire House and kept a constant vigil at her bedside. I have endured a great deal of sickness in my life—both my own and that of others—but I'd never seen anything to compare to the agonies Georgiana suffered. The operations performed on her were excruciating—I held her in my arms throughout the awful procedures, when she screamed and screamed, until I thought such tortures would send me mad.

It was a living nightmare, but, just as I feared exhaustion must put an end to her existence, the doctors announced the worst was over. Thank God they were right: little by little, Georgiana's eye returned to its usual size. But she never fully recovered. Her sight was blurred forever after, and her eyelid drooped, ruining the perfect symmetry of her beloved face. For a long time, she could not see clearly enough to look in a mirror. When she was finally able to see her reflection, it was a terrible blow. She refused to allow anyone outside her immediate family to visit and didn't leave the house for nearly a year. During that whole time, she never complained, never railed against what had befallen her, but was humbly grateful for our care and compassion. If ever I'd needed proof that my sister was an angel in human form, her conduct during this cruel sickness provided ample evidence of it.

As Georgiana had no other means of occupying herself, I sat with her most days, reading aloud if she wished it, and chatting quietly when that palled. One afternoon, when we were alone, she confessed how touched she had been by the depth of her husband's concern for her.

"If I hadn't seen it for myself, I'm not sure I'd have believed it. I never imagined he cared so much for me."

"He was beside himself with anguish," I replied. "It was plain he couldn't have borne to lose you. Lord B was just the same. When he thought I was close to death, suddenly he discovered what he felt for me."

"How strange men are," she mused. "I've turned it over and over in my mind, lying here in the dark. It's made me reflect on how little we understand the workings of the human heart, even in those who are closest to us."

"Perhaps we understand them least of all—they're both too near and too familiar to see clearly."

"Because the Duke never spoke to me of love, I thought he felt nothing for me. Now I'm not so sure. There's something there, I think—buried very deep and not easily expressed—but something nonetheless."

I smiled. "Of course he loves you. How could he not?"

"Whatever it is, it has made me very conscious of what I owe him—how wrong it would be for me ever to betray him again. Have you felt something similar about Lord B?"

I very much disliked the direction of this conversation but couldn't see how to deflect it.

"I know only too well how much I am in his debt."

"I thought, when we were in Italy, your relations with him seemed so much warmer than before. It made me so happy. I hoped there was a chance you'd found a way of living more comfortably together."

"I'm no longer afraid of him, if that's what you mean."

"I know he was unkind to you. But I thought he'd changed. He seemed genuinely to wish for some reconciliation."

I turned away.

"Oh, Harriet, please don't tell me you've rejected him?"

"I wouldn't say that, exactly. But we're no longer as well disposed to each other as we were in Italy."

Her face fell. "I wish you'd think again. Imagine how much easier your life would be if you could just resign yourself to him."

"I know. Believe me, I've tried, but I just don't love him. I don't love him at all."

"And you hope someone else will supply that love? Lord Granville, perhaps? You're very much talked of, you know."

This was the first time she'd mentioned him so directly.

"If there's gossip," I replied, as steadily as I could, "it's very unjust. I've done nothing of which I'm ashamed."

"Not now, perhaps. But that may change."

"Do you think so little of my resolution, then? Of my honesty? My self-respect?"

"Oh, Harriet—believe me, all those admirable qualities will dissolve into thin air once you surrender to a man who awakens all your most passionate feelings. If Lord Granville is that man—then I beg you, run away now, before it's too late. You saw for yourself what happened to me with Grey. Please, I beg you, don't follow in my miserable footsteps. I don't think I could bear it."

I took her hand and held it tightly. I hated to see her so distressed.

"Once you let a man like that into your heart, there's no going back. It can only ever end in disaster. And the worst of it is—after all the suffering your folly has brought upon you and everyone you care for—despite everything, you'll still love him—and will continue to do so, long, long after he has stopped loving you."

"Oh, G, please don't cry, it will hurt your eye."

"You're right, I mustn't give in to grief—even tears are forbidden to me, it seems."

With a great effort of will, she composed herself.

"Well—I promised myself I would speak," she continued, "and now I've done so, for all the good it may do. I shan't mention him again. You must make your own choice. All I ask is that you learn from my example—that you consider what the pursuit of love has done for me before running so heedlessly after it yourself."

She drew her hand away, and we sat in silence until she asked me to read to her once more. Soon we were lost deep in Miss Burney's *Camilla*, where the virtuous heroine was certain to be rewarded with the happy ending she so richly deserved. If either of us felt the contrast with our own situations, we did not mention it. Soon Georgiana was asleep, so I rose and went home.

I returned to Cavendish Square in a very subdued frame of mind. All I could think was that Georgiana would never be the same again.

She was not yet forty, but had lost the vivacity and spark that had always been such a vital part of her nature, and who could say if it would ever return? She seemed frail, with a crushed and defeated air. I could never love her any less, but I grieved terribly for the loss of the Georgiana I had adored for as long as I could remember.

For that reason, perhaps, her warning weighed particularly heavily upon me. Was I really so far gone in wickedness that I could ignore the plea of a sick and much-loved sister? I spent a long time alone in the days that followed, struggling to reconcile the contradictions in my heart. I knew I was teetering on a precipice, hurtling toward it with my eyes closed, my fingers in my ears to drown out those who tried to alert me to my danger. It could not go on. No more vacillations, as Lady Melbourne would say. I must put a stop to it and now was the time.

I went to my desk, took out paper and pen, and began to write to Lord Granville.

It was the sternest letter I'd ever sent him, for I wanted there to be no mistaking my position. I told him once more in the firmest terms that I had nothing to offer him but friendship. I regretted if my weakness—my repeated, foolish, guilty weakness—had encouraged him to conceive some other impression—but I must now correct that misunderstanding.

If he still wished to see me, we could meet only if we obeyed the strictest possible rules. We must never be alone together. He was to alter his manner toward me, making no more loving declarations; and he must promise never to behave in any way likely to encourage such a response from me. If he could accept these conditions, we might continue to see each other—but if they were unacceptable—if he continued to push and push for an intimacy I could never grant him, to take advantage of my own frailty—then I would be compelled to put an end to a situation that could only be productive of frustration to him and the deepest remorse and regret to me.

20

I knew that once he received my letter, Granville would do everything he could to see me. At first, I resisted his plaintive notes begging for a rendezvous, but his persistence wore me down. I was deeply affected by the hurt and disappointed tone in which he wrote and eventually concluded that perhaps a meeting might help him understand the seriousness of my intent and, as a result, would persuade him to agree to all I'd asked of him.

We met once more in a hackney coach—where else could we talk of such things without fear of being observed?—and drove out toward Kensington, where I thought we'd be safe from notice. I saw immediately how unhappy he was. I'd determined not to be the one to begin, and we sat in silence until finally he spoke.

"Your letter was a great shock to me," he began. "I could hardly believe it was from you, its tone was so cold."

"I intended it to be taken seriously. I hope it will have some good effect."

"It was very unkind."

"I thought it resembled all my behavior to you, in being far, far too kind."

I couldn't look at him, but fixed my eyes on the floor of the carriage. "I've allowed you liberties I should never have permitted. No wonder you treat me as you do. But now it must stop."

"If that's what you want, I'll do my best to be as correct and distant as you ask."

The carriage jolted over a pothole, and in the confined space of the carriage, his knee touched mine.

"But it's very painful to be so near you and yet held at such a distance. It doesn't bring out the best in me. A man in love is a very selfish being."

I began to cry. "You cannot speak such words to me, Lord Granville. You mustn't say them, not now, not ever."

"Don't send me away," he whispered. "I couldn't bear it."

Before I could reply, he raised up my head and kissed me. It was exactly as I remembered it, just as delicious as it had been that first time. All I wanted was for us to stay exactly as we were forever. My rational mind protested, but it was no match for my desire. I should have pushed him away—but instead I raised up my arms to embrace him, and there we remained, entangled together, his hat on the floor, my hand in his beautiful hair, as eager for each other as it was humanly possible to be.

Eventually—when we both knew matters must go no further—I pulled away. We sat looking at one another, both conscious we'd crossed a line from which there was probably no return. He smiled.

"Now you see the strength of what I feel for you."

"Yes. And, to my shame, the utter weakness of my resistance." I put my head in my hands. "I simply haven't the self-control to refuse you."

"I'm very glad to hear it." He reached out for me once more, but I refused any further embraces and asked to be taken back to the place where we began.

As the carriage bowled back toward the park, there was no more talk of my sending him away. I saw with a painful clarity that all the promises I had made to give him up were written on water. He saw it too, although he was too gracious and gentlemanly to allow any hint of his triumph to show. As for me—when I thought of those whom I had sworn never again to betray, I was genuinely horrified by what I'd done.

But there was that other part of me—the selfish, animal, yearning part—which was exultant. When I asked to be let down in some quiet place away from Cavendish Square, there was a spring in my step. So this was how it felt when pleasure was given and returned without sufferance or pretense, when the desire of one lover was met by the excitement of the other. All my life I had longed to experience this. Well, now I had—and for the first time I felt truly and joyfully alive, woken up to a host of sensations I hadn't thought I possessed.

I knew this elation would be quickly overtaken by remorse—but on that bright London day, for a few hours at least, I gave myself up to the knowledge that I shouldn't die without experiencing such joy. When I arrived home, Sally commented that I looked very well, that the air had clearly done me good. I smiled and turned away to hide my blush. I was already calculating how long it would be before I could meet him again.

$\mathcal{I}$t might be imagined, from what I've described, that my whole existence was given up to my feelings for Lord G—but everyday life has its way of going on, even as passion shakes you out, spins you around, and turns you upside down. At the same time as I tiptoed ever closer to becoming his lover, I did my best to remain, in the more sedate aspects of my life, the picture of diligent, matronly womanhood. I was, I hope and believe, an affectionate and attentive mother to my children. My elder sons, John and Fred, fifteen and thirteen, were almost young men; even young William was at school now. Only Caroline remained at home with me. I loved her dearly but was often puzzled to know how to manage her. Her moods were so variable—one moment she was gleeful and quite impossible to control, the next, she was sunk in gloom. My mother thought I was too soft with her and advised stricter discipline; but I hadn't the heart to punish and, besides, had never observed it did much good. So I indulged her, perhaps more than I should have done.

In fact, both my sister and I were known to have particularly tender feelings toward children and babies. Once our susceptibility became known, infants of every description were often left at our doors, by poor wretched parents who could no longer provide for them. We gladly took them in, unable to look upon them without trying to help. Any mother, I think, feels acutely for the sufferings of a neglected child, and I don't doubt our sympathies were heightened by reflecting on what Eliza's fate might have been, or, indeed, what might have befallen Granville's young son, had they been born into more straitened circumstances. The tiniest babies we fostered out, bringing them back into our households when they were older, and raising them as best we could. I had the girls trained up to go into service, and tried to place the boys as apprentices as soon as they were of an age. For a time, I even ran a little school at Roehampton, our country house just outside London, to equip them with the rudiments of reading and writing. As a result, there were always children of every age to be found roaming about our different houses. I enjoyed having so many young people around us; the amount it cost to maintain them was a heavy drain on my often scanty resources, but it felt a small price to pay for seeing them thrive.

I was, indeed, very much occupied by the precarious state of our finances. Our situation had not much improved at all since Lord B had inherited his father's title and property. Some of the most pressing debts had been paid; but a mountain of others remained, and servicing them was a terrible burden upon us. There were times when I couldn't lay my hands on five pounds in cash to pay our dairymaid, which was enough to raise a bitter laugh as I surveyed the grand circumstances in which we lived, so rich in assets but with barely an unmortgaged penny to our name.

I was frequently dispatched by Lord B to make a tour of London's many banks and moneylenders to see what credit I could raise to keep us afloat. He thought I made a better impression upon them than he did himself, and he was probably right, for I soon became a very good judge of who was likely to lend and who would not. I disliked the whole business extremely, but I knew it must be done and steeled myself to smile beseechingly through the many humiliations this odious task required of me.

Thus it was, that during those restless months, when in my heart I knew I'd reached a point of no return with Lord Granville—when I understood that all my protestations were hollow, that I was too infatuated ever to send him away—at the very same time, I strove to be a loving mother to my own children, a benefactor to other infants most in need, and even, at times, a helpmeet and companion to my husband.

For yes, there were occasions when Lord B and I still behaved as a married couple—when I presided over his dinner table, acted as hostess to his friends when they visited us, or traveled with him to stay at the houses of people we knew. Sometimes we even went shopping together. Though I did my utmost to hide it, I was very ill at ease and nervous in such situations. I thought it impossible that he could be completely ignorant of the rumors about Granville and me, supposing that, for reasons of his own, he chose not to raise the subject. But I was always waiting for him to do so and lived in constant dread of the moment of truth being sprung upon me.

I've often thought how much easier it would have been if he'd had a steady mistress of his own, some kindly woman who made him happy. I shouldn't have minded. His attentions had always been unwelcome to me, so how could I resent his bestowing them elsewhere? But if there was such a lady, I never heard talk of her; and as it's inconceivable some concerned friend would not have alerted me to her existence, if she did indeed exist, I'm forced to conclude there never was any such person.

I suppose he must have paid for his pleasures, as men readily do; but I think a more regular connection would have been better for him, soothing his hurt pride, focusing his mind on someone other than myself. I'm convinced he would have cared far less about my transgressions if he'd possessed a love of his own to make up for my betrayal. This is poor moralizing, but I was convinced of the truth of it. If Lord B had only found a mistress who suited him, we might both have been much happier for it.

I'm aware, as these thoughts occur to me, how very worldly and amoral I sound, exactly like Lady Webster or Lady Melbourne. These were the easygoing principles on which they conducted their lives; and, as both liked to tell me, it would have spared me a great deal of grief if I'd been able to embrace them myself.

Instead, shame at my conduct weighed heavily upon me. I could never rid myself of the belief that I was betraying every duty, every obligation that I owed to those around me, that I prized my own gratification above their happiness, and that I deserved to be condemned as the most selfish of beings. As a result, I became in effect two people in a single body—one only too aware of her guilt, doing all she could to preserve the decencies of a family life she knew was threatened by her desires; while the other was thrilled to find herself the object of a beautiful young man's passion, alternately dreading and longing for a consummation.

*I*t was at about this time that Lady Webster arrived back in London.

I hadn't seen her since our days in Naples. Then she'd been pregnant with Webster's child; now it was Lord Holland's baby she was carrying. She'd executed her plan exactly as she'd said she would, taking the compliant Holland as her lover, announcing her condition to her husband, who had promptly commenced divorce proceedings against her. Once these were complete, she and Lord Holland were to be married. But as she sat in my drawing room, her accustomed brisk confidence was somewhat less in evidence than I remembered.

"Do you have any apples?" she asked as she eased herself against the cushions. "Or is it too early for them here? Last time it was peas I craved. I ate more of them than any woman in Christendom. I'm surprised I didn't turn green."

I sent a servant off to look for some, offering tea in the meantime. How, I asked, had she been treated upon her return?

She frowned. "London society has not been particularly welcoming. I confess I underestimated quite how chilly and disobliging my reception would be."

"I'm sorry to hear it—but you know how much people enjoy being censorious."

"Yes—the unpleasantness comes as no surprise. But it turns out I'm not quite as brave as I imagined. I've found the whole experience most distressing."

"That isn't like you. You've always been a fighter."

"I don't think I'm easily cowed. But the inconvenience of being between husbands has exposed me to the spite and condescension of every purse-lipped prude who chooses to find herself offended by my conduct. I have been ignored, dismissed, sneered at, and cut in the most brutal manner. It lowers the spirits."

"I'm sure it will improve once you're safely established as Lady Holland. And your condition perhaps makes you feel more vulnerable than usual."

"I'm afraid our timing was a little off in that respect. The divorce proceeds more slowly than I'd imagined and I'm afraid will come too late to benefit this poor child"—she pointed at her burden—"who will be deemed illegitimate, if it has the misfortune to arrive before Holland and I can say 'I do.'"

She put down her teacup.

"Anyway, it has all been very vexatious. You're one of the very few people who's prepared to see me at all."

"I've been the subject of too much unpleasantness myself to let it affect my opinion of anyone I care for. I'd never abandon a friend because they were gossiped about—and I shan't do so now."

Lady Webster wiped her eyes on her napkin. She was a tough little creature, and I had never seen her shed a tear before.

"You're very kind—and in return, I'll tell you something I heard yesterday which I think you should know. One of the ladies leading the charge against me is the mother of your beautiful young friend."

"Lady Stafford? I've never heard she was a particularly vindictive character."

"Perhaps she's usually as nice as pie. But I imagine the news of my elopement with Holland touched her in a very sensitive place. I'm a terrifying example of the dreadful consequences that lie in wait for young men who form alliances with married women of loose morals and Whig principles—all of which strike very close to home in her case."

I was too taken aback not to let my surprise show.

"So the Staffords know all about my closeness to Lord Granville?"

"They do indeed—and they don't like it at all. From what I hear, Lady Stafford is doing everything in her power to make him aware of the risks he runs in continuing to see you."

"How do you know all this? Has anyone spoken to you about it?"

"Lady Stafford wrote to Lord Granville when she heard about us running off. He showed it to Holland, and I gather it was a stinker. Father's disappointment, her own broken heart, et cetera, et cetera. Every line was intended to convince him of the horrors that must result if he doesn't free himself from his connection with you."

I sat like a stone, not sure what to say.

"I'm sorry if I've upset you. But I meant it kindly. It's always wise to know who our enemies are."

"I should hate to think of Lady Stafford as my enemy. Lord Granville loves her, and I couldn't think ill of anyone he cares for."

"Well, I'm only the messenger. Personally, I'd be tempted to poke out my tongue if I saw her in the street, but you are a far better person than I and will never sink so low."

I decided to mention nothing of this to Lord Granville. If I were to complain, what was he to do? I could hardly expect him to repudiate his mother's criticisms. But Lady Webster's warning worried away at me, like a pebble caught in a shoe. What if Lady Stafford should prevail? Lord Granville was her only son, and I knew how much she loved him. What if her admonitions gradually turned him against me? I had tortured myself half to death wondering if I should be the one to put an end to our connection; but I'd never seriously considered that, swayed by his mother's pleas, he might be the one driven to do the right thing and decide to see me no more.

*I*t was in the autumn of 1796 when Lord Granville first mentioned the possibility of his being sent as a very junior member of a diplomatic mission to Paris, to explore the prospect of a negotiated peace with France. Little progress had been made in a war that had turned out to be as expensive as it was ill conducted. None of the promised military victories had materialized despite the terrible casualties that had resulted from the vicious fighting in the Low Countries. I was myself very much in favor of peace—it was exactly what Mr. Fox had sought for so long—and was therefore glad to hear talks were to be attempted. They were to be undertaken by Lord Malmesbury, an experienced diplomat and loyal Pittite Tory, who'd offered Lord Granville a junior place in his entourage. The commission arrived completely out of the blue—Lord Granville was as surprised by it as I was and sought my advice about what he was to do. I found myself torn in two when I considered how to reply.

I'd long urged him to fix upon some career, for as a younger son he could expect little by way of inheritance. He had an elder half brother, who would in time inherit all the family property, with only a small allowance remaining for him. It would eventually be necessary to commit himself to some profession, if he wished to retain any standing in the world. His experiences at Plymouth had convinced him he wouldn't prosper in the army, and I thought him unsuited for either the law—too little application—or the Church— too much love of pleasure. His parents wished him to enter politics, and in this, at least, I entirely agreed with them.

When, some months before, a parliamentary seat had opened up in the borough of Litchfield, Lord Granville's father decided his son should stand for it. The Stafford influence was very strong there, but Lord Granville would nevertheless be required to show himself to his prospective constituents and convince them he was worthy of becoming their member. He didn't much care for the prospect.

"I'll be obliged to drink with the electors—dance with their daughters at some local inn—make speeches to all and sundry. Everyone will insult me, I'll be shouted at and abused—and on top of that, I must give the impression I'm enjoying every moment of it."

I'd had no patience with his objections. I'd been involved in elections all my life and understood exactly what was required of a parliamentary candidate.

"Yes indeed. And I most heartily recommend you throw off that proud expression you too often adopt. It doesn't pay to seem haughty. Your electors won't like it."

"Perhaps I should kiss a few butchers while I'm about it—as you and your sister did for Mr. Fox."

"That's an old canard, and I shan't dignify it with a reply. I know well enough you and your Tory friends think no woman has any business involving herself in politics. But I've been around politicians all my life—and let me assure you, you must accustom yourself to going among your constituents, if you truly wish to represent them."

He sighed and said nothing; but I knew he felt the truth of what I said.

"Take my advice and you won't regret it." I smiled. "It's particularly selfless on my part to offer it, since when you enter the House, it will only be to vote against all my opinions."

Well, he won the seat, which pleased me, for a while at least. But I can't pretend he proved particularly diligent in attending to his parliamentary duties. I began to fear he'd never rise above the trivial round of pleasures that occupied him whenever he wasn't with his regiment: playing tennis—he was inordinately fond of that—attending parties, assemblies, and dinners, and above all, spending long nights at Brooks's club, where he continued to gamble away his limited means, paying no heed at all to my pleas to give it up. I was desperate to find for him some occupation that would call forth his ambitions and galvanize his talents—and when he told me about Lord Malmesbury's offer, it struck me as exactly the opportunity that might set him at last on the road to a worthy position in public life. So how could I do anything but urge him to accept it, as quickly as possible, for such a chance might not come around again.

My private thoughts, however, were not so selfless. I knew enough of the world to understand there was more to this offer than met the eye. This plum appointment would never have fallen into the lap of an untried young man without some private urging behind the scenes. I saw Lord and Lady Stafford's hands at work in the business and had no doubt Lord Granville had been offered the place entirely because of their efforts. To secure it, they must have pulled every string at their disposal, calling on all the ties of friendship, gratitude, and party interest that existed between themselves and the Prime Minister, Mr. Pitt.

It seemed equally plain to me, in the light of what Lady Webster had said, that the Staffords' real purpose in attaching their son to the Malmesbury mission was only partly to do with building his career—its real intent was to get him away from me.

24

I think it much to my credit that I kept all these suspicions to myself and unhesitatingly insisted that Lord Granville should accept the post. I honestly thought it would be good for him; and that it might be of benefit to me too, as I should no longer be constantly tempted and teased by my feelings for him. A little time apart might enable me to see things more clearly when he returned. Providence—in the shape of Lady Stafford—had separated us again, for which, I supposed, I ought to be glad.

At least, that's what I told myself. In truth, I suspected that, much as my better part might wish it otherwise, the strength of my attachment to him was unlikely to change, however long he was away—but what about his feelings for me? His new life would be full of temptations, impossible, surely, for a young man to resist. I knew Paris very well and had no doubts of how he, with his striking beauty, would be received there. Parisian ladies are bolder than we are. They're not afraid to pursue very openly the objects of their desire—and how should I feel when they turned their attentions to him?

I thought I could bear a dalliance or two, but what if he should meet with someone he really liked, someone younger and more beautiful than I, without my constraints of situation? What if she did not whine and cry as I did, but was eager and free and determined to have him? How should I feel then? I was terrified that someone with fewer scruples than I had might rush in and take possession of what I'd come to believe was truly mine.

Jealousy isn't an attractive emotion. It made me anxious and suspicious; but I was mortified to discover it had yet another danger-ous effect, which I hadn't in the least anticipated. I will be candid—it very much increased the desire I felt for Lord Granville. I'd never found him so enticing as I did now that he was about to go away. I couldn't catch sight of him across a dinner table or at some other crowded gathering without recalling all I had felt when he held me in his arms.

I knew I must see him alone, for one last embrace before he went, for who knew when we should have the chance again? His mis-sion was to stay in France for as long as there remained any hope of success; he might be away for months. I believe the thought of so long a separation sent me more than a little mad. Certainly, it encouraged me to take a very great risk. I approached my old friend Lady Anne, who'd known about my connection to Lord Granville since our time at Teignmouth, and asked if I might meet him in her apartments before he left. I shouldn't need long, I said. It was just to say goodbye. She agreed—with a knowing smile—to be absent for an hour, after which time she would return and carry me away to supper with Lord Boringdon, our arrival together suggesting we'd spent all evening innocently in each other's company. Lord Granville and I should thus have a short time together in which to bid each other farewell. I told myself this would allow us to exchange some tender words, and perhaps even a few kisses. I would let him stroke my hair. We shouldn't be alone for very long; and surely, we had enough discipline between us to prevent the occurrence of any-thing more.

This was what I imagined. The reality was very different.

25

When I arrived at Lady Anne's apartments, Lord G was already waiting for me. He took my coat and hat and poured me a glass of wine. We sat on Lady Anne's hard-backed chairs and drank to each other's health. I remember we were self-conscious and silent; we must have had some conversation, but I can't recall a word we said. Then, just as I wished him to do, he came to sit beside me and kissed me. I sank into his embrace, not attempting to free myself, and a short time later, he took my hand and led me to the bedroom. I should have protested, but to my shame, I did not. It was the first time we'd ever been together on a bed and the very act of lying down together indicated only too clearly what was to come.

It was then he finally spoke the words I had yearned to hear for so long.

"I love you, Harriet. My dearest, dearest Harriet."

After that, any idea of putting an end to this joy was utterly impossible. I looked into those beautiful turquoise eyes and drew him toward me.

I thought I understood what to expect, but I was quite wrong. The other men I'd known had required only my acquiescence.

Nothing more was asked of me, and very little given in return. I had never dreamed a man and woman could truly be partners in the act of love. It was nothing short of a revelation to discover how that felt.

We often say, "I don't know what possessed me," lightly, with a laugh, as if possession is not an idea to be taken too seriously. But when I was with Lord Granville that night, for the first time I understood its true meaning. For when he held me, I felt myself no longer in control of my own senses, but obedient only to what my body demanded. I can't describe it other than to say I was overcome by an eagerness, a drive toward a fulfillment that my senses insisted was waiting for me, just out of my grasp, if only I could get there. When I finally did so, I couldn't believe what it was like. I had never known such a thing before—but now I understand that this is what true desire feels like, that it is this sensation, in all its unstoppable power, which is the right true end of physical love.

I should add that passion of this kind does not leave much room for delicacy. Once it has you in its grasp, it is selfish, with no regard for the proprieties. It drives out shame, drives out modesty, drives out anything except the urge to be one with the man who is the source of so much pleasure; or at least, that is how it was for me. I couldn't have stopped for the world. It was Lord Granville who, at the very last moment, found enough self-possession to draw back from the final consummation of love. I was left breathless, almost tearful with gratitude, both for what he had given me and for what he had held back from taking.

When it was over, he lay beside me, telling me how glorious it had been, how much he loved me. I didn't know how to reply. I felt myself slowly returning to the world, and with consciousness came remorse. I couldn't believe what I'd done. My first thought was that he must leave, as quickly as possible. At first he protested, but finally I persuaded him. Once he'd gone, I smoothed down the bed, threw water on my face, and arranged my clothes. Then I went to the little sitting room and waited.

To be left alone at that moment was probably the worst possible situation for me—my nerves all jangling, my emotions stretched as taut and thin as a string on a violin. Once the fit of passion passed, my ferocious joy was replaced by something like horror. How could I have acted in such a profligate way—what must he think of me? I was horribly ashamed, overwhelmed with remorse. By the time Lady Anne arrived, I had worked myself almost into hysteria, crying and wringing my hands. She guessed immediately what had passed.

"Oh, my dear, what is this?"

She ran to me and took my hand, which only made me cry harder. I laid my head on her shoulder and wept, until she removed me from herself, stood me at a little distance, and spoke to me very seriously.

"Come, Harriet, this won't do. You must take hold of yourself. If you've enjoyed what's just passed, then be thankful for it. If not, don't do it again. It's a simple choice—there's really no need for so much misery."

Her words rallied me a little. I wiped my eyes and swallowed the cordial she offered, and together we went to Lord Boringdon's, as arranged. But my poor attempts at concealing my distress did not last long and, blaming illness, I soon left for home. I was in such a state that I was required to be put to bed immediately.

I think Sally suspected what had happened. She'd watched Lord Granville's pursuit of me since our return from Italy with increasing apprehension. It was impossible she hadn't observed the cooling of relations between myself and Lord B; so far, she'd said nothing, although her expression often told me all I needed to know of her true opinions.

This was not the moment for me to take her entirely into my confidence. I was too distracted for that. We hardly spoke while she measured out some laudanum to calm me down and make me sleep.

While I waited for it to take effect, I found pen and paper and scribbled a note to Lord Granville.

It was a sad and desperate piece of work, babbling and incoherent with guilt. I was a wretched and abandoned woman, wholly unworthy of any regard or consideration; nothing could excuse what I'd done. Since I'd told him so often I could never be his lover, he must surely despise me for having surrendered—it made all my previous protestations seem insincere—as did the shamelessly obvious pleasure I'd taken in the act itself. I took little consolation in the knowledge that we hadn't proceeded to the final culmination of love. I was grateful for his restraint; but we'd gone so far that I couldn't deceive myself about the reality of my guilt. All I wanted was to hide myself from the face of every human being I knew, and most of all, from him.

As soon as he received my note, he wrote begging to see me. I refused; but he was so shocked by the violence of my misery that a few days later he arrived uninvited at Cavendish Square at a time he knew Lord B had already left for Brooks's. Reluctantly, I came to the drawing room to meet him. I insisted, however, that the door remain open during our conversation, and that he must not stay for longer than ten minutes.

I saw that my appearance shocked him. I was pale and drawn—the laudanum I'd taken over the last two days had not been kind to my looks. I endeavored to compose myself, but found it hard to meet his gaze, painfully conscious of what had happened between us the last time I'd seen him. With his back to the open door, so that no passing servant could see his expression of concern, he spoke fast and low, his eyes always fixed intently upon me.

"I am come here for two reasons. First, I wanted to know how you do; and I see for myself the answer is not very well. Please, please, for my sake, if not your own, don't torment yourself in this way. It's terrible to see, and very painful for me to think I'm the cause of it. Throw off this unhappiness, I beg you."

He waited for me to speak; when I did not, he continued in the same intense tone.

"Also, I'm here to tell you none of the fears you describe in your letter have any foundation in truth. You use such cruel and dreadful words about yourself—'abandoned,' 'depraved,' 'criminal'—and say you believe this is what I must think of you now. Let me assure you that's quite impossible. You know what my feelings are—you must recall, at Lady Anne's I told you I loved you. You haven't forgotten that?"

I shook my head. I had not forgotten.

"Then how can you think what we enjoyed together could make me judge you in such a despicable way? The truth is quite otherwise. My feelings are unchanged. I care for you just as deeply as I always have—and to be candid, perhaps a little more. I'm proud of what happened. I wanted to give you pleasure and am glad I succeeded."

"You are very direct, sir."

"A little frankness seems necessary at this moment. I promise you most sincerely I think nothing less of you because of what we did. I'm pleased I made you happy—happiness is all I want for you. You must understand that."

If I hadn't been so afraid of being seen, I would have reached out my fingers and touched his cheek.

"It makes my heart very full to hear you speak so." I clasped my hands tightly together to keep them away from him. "But you know I can't feel as you do about the connection between us. My situation won't allow it. For me, there can be no happiness, no pleasure between us that doesn't come with a weight of guilt attached to it. So if you really care for my happiness as you say you do—and for my health, my self-respect, my ability to look the world in the eye—we both know there is only one certain way of ensuring it. Promise me we will never, under any circumstances, repeat what passed between us the other night. And yes, I don't deny the pleasure you give me is like heaven at the time, but when I come to my senses, it can never be anything but a source of misery to me. I beg you then to ignore my moment of weakness—and to assure me that, despite everything, you won't think of me as your lover—but rather, as I've so often urged, as a tender and affectionate friend."

"So we return once more to friendship, your favorite word?"

"I think we must, if you do not wish to see me torn apart by feelings I cannot bear. Would it cost you so much to agree we would never again exceed the bounds of a loving friendship? Perhaps you could attempt to think of me exactly as you do your sisters?"

He looked incredulous, as though he was about to laugh—but when he saw I was hurt, his expression became grave.

"Listen to me seriously now. It would be easy for me to agree to what you ask, to salve your conscience and make you feel better; but I can't do it. I have shown you time and time again the strength of my attachment. It has withstood all you have thrown against it. This is no passing whim for me. I must therefore refuse what you ask—much as you say you want it. I shall never think of you as I do my sisters. I cannot make that promise, nor any of the others you ask for, because I know I could never, ever keep them. My feelings for you stand in the way."

"Perhaps you don't love me enough to try? Surely there can be no greater proof of your affection than to rein in desires that can only be gratified by plunging me into wretchedness?"

"That may be so for another kind of lover, but it won't serve for me. Our time together the other night was exactly what I have long wished for—and I must tell you that, far from thinking it something not to be repeated, I hope very much it will happen again—it cannot do so soon enough for me. There—I have been as sincere as even you could ask of me."

He smiled. "But now it is time for you to be equally plain with me. If you genuinely believe that except on the terms you suggest, our connection is impossible, then this is the time to say so. If you can truly and honestly swear you wish us to be together only as brother and sister, then declare it now. But do so in the knowledge that I can never be with you on such terms. So you must choose—if you genuinely have nothing to offer but friendship—this is the moment to break with me, now and forever."

I've never been so shocked in my life. I sat stunned, not knowing what to say. But he seemed not to expect a reply; instead, he rose to leave. I stood up to bid him farewell—and when we reached the door, before I knew what he did, he gently closed it—and just as swiftly, bent his head to mine and kissed me, not gently this time, but with a force my body remembered. I should have resisted—instead, I'm afraid, I boldly returned his embrace.

It was the act of a moment, but we both understood what it meant. I'd given him the answer he hoped for, had shown in the plainest way that I could never give him up. We didn't speak again—and then he was gone. I heard his voice in the hall, as a servant rushed to open the front door and see him out. I doubt our meeting lasted much more than ten minutes in all, but in that short time my life was changed forever.

Now our attachment was no longer something uncertain, ambiguous, undecided. I had pledged my future to him, doing so in the full knowledge of the risks I ran, of the betrayals I would inflict, of the hurt, shame, and guilt I would suffer. But, as I sat stupefied in the silent drawing room, dazed by what I'd done—I knew that if I'd been offered one last chance to reconsider, to run after him and take back the consent my kiss implied, I wouldn't have taken it. Love makes fools of us all.

26

*B*efore he left for Paris, I extracted from Lord Granville a promise that he would write to me as frequently as his duties allowed. I gave him strict instructions about what I expected—a few lines every day, telling me everything he saw and did, for nothing was so engaging as hearing from a distance the details of his daily life; and nothing was so dull as a correspondent who began his letters, as he so often did, with "I have nothing to say." I knew France very well, loved the country and its people, and was curious to discover what he made of it. Of this I heard a little—Paris looked very much as it did formerly, although there were fewer carriages in the streets; no one used the word "citizen" anymore, and the people appeared, he thought, rather less democratic in their appearance than in England. I was also keen to hear how he liked his new profession and whether he thought the diplomatic life might suit him, but he told me nothing at all in this respect, declaring that Lord Malmesbury had forbidden any mention of the progress of their mission in private letters home. I did, however, learn a little more on a subject of even greater interest to me. I will be honest and confess that I was extremely eager to find out which ladies had thrown themselves in his way, and to what extent he'd surrendered to their charms. I'd urged him to be absolutely candid in this respect, describing every flirtation and encounter, in as much detail as decency allowed. I assured him I shouldn't be jealous; I didn't expect him to live like a monk and should much prefer to hear of any adventures directly from him than from the gossip of others.

To some extent, he did as I asked. Thus, I heard a great deal about the attractions of the fascinating actress Madame Talma, perhaps, as he told me, the cleverest woman he had ever met, who lived openly in an attachment not, as he delicately put it, sanctified by the rites of marriage. She seemed to enjoy his company very much. He visited her so often that perhaps it appeared as if they were about to embark upon an affair, though he assured me this was not the case. Then there was Madame Tallien, very beautiful, very elegant, and very brave—she'd saved many unfortunates from Robespierre's persecutions during the worst days of the Terror. She was now under the protection of a powerful politician, but she was still much sought after for her favors, which, Lord Granville had been told, she bestowed entirely as she thought fit, with a freedom he couldn't help but admire.

Neither of these ladies was in her first youth. I couldn't decide whether that made them more, or less, dangerous to me. I knew callow, immature girls weren't much to Lord Granville's taste, and that he preferred older, more experienced women of the world. So how long, I asked him, would it be before he declared himself to one of them? Or perhaps to both at once? He replied that his morals were so far uncorrupted; but, as he added that Paris was without doubt the most dissolute and scandalous city he'd ever known, I was not entirely comforted by his assurances.

At the end of 1796, it became clear that nothing was to be hoped for from Lord Malmesbury's mission, and by December he and Lord Granville returned home. In his absence, I'd lived quietly down at

Roehampton with my family, doing all in my power to persuade myself I would never give way again to the passion that had overwhelmed me before. But I was weak. Once he was back, once I saw him again, all my resolutions failed me. Whenever we met alone—encounters I should never have allowed—my feelings overpowered my good intentions, and all our former intimacies were renewed.

Such was the torment between the strength of my attraction to Lord Granville and the guilt I felt in surrendering to it that I was almost glad when he was sent back to France the following summer. The state of politics in Britain was desperate. Great mutinies by sailors at Spithead and Sheerness had shaken Mr. Pitt's government and threatened the security of the seas; my brother George, who was First Lord of the Admiralty, left us in no doubt as to the seriousness of the situation. It was perhaps no surprise that Mr. Pitt thought it worth another attempt to negotiate a peace; and Lord Malmesbury was dispatched again to France, with Lord Granville accompanying him.

Just as I had before, I told myself our separation was not to be regretted, as it removed me from the temptation of Lord Granville's presence; but for all my efforts to cultivate serenity, I was very unsettled while he was away. Lord B had taken a house at Bognor, on the Sussex coast, and I was lonely there. He was out all day, leaving the house early each morning, weighed down with paper, paints, and brushes, to sketch the beauties of the sea, sky, and cliffs. I was left alone—and as was always the case when I was solitary, my conscience pained me sadly. I concluded I was both too good and too bad to behave as I did. If I was more of a sinner, I shouldn't care—and if I was what I should be, I'd have never considered it. But instead, I was trapped between the two imperatives of duty and desire—and destined to suffer as a result.

Eventually, I asked Lord B if my old friend Lady Anne might come down to keep me company. He agreed, and she duly arrived—but if I hoped her arrival would raise my spirits, I was very much mistaken.

She was not her usual giddy, chattering self, but altogether more subdued, silent on our walks along the cliffs, and withdrawn when we sat together after dinner. When I asked what the matter was, she shook her head and refused to say; but one afternoon, as we sat on the seashore, watching the waves smash against the wet rocks, she opened her heart to me, quite out of the blue.

"I don't think Morpeth will ever marry me now."

She'd been entangled with Lord Morpeth, one of Lord Granville's closest friends for years, almost as long as I'd known her. I didn't know what to say, for it had never occurred to me she might have expected him to do so.

"When I ask him what he intends, he changes the subject or refuses to reply at all."

"Well—" I stammered, gathering my thoughts, "most men assume that is a question only they can raise. Perhaps he was surprised by your mentioning it to him."

"I'm sure he was," she continued. "It was plain enough he'd never thought about it at all."

She picked up a pebble and threw it with all her force into the sea.

"We've been together for four years, and not once in all that time has he told me he loves me. Has Lord Granville ever said anything of that nature to you?"

I turned swiftly away, trying to hide my expression, lest it reveal even the slightest hint of triumph. But she understood well enough.

"Then you're luckier than I." A tear rolled down her face and she brushed it away angrily. "I suppose I'm too old for him. Is ten years so great a difference? No, don't reply, we both know it is. Not for a mistress, perhaps, but definitely so for a wife."

Then she remembered the thirteen years between Lord Granville and me.

"Ah, but perhaps not for you. Your case is entirely different from my own. I believe Lord G really cares for you."

"Of course he knows I can never marry him," I said softly, "situated as I am. He need have no fear of that."

"That's why they pursue us so eagerly," Lady Anne cried; "we older women are such a convenience for younger men. They can enjoy everything we have to offer, with no fear of being held to some greater obligation—and then, when it suits them, we can be dismissed with a smile and a thank-you, like a servant being turned out of a place."

"Will you leave Morpeth, then? If he makes you so unhappy?"

"The worst of it is, I don't think I can. I haven't the strength to do it. I expect I'll stay until he gives me my marching orders."

I took her hand, and we sat silently for a moment.

"But make no mistake, Harriet, these lovers we've allowed into our hearts consider no one's feelings but their own—partly because they're men, and that's how men are—but even more so because they're young, and youth makes them merciless. I don't doubt Lord G cares for you—but don't ever allow yourself to rely on his affection. None of them can really be trusted."

She cried there for a little, perched on the rocks. When she was calmer, we walked back to the house, where she brightened a little. Her mood seemed to have been improved by her outburst, as if some long-pent-up frustration had been released, leaving her more like her old self. We sat down with Lord B for dinner that night, and the conversation flowed as freely as anyone could have wished, as he told us where he had been all day and even showed us a few rough drawings he had made. To anyone who didn't know us, we would have seemed a tolerably cheerful little party—but the truth could not have been more different. When I looked around the table, I could not help but see us as we really were—an aging, unloved mistress, waiting for her inevitable dismissal; a bitter, angry cuckolded husband; and a scheming, deceitful wife, blinded by her passion for a much younger man. What a pretty picture we made. Suddenly I was overwhelmed by disgust and could bear it no longer. I took myself to bed and swallowed some laudanum. It sent me to sleep but gave me bad dreams in which Lord Granville introduced me to a French lady with whom he was very much in love.

27

A month went past. The weather grew chillier. Lady Anne had long since returned to London, and I was alone and sunk in a melancholy frame of mind. Lord Granville had sent me a little picture of himself, which I kept closely wrapped up, bringing it out only when I was sure it was safe to do so. I'd hoped it would raise my spirits, but in fact it merely served to depress them even further, by emphasizing the distance between us. And then I received a letter from him that lit up my gloom like a bolt of lightning—the diplomatic mission had failed—the negotiations had collapsed—and in consequence, he expected to be back in London within the next few weeks.

It took every effort of mind and body for me not to betray the excitement I felt. I should see him again—and perhaps quite soon! But once the first exhilaration passed, I was perplexed to think how we were to meet. There was no possibility of my rushing up to town. On what pretext could I go? My husband would never allow it. In the interlude between Lord Granville's two missions to France, there had been moments when I feared I'd been incautious, when a change in Lord B's mood alarmed me into taking greater care. But in general, his demeanor had been calm, even good-natured, to such an extent that it redoubled my already profound sense of betrayal. Nothing further had passed between us on the subject of Lord Granville since that last terrible conversation; and in its wake we had settled into a fragile peace that I was keen not to disturb.

But I had learned from experience not to mistake Lord B's outward calm for ignorance. His temper was always better when he knew Lord Granville was safely out of my reach, and that knowledge had no doubt contributed to the placid months we spent together at Bognor. His feelings would be quite different once he knew Lord Granville had returned.

I told myself I must take the very greatest care. I must never suggest, by any expression or word, that I had any wish other than to remain where we were, until it pleased him to announce we were to go home. After all, I thought, how long could it be? The holiday season was over, the little resort was empty, autumn was almost upon us. Lord B, however, showed not the slightest intention of leaving. On the contrary, he told me he enjoyed the darker weather, for it offered entirely new perspectives for his sketching.

Lord Granville had been back in London for some time by this point, eagerly anticipating my arrival there. But soon, he explained, he'd be obliged to return to his hated regimental duties at Plymouth. There was no chance of our meeting once he was exiled there again. I thought I should die of sheer frustration.

There were moments when I wondered whether Lord B was deliberately tormenting me in the way he knew would hurt me most. I studied him intently as we sat opposite each other at breakfast and at dinner, searching his bland, closed features to discover whether he was carrying out some plan. Then, just as I thought we should never leave, he informed me in the most matter-of-fact manner that it was time to go. We were sitting in the snug little sitting room, both of us reading. I put down my book very carefully. I knew I must show not the slightest evidence of elation.

"That seems a good idea," I murmured, as if it had just occurred to me. "There's nothing to keep us here now the weather is so unkind and everyone else has gone."

"I feel we've exhausted what Bognor has to offer us." His expression was unreadable. I should have left it there—but I was emboldened to make one sly remark, in the hope of uncovering some reason for his actions.

"We certainly hung on as long as we possibly could."

"Yes—I was resolved we shouldn't be forced out before it was necessary. I took this house at enormous cost, until October. And whatever might happen, I was determined we should remain here until the lease was up. Now that it is, I'm ready to leave."

Did I believe him? Had we really dallied pointlessly for so long, merely because he could not bear the idea of wasting money on rent? Or had it really been his aim to keep me secluded down in Bognor until he knew Granville was no longer in London? But whatever the reason for his actions, the whole episode was a timely reminder that it would be fatal to underestimate him. Vigilance must remain my watchword. But I could not remain depressed in spirits for long. I was going back to London—and once there, I would find a way of seeing Lord Granville. I didn't know how it would be done, only that if I had to move heaven and earth to achieve it, I would somehow make it happen.

I arrived back in Cavendish Square to find the house in brilliant order. Sally had gone on ahead and made all the arrangements to ensure everything was just as I liked it, so that I settled back into my home with all the pleasure of a cat returning to a favorite basket. On my first night, I lay on my bed and stretched out with delight, gazing around fondly at the familiar comforts of my room—the well-polished furniture, the fire lit in the gleaming grate, the fresh linens in the wardrobe, my brushes and combs and creams laid out before the mirror. This was my favorite place, and I greeted it all like a long-lost friend. I noticed on my writing desk Sally had left me a small pile of letters that had arrived during my absence. I riffled through them quickly, until I came to one that looked grubbier than the rest. It was addressed in a hand I did not recognize. I hesitated before opening it—and once I saw what it contained, I wished with all my heart I had not done so.

It was an indecent print, a crude drawing of a man and a woman engaged in the most lewd and disgusting act. Beside these obscene figures, someone had written Lord Granville's name and my own. I was so shocked that at first I could not get my breath. I sat, unable to move, transfixed with horror at the nastiness of it. Then I was overwhelmed by disgust—I could not bear to look at it for another second—its very presence repulsed me—I screwed it up and threw it in the fire, watching until every scrap had been turned into ashes.

I was shivering as I lay back on my bed. Who could have sent me such a loathsome thing? I could not imagine who among my acquaintances could have wished to humiliate and upset me in such a cruel way. It was terrible to think that some smirking, anonymous coward hated me enough to abuse me in this foul manner.

More than that, it was proof that my liaison with Lord Granville was more widely known than even I had suspected. God knows, the list of those in on the secret was already long enough—there were my friends Lady Anne, Bess Foster, Lady Melbourne, and Lady Webster—or Lady Holland, as she'd now triumphantly become. There was my sister, too, who'd shared with me her suspicions and fears about our connection, but in whom I'd confided nothing definite about the progress of our affair. Then there were Lord Granville's closest companions, Lords Morpeth, Boringdon, and Holland. That was number enough, without even considering those with whom they might have shared their knowledge. And then there were the inveterate gossips outside this inner circle, who made it their business to dig up any scrap of scandal—men like my old lover Richard Sheridan, who had wormed out the story from some thoughtless person and teased me about Lord Granville unmercifully whenever he saw me.

As I counted these names, I grew more and more afraid. Every new addition made me more vulnerable. And to have received something so depraved—was that not warning enough of the ever-increasing risk I ran? But horrified and disgusted as I was, I confess I was so far gone in my passion for him, that a terrible thought occurred to me. If I was obliged to be the victim of such a low piece of obscenity, it gave me some strange satisfaction to know that the name I was linked with was his. I could not have borne it if it had been anyone else.

28

*I*t was some time before Lord Granville was able to secure leave from his duties and return to London. I was obliged to be patient, a virtue that has never come naturally to me—but I sought to distract myself as well as I could. I played with young William, riding out with him in our carriage to take the air when the weather allowed it. I spent wet afternoons teaching Caroline to draw—she had a real gift for the art, inherited perhaps from Lord B. She never had much application and couldn't be brought to study technique; but there was a freshness to her work that I knew wasn't present in my own. In just a few lines she could capture the energy of her pet dog or the expression of some character she had invented. She had talent, but not the discipline to hone it, which I very much regretted.

I confess I also devoted myself to more selfish occupations. I began to give serious thought to the image I presented to the world. I've never been particularly vain of my appearance. Even when young, I wasn't considered a beauty. My figure was never as lithe and girlish as Bess Foster's, and there was nothing in my face as fragile and beguiling as hers. Nor had I inherited any of my sister's star- tling charismatic appeal—but my complexion was clear, my teeth good, and my lustrous brown hair much commented upon. The men who pursued me talked of my melting eyes, of the lushness of my figure, of the air of generous kindness they sensed in me—and gradually these were the features I learned to appreciate in myself. It had been a long time since I'd sought to do much to improve them—my bad health had dissuaded me from any such vanities. But now I was so much better—my cough reduced to an occasional annoyance; no more spitting of blood—I felt the time was right to take myself in hand. I don't need to add that I also wanted to look my best for Lord Granville. That was uppermost in my mind, and therefore very obvious—and, as I quickly understood, not only to me.

I'd set Sally the task of reviewing my wardrobe with me—taking out all my clothes to consider whether they might be altered or improved in some way. This took us the better part of a week; and once that was finished, I sat at my dressing table and asked her to consider whether there were any more flattering ways in which my hair might be dressed. It was this, I think, that finally compelled her to speak.

"I know you won't care for what I'm about to say, but I can't stay silent any longer."

I saw she was agitated; and I knew only too well what was coming.

"I see how things are with Lord Granville—and it makes me afraid for you."

There was no use in my attempting some half-hearted denial. I merely bowed my head and sighed.

"I shan't lie to you, Sally. I respect you too much for that. I do—I do feel for him—" I couldn't continue and choked on my own words.

"I wish you'd give him up. I know you won't, but I wish you would."

I took a deep breath. "I think it can be managed. I think I can control it."

"I wish I thought the same. I can see already the power he has over you—and it frightens me."

I couldn't meet her gaze. I had no need to ask whether I could trust her—I never for a moment doubted her loyalty, nor indeed the truth of what she said. Here was another person I loved warning me to think again about the perilous path I was embarked upon. I should have listened, should have heeded her. In the moment, I knew she was right. I brooded on her words for a long time—right until the day Lord Granville reappeared in London. Then I brushed them away, absorbed instead in the task of finding somewhere we could meet alone.

❧

Once more it was Lady Anne's generosity that made our rendez-vous possible—and oh, what a reunion it was! It is impossible to express all I felt and enjoyed, how moved I was in both mind and body by the sheer delight of our embraces.

After, as I was arranging myself before Lady Anne's mirror, he lay on her bed, lazily watching me. He had cut his beautiful hair in France, replacing his long queue with the new short style—the Brutus, it was called—which was supposed to suggest republican severity. I was angry at first, mourning its loss. But if anything it looked even more becoming than before.

"I have a question for you," he began, as I struggled with my hairpins. "When am I to leave off being Lord Granville and become merely Granville to you? Given the terms we are on, it seems strange to hear you speak to me so formally."

It was the very last thing I had expected him to ask. I laughed and returned to my hair, but he persevered.

"I doubt you'd like it much if I still called you Lady Bessbor-ough, as if we'd just been introduced."

"No," I agreed, "I wouldn't like it at all. I love to hear you call me Harriet."

"Exactly—the names we use should reflect what we feel for each other. So if you are Harriet to me, why cannot I be Granville to you?"

"I don't know. I've always addressed you as Lord Granville and I'm used to it now. To call you by your name suggests a great deal of freedom on my part—it would seem very familiar."

"But we are familiar." He gestured toward the crumpled bed. "It's hard to imagine how we can be more so."

"I suppose if I were to do as you wish, every time I used your name I'd be reminded of what we are to each other. It would be an admission of our connection."

"But that's precisely why I want you to say it. I want you to acknowledge the terms we're on. No more hiding behind Lord This and Lady That."

He rose from the bed and took me in his arms.

"I should like it very much. Isn't that enough to do as I ask?"

He showered my face with the gentlest of kisses.

"Harriet," he said softly. I could not resist him.

"Granville," I replied. "My very own Granville."

Already it was easier to say. I liked the shape of it in my mouth. Now that I'd begun to use his name, it would quickly become habitual—and with that came fresh dangers. It was, as he said, a sign of our closeness, and was not to be used thoughtlessly or by accident. But I didn't care, if the reward for taking such a risk was hearing him speak to me with such tenderness. I was putty in his hands, and glad to be so.

29

*I*t had long been my sister's custom to host a large family party each autumn at Chatsworth. It had been my habit to join her there, often for several months, to keep her company during the cold winter months. I'd hitherto looked forward eagerly to the time we spent there together; but now, I'm ashamed to say, the thought that my stay would remove me from Granville's company made me view it in a very different light.

It was Granville who suggested a possible solution. If Georgiana could be persuaded to include him among her guests, perhaps we might find opportunities to see each other during his stay. Chatsworth was a huge and rambling palace, with a surfeit of rooms and wild and beautiful grounds. Surely among all that we might seize the occasional moment to be alone. My greedy lover's heart leaped at the slightest prospect of seeing him, but Sally's warning echoed in my mind, and at first, I was wary.

"Lord B will be there some of the time. My mother too. And I've never confessed to Georgiana exactly what we are to each other."

Granville was undeterred.

"It wouldn't be for long. I doubt I could get leave for more than a week. And we needn't do anything to draw attention to ourselves. Just to walk and talk together sometimes would be enough."

This was too enticing a prospect for me to give up, so, after a great deal of anxious deliberation, I decided I would speak to Georgiana.

I went to Devonshire House on one of those dark London afternoons when the candles are brought in with the tea things. Georgiana seemed in better spirits, although still much reduced by her illness. I noticed with a pang that the arrangement of her hair was designed to draw attention from her poor injured eye. It wrung my heart to see her so changed, but I knew she hated pity, so I gave no sign of my distress. We talked quietly for a while about the arrangements for my visit, until I decided that if I was to make my request, I must do so now, before my courage failed me.

"I wonder if you'd consider inviting Lord Granville to join us at Chatsworth. He's pining away at Plymouth, desperate for interesting company. It'd be a real act of charity to ask him."

She frowned. I saw she wasn't pleased.

"I think of this as a family gathering." She paused. "I no longer have much appetite for entertaining people outside our circle. It makes me uncomfortable when strangers stare. I only see people now I'm sure I can trust."

"You've met him many times. He likes you very much and would never do anything to distress or embarrass you. I thought you liked him too."

She sighed. "Of course I like him. He's very charming, as you well know. But it's your feelings for him that most concern me. I hoped—I really and truly hoped—that you'd taken to heart what I said about not following in my footsteps. It pains me very deeply to think my connection with Lord Grey might in any way have led you to think such affairs are permissible, that they can ever end in anything but the ruin that engulfed me."

"Oh, Georgiana, please don't distress yourself. That isn't what I think at all."

"All I wish," she continued, "is that you should never suffer as I have. It might make my unhappiness easier to bear if I felt the knowledge of it had persuaded you not to do as I've done."

I felt the tears rise in my own eyes. "I think every day of what you went through. I have it before my eyes always."

"But it isn't enough to make you act more wisely. To make you turn away, as I should have done, from a man who is bound to disappoint you in the end."

"Don't say that. Please don't say that."

"I see plainly there's nothing I can say—you're already too far in for my words to have any effect." She gave me the ghost of a smile. "I suppose I'd have been just the same if anyone had offered the advice I've tried to force upon you. Well, we must all make our own decisions in matters of love. You've made yours, and I won't question you further about it."

She sighed once more, and walked to the window, looking out into the dark streets beyond. "If you wish it, I'll invite him. But if I can't make you stop loving him, at least promise me you'll take care. Do everything in your power to make him behave discreetly, and ensure you do so yourself. People are already talking about you. Don't do anything that might confirm their suspicions."

She turned back to look at me. "And perhaps this is one secret we can't share, as we've been used to do with so many others. It breaks my heart, Harriet, to imagine you experiencing the same desolation that has been my lot for so long. If I can't dissuade you from the path you're set upon—I don't think I can be your confidante as you go down it. I'm ashamed to say I haven't the strength. I'll never betray you, never do anything to hurt you—and if and when all is over, I'll be here and ready to support you in any way I can."

I rushed to her side, took her hand in mine, and we stood there together in silence for some minutes. It hurt me terribly to think my feelings for Granville had come between us; but the truth was, I'd known for some time that they were a subject too closely associated with her own remorse for her ever to acknowledge them openly. I had long ago accepted this was one subject that must always remain ambiguous between us, both admitted and concealed. I regretted it intensely; but it wasn't enough, as Georgiana had ruefully conceded, to make me change my mind.

30

I 've always loved Chatsworth, as much for its situation as for the house itself. It's set among the most beautiful country: great crags, deep dales, and mighty peaks, begging to be explored. The house itself is the size of a palace, with rooms for every occupation, each full of treasures to admire, with space for everyone to be as social or as private as they wish. Georgiana was a brilliant hostess; the food was always sublime and the conversation lively. I couldn't wait to see Granville in such a setting.

He arrived with Lord Morpeth, who was traveling on afterward, to his family's house in Yorkshire. This was very fortunate, for arriving with his friend took off somewhat from the singularity of Granville's being invited; Morpeth's presence also enabled us to spend time together under the protection of his accompanying us. We three often went out riding, but he would hang back to give us the luxury of some short time alone. Otherwise, when we were in company, I was scrupulous in my self-control, doing everything in my power to conceal any longing looks or affectionate glances. And anyway, Lord B, at least, was rarely around to notice. Like many of our fellow guests, my husband habitually drank deep, stayed up late, and slept well into the next day. My sister had given us separate rooms, which she knew I preferred, so that luckily there were many hours in which we didn't see each other at all.

Granville and I were constantly exchanging little notes, in which we confided to each other all the tendernesses we could never have expressed where there was any danger of their being observed; and though I tried to be grateful, merely to see and be near him, I longed for a more private communion with him—just once—if only I could think how to manage it.

It was my sister who gave me the solution. She mentioned that Hardwick Hall had been cleaned and put in readiness for anyone who chose to stay there. Immediately I asked whether I could visit it. I have always loved the place. It's a very old house, some few miles from Chatsworth, built in Tudor times for one of the Duke's ancestors, the formidable Bess of Hardwick, who outlived four husbands and died one of the wealthiest women in England. It has no modern comforts but looks very romantic, with its lofty brick chimneys, high glass windows that rattle in the wind, wood-paneled rooms, and rather gloomy tapestries.

"May I take Lord Granville and Lord Morpeth with me? It would be a neat little excursion for us—I doubt they've ever seen anything quite like it. We could ride over tomorrow."

"Well—of course, if you think it could possibly interest two such young men. But make sure you're all well wrapped up; it is like an icehouse inside."

Morpeth selflessly agreed to accompany us and even volunteered to disappear for an hour. Thus, the next day, I found myself conducting Granville through the empty house, striding down the creaking corridors and up the stone stairs, pointing out everything of interest until we reached the stateroom, with its elaborately curtained bed. The house was indeed very, very cold.

"I think," he said, "I'll freeze to death if I don't find something to keep me warm."

I saw Granville's eyes stray to the bed. There we stopped.

"Let's slide under the cover." He indicated the great bed. "Just for a moment."

I can't believe I was so bold, but I did as he asked. I was so happy there in his arms that I did not protest when he began to kiss me, but instead received him with the greatest pleasure I had ever enjoyed. On this occasion he did not hold back, and for the first time we were completely united in the act of love.

It was not the most comfortable or elegant consummation—it was impossible to take off our clothes, and the ancient bed was not the most welcoming—but none of that mattered to me. I was entirely his now and was glad of it.

Afterward, it was he who spoke first. "I have a question to ask you, which I've been turning over in my mind for some time. I beg you to consider it very seriously before you reply."

He held me a little tighter under the heavy velvet coverlet.

"I want you to leave Lord B and come away with me. We could go abroad for a while, until he divorces you. Then we could be together."

A chill ran right through me that had nothing to do with the temperature of the room.

"What do you think?" he asked gently.

I raised myself up to look him directly in the eye. "That can never happen. It's quite impossible."

His face fell. "Take a little time—I know it is a great deal to absorb."

"There's really nothing to consider. I can never do as you ask."

"Don't you want to be with me? Don't you believe we'd be happy?"

"In my dreams, there's nothing I long for more. But in the real world, our happiness would be paid for by the suffering of others—the humiliation of Lord B—the shame of my mother and sister—the misery of my children—to say nothing of my own guilt and degradation. I couldn't enjoy a happiness bought at such a cost. If you're indeed the man I think you are, I don't believe you could do so either."

He sat up and swung away from me, moving angrily to the edge of the bed. Without even a glimpse of his expression, I understood the depth of his disappointment.

"You say you love me—but it sounds as if you love Lord B much more, since his comfort means more to you than the happiness we could have together."

I reached across and touched his arm. When he didn't shake it off, I moved to his side, but couldn't look at him. I intended to be very frank in what I was about to say and thought it would be easier if I could not see his face.

"I promise you most faithfully that I've never really loved him— not with the love I feel for you. I knew as soon as we were married that he wasn't the right man for me. But as I've told you before, I owe him a great deal. He's been very indulgent to me, forgiving errors and follies that few other men would have borne with."

"So all you feel for him now is gratitude?"

"Gratitude, yes, but pity too. God knows, he didn't behave well when we were younger. But I believe he sincerely loves me now, in his own particular way, even though he knows I'll never return that love. I don't think he can imagine life alone. We've been together for sixteen years, and for all my faults, he'd be miserable without me; and I confess that, after so long a time together, I would be unhappy to think of him alone and deserted."

"So the habit of being with him means more to you than coming away with me."

"That's not what I meant at all. It isn't just him. I'm bound to my life by a thousand ties that I could never tear away. My obligation to Lord B is only one of them. But, in part at least, ours is a bond of friendship, not love."

He turned and gently lifted my head toward him, very grave and serious now.

"Do you truly live as friends, then? Or are your relations still those of husband and wife?"

I didn't at first understand exactly what he meant, and when I did, I couldn't believe he could put such a question to me.

"Do you really expect me to tell you?"

"You can't be surprised that I ask. Situated as we are, I think I have a right to know. You've demanded that I be honest about my own connections; you can't resent it when I inquire about yours."

I closed my eyes. I was reluctant to admit the truth, but I knew I couldn't lie to him.

"Yes. On occasion. If he requires it, there are times when we live as husband and wife."

I heard him take a deep breath.

"I prefer not to speak of it," I continued. "It isn't a matter in which I have much choice."

He did not reply. His silence first made me fearful—and then suddenly I was angry. "Believe me, it's far worse for me to endure than for you to hear about it. But what do you know about what women must bear? I try all I can to avoid it. I refuse whenever possible, which is no surprise to him because he knows I've always hated it."

I had begun to cry now, bitter ugly tears, for this was a truth I had never confessed or spoken of to anyone before.

"It never worked between us, from the very beginning. I disliked it extremely. It was only with the greatest reluctance that I could be persuaded to surrender to him. I certainly took no pleasure in it."

I hated even to think on this subject—to hear myself speaking of it aloud was terrible to me. For a long time, I thought my aversion a fault in myself. I feared there was something unnatural in me; and, moreover, that it was my distaste for the act that was the cause of all his anger against me—that, in injuring his pride in so delicate a place, I was responsible for souring his temper. I'd have done anything to change how I felt, but it was impossible; I was simply incapable of hiding my dislike. Sometimes I almost pitied him. No man likes to think his wife finds him repulsive.

I should have thought better of him if, after I'd provided him with four children, he'd left me alone. But no, he was persistent. Even now, I still wasn't free of his attentions. Sometimes, to discourage him, I took Caro into my bed, which was usually effective in deflecting his attentions. Otherwise, I was simply obliged to bear what I could not enjoy.

Finally, Granville turned to look at me.

"I hate to hear this, Harriet, and not only because it's painful for me to think of you with another man. I hate it because you hate it—and would do anything I could to prevent it. And I want you to understand very clearly the terms I propose—the very moment Lord B divorces you, we could be married. Exactly like Lord Holland and Lady Webster. They managed it cleanly enough. Why shouldn't we do the same?"

I hadn't imagined this. He wanted to marry me. My secret response was an incredulous joy, but my wiser, cooler head knew it was quite impossible.

"The case is not the same. Lady Webster had no family to suffer at the sight of her becoming Lady Holland. No mother to shame, no sister to disappoint. She hated her husband with a furious passion, which I do not. And she is such a detached and distant mother that I'm sure the feelings of her children never crossed her mind."

"So is our future always to be decided by the feelings of others? What about yours? What about mine? Do I merit no consideration in that long list of people who must never be hurt? I love you with all my heart and long for us to be together. Can you honestly say the same?"

"Oh, Granville," I murmured sadly. "I've never loved anyone the way I love you. You occupy my every waking moment. Only in death will I stop loving you."

"Then why won't you do as I ask?"

"Because I care for you too much to agree. In other circumstances,

I should have loved to be your wife; nothing would have made me happier. But not if the number of years between us remains the same."

He tried to interrupt, but I would not allow it.

"You think we'll always be as we are now—there isn't such a gap between thirty-six and twenty-four. But you'll feel very differently when you're forty. I'll be fifty-three then, no doubt very much altered, perhaps old and infirm. Worst of all—we would look ridiculous. It's one thing for a young man to have an older mistress; it's quite another for him to have an aging wife. I won't do it—I love you too much to ruin you in such a way. I have to protect you from yourself."

"And am I to have no say at all in a matter that's important to me?"

"If we discuss it, you'll persuade me out of my resolution, and I'm determined that won't happen. The decision is mine alone."

"And would these same conditions apply if you were to find yourself free by natural means?"

"You mean if Lord B were to die? It wouldn't alter anything I've said, unless I were to become twenty years younger at the moment I was widowed."

"So then I must ask—if you won't come away with me, won't agree to divorce from Lord B, won't marry me, indeed won't countenance anything I've offered—how are we to go on together?"

At that, all my firmness of purpose deserted me. I had no answer.

"Is it to be merely one day after another, as it is now?" He stood up, more downcast than I had ever seen him. "More assignations in cold rooms?" He sighed. "I wanted more for us than this."

"I know," I said. "I'm sorry."

It took all my self-control not to shout out loud that I'd changed my mind, that we should go away as quickly as we could, that there wasn't a moment to lose. I believe it's much to my credit that I did not utter these words, and that I was strong enough never to waver from my resolution. But in the time that followed, I've often wondered what those few years of happiness we might have had together would have been like, and there are moments when I imagine them still.

We had a few more days together at Chatsworth before Granville was obliged to return to his regiment. I dreaded the moment of his leaving; our conversation at Hardwick had thrown a shadow over our remaining time together, and we could not recapture the joy we had both felt when he arrived. It was terrible to me that we should part on such sad terms. My anguish must have shown on my face, for on the very evening before his departure, Bess Foster bore down upon me as I sat alone and began to tease me about him.

"You'll hate it when he goes, but it's really for the best that he does."

Her manner was playful, but I was too low to respond in kind.

"I wonder why you think so?"

"Because otherwise, you'll never escape, particularly since he cut his hair, which makes him even more beautiful. What a risk he poses to us all!"

When she saw the depths of my unhappiness, her face fell. "Please tell me this isn't serious. I imagined it was just a passing flirtation."

I gathered my features into what I hoped was a semblance of a smile. "That's all it is." I even tried a little laugh. "That's all it must or ever can be!"

Bess frowned. "It would certainly be much better for everyone— and most especially yourself—if you can keep it that way."

I nodded. She sat looking at me for a while, as if deliberating what to say, considering whether any advice of hers could possibly change my feelings; then, concluding that there was nothing to be done at this time and in this place, she kissed my cheek, patted my hand, and left me.

I decided I wasn't equal to any more such encounters that evening. Instead, I thought it advisable to take both myself and my unhappiness to a place where it would not be remarked upon and went off to bed.

There at least I could give way to my grief undisturbed; but much later that night, Lord B arrived in my room, his intentions unmistakable. I buried my tearstained face in the pillow and hunched myself into as unenticing a position as possible, hoping to repel his advances.

"Harriet." His voice was slurred; he was probably drunk. "Harriet," he repeated. "Are you awake?"

It was simply impossible for me to receive him in my current wretched state of mind. I couldn't do it. I turned over to look at him.

"I can't," I said. "I'm not well."

He held up a candle and took in my distressed state. "You've been crying."

"Yes, I'm nervous and tired. I don't know what's wrong with me, but I cannot help it."

He blew out the candle and, without another word, strode out of my room, slamming the door in anger as he went. It was at least an hour before I went to sleep, and when I did, I had a terrible nightmare. I dreamed Lord B had found one of Granville's letters, that he came to my bed, sword in hand, and asked if it would be Granville or myself who would die. I replied that it must be me—I felt the cold point of his sword on my breast—I shuddered as he drove it in—and woke in such distress that I was forced to call Sally, who found me in such a state that she was obliged to sit with me for hours until I fell asleep once more.

31

There was a change in Granville's attitude toward me after Hard-wick. I noticed in his letters that he'd begun to ask me increasingly often whether I loved him. At first, this made me glad, because it seemed like an encouragement to declare all I felt for him. I liked it less, however, on the rare occasions he was in London, when the insistent passion he expressed on paper became reckless behavior in my company. He threw all caution to the wind, staring at me pointedly across a crowded room, taking my arm in the presence of others, hurrying me into corners, indulging himself in a thousand little gestures guaranteed to excite the unwelcome suspicions of those around us. He ignored all my pleas to comport himself more decently, and I eventually had to conclude that he was determined to flaunt our connection, with the aim of bringing on an exposure that would compel me to run away with him. There seemed no other explanation for the carelessness of his behavior—certainly, when I taxed him with it, he was sullen and had nothing to say in his defense. So when in the new year he was offered another diplomatic commission, I thought it not the worst thing for him to be removed from my society for a while.

It was on the face of it an undemanding assignment: to go to

Berlin and present formal congratulations to the new King of Prussia on his accession to the throne; but he would also be expected to explore the possibility of the Prussians allying themselves with Britain against France. And this time, he was to go alone, an encouraging sign of trust in his abilities. It was a good step up for him, and an enterprising young man would have seized eagerly upon the opportunities it offered for advancing his career; however, Granville did nothing but complain.

"I'm to travel across Europe in the depths of winter to spout a few empty formalities. An utterly pointless task. Anyone could do it. Why must it be me?"

"You know it's much more than that. It's a sign of favor and a chance to distinguish yourself," I replied. "And what will you be doing if you remain at home? Playing at tennis? Visiting your boot maker? Gambling with money you don't have, running up debts you can't pay? A month or two away from gaming would be a virtue in itself."

Granville's obsessive love of play had become far worse that winter. His losses were huge—he owed money all over London, with no real chance of repaying it. I'd even arranged loans for him myself on occasion, when he couldn't meet his obligations. It broke my heart to see him hurrying down the same hopeless path that had ruined Lord B, me, my sister, and so many others I knew; but to those possessed by the gambler's mania, all warnings are useless.

"I believe there are tables in Berlin for those who want them."

His derisive tone provoked me, just as he intended it should, and I lost my temper.

"If this post isn't good enough for you, I wonder what you think you deserve? You have very high ideas of yourself and your capacities—perhaps this is the chance to prove whether they're justified? Or are we to accept your powers solely on your own assurance that they exist?"

"You sound," he said, with a faint, cold smile, "exactly like my mother."

I felt the force of his words like a blow to my chest; but I would not be diverted.

"If that's so, I'm glad to hear it, because in this matter, if your mother thinks as I do, she is right. I might add," I continued, "that it's very harsh for you to throw my age at me in such an ill-mannered way. I warned you of all the evils it brought in its wake—but you chose to love me—you cannot now complain of what I am."

All at once, his expression changed; he threw off his languid air and took my hand urgently in his.

"Don't you understand, Harriet—it's you—you're the reason I hesitate to go to Berlin? I can't bear for us to be parted. I'm amazed you don't see it."

"But it isn't for very long—and I shall be here for you when you return."

"But will you? The truth is, I'm no longer sure of you. And the more you urge me to go, the more I think my worst suspicions might be true—that you don't love me as much as I love you."

"You can't possibly believe that," I cried. "You must know how very deeply I love you. What could I say—what could I do to prove it more than I have already?"

"There is one thing. You know what it is."

"Please—let us not return to that."

"But it plays on my mind. I think—'Ah, if she really loved me, she would want to be with me always.' And then, when you tell me I should go away—then yes, I fear you don't feel for me what I do for you."

"Oh, Granville, you couldn't be more wrong. Of course I shall hate it when you're away. But I'll never allow myself to become a drag upon your prospects. My duty—but not my pleasure—is to push you forward, not to hold you back."

I leaned over to kiss his mouth, and I thought he seemed reassured. Certainly, I was pleased when he told me a few days later he'd accepted the offer and would be leaving very soon for Berlin.

I genuinely hoped the change of situation would do him good and stop him brooding on my refusal to leave Lord B; but regrettably, that was not the case. It stood between us like some great bleak wall, which could be neither surmounted nor ignored. It was still uppermost in his mind when he came to say goodbye.

"Harriet, when I'm away—promise me you'll think again about what I've asked?"

I laid my head against his shoulder, but said nothing, for I would not, could not be moved on this subject. I felt him stiffen as he drew away, frustrated by my silence. I hoped, nonetheless, that a little time and a little distance would return him to a more reasonable state of mind, so that we might talk more sensibly about our situation when he returned.

32

*H*e was away for three months. On his return, Lady Anne
kindly allowed us to meet as before in her apartments—and
our reunion, after what seemed to us so long a separation, was as
passionate as either of us could have wished—although it seemed to
me not quite as tender as our past encounters. I sensed some darker
emotion behind his desire—anger was too strong a word for it—but
there was something new there, something more driven and less generous than before. When I asked him if he was happy, he assured me
he was; but as the days passed into weeks, this seemed increasingly
untrue.

Whenever we were in society together, his conduct was just as
reckless and inconsiderate as it had been before he left—possibly
even worse. One night he called at Cavendish Square when he knew
Lord B was at Brooks's and stubbornly refused all my entreaties to
leave before he returned. Such was the danger that Sally came to me
with tears in her eyes and begged me to make him go.

"He can't stay another minute. One of the servants has already
seen him, I'm sure of it. You must make him listen to you. It will end
in ruin if he's found here."

But nothing I could say moved him, until I finally lost my temper.

"Have you no idea how your selfishness exposes me? Of course not, our situations are so different."

He sat before me, stony-faced and silent.

"Discovery to you is nothing," I cried. "No man suffers from the knowledge he has a lover. But a woman must be cautious—a single careless act is enough to destroy her."

"The world is unfair," he observed in a detached tone. "I understand that."

"I don't think you do. Or you wouldn't conspire to make my situation intolerable!"

He stood up, angry now. "I dislike this deceitful hole-in-a-corner existence as much as you. But I've offered you an alternative, a way we might be together without fear. You have only to accept it for all this to be over."

"You know I can't do that."

"Then this, it seems, is the way things must be." He picked up his hat. "I should leave by the back door, I suppose, like a thief who's stolen the silver?"

He went without another word, leaving me shaking with fear. I endured days of anxiety, watching Lord B's every expression, sneaking glances at the servants to see what they knew. It was a week before I breathed more easily. But it was the temporary relief of a wrongdoer who knows she's escaped justice by the skin of her teeth. My luck might not hold next time. There was only one way to minimize the dangers to which I felt increasingly exposed—I must thrash matters out with Granville before his foolhardiness engulfed us both in disaster.

I arranged we should meet in the park. I should be there, walking with Sally, Caro, and William; what could be more natural, then, that our paths should cross with Lord Granville's, and that we should enjoy a little decorous conversation before we parted? It was a risk, and I knew it, but one I felt I had to take. I was determined, however, to limit my exposure, so once we were walking together, with Sally and the children striding out before us, I wasted no time on pleasantries, but jumped right in.

"I must know why you are acting as you are," I began. "You resist every little prudent action that might keep us safe, even when I beg you to do as I ask. Why are you doing this, Granville?"

Silence.

"Do you want to see me exposed—would you enjoy seeing me miserable and humbled? Will you only be satisfied when everyone we know is aware of my guilt?"

"You can't possibly believe me capable of such a thing."

"What else am I to think when you have no care at all for my reputation? Tarnished as it is, I value what's left of it—and won't allow you to trample it in the mud."

"Why would I want to do that?"

"I think you may have conceived a mistaken idea about what I should do if we were discovered. I must tell you now that even if our connection was exposed to all—if I were cast off by my husband and rejected by my mother, my sister, my children—I still wouldn't run begging you to marry me."

He beat the path with his stick, but did not speak.

So," I continued, "if what lies behind all this is some attempt to force my hand—to coerce by exposure what I will not freely agree to—I tell you now, it won't work. For your sake as much as mine. I love you too much to become a burden to you. Whatever happens, I will not be driven to that."

"Yes," he replied, evenly. "You have said so before."

We walked on a little farther.

"You'll never leave him, will you?"

"No," I replied. "I never will."

"And there, in that single no, is all you need to understand why I feel as I do. It's my powerlessness that drives me to distraction."

"In what way are you powerless?"

"The one thing I want, you won't give me. You make it very clear you'll never be wholly mine."

"Not in the way you wish, no. But we could be together in a different way if you'd only do as I ask. I know a man likes to feel his lover is subject to his commands and should do all she can to satisfy them." I smiled, hoping to soften his severe tone. "But would bending a little to my wishes in this really take away from your authority?"

"My authority? What authority do I have? All the decisions are in your hands. You will not leave Lord B. You see me only on terms that suit you. You hold all the reins, Harriet. All I'm to do is gallop in the direction you require."

I was genuinely taken aback. "I spoke jestingly. Really, who thinks of power where two people love each other?"

"You are in command. All I am to do is agree."

I laughed wryly at this. "For all our intimacy, how little you really know me. You have a far greater power over me than I can ever possess over you—that of withdrawing your love. My affection, once given, is fixed and eternal—it will never change, except with death. But you are a man and therefore inconstant. Your love will never be as deep or as lasting as mine. It's not in your nature. For a woman, the fear is always there: When will he tire of me? When shall I be dismissed?"

He tried to interrupt—but I was not to be diverted.

"So let's not talk of power between us, when you must see mine is built on such fragile ground. The one who loves the most is always at a disadvantage, however it may appear to the contrary."

At last, I had coaxed from him something approaching a smile.

"I'm glad to hear you love me enough to think you love the most.

I shan't contest with you any further for the title. But I ask you to think, Harriet, about the truth of what I've said. Our relations are, it seems, to be conducted entirely as you decide. And I admit, I bridle at the thought that I am always to do and behave as I'm instructed. No man likes to feel himself placed in such an invidious and dependent place."

"So," I thought, "you find yourself in the position a woman occupies for the entirety of her life and feel it not to your liking?" But I thought better of saying this out loud. We parted soon after, and as I walked home, I brooded on our conversation. The best I could say was that we had both stated our feelings with as much clarity and plainness as was possible. I knew Granville was to be in London for a little while longer. Perhaps if we could talk more, I could work gently upon his injured pride and thwarted desire, make him see there might be some middle way between his desire to possess me entirely and the reality of my situation.

Could that have worked? I'll never know, for I was not allowed to find out. At dinner that evening, Lord B announced he had a surprise for me.

"I have taken a house in Margate for a while—a good one, I think. You've looked pale lately. I thought the sea air would do you good. Caro will enjoy it. What do you think?"

I was well used to having such surprises sprung upon me. It was Lord B's habit to arrange such trips, without the slightest hint of his plans, until they were almost upon us. I was never consulted—all that was required of me was to show my gratitude, which I duly did.

"I should like that. When do we go?"

"In a few days. I thought we'd stay a month and see how we get on. Caro's very excited."

I smiled and twittered about how enjoyable it would be, trying not to let my disappointment show. Granville and I would be parted again—and all the good work I'd begun this morning would count for nothing. There would be no chance now for the careful management of his emotions, which I'd hoped would steer us little by little to a calmer understanding of our situation. I allowed myself a sardonic reflection. Granville thought me powerful, but here was the sad reality—like a child, I was told where I was to go and for how long, with nothing more to say about it than to exclaim with delight at the prospect.

I was less angry when we arrived, for our house was in a particularly fine position, high up on a cliff, with the sea breaking onto rocks beneath. In bad weather, I watched the ships beating up and down the English Channel from the great windows that overlooked the coast; when it was fine, I walked down to the beach, sat on the sands, and let the waves dash up almost to my feet. The air was fresh, and the great blue sky, the silvery light, and the salt tang in the breeze soothed me, at least until the post arrived.

Then it was only too clear that all Granville's resentments and suspicions had resurfaced in my absence. He was unhappy, plaintive, suspicious. He was sure my feelings had cooled. Did I truly still care for him? I tried everything in my power to convince him I loved him with all my heart, but it was all in vain. He refused to be consoled, and soon his misery took a darker turn.

Margate was a sociable place, offering many pleasant amusements—dinners, musical concerts, all manner of outings and excursions. I hadn't wished to come, but now I was here, I resolved to make the best of it and went out most days into its simple society. Granville did not like this at all. He was jealous of every gentleman whose name I mentioned—and little by little he adopted an increasingly lordly tone, ordering me to stay at home and avoid men's company altogether, as not one of them was to be trusted. I bridled at this. The picture he had conjured up in his mind was so far from the truth that I felt obliged to protest, asking upon what grounds he thought himself entitled to tell me what to do. He didn't deign to argue with me, but merely replied that his commands were absolute, and he expected me to obey them.

This was not the first time I'd been told by a lover that my first duty toward him was submission. The truth is, all men long to enforce their will over the poor woman who loves them, demanding she look to them to know where she can go and whom she can see. So while it was painful to hear Granville use such language to me, I cannot honestly say I was surprised. I'm afraid even the best of men share this wish for dominion over those they love—it is as natural to them as breathing.

But I understood, too, that the appearance of this uncompromising stance was intimately connected to my refusal to leave Lord B. It was as if, having met with such an inflexible refusal on that subject, he was determined to make his power over me felt in every other aspect of my life.

I tried—God knows I really tried, with all the strength at my disposal—to resist his attempts to bring me to heel. I thought it a shameful thing to put myself so easily under the control of another, even one I loved as much as Granville. At first, I fought back by refusing to take him seriously, teasing him for his pretensions. But it made not the slightest difference to his conviction that he had an absolute right to tell me what to do—I'd put myself under his command when I surrendered to him—why was I so reluctant to acknowledge this simple truth?

Once I saw he was not to be soothed or charmed into retreating from his position, I resorted to more serious arguments. I repeated my belief that, between two people who loved each other as we did, there was really no place for questions of mastery; our absolute confidence in each other should be enough to make all such questions irrelevant.

He replied that if I really loved him as I said I did, it should be no sacrifice to acknowledge his authority over me. Wasn't it natural for a woman to wish to please the man she loved? Was it really such a hardship to put myself under his affectionate command? My reluctance made him wonder whether I truly cared for him at all. Clearly, despite all my protestations, I meant to give him up.

I was beside myself with anger when I read this. Hadn't I already shown him the greatest proof of affection a woman could give? What greater evidence of my devotion could he possibly require of me?

Surely, he wrote, I could not be ignorant of the answer to that. How could I say I loved him, yet turn my back on the chance of our living happily together? And now, to add to his sense of rejection, it seemed I was determined to refuse his natural authority over me. It was a proof of devotion most women were happy to give, yet I resented it. Was it any wonder he doubted me?

Well, he wouldn't continue to force his opinions upon me. He'd made his feelings clear—now I must decide for myself how I wished to continue.

Was he really suggesting he would give me up if I continued to resist him? I began to think so. I dashed off a frantic reply—with respect to Lord B, I begged him, if he loved me at all, not to ask me to do what must destroy me. And on the question of the authority that meant so much to him—I pleaded for a little time to consider it. It was a desperate letter, my fear and anxiety painfully apparent in every word. I waited with the greatest possible apprehension to hear what he would say. And then—there was silence. No reply. Day after day went past with no word from him at all. A week went by and then ten days. Still silence.

There had been gaps in our correspondence before, but this felt very different. It was a calculated gesture. He'd laid his cards on the table and was now waiting for me to make the next move. Nothing would happen until I did so.

I began to panic. The prospect of his withdrawing his love from me was terrible to contemplate. But the thought of putting myself utterly under his authority was deeply humiliating. I'd been under the control of men all my life—and I suppose I'd allowed myself to imagine that with Granville it might be different, that the strength of our feelings for each other might make us more equal partners in love.

But I understood painfully now that no passion is strong enough to entirely wipe away imbalances of power between lovers. There is always one who knows that they to hold the reins, as it were. In the early days of our liaison, that person had been me; then Granville had been the desperate suitor who turned himself inside out to gain my affections, while I was the queenly bestower of favors who held his heart in my hand.

All that changed when I fell head over heels in love with him. Then everything was reversed—my power over him was revealed to be as fragile as the towers of wooden bricks my children had loved to build when they were small—any change in his feelings was enough to bring it all crashing to the ground. The depth of my passion undermined its foundations—for if you're to have any authority over a lover, you must be prepared to give them up if you wish to maintain a semblance of control. And here, finally and most reluctantly, I was obliged to confront the truth of my situation: unless I was prepared to give him up, none of my objections had any force at all.

Was I capable of leaving him? I spent many painful hours walking alone on Margate's damp and tussocky cliffs asking this question of myself again and again and again. But however many times I did so, the answer never changed. For me now there was only Granville. He was like some bright light that scorches away every other image in the power of its glare. Without him, there would be no pleasure, no warmth, no satisfaction, no joy, no purpose to my life. While he still wanted me, it was inconceivable I would ever willingly abandon him.

Once I understood this, I had no doubt what I should do. If I wanted to keep him, I must offer what he wanted. I didn't do this lightly, and I confess there were times afterward when I asked myself whether I had made too great a sacrifice—for who wants to know themselves so abject that they would relinquish so much to keep a lover? But I couldn't bear to lose him; therefore, I did what I thought love required of me, and one sunny afternoon, with the sound of the sea in my ears, I sat down to communicate to Granville the terms of my surrender.

The words came easily from my pen as I wrote. I placed my life in his hands and gave myself up entirely to his authority. I would obey his commands and never dispute his entitlement to issue them. When we differed, I should express my opinion but would not dispute his will on the subject. He should never again have the slightest cause to doubt that he was indeed the master of my heart. To close the letter, I had a special seal made—it read in Italian *Ubbidisco*: I obey.

Could the most tyrannical potentate have asked for more?

Just as I'd hoped, Granville was gracious in victory. His injured pride was mollified, his amour propre restored. What he didn't know, however, was that there was one crucial point upon which I did not consider myself bound by my pledge of obedience—it did not extend to the question of my leaving Lord B. On this, I remained immovable. How Granville would react, I couldn't say. I hoped he wouldn't force me further; but I shouldn't know until we were together once more.

That time approached fast. The Season drew to a close as winter approached and we prepared to return to London. Just before we left, Lord B declared he should like to attend one final dinner in town. I was against it, as I did not like the journey back to our cliff-top house at night; but my wishes carried no weight. After the dinner, Lord B drove us back in the dark; we were alone, the servants having gone on before us, with no one in the carriage but Lord B, Caro, and me. There was no moon to light our way, and we didn't know the roads. Soon it was plain we were lost. The horses were restive, disturbed, finally stopping suddenly and refusing to go on. We couldn't see what had frightened them—but when they reared up in terror, it was plain it was something very bad. Lord B, alarmed now, peered into the darkness to see what was amiss. He drew back, appalled.

"Keep still!" he cried as he slid carefully back into his seat. "On no account move—not even an inch."

"We're in a very bad place indeed," he whispered, so that Caro would not hear. "Off the road—and there's a huge chalk pit right in front of us. We're at the very edge of it—that's what upset the horses. One wheel is barely on the path. I can't risk trying to turn them. A single stumble might hurl us in."

In low, anxious voices we discussed what to do next. We were so preoccupied that neither of us heard Caro slip silently away. She disappeared into the darkness, running in her light shoes down the path and onto the road. She walked for over a mile until finally she came upon our servants desperately searching for us. What bravery! Caro always had a fearless heart. I honestly believe it was entirely owing to her courage that we were saved. Before strong men arrived to haul us safely away from danger, Lord B and I spent a very perilous hour or two, perched fearfully in the darkness. We said little, afraid of provoking by our voices some sudden movement from the horses; and in those tense and wordless moments, it occurred to me that my perilous predicament closely resembled my wider situation in life—unable to go forward or back, hanging, as it were, between safety and destruction, with nothing to do but whistle in the dark, hoping all would come well in the end.

34

*A*s it turned out, my submission to Granville ushered in some of the happiest few months of my life. He seemed assuaged and content, and I resolved not to brood upon future dissensions between us until, and if, they arrived. He didn't raise the subject of my leaving Lord B, and I therefore attempted to put the alarming prospect of his doing so far from my mind, seeking to convince myself he'd perhaps even resigned himself to our existing situation.

While that terrible subject remained unspoken and didn't rise up to divide us, I felt more deeply connected to Granville than to anyone I had ever known before—and I'm not ashamed to say the physical pleasure we enjoyed together contributed greatly to my sense of being totally and utterly his. Women are not supposed to admit to feelings of this kind—we're taught nothing at all about our desires, other than the need to rigorously suppress them.

That had certainly been my own case. It might seem strange, that someone with my reputation—an experienced woman of the world, a veteran of several affairs—knew so little of the physical pleasure of love; nevertheless, it was so. At heart I was still an innocent, a blank sheet of paper, somewhat scribbled upon at the edges, it's true, but otherwise, untouched, unawake, unaware.

It was Granville who changed all that, introducing me not just to sensations I'd never known before, but also to the idea that lovers might talk with one another about what they enjoyed. I'd blushed and hidden my face when he first encouraged me to speak of such things—but little by little, my embarrassments were overcome, and I allowed myself to reflect on aspects of my nature I should never have acknowledged without his guidance.

During our conversations, he introduced the subject of erotic books, telling me that many lovers enjoyed reading them—should I like him to get some for me? I knew of their existence but had always thought of them as men's business, never imagining any decent woman could possibly read them. I'd been swiftly disabused of this naïveté one night back in Naples, at a supper with Granville and his young friends, when the wine flowed, and the conversation became more frank.

These books were mentioned, and I was asked which I considered the most accomplished. When I was compelled to admit I'd read nothing of this kind, the table erupted in disbelieving laughter.

I confess I was annoyed by their amusement, ashamed that so many young people—for I was at least a decade older than the others at the table—were so much more worldly than I in this respect.

So when Granville offered to supply this deficiency, my curiosity had already been aroused. I was a quick study, as the tutors say, and to my great surprise I discovered a liking for a certain kind of impropriety. I began, as everyone does, with *Les Liaisons Dangereuses*, and went on from there. I should be clear here that I never plumbed the depths of depravity. When Lady Holland, who is infinitely more wicked than I, made me a present of the Marquis de Sade's *Justine*, I sent it back immediately. Cruelty was never to my taste.

But when Granville and I were apart, it became his custom to send me books we might discuss later at our leisure, and it was my delight to receive them, believing our candor in this respect was another tie

that bound us together and secured me even closer to him. I was satisfied in every possible way, such that my feelings for Granville reached
new heights of intensity. Indeed, I was so hypnotized by my passion,
so dazed by the strength of my love, that, for a while at least, I no
longer resented the measures I'd taken to secure it. On the contrary, I
reveled in my submission, delightedly brandishing my *Ubbidisco* seal,
proud to belong to a man who made me so completely happy.

Very occasionally, the clouds of my infatuation parted long enough
for a little light to shine in. There were moments when I was obliged
to acknowledge that, however closely I felt myself bound to him,
there were many matters upon which we would never agree. Most
of these were political. Thus, when yet another bill was introduced
into Parliament in 1799 to limit the extent of the slave trade, I was
grieved but not surprised to discover he had not supported it. When
I tackled him on the wrongness of his position, he had nothing to say
beyond the usual platitudes—the time was not right, the state of politics was too dangerous just now—all the familiar, feeble arguments
so often heard before.

I thought much the less of him for it and told him so; but to my
shame, that was the limit of my protests. There were many other
issues upon which our opinions were very different—the continued
prosecution of the war against France, Mr. Pitt's increasingly tyrannical attempts to suppress the desire for reform at home—and sometimes we argued about them, although I knew I was quite powerless
to change his mind on such questions. I never pretended to agree
with his views; but now I sometimes ask myself whether I should
have argued against them more forcefully. Yes, I teased and mocked
and laughed at many of the things he held dear—but the truth is, I
shied away from allowing them to define our relations. I was more
keen to keep his love than to win arguments against him. I didn't
appreciate it then, but that was perhaps one of the greatest prices I
paid to secure his affection.

35

$\mathcal{I}$ knew, I suppose, that these happy times could not last forever—that at some point, the issue of my leaving Lord B would be raised once more. It was as if the sword of Damocles was poised above my head—as time went by, it seemed increasingly likely that it could not remain there forever—but I had no idea what might eventually make it fall.

In the end, it was the plight of Granville's friend Lord Boringdon. He'd been for many years the lover of Lady Elizabeth Monck, sister of that Lady Anne who'd so generously assisted Granville and me in managing our own affair. (Yes, ours is such a small world that our lives are endlessly entangled.) Lady Elizabeth was unhappily married, with two daughters, to a man she very much wished to leave. She'd already had one child by Boringdon, whose existence they had successfully concealed. Now she found herself pregnant again and didn't know what to do. Should she continue in her deception and attempt to give birth to this child, too, in secret? Or was this the moment to throw off all pretense and acknowledge the truth of their predicament, with Lady Elizabeth leaving her husband and setting up house with Lord Boringdon?

In their agitated state, Boringdon and Lady Elizabeth turned to Granville and me for advice.

I wished they hadn't, for this was a subject I would much rather have avoided; but Lady Elizabeth seemed in such need of help that I couldn't refuse.

Their own preference was for an elopement, which Granville readily supported. I said nothing for as long as I could, but when they began to discuss how and when it should take place, I could stay silent no more.

"I do urge you to think very hard before taking such a step. Mr. Monck is a dull man, I agree, but not a cruel one—can you really wish to subject him to such a terrible humiliation?"

I saw Granville frown at this, but I could not stop myself.

"And what about your daughters? They're still very young—much in need of a mother's care, which will surely be denied them if you leave, for Mr. Monck may never permit you to see them again." I took a deep breath. "It's a terrible thing to destroy a family who've done nothing to deserve such a fate. In the heat of the moment, you mustn't forget what you owe to those who depend upon you."

No one said anything for a moment. My words hung heavy in the air, and I wished very much I had not spoken them. Then the discussion resumed, though in a more subdued tenor, until our little party broke up, no nearer finding an answer to Lady Elizabeth's dilemma. Granville said nothing about my outburst, but I saw he had taken it to heart and understood it would not be long before he challenged me on it.

He did so one afternoon when we were at Lady Anne's apartments. Both of us were in a pensive mood, as is often the case once the throes of passion are over. It was Granville who began upon it, watching me from the bed as I brushed my hair.

"I've been thinking about Lady Elizabeth and wondering what you would do if you found yourself in her situation?"

"You won't like what you hear, so perhaps it is best to say nothing at all."

"Try me."

I was genuinely reluctant to speak. I'd reflected a great deal on this question, and none of my conclusions were anything but bleak.

"There's one remedy a woman might think of in such a situation—the most severe that can be imagined—but one she would consider if it would save her family from disgrace and preserve something of her good name."

Granville raised himself up, shocked. "Are you seriously saying you'd kill yourself?"

"I've sometimes thought of it. Others have done it."

He shook his head, astonished. "What could you possibly hope to achieve by so pointless a gesture?"

"In protecting those I love, it would not be pointless to me."

"This is quite mad," he declared, exasperated now. "And once you were gone, what would you imagine I'd do? Did you think of the pain and grief I should feel?"

"Of course," I replied, feeling tears well up in my eyes. "But you're young, and eventually it would wear off."

At that, he took me in his arms, holding me so tightly that I could barely breathe.

"Harriet, that's enough. It is terrible to hear you speak in this way. You cannot really believe you would do such a thing."

I was shaken. Lady Elizabeth's troubles had affected me very deeply. I was overwrought and terribly anxious.

"What would you have me do instead?"

"You know very well what I think. There'd be no need for such dark thoughts if you would only do as I wish and come away with me."

He released his hold upon me, and I slumped away from him. I'd known as soon as the subject was raised that this was where we would end.

"Lord B would divorce you," he went on, urgently, "we should be married and there would be no need for any of this anxious misery."

I sat up straight and composed myself. It was important he understood what I was about to say.

"I've told you before I cannot do that. I know how much you wish it, but for all the reasons you already know, it can't happen."

"But you told me not long ago that the love you felt for me made you happy to bow to my will. And this is what I wish for."

"In all other things that is true. Ask me anything else and I will do it. But this is one order I cannot and will not obey."

He turned away from me, angry now.

"If you really care for me," I murmured, "you would not demand something from me that can only make me wretched. You wouldn't ask it, out of love for me."

I laid my head on his shoulder—he did not, as I had feared, pull away—and thus we remained for some minutes. When finally we parted, both of us were polite and more composed; but we knew, too, that nothing had been resolved, and the struggle between us on this point was anything but over. Very far from it.

I'd said what I knew I must, but I had no idea what the conse-quences would be. My deepest fear was that Granville would stop seeing me; to my relief, he never suggested that, but I soon dis-covered that all was not as it had been. The glorious few months I'd so enjoyed were definitely over. His mood soured, until it seemed everything I did or said irritated him. When we were occasionally together in company, I saw him sometimes staring at me with disap-proval at some chance remark I'd made.

I think when he understood I would not be moved on the issue of leaving Lord B—that on this question, I wouldn't surrender, as I had done regarding so many others—his anger and frustration rose to such a degree that he was no longer in full control of his emotions. Sally had observed to me long ago that Granville gave the impres-sion of a man used to getting what he wanted. He couldn't quite believe, I think, that his first experience of not obtaining the dearest wish of his heart came from the woman who professed to love him more than anyone on earth.

I wonder now if his frustration was made worse by the realiza-tion that he couldn't take the simplest way out of his dilemma and simply put an end to our connection. I believe that if his feelings had allowed it, he'd have left me. But when it came to it, he couldn't do it, couldn't find the will. I suspect he was a little ashamed of his inability to walk away—and that only served to worsen his temper, especially as it was directed against me.

Gradually, his baser instincts got the better of him, and he began to talk of ways I might be compelled to do as he wished. He started to use language I did not care for—I was horrified to hear him assert that a man might be entitled to strike a woman in order to enforce his authority—a remark that elicited from me a most freezingly dismissive stare. All men, I think, like to believe that in any struggle with a woman's will, might—not right—must have the final say. Did I think Granville would ever have been capable of such an act? I really could not tell. But I had no desire to live once more in an atmosphere of threat and fear—I had seen enough of that with Lord B. So when one day Granville and I were arguing—over some trifle, some letter he wished to see that I refused to show him—and he made reference to the efficacy of beating in such instances—that surely I'd drive him to it one day—I decided I could stand for this no longer.

"Are you seriously saying you would beat me?" I asked, icily calm.

"There are times when I think you'll provoke me to it."

A shiver ran through me. I had thought there was nothing I wouldn't do for him, nothing I wouldn't surrender to keep his love. But I knew in that moment this was too much.

"You wouldn't dare. And if you did, do you really imagine I'd allow it? I warn you not to try. I'm shocked at your thinking of it at all."

He tried to speak, but I wouldn't allow it. I turned on my heel and left him.

My indignation carried me home and supported me through that night on a buoyant wave of outrage. I only wish I could say I continued to behave in so bold and decisive a manner, but I'm afraid that was not the case. When a note arrived from him the next morning, I tore it open with trembling fingers, hoping for some apology for his words—but it was nothing of the sort. He told me in the coldest possible terms that I had laughed at his anger, as was always my way; and that perhaps it would be better if we did not meet for a while.

All my fury drained away, to be replaced by a kind of desperation. What if this was the end? I would not consent to being beaten—but nor could I bear to give him up. I thought, I hoped, I prayed that I'd made my horror at the mere idea of such an act sufficiently plain—and that having done so, we might never speak of it again. But first I knew he must be mollified a little, soothed and reassured—and I understood very well how best to achieve this. I sat down and wrote a very humble letter, asking for his forgiveness if I had indeed offended him. Yes, it was abject, and I confess I blushed a little when I recalled its contents just now; but it was true to my feelings at the time. I could not imagine life without him, and I was prepared to sacrifice a great deal of my pride to keep him in my life.

My reply had the effect I desired. He graciously accepted my apologies, and soon we were tolerably good friends again. Or almost so—for we both knew nothing would ever make up for my refusal to leave Lord B—and while I refused to grant him this, there would always be something bitter and angry in his feelings for me, which nothing I said could ever efface.

To my great relief, there was no more talk of beatings; but I soon discovered there are other ways of expressing deep-seated resentment than laying about oneself with one's fists. When, in the act of love, tenderness is replaced by a fevered urgency, a hunger to possess a lover so completely, to own and overwhelm them by the strength of one's need—that, too, is a kind of domination, for all that it appears in the guise of desire. When passion becomes a weapon of will as much as an expression of love, it leaves its traces on the body as distinctly as any slap. After a night together, my arms were sometimes black-and-blue from the tightness of his clasp, the force of his embraces, so much so that I was obliged to hide them from Sally, or account for my bruises by blaming them on a tumble I'd taken beforehand.

I didn't protest, for terrible as it is to admit, I preferred an excess of desire to the alternative. If he wished to possess me completely, there was part of me that yearned to be just so possessed.

There's a kind of attraction so powerful that it takes lovers into a world where nothing matters but the feelings of the moment, when all other considerations are forgotten. They call it amour fou, mad love, and I think it was something of this kind that had Granville and me in its grip throughout that summer. Whatever it was that overcame us, we were far less careful in one vital respect than we had hitherto been; and by the autumn, I could not deceive myself any longer as to my situation. I was pregnant with Granville's child.

*T*here couldn't have been a worse moment for me to deal with this news. In every possible way, 1799 was a bad year for our family. Lord B and I had teetered for years on the edge of bankruptcy—the malign legacy of our reckless younger days, his gambling, my extravagance, much of which had never been paid for—but this was the moment when the threat of ruin became real. The day of reckoning had finally arrived. Our credit, on which we had survived for so long, was finally exhausted, and there was not the slightest chance of our paying what debts we owed.

We would have been lost had not the Duke of Devonshire stepped in to rescue us. He proposed setting up a trust, to which he would contribute, along with our relations and friends. They would raise the money to cover our most pressing liabilities; but their help came at a cost. Savings must be made, and the conditions imposed on us were harsh indeed. It was suggested we leave our homes at both Roehampton and Cavendish Square, with a view to their being rented out; once tenants were found, it was intended we should quit London as soon as possible and live for while at Hardwick Hall, deep in the Derbyshire countryside, safe from expensive metropolitan pleasures, with a much-reduced establishment of servants.

As if this forced exile were not enough, Lord B was also instructed to dispose of the great collection of art accumulated by his father, to which he had added so prodigiously. This was a great blow, from which I think he never quite recovered. He was immensely proud of the paintings, drawings, and sculptures in his care, and never stopped regretting the loss of those he was compelled to sell. Watching them go under the hammer at Mr. Christie's auction house was terrible to him, especially as they went for sums far less than their true worth.

Alongside the art, we were also forced to dispose of several smaller properties, farms, and tenancies. We could only hope all this would be enough; for if there was a shortfall, there remained one further sacrifice to be asked of us. If we could not rein in our expenses, then we were to understand it might be necessary to sell Roehampton. The jewel in the crown of the Bessborough patrimony would be gone, no longer available to pass down to John, our eldest son and heir.

Lord B understood only too well that he'd failed in the first duty of a responsible parent—that of good stewardship. It had been his task to protect the inheritance, to increase it if he could, but instead, he would leave behind him a sad and sorry mess.

He didn't speak of it, but I knew he was consumed with guilt and humiliation. I caught sight of him once, standing in the drawing room of Cavendish Square, staring blankly into the street, clasping and unclasping his hands behind his back, the very picture of a lost and defeated man, and suddenly, I felt overwhelmed with sympathy for his situation.

It was only too plain that the wreck of our fortunes had all but destroyed him, that he thought his humiliation complete. "He has no idea," I told myself bitterly as I gazed at him, "how much worse matters really are. He thinks this is a catastrophe—what would he say if I were to confess to him that his middle-aged wife"—I was thirty-eight years old that year—"to whom he'd been married for nearly twenty years, was pregnant with another man's child, and beside herself with worry as she tried to decide what to do next?"

38

T told Granville the truth about my situation one night as we drove together in a hackney carriage through the park, one of the few places I felt safe enough to confess such news. During the previous few days, I'd allowed myself to imagine the very worst responses from him. Instead, he gently took my hand and looked very earnestly into my eyes.

"Before I go on, I have a question to ask. You told me not long ago that if this should happen, you would consider taking your own life."

"Yes," I replied, in a small, hesitant voice. "I did say that."

"I want you to promise me now that under no circumstances will you think of doing such a thing."

All I could do was to clasp his hand more tightly.

"Come, Harriet, must I ask again? Promise me."

"I am not sure I'd have the courage to do it."

"That is not what I'm asking. I want you to promise you will not do it."

"I will not do it."

"I *promise* I will not do it."

"I promise I will not do it."

At that, he threw himself back against the seat of the cab.

"Can it be managed, do you think?"

"I don't know, Granville. Not until you tell me what you intend to do."

"What I intend?"

"Do you mean to desert me?" My voice shook. "If so, I had rather know now."

"Surely you don't think me capable of such a dishonorable act?"

"I hope you won't, for I love you so very much."

He moved to sit beside me and took me in his arms.

"No, Harriet, I will not desert you."

I felt him stroke my hair. It had been a long time since he had bestowed upon me such a tender gesture.

"Think of what you want to do, and we'll talk again," he continued. "But in the meantime, don't speak of this to anyone until you're absolutely sure how you want to proceed."

"If I'm certain of your love, then anything is possible. But I've one thing to ask of you before we part."

I pulled myself away from him and sat up a little straighter. I had something important to say, which I knew I must get out before the moment was lost.

"I can't go through everything that lies before me if you're to use my condition as a reason to bully and harass me with demands I should go away with you. It will distress me beyond measure and may have the gravest consequences for my health. I beg you not to do it. Can you agree to that, do you think? For my sake, if not your own?"

I saw he didn't like it; he frowned, as if it was a great struggle to do what he knew he must—but in the end he nodded bleakly.

"If that is truly what you wish."

I buried my face in his coat and stayed there wordlessly, until we reached the place where I was to set him down. As the carriage drew to a halt, he kissed me, and then he was gone.

---

*I*n the days that followed, my overwhelming feeling was one of relief. I was not to be abandoned. I shouldn't have to endure whatever was to come alone, with grief at losing Granville added to the burden of guilt that already weighed heavily enough on my shoulders. This knowledge was itself enough to rally my spirits, enough to make me put aside all thoughts of resorting to destruction—not only of myself, but also of the new life growing within me.

I knew there were remedies to which desperate women turned in their troubles. I'd seen them advertised in newspapers, tiny paragraphs sandwiched between appeals for the return of lost dogs and recommendations for tooth powders. They sold themselves as treatments for female disorders—but we all knew what they really were. There were also certain herbs said to bring on the desired result, if one knew where to find them. I can't say whether I would have fled to such an extreme solution if Granville had rejected me; but I understood only too well the panic and terror that made women in my situation do so, and I would never judge harshly any poor soul desperate enough to have recourse to them.

I only knew that, once sure of him, there was no question of my destroying the little creature we had made between us. I would and must find a way to preserve it—but how this was to be achieved without shattering the happiness of everyone I cared for—I had as yet no answer.

I knew I'd soon have to tell Sally. She lived with me so intimately that she would have discovered the truth of my state pretty quickly, without any confession on my part. But I trusted her absolutely, and it was a great relief to open my heart to someone. When I told her, she sat down heavily on my bed as if all the breath had been knocked out of her.

"Oh, I'm so very sorry. That is—I'd begun to wonder—but I'd hoped I was wrong. I'm very sorry indeed."

"No, you can hardly offer me congratulations."

"You are quite sure, I suppose?"

"Oh yes. And I'm long past the time when I've miscarried before."

She nodded; she remembered those times. I'd lost at least two babies that way, perhaps more; it's hard to tell, when it happens very early. And then there were my four successful confinements. Sally had been at my side through them all.

"I hope," I began, trying to keep my voice steady, "I hope I can depend on your kindness—on your loyalty—and, above all, on your discretion—to help me through what is to come?"

She rose from the bed and took my hand between hers.

"You need have no doubts about me. I won't falter. I'll be with you through it all."

Sally's soundness was a huge comfort to me. Once I had decided how to proceed, she would do everything in her power to assist me. But only I could say how I wished to manage what lay before me. I grew more and more anxious as I turned it over endlessly in my mind. The agitation was terribly bad for both the child and me, but I knew I couldn't settle until I had some definite scheme to hold on to.

I had already ruled out the first possibility, that of putting an end to the pregnancy by my own hand. Nature might still intervene to produce the same result, but I was adamant I would not hurry it on.

The second choice was concealment—to hide my swelling figure and go away as soon as possible to deliver my baby in secret. Georgiana and Bess had both taken this road—but my situation was very different. It was impossible I should flee abroad—the wars had made any traveling on the Continent impossible. Even if I were to find some retired place in England where I might be confined, I doubted Lord B would allow me to go any distance without him, let alone stay away for any significant time. It might have been easier if I'd felt able to ask Georgiana's help—but then I should have been required to confide in her, which I was determined not to do. The birth of Eliza had been the most painful ordeal of her life, and, as I knew only too well, she suffered from the consequences of it every day. I would not inflict upon her the knowledge of my own situation, which would only remind her, in the most painful way possible, of her own grief and remorse.

It would be far, far harder to manage a secret birth if I was confined to home. For months I'd be obliged to hide the truth from my family, friends, and relations who knew me best, who saw me every day. The smallest slip, the slightest accident could result in instant disgrace. The very thought of it terrified me—the measures I would need to adopt, the constant vigilance, the great improbability of no one noticing, especially in the latter stages—I couldn't think of it without dread.

That left the third solution. I could simply pass off Granville's baby as Lord B's child. This wasn't impossible—Lord B still came into my bed when I felt myself obliged to receive him; the dates were perhaps a little awry but might be massaged into truth. This was by far the safest course of action. But there was a cynicism about it, a calculation which I disliked extremely. I'd already made my husband a cuckold—was I so abandoned as to impose on him another man's child? He'd done nothing to deserve it, yet he was to be the one injured. Although I saw the advantages of this tried-and-tested subterfuge, I was extremely uneasy about resorting to it.

So, what was I to do? The decision was left very much to me. Granville declined to force my hand, declaring that as I was the one who would bear the consequences, it was only right that I should make the choice. I appreciated his candor, but as the weeks went on, and the familiar symptoms grew increasingly apparent, I felt more and more strongly the desire for some trusted female ally to whom I could speak frankly. It was very fortunate for me that just when I needed her most, the best friend imaginable for one in my situation presented herself to me.

$\mathcal{I}$ 'd grown closer to Lady Elizabeth Monck since our difficult conversation about her own pregnancy, and the better I knew her, the more I liked her. She was a calmer presence than her volatile sister Anne, with a sympathetic warmth that was a balm to my anxious mind. I thought she must know, both from Boringdon and Lady Anne, exactly the terms Granville and I were on—but she had never alluded to it directly. I respected her tact, convinced myself she was trustworthy, and decided to take advantage, if I could, of her experience in these matters.

I took to visiting her in the afternoons as the moment of her delivery approached. In the end, she and Boringdon had decided against eloping, as being too fraught with danger to proceed. Instead, she'd hidden herself away from society until she was delivered, when the new babe was to be taken to some retired country place where it would be raised quietly.

She'd never made any attempt to hide these arrangements—so I ventured to ask if she was happy with them.

"The child will be safe in the care of kind people who will know nothing of its parentage. I'll visit as often as I can, in the guise of an interested benefactor." She smiled ruefully. "I believe it will work as well as any other solution I could contrive." She turned her mild gaze in my direction. "Forgive me if I trespass upon delicate ground—but do you find yourself in the same situation as I?"

I sighed. If I was to ask for her help, there was no point in dissembling. "Indeed I am. Perhaps three months gone, maybe four."

"And you aren't sure how best to go forward?"

I nodded.

"In which case, let me give you the benefit of my experience. The choice was to some extent forced upon me, for my husband and I are very rarely together, if you take my meaning."

She straightened her back a little and shifted in her chair—I knew that feeling very well from carrying my own children, and wondered when I should begin to experience it once more.

"But if we hadn't spent so long apart, I shouldn't have hesitated to assure him the child was his, had he ever asked. Which, as he is really a rather innocent and unsuspecting man, I doubt he ever would."

"And you honestly think that would have been the better course?"

"Undoubtedly. I would always have had my child in my company, rather than placed with others, however indulgent they may be."

I thought of Georgiana's Eliza, placed with her grandparents in Northumberland, where her position in the family was said to be as chilly and unwelcoming as the northern weather outside. I compared my sister's situation with that of Bess—whose children by the Duke were brought up in her sight, under her care—and there could be no doubt which of the two was the happier.

"Excuse me if I speak directly," I began, "but your frankness encourages me to be bold. Would it not have troubled you to think you were imposing another man's child on poor Mr. Monck? Isn't there something very dishonest about it?"

She smiled and reached out her hand to me.

"Oh my dear, I should have done it without a qualm! Really, what is parentage when you come down to it? Don't you think we're surrounded by proud fathers who have no idea that their son and heir is not truly their own? It's been going on as long as time. And what difference does it make in the end? No—in my opinion, if you are on such terms with your husband as will admit of it, it is by far the best, the safest, and the least troublesome answer to your dilemma."

I went away from Lady Elizabeth almost convinced by her argument—but something in me shrank from it nevertheless. It was easy for Lady Elizabeth, who clearly felt nothing at all for her hapless husband, to brush away any sense of betrayal. This was not the case for me. Lord B's miserable state weighed heavily upon me. Was I really prepared to add to his many humiliations by foisting upon him a child that was not his own?

And yet—for all these misgivings—when I thought of the alternative, my heart quailed. Did I really have the strength, the sheer determination to commit to a prolonged course of deception, which would require the utmost vigilance on my part and must culminate in circumstances of the greatest risk? I wasn't sure I did. I steeled myself to follow Lady E's advice, telling myself it would be for the best. Several times I attempted to take the first step and inform Lord B of my condition as if it was his own doing—but I simply couldn't manage it. My gratitude, my conscience, my heart—call it what you will, something within me made it impossible.

For some weeks, I flailed about helplessly, too delicate in my morals to take the easier path of deception, and yet too afraid of the risks involved in attempting to conceal my state. What was I to do? I thought of nothing else almost every waking minute, but my fretfulness brought me no nearer a solution.

In the end, a chance memory showed me the way forward. As I lay sleepless one night in bed, my mind wandered back to our last stay at Margate, and an extraordinary event I'd witnessed there.

The little port was entirely occupied with the frantic business of transporting soldiers to the battlefields of the Low Countries, where the fighting was particularly intense. I often walked down to the quay to watch them as they waited to embark, joining the crowds that gathered to see them off. It was very lively—sometimes there was even a little band of musicians playing martial tunes, while boys ran in and out of the throng, waving paper flags.

It was all very stirring; but my eye was always drawn to the more melancholy scenes, where young men bid their tearful farewells to families they might never see again. Some of their wives seemed resigned to their fate; but others simply refused to be separated, declaring instead they would follow their men to war. Most troopships allowed a few of these doughty females to go on board with their husbands, but there were always more women wishing to go than there were spaces to accommodate them; so the ladies had settled on the drawing of lots as the fairest way to decide who should go and who should stay. I arrived one morning just as the lots had been drawn, to see one poor unlucky woman, who had not been successful, beside herself with grief. She ran back and forth along the harbor's edge, crying and sobbing, a baby at her bosom, a small child holding her hand, refusing to be consoled.

She carried on in this fashion until the soldiers were all on board, the anchors drawn up, and the ship beginning to move. Then, at the very last minute, she ran forward and threw the elder child into the arms of her husband, who was waiting at the rail to catch him, before jumping down into the ship herself, holding the baby tight in her arms. There was a sudden silence, as if all of us watching held our breath—but both survived the precipitous leap. Everyone's eyes then turned to the officer commanding the transport to see what he would do—would he have the woman and her children turned away? But no—he was so touched by her courage and perseverance that he immediately gave the signal for her to remain. The crowd erupted—

huzzahing and cheering, waving their hats in the air, delighted at the bravery of this nameless woman.

This extraordinary event made a great impression upon me. I can't say why it should have come back into my mind again so forcefully, but it did so at a moment when I was much in need of a little courage. The bravery of that woman put my own vacillating spirit to shame. She'd been fearless in refusing to take the path of least resistance. What a contrast with me—I knew in my heart it was the coward's way out to consider placing Granville's child like a cuckoo in another man's nest—that it was wrong, not just to Lord B, but also to the child itself, who could never be told who truly gave it life and would be obliged unknowingly throughout its whole existence to live a lie. Could any good come from such a falsity?

I think I'd always known what I ought to do. All I required was the resolve to undertake it. A woman in love has resourcefulness and enterprise she scarcely knows she possesses until she is required to exercise them. I was clever, I was bold, I was determined—why should I not enjoy the same success as the soldier's wife? It would not be easy. But I'd made my decision. I should conceal the pregnancy and give birth to the child in secret, having sought out some kind persons to take care of it until decisions could be made about its future.

When I told Granville what I'd resolved, he accepted it without argument. My feelings overwhelmed me, and I once more I buried my head in his shoulder until I could speak again.

"You must know, dearest Granville, it wasn't only on Lord B's behalf that I came to this conclusion. It was as much for us as for him—for how could we have borne to see our child raised by another man, never able to express everything we thought and felt for the little creature? I couldn't have endured it, and nor, I hope, could you."

He smiled at me.

"I told you the choice would be yours and I meant it. You know far better than I ever can what lies ahead. Can you really do it, Harriet?"

"I believe I can. Anything is possible when one is truly determined to see it through. And consider what I'll have to drive me on—the thought of our child coming as honestly as is possible into the world, of my holding it in my arms and knowing it to be ours— how can I fail with those thoughts to sustain me?"

"You're very brave."

"But there's one last thing I must know, if I'm to have any chance of succeeding—that when it's born, you'll love the child."

"I promise to love it."

"Now that you've sworn, I'll confess something very shameful. For all my fear at what's to come, I'm thankful for this scrap of life we have brought into being—it makes me feel more belonging to you. And for that reason, whatever the world might say, I rejoice in it."

I think my words must have moved Granville very deeply, for the next day, I received from him a little note. It was short and to the point, telling me simply that he would love our child just as much as he loved me. No profession he had ever made before gave me more pleasure. I cut that line out of his letter and placed it in my locket, where it remains to this day.

40

I've always found the earliest months of pregnancy to be the hardest, and this was no exception. My sickness was such that I could eat nothing at all, except a little thin chicken soup from time to time. Although I had begun to sense the tiny movements that announce life, I felt so ill that I was afraid I should not go on, which filled me with despair, as I wanted so much to see things through.

Then, as is so often the case, I suddenly felt better; and by the end of the year, I was well enough to accept an invitation from my sister to go to the theater with her one evening. It was a very unlucky decision. The audience that night was rowdy, there was a great deal of drunken shouting—and suddenly, without the least warning, some fool fired a pistol right next to our box.

The noise was terrific, so loud that it seemed to go right through me. I was standing at the time, and fell backward with shock, all the breath knocked out of me. I didn't think I was hurt until I began to feel terrible pains in my stomach, which distressed me beyond measure. I made haste to leave—Georgiana must suspect nothing—and went straight back to Cavendish Square, where I took to my bed, dreading that some great hurt had been done to my child.

I begged Lady Elizabeth, the only friend aware of my situation, to come and keep me company, and of course she obliged. I felt the babe move once or twice, and that gave me hope; but Lady Elizabeth was pessimistic.

"I am sorry, my love, but I fear there's only one way this can end. It may take a little longer, but the outcome will be the same. You must try and prepare yourself, if you can."

She was right. A few days later I knew I was in labor. I asked that no help be summoned; but hearing I was ill, though ignorant of the cause, my sister sent her doctor to see me. Dr. Farquhar was an excellent physician, but there was nothing to be done in my case. After twelve hours of pains, the child was delivered dead, long before its time. She was a little girl, perfectly formed. I thought my heart would break with grief—how I regretted her—so much trouble and anxiety, so much love and hope invested in her, and now all for nothing.

I didn't want her carried off by strangers, to be disposed of in who knew what manner; and having no other idea of what else might be done for her, I asked Sally to place her remains in the garden, under a rose tree, where she lies to this day.

Afterward, as I lay speechless and exhausted in bed, Lady E stroked my head and whispered to me that although it was impossible I should think so now, later I might consider my loss as a blessing in disguise. She meant to console me, but I couldn't agree. I mourned the little girl extremely and was very low. I'd bled a great deal and continued so unwell that Dr. Farquhar was obliged to speak to Lord B and tell him I had lost a baby.

I waited very apprehensively for my husband to visit me. Farquhar had not mentioned that he'd shown any signs of surprise or anger when he delivered his news; but I wouldn't know until I saw him exactly what he felt. He arrived some hours later, and, though he seemed a little perplexed, was kindness itself. If he had any suspicion that the child had not been his, he did not voice it directly; and, in the circumstances, I saw no reason to enlighten him.

"I'm surprised you didn't tell me how you were situated. You've always done so before."

"I had some doubts whether I should go on—and decided to say nothing until I was sure."

His expression softened, and he sat down on the bed.

"I'm very sorry, Harriet, to see you so unwell."

"I've been very unlucky."

"You can't have been with child very long, by my reckoning—is it usual to be so ill in such cases?"

I dropped my eyes. "Farquhar says babies grow at so different a pace—especially in the early days—it's impossible to say."

He looked at me quizzically for a moment, and I dreaded him pursuing me further; but he stood up to leave me.

"Well—I hope to see you recovered very soon."

He said no more and went away. I had no idea what he really thought, only that he'd decided to ask no further questions. Did he believe what he'd been told, or did he prefer not to uncover the truth? Perhaps he was as keen not to know, as I was not to be found out. I couldn't say. Overcome with misery, I sank my face in the pillow so that no one could hear and sobbed and sobbed and sobbed. Eventually, Sally came in, held my hand, and stayed with me in silence until finally I fell asleep.

41

A few weeks later, I asked Granville to have a black mourning ring made for me to mark the death of our poor little girl. I couldn't wear it anywhere it might be seen, but it was a comfort to me; and anyway, I saw hardly anyone after my sad loss. I was much troubled with bleeding, a complaint that had often affected me after my confinements, and which made me so weak that I saw no one but Lady Elizabeth and Sally, who took care of me as well as any nurse. In the long hours I spent alone, I thought of nothing but Granville. I treasured the kindness he'd shown me throughout my ordeal. All the pain I'd endured only made me feel more deeply united to him, more truly his than I'd ever been before.

My only desire was to be alone with him once more; and as soon as I was up and about, I began scheming to make it happen. Weak and tottering as I was, I couldn't wait to hold him in my arms once again. As soon as my health would stand it, I began making all the arrangements—carriages were appointed, Lady Anne's apartment spoken for—and in no time at all, my dearest wish was granted. In his arms I was happy, and in my delight, I forgot there's always a price to be paid for pleasure. I suppose I was careless or hadn't thought it possible—certainly I could hardly believe it at first—but soon there was no mistaking what my body told me. Barely a month after giving birth, I was pregnant again.

I was so embarrassed I could barely confess the truth to either Sally or Lady Elizabeth. But I was obliged to do so, for I knew I would be dependent on their support once more to carry me through the next nine months. I was curiously composed at first, with none of the floundering uncertainty that had plagued me last time.

The biggest decision was made for me, since there was no chance at all that the child could belong to Lord B. Concealment was the only way forward, and I suppose I'd grown used to the idea, for it didn't terrify me as it had before. Granville promised me his love and support, and I began as well as I could have done, considering the circumstances; but then my health failed, and matters took a very different turn.

Once more I was horribly sick and could keep nothing down. I have always been a well-upholstered sort of person, so it was a shock to look in the mirror and see myself so thin and haggard. Soon I was prone and feeble with exhaustion, feeling every one of my thirty-nine years, and desperately afraid my illness might be harming the little creature within me. I think I hadn't properly recovered from my previous delivery, and I began to imagine I was about to repeat it and miscarry once again.

First Sally, then Lady Elizabeth, and finally Granville himself urged me to see a doctor. I resisted as long as I could. I have in general a horror of being under a doctor's care, for it does give them such a power over you; and in my condition, I had even greater reason for fear, since I was as vulnerable and exposed as it was possible for a woman to be. The very idea of confiding in some medical man—of throwing myself upon his promise of silence, of owning to him my deepest secrets, appalled me. But when Granville told me to conquer my fears for the sake of our child, eventually I gave in.

I turned over and over in my mind whom I could approach to help me. The doctor I chose must have excellent skills as an accoucheur, for I was no longer young and could not count on health and vitality to see me through. He must also be of sufficient standing for it not to appear unusual when I wished to consult him at home—his drawing-room manners must be as exceptional as his medical expertise. Finally—and most significantly—I must feel able to trust him, utterly and absolutely, for I would be required to share with him intimate details of my life which could end in my ruin if divulged to any other person.

After much thought, I settled upon Sir Walter Farquhar as the physician best suited to my needs. He'd cared for me very well after my last sad loss, and before that had attended my sister for many years. He had many other rich and influential patients and would never seem out of place at my bedside. Much of his practice was among ladies, for he was greatly in demand for the treatment of women's complaints. I'm sure many of these cases were exactly what they seemed to be; but I'd also heard he was particularly experienced with situations like my own.

I wasn't sure whether to think of these stories as a recommendation or a deterrent to placing myself in his hands. They suggested he had experience with such predicaments and must have enjoyed some success in managing them, for I never heard of any of his patients coming to ruin. But it worried me to think that in merely attaching myself to him I might be casting a shadow over my already tarnished reputation, declaring my dilemma to anyone who'd heard the same rumors as I had.

Finally, there remained the most important question of all—could he be trusted? Certainly, he'd been tactful enough with me before. But he hadn't known the full story of the child I'd lost; he may have suspected the truth, but he never mentioned it. Now, there would be no room for such ambiguity. I should have to tell him that this was not Lord B's baby—that I looked for his help in hiding its presence from the world and in delivering it in total concealment when the moment arrived.

I concluded Farquhar would not deliberately expose me, that there was no risk he would hurry off to Lord B and repeat everything I said. Too much of his practice involved tending to ladies with secrets for him to risk undermining their confidence by betraying a trust so publicly.

But he did have one great weakness—he could never resist the temptation of hinting at what he knew. Sitting at the bedsides of his bored convalescent patients, he would sprinkle his conversation with anecdotes of various extraordinary instances he had encountered in the course of his professional duties. He'd never reveal a story in its entirety—he understood he wouldn't have lasted long among us if he had—so no names were ever used, and he was adept at knowing exactly where to draw the line. Nevertheless, I blanched a little at the prospect of becoming a character, however disguised, in one of his salacious sickroom bedside tales.

But when I ran the names of other doctors through my mind, I saw my difficulty. They might be less inclined to gossip, but none were as willing as Farquhar to be of service to a woman in my state. It seemed I must take him as he was, with all his faults.

I was still turning over how best to approach him when, a few nights later, I went to supper at Devonshire House, and there was Dr. Farquhar, appreciatively surveying the table of cold meats. It was the perfect opportunity to engage with him. I was nervous but made myself speak, saying that I would much appreciate a few private words with him. Perhaps he wouldn't mind dismissing his own carriage and accompanying me home in mine, where we would not be overheard?

A little later, I found myself sitting across from him in the rattling darkness, wondering however to begin.

"I find myself in a very difficult situation," I murmured, unable to meet his eye. Before I could go on, he held up his hand—

"You needn't say any more. I can see your difficulty for myself."

"Is it really so obvious?"

"Probably not to others, but the trained eye notices things."

He leaned toward me. "If you want my help, I'm happy to assist you if I can—and I shan't bother you with unwelcome questions along the way."

His tone was businesslike, which I found reassuring. And now that he'd offered his services, I realized how much I longed for someone to support me in this fearful and uncertain business.

"Yes," I replied firmly, "I should like that."

"Very well. So let us see where we are. How many months gone are you?"

"Five months, I think. Perhaps six."

"Really? Will you open your coat for me, please. I must touch you now."

I closed my eyes as his hands ranged over me.

"I should say closer to seven."

"No!" I exclaimed. "That's quite impossible!"

"Well, if you're so sure—perhaps you're carrying an unusually large and lively child."

He withdrew his hands, and I buttoned up my coat.

"When you get home," he continued, "you should let it be known that you're not well—not gravely so, but enough to require my attendance. I shall arrive tomorrow, and we can speak more then about how to proceed."

Only now that I'd committed myself entirely to him did my emotions rise up, so that a single sob escaped me.

"None of that, if you please," he declared briskly. "The most important thing just now is to keep up your spirits. I've helped many other women through difficulties of this kind and will get you through it too."

"Thank you," I murmured, with a weak smile.

"Now, I shall hop out here." He gathered his gloves and stick. "I'll see you again in the morning—shall we say eleven?"

42

*L*ord B was not awake when Farquhar called, so he was able to explain his proposals to me with no danger of our being interrupted.

"The first and most important consideration is to provide some reason for your retirement from the world. We must turn you into an invalid, I'm afraid. You must begin by telling Lord Bessborough that you've been concerned for some time about your health, having noticed a tendency to swelling throughout your body. Explain that you've consulted me—that I've examined you and have suggested a course of treatment."

I frowned. It made me uncomfortable to hear the terms of my deception set out so baldly, but Farquhar took no notice.

"Then you may give him this letter—in it, I explain to your husband that your sickness requires you to rest as much as possible, either in bed or upon a sofa, until the disorder has subsided. You may show him your ankles, as evidence of the swelling, if you wish. They ought to prove how harmful any form of exercise or indeed of constriction must be to you at present. I recommend that you are to wear only loose and easy garments, and on no account attempt to put on a corset. I end by assuring him I have every confidence in your making a complete recovery, but only if my instructions are followed with the greatest possible exactness."

Later that day, I gave the letter to Lord B. I thought I must die of guilt and shame as he took it from my hand and read it with obvious surprise. His kind expressions of concern, his immediate willingness to do anything that might contribute to my improvement, made my sufferings a thousand times worse. Once again, I berated myself as the most base and deceitful of creatures; but really, it was too late for all that. The best I could do now was to keep him from knowing the true extent of my betrayal.

Over the next few months, I obeyed Farquhar's orders as minutely as he'd commanded. I lingered long in bed, rising late in the mornings and retiring early in the evening. When I did venture downstairs—carried there by two strong servants—I wore only my most voluminous dresses. I was much assisted by the style of dress that prevailed at that moment—the Empire line, so universal in those days—which raised the waistline so high under the breasts that even the most slender woman sometimes appeared as if she were with child. I firmly believe that I owed much of the success of my deception to fashion, for I have no idea how I should have managed if the silhouette had been less forgiving. Once established on a suitable sofa, there I remained, swathed in shawls, disguising even further my rapidly increasing figure.

I saw only Sally and my children, to whom I explained that I'd been told to rest until my disorder was cured, which I fully expected would be the result. I hardly ever ventured out, and I discouraged my friends from calling upon me. I doubted I was equal to the beady-eyed scrutiny of Lady Melbourne, or to the unashamed curiosity of Lady Holland. When I felt myself obliged to see them, I did so only at nighttime, in the sheltering darkness of candlelight. I couldn't impose similar restrictions on Georgiana or my mother and had been at a loss to know how they might respond to the sight of me—but Farquhar had smoothed the way there too, warning them not to be surprised by my appearance, sharing with them the nature of my disorder while promising them he had every hope of a cure. He spoke with such conviction, and their faith in him was so strong, that they seemed to accept his explanation and didn't press me further.

There were times when I marveled at the effectiveness of Farquhar's strategy; but such is human nature that its success, upon which so much depended, was at the same time a source of great pain to me. I felt myself falling deeper and deeper into a mire of lies, acutely aware that the falsehoods on which I was obliged to rely had opened a yawning distance between myself and those I loved best— particularly Georgiana.

Granville often pressed me to confide in her, thinking it would be a comfort to have an affectionate sister to depend upon. I was adamant that she was not to be told. I understood, as he never could, how the knowledge of my state would open up the deep unhealed wounds inflicted upon her by the loss of her own secret child. I knew how sincerely she yearned for her little daughter, kept so far away from her anxious mother's eye; and I was determined I should not be the one to stir up those barely suppressed memories, which continued to torment her. There were times, I admit, when I longed to tell her, when the yearning to throw myself tearfully into her arms was almost too strong to resist; but I would remind myself of the bleak warning Farquhar had issued to me when he first agreed to take on my case.

"I can do a great deal for you, and believe that with my help, you have as good a chance as any of seeing this through. But this is a solitary road you're set upon, and you'll be obliged to travel much of it alone. I understand how it will be—you will long for sympathy—to open up your heart to someone—but I beg of you, on no account give in. You can't trust anyone, even those you love. They may not mean to betray you, but they might. So tell no one. You must keep silent if you wish to stay safe."

He spoke so sternly that it made a deep impression on me. As a result, I condemned myself to an isolated summer, separated from my friends and everyone I loved. I refused to allow even Granville to visit me. It might have been contrived, if he had arrived with friends under the guise of some general invitation; but I didn't like the idea. The prospect of seeing him, in my sad state, under my husband's unknowing gaze, was too much to contemplate, and I refused all his pleas to arrange a meeting.

***

Mostly I kept to myself, shrinking from all company, fearful that, through some unconsidered movement, I should somehow expose my true condition to the world. Lord B was sympathetic to my situation, showing the greatest concern for my well-being and never quarreling with Farquhar's regime. He seemed to accept my withdrawal without complaint, entertaining his friends without me, until one day he inquired whether I felt well enough to make an exception to my rule. He'd arranged a dinner at which he particularly wished me to be present, for he'd invited several senior politicians, and would be grateful if I could be there to support him. He asked so humbly that of course I agreed. I thought it might be managed without undue risk, if I arranged to have myself seated at the table before the other guests arrived and arrayed in my usual shawls.

I didn't like it when I discovered that one of those present was to be Charles Grey, the man who had broken my sister's heart; but I told myself I could control my dislike of him for a single evening. The dinner would last perhaps three hours at the most before everyone dispersed to drink and talk elsewhere—surely, I was equal to that?

At first, things seemed to go smoothly enough, Grey was loud and hectoring, but I was seated at a distance from him and not too much troubled by his boorishness. Then, just as I began to think the evening might go on without incident, he began to relate the terrible story of the unfortunate Mrs. Scott. This poor woman, who was even older than I, was said to have discovered she was pregnant with a child not her husband's and had killed herself as a result. This horrible tale had been much gossiped about, but for obvious reasons I had steadfastly refused to entertain it in my mind. Now I had no choice but to listen as the men around the table, dead to any sympathy for this sad woman's sufferings, attempted to turn her misery into gross and heavy-handed humor.

Needless to say, it was Grey who led the way. He didn't believe the story, he declared, for no woman was obliged to do away with herself when there were a thousand ways of concealing her guilt. Some women even gave birth in their own homes, or so he'd heard. He smirked as he gazed around the table. "I promise you, it happens all the time."

All of the men, including Lord B, laughed very heartily.

For a terrifying moment, I honestly thought my heart would stop. I imagined everyone turning to me as one, as if to say, "We know your secret; you can't hide it from us." I took a few deep breaths and closed my eyes. When I opened them once more, the men were still tossing the story about like dogs with a bone. A cold fury swept over me as I looked at their cruel eyes and ugly braying mouths, repulsed by their willingness to turn a tragic woman's story into an excuse for a wicked, heartless joke. At that moment, I had never hated the male sex more.

Eventually even they saw the subject was exhausted and moved the conversation in a less distressing direction. The dinner inched its way forward—course after course was served, bottle after bottle drunk, until it drew at last to a close. Lord B shepherded his guests away, and I was carried back to my room by the burly servants, telling myself that, unpleasant as it had been, I had done my duty as I saw it.

That really should have been the end of it, but it wasn't, somehow. I simply couldn't shrug off the horror of Mrs. Scott's story or forget the relish with which the poor dead woman had been attacked. It left a dark chill upon my mind that nothing effaced. I know now that it marked the beginning of my descent into a melancholy that very nearly destroyed me, for nothing is so fatal to a woman in my situation as despair.

*U*nder the cold shadow of Mrs. Scott's harrowing story, I came to see everything in the blackest terms. I was like a snowball rolling down a hill, accumulating wretchedness as I went, until it seemed nothing could prevent the total collapse of my spirits.

One of the few people I could depend upon as I felt my mood alter was Lady Elizabeth Monck, whose calm presence always soothed my anxious mind, and who was one of the select few in whom I'd confided my trouble. Her sister Lady Anne, however, was a very different matter; I loved her dearly in those days but she was always an excitable soul, one day on top of the world, the next sunk in the deepest depression. No one could call her the best company for a nervous, agitated person. Although she'd known about Granville and me for many years, I thought her too volatile to trust with my secret and had asked Lady Elizabeth to keep her away from me until I felt strong enough to see her again. I was therefore very surprised one afternoon when Sally announced that both sisters had come to call. I gathered my shawls about me as best I could to conceal my guilty figure and composed my features into an expression of concerned sympathy; I knew something must be wrong, and when Lady Anne appeared in my drawing room, I saw immediately that that was the case.

Most unusually for her, she wore a veil; when she threw it up, her face was blotched and her eyes red from crying.

"She would come," murmured Lady Elizabeth softly, "although I told her it would serve no purpose, since there's nothing to be done, and it will only distress you."

"I don't want her to do anything," Lady Anne replied. "I'd just like her to know."

"What must I know?" I asked, anxious now. "What can have happened to make you so upset?"

"Morpeth has left me. He told me last night."

"Oh, my dear Anne, I'm so very sorry." I took her cold hand in mine. "But you've been here before—the two of you are always parting and then returning to each other. Are you sure this is final?"

"He left me in little doubt. His explanation was such that even I would be obliged to accept it."

"He wants to get married," interjected Lady Elizabeth. Her sister glared at her.

"Yes, he does. But not to me."

She tugged angrily at her veil until it came off, and she threw it on the floor.

"He's twenty-seven this year, and he wants to settle down with some nice young wife, with whom he can start a family. Note, I beg you, that horrible little word 'young.' It's that which rules me out. He has no desire to permanently attach himself to a woman ten years his senior, who may not have many years of pushing out babies left to her."

She wiped the tears from her eyes, her hand shaking a little.

"I was good enough to be his mistress, but never to be thought of as his wife."

There was no answer to this; we all knew it to be true, and were silent.

"When I asked him if he had some lucky female in mind, he wouldn't be drawn, but admitted there was one young woman who had caught his eye."

"We don't know who it is," said Lady Elizabeth, "and wondered if you'd heard a name—Boringdon looked blank when I asked him. Has Granville perhaps mentioned anyone—"

"It really doesn't matter at all," interrupted Anne. "I'm quite resigned. I've no intention of mooning around like some lovesick girl, desperate to know who's supplanted me. I simply refuse to be humiliated in that way."

"Quite right," murmured her sister. "Never let them see they've hurt you."

"The truth is, I fully expect to be married before he is. A gentleman has been pursuing me for some time—he has offered more than once to make me his wife—and this seems the perfect time to finally say yes."

"It's the Earl of Abercorn."

"Really, Lizzy, am I never to say anything for myself?"

"Is it truly him, Anne?" I spoke as gently as I could. "If so—he's a very cold and formal sort of man—do you think the pair of you could possibly agree?"

"They say he makes the housemaids wear kid gloves when they change his bed," declared Lady Elizabeth scornfully. "I don't think she should do it."

"Could he make you happy?" I persevered. "What does he have to recommend himself to you?"

She laughed. "I don't expect to love him, if that's what you mean. He has a great deal of money and a title. I think I shall enjoy being a countess. That will be enough for me."

She picked up her discarded veil and began to run it through her hands, smoothing it over and over.

"And do you know—terrible as the blow is, there's part of me that's relieved it has fallen at last. It had to happen. It's the fate lying in wait for all of us foolish enough to involve ourselves with younger men. One day our lover will come to us with a serious face and say the dreadful words we've always known are coming—'settle'—'marriage'—'family.' We know not the hour, but it's coming. And there isn't a thing we can do about it."

Calmer now, she picked up her veil and attached it to her hat.

"That's all I have to say, and I don't want to cry again in front of you, so I'll wish you goodbye and be gone."

She held her veiled face to mine, I kissed her cheek, and she bustled away without another word.

Lady Elizabeth sighed and began to gather up her things. "I'm so sorry. There was nothing I could do to stop her coming. And to what end? All she's done is spread her unhappiness around, like mud on a clean floor, without being any better off for it herself."

"You can't argue with her conclusions, though." I was agitated now, clasping my hands together in my lap. "The clock is ticking—nothing can stop it—Anne's right—the moment will come when our lovers will want what we can't give them, and then they'll be off." I blanched at the very thought. "We'll be dismissed—and then there'll be only one question left for us—how graciously can we step aside? Can we do it with dignity, accepting our fate with resignation? Will we go angrily, spitting and furious at the injustice of it all? Or will we simply turn our faces to the wall and give up?"

I felt the baby move, as if it shared my distress.

"And what of the little creatures we've brought into the world? They can't be so easily set aside, can they? Oh, Elizabeth, what will become of them when their fathers have legitimate children to consider? Will they be utterly forgotten?"

"I don't think any of our lovers is dishonorable enough to abandon a child. And the babes will always have us to watch out for them."

"But what if we die? What if—"

"Harriet, I beg you, don't give way to these thoughts. It's bad for the baby and for you. You cannot allow your feelings to overwhelm you in this way."

"How am I to stop it, then, when the future looks so bleak?"

She took my anxious hands in hers. "I can only tell you how I deal with it myself. I knew when I became Boringdon's mistress that our affair couldn't last forever. The end will be painful, and I shall be sad, but I am determined it won't destroy me. I shan't allow myself to be shattered into a thousand pieces because our connection is over. Where would be the sense in that?"

"Good advice if it's possible to follow it—but do you really think you could keep your feelings so firmly in check?"

"I suppose I shan't know until I'm called upon to try. It might be impossible—from the moment of our births, we women are encouraged to think of ourselves as slaves to our emotions, and I suspect the habit runs as deep in me as in any other lady. But there are times when I imagine how much easier it would be to behave more like a man in such a situation—calm and rational, regretful yes, but not overwhelmed. Oh, it all seems so much less exhausting than the tears, pleas, and agonized remorse with which we torment ourselves when all is over."

She stood up.

"I can tell from your expression that I haven't convinced you. And perhaps it was hopeless to try, for your heart is, I am sure, far more tender than my own dried-up article. But much as you love him, do, I beg of you, have a care—cultivate a little toughness in your soul, something to rely upon when all is over. It's that which will save you in the end."

She bent over and kissed me lightly on both cheeks.

"I firmly believe Anne would not be in such a sorry state now if she'd listened to me—but no, she offered up every single part of herself to Morpeth, tied up with a great red bow. And now he has declined her gift, all she can think to do is make haste and offer it to

some other man, even one as wholly without charm as Lord Abercorn."

Hat on her head, gloves in hand, she was ready to go in search of
her unhappy sister. But at the door, she turned on her heel to leave
with one last word.

"Promise me you'll think about what I've said."

I nodded. But once she was gone, I hauled myself upstairs and
lay on my bed, staring blankly up at the ceiling. Lady Elizabeth's
attempts to rally my courage had failed in every respect. All I could
think of was the inevitability of our fate. We were all of us destined
to hear the same words from the men we loved. The only question
was when.

44

Over the next few days, I felt my spirits sinking, sinking, sinking, as if I was tied to some great stone, descending ever deeper into fathomless black water. I knew I should exert myself—but it was quite beyond my capacity to do so.

I couldn't remember when I had felt more alone. I missed my friends, I missed my sister, and, above all, I missed Granville. It was so long since I'd seen him. He'd been obliged to go up to Staffordshire to fight yet another election, and once he'd emerged victorious from the campaign, he'd written begging to be allowed to visit me. With a heavy heart I had declined, for all the reasons I had refused him before—fear, delicacy, and shame, the same old guilty triumvirate that weighed upon me so heavily.

Naturally enough, he'd gone elsewhere—to his family, to house parties, shoots, dinners, and sociable gatherings. I couldn't resent it, as I wouldn't let him come to me, but I turned myself inside out with jealousy, imagining the women he met at these cheerful gatherings, all younger, livelier, prettier than I, with something to discuss beyond the tribulations of the sickroom. I had no doubt they chased after him. He was always pursued, wherever he went; and sometimes, I knew, he was happy to be caught. I knew he had other women; sometimes these interludes were no more than pleasurable flirtations, but on other occasions, I knew, they went further. I'd always insisted I wouldn't object, as long as he never deceived me, nor failed to tell me about the progress of his amours. I believe he kept to our bargain, most of the time at least—but oh, how it pained me, isolated as I was, when he wrote describing whom he sat next to, with whom he had danced, and whose conversation he had particularly enjoyed.

Then suddenly the letters stopped. At first, I didn't think too much of it; the getting and sending of our correspondence required a great deal of careful arrangement, at my end at least, for it was impossible that Granville should simply write to me as often as he did without attracting attention. In most houses, letters were laid on a plate in the hall to be either sent out for the post or collected by their recipients. Such a regular correspondence as passed between Granville and me was bound to be remarked upon eventually, by the servants if not by Lord B. This was far too great a risk for me to contemplate. So sometimes Granville sent his letters to Sally, who passed them on to me; or had them delivered to some nearby coffeehouse or other safe place, from which Sally would collect them. Once, when we were both staying in some great house, but could not risk too many private conversations, we hid our notes to each other inside the piano. When all our usual stratagems were exhausted, I was sometimes reduced to asking him to disguise his hand on the envelope, so that it shouldn't be recognized.

All this meant that it wasn't unusual for letters to be delayed; and for a while I continued to send my little packets of news to Granville's family house at Trentham, where he'd told me he'd be staying. But his silence grew longer—days passed, then a week, with no word for me. Had some accident befallen him? Surely, I would have heard about it if that were the case. After a fortnight I was frantic with worry and would have ridden north myself to discover the truth, if my health had allowed it. But in the end, it was Lady Anne who unwittingly told me what had happened. We were sitting together, dolefully drinking tea, when she asked me whether I'd heard from Granville. My heart missed a beat, but I merely replied that I expected to hear imminently, desperate not to reveal my agitation even to as good a friend as she was.

"That's a shame. I thought you might have had some account of the house party at Bulstrode. I hear it's been a great success. No one wants to go home. Granville's been there for nearly two weeks and shows no signs of leaving."

She chattered on for a while, regretting she hadn't been invited, for it would have done her a world of good, as things were; if she noticed my frozen, horrified expression, she did not acknowledge it. I swallowed hard. Now I understood why Granville had not answered any of my letters. He had never received them. They were still at Trentham where I had sent them, accumulating into an embarrassingly large, unopened pile. Why hadn't he told me he was going to Bulstrode? I could have written to him just as easily there.

Did he not understand how I lived for his letters, how they and they alone sustained me in my isolation? Apparently not, for he had unthinkingly severed the only tie between us, apparently without a qualm. My comfort, my happiness had not been worth the moment's consideration required to keep us connected. I couldn't believe he was capable of such selfishness, and when Sally readied me for bed that night, I was still shaking with shock. When I confessed to her what had happened, she refused to see it in so dark a light.

"He may have had to change his plans quite suddenly. Something may have drawn him away that he didn't expect. Perhaps a political matter of some kind?"

If I'd had the energy, I should have laughed. I doubted politics was the attraction. Bulstrode was home to my friend Lady Charlotte

Greville, and I had no doubt it was her company that kept Granville there. There had long been a mutual attraction between them. She was exactly the kind of woman he liked—clever, worldly, unhappily married—everything I was myself when in health—and I was terribly, horribly jealous of her. Was it possible that even now she was planning to take my place? I could feel my agitation rising, and Sally saw it too, for she begged me to call for Farquhar. I refused. Nor would I take the laudanum she urged upon me. It would fog my mind, and I wanted above all things to think clearly, for I intended to write Granville a letter, such a letter that would drive home to him the depths of my hurt.

I had to ask Sally three times before she agreed to bring me pen and paper. Once I began, the words flowed with an awful fluency—it was as if a dam had broken within me, releasing all my deepest fears. To others, his thoughtlessness in not writing might seem a small thing, but we both knew it was much more than that. It was a sign of his indifference, I told him, a confirmation of what I had long suspected, that he was tired of both my letters and me.

I couldn't really blame him for his change of heart. I knew only too well what I had become—miserable, dull, and above all, old—for my age had never pressed upon me more heavily than it did just now. I had become the drag upon him I had always feared, a clumsy, fretful weight, tearfully clutching at his sleeve, begging him to love me. What kept him with me was no more than habit—and a little compassion, for I believed he felt some pity for my sufferings. I did not complain, for I didn't think he meant to be cruel. I was only sorry that he had never loved me as deeply and as completely as I had loved him. As soon as the ink was dry, I sealed it up and gave it to Sally to send on to Bulstrode. I wanted Granville to read it while it was still raw with the despair I had suffered in writing it, hoping to provoke a truthful reply from him. I knew I could expect nothing for at least three or four days. All I could do now was wait.

I wish I'd been able to do so with the resignation Lady Elizabeth had urged upon me, but I was quite incapable of that. I wanted desperately to bring this baby alive into the world—as Granville and I had together created the little creature, how could I not long for its safe arrival? But try as I might to concentrate on that thought, everything around me conspired to depress my spirits further. I heard of nothing but terrible childbed sufferings. A poor woman in the village died in labor; Lady Downshire was all but given up after delivering an enormous baby at great cost to herself; and one morning, as I took a rare airing outside, I met poor Lady Burford's funeral coming the other way.

Pregnant women are instructed not to brood on such things, but they played on my disordered mind until I could think of nothing else. I stopped eating; I was listless, pale, and very, very low. When Farquhar came to visit me, he was appalled by my appearance.

"Come, my dear, we must do better than this. You'll need all your strength to get through what is to come."

I closed my eyes.

"If I may?" He parted the layers that covered me, gently felt my belly, then sat back and looked at me very earnestly.

"I'm aware we disagree about when this baby will arrive—you insist upon September—but I think he'll make his appearance far sooner than that. It could be as near as a fortnight."

This jerked me out of my stupor. "But that would make him a seven-months' child!"

"Yes, if your dates are correct. But judging by what I feel—I should think him a good month older than that, at the very least."

I was too tired to argue.

"I must urge you to exert yourself," Farquhar continued. "Time is running out, and you must draw up a plan for your delivery. Nothing will be achieved without one."

"Yes," I replied, "I understand."

"I will tell Lord Bessborough your health is worse—he shouldn't take much convincing, looking as you do just now—and that I think it best I call more often to check on your state."

I watched him through half-closed eyes as he gathered up his bag. I was so exhausted I couldn't summon up a single word, even for politeness' sake. He leaned toward me and spoke very quietly in my ear.

"In my experience there is no such thing as too much preparation. Sally is a capable woman and trustworthy. Speak to her about it as soon as possible."

I knew he was right, and that I must stir myself—but misery lay so heavily upon me that I couldn't find the energy to do it. I really believe I should have slid into disaster if the longed-for letter from Granville had not finally arrived.

As soon as I saw the beloved writing on the cover, I tore it open, my hands trembling at what I should find there—but in an instant, I saw all was well. He apologized profusely for the pain he had caused me, taking all the blame upon himself—he had been regrettably stupid and inconsiderate—but I must understand it was merely carelessness on his part and nothing more. I was very wrong to conclude from it that he loved me any the less. That would never happen. And then, in words I had so longed to hear, he told me plainly I was loved—that I was cared for—and that he hoped I would never have cause to doubt his feelings ever again, either for myself or for the child that was to come. It was short and unadorned—just a few simple pages—but it was enough to lift my heart and restore all my happiness.

While Granville loved me, what did I have to fear? Secure in his affections, I could bear any pain and suffering. I was equal to it all. It was only the thought of losing his love that had driven me close to despair—now I had no reason for doubt, I should prove myself as active and ingenious in all my exertions as even Farquhar could wish of me.

45

Sally and I agreed the birth should take place in our country home at Roehampton, which, fortunately, we had managed to hang on to despite all our debt. Everything was more private there, but as it was only nine miles from London, I wouldn't be too far from any specialist medical help, should that be required. My sons would be away at school, and I could send Caro off to stay with her grandmother. Lord B and I were to travel down together quite soon, and my plan was to persuade him to leave me there alone, once my time drew near. For this reason, I was delighted when Lady Anne—or Lady Abercorn, as she was now—invited Lord B and me to visit her at the Priory, her new husband's home, to mark the occasion of their marriage. I urged Lord B to accept, but warned him my delicate health meant I couldn't be sure whether, on the day, I should feel well enough to attend. I hoped he'd be persuaded to go without me, leaving me behind. Then, with everyone out of the way, it should be safe enough for me lie in.

I arranged with an apothecary at nearby Putney, who understood the care of babies, that he should take my child as soon as it was born and look after it in his house; and Sally found a wet nurse of good reputation, who would give the little creature the nourishment I would be prevented from offering it myself.

With all now in place, I appointed Farquhar to attend me in early September. He looked askance once more when I told him the date, but I refused to debate that vexed question again, and he was obliged to submit to my will, though he did so with a great deal of huffing and puffing. I didn't care. I had gone from the depths of misery to a breezy ebullience that made me feel as though I could conquer the world.

Then a terrible misfortune befell me—I fell down the stairs. I was standing by the balustrade on the first floor, when I felt a great pain run through me—my ankles, weakened by my size and condition, gave way—and I tumbled down the steps to the bottom.

Sally saw me go—I think I heard her scream—and she was all over me in a moment, covering my body so that no one should see the state of me. Thank God I was only stunned, so that she and one of the servants could assist me back to my room. I was shaking with fear as they laid me on the bed—what if my husband had discovered me unconscious, my guilty condition obvious to all the world?

As soon as he was told, Lord B hurried to my room, and finding me in such a state, immediately summoned a surgeon, who bound up my head in a large bandage—I refused to allow any further examination—and gave me laudanum to take. I complied with anything he proposed, desperate to be rid of him before the real nature of my condition became apparent. To my horror, I had begun to feel the first pains that I recognized only too well and was seized with terror at what they implied.

I beckoned Sally to me and whispered in her ear.

"My labor is beginning, I'm sure of it. The surgeon must be got rid of—as soon as possible—say whatever you think will make him go."

Once Sally had disposed of him, I tried to think of what I should do next.

First, Farquhar must be sent for and asked to get to Roehampton as fast as he could. Then Lord B must be persuaded to leave for the Priory as soon as possible. This wouldn't be easy, for he'd been very alarmed by my fall; and if he believed I was seriously hurt, would probably refuse to go at all. I knew he wouldn't listen to anyone else, so it fell upon me to convince him I was not well enough to travel, but not so sick that I couldn't be left.

I wasn't sure I could do it, as my pains were coming more regularly now; but I had Sally wash my face, arrange my hair, and seat me in my favorite armchair, covered up with wraps. I even managed a feeble smile when Lord B came tentatively into my room. He stood looking at me for moment, obviously distressed by what he saw.

"You look very white. Shall I call the surgeon back?"

"Oh," I said, as lightly as I could, "I believe it looks worse than it is. What I need is rest and silence, a few days in a darkened room with no one to bother me. Then I'm sure I shall improve. But as you see, I'm not fit to travel just now."

"I shouldn't dream of asking you to do so." He pulled up a chair from my dressing table and sat opposite me, perching uncomfortably upon it. "Should you like me to stay? I needn't go to the Priory if you don't want to be alone."

"You're so kind, but I don't think that's necessary. I doubt I should even see you, for I intend to shut myself away. It'd be very dull for you. And Sally has asked for Farquhar, so if there's any reason for concern, we can summon you back instantly."

My heart was in my mouth as I saw him turning the matter over in his mind. He stood up, pushing the chair away.

"Well, if I can do no good, I suppose there's no reason for me to stay."

I saw that he was disappointed, but I couldn't allow myself to feel sorry for him. "I might as well go today, if there's nothing to keep me here."

Relief washed over me, but I knew I mustn't show it.

"I hope to be much better when you return," I answered, gritting my teeth against another wave of pain. "Do give Anne my love. I long to know how she likes her new married state."

"The happiest state in the world," he replied, "as I'll be sure to remind her."

I hated myself for the lies I told so glibly, but I had no time to brood upon them. I must be put to bed, for the pains were coming on more regularly now. And as they did, I was seized by another fear—that I should lose this baby exactly as I had done the last—that everything I was to suffer would be in vain—that the poor little thing would die and there was nothing I could do to help it.

I don't remember much more about that day. I believe I spent most of it fainting away, only to be revived by the return of the pains. When Lord B came to bid me goodbye, Sally told him I was sleeping and could not be disturbed, and he duly went away.

I don't believe I was truly myself for some hours after that. When I did recover my senses a little, Sally had only bad news to tell me. Farquhar couldn't be found—he'd gone out of town, and no one knew when he'd return. Messages had been left asking him to come to me with all speed. But there was no saying when that might be.

I was so shocked at this, I cried out with fear—what should I do without him?—but Sally took my hands in hers and spoke to me with such quiet authority that I was compelled to compose myself and listen.

"I know it's a blow, but we mustn't give way to panic. Nothing is worse than that. So I've taken it on myself to make other arrangements. I've asked the midwife from the village to come up—"

"But she'll know me, I can't let her see—"

"No, she won't, because we shan't have her in here. You know the little box room at the end of the hallway, where the maids sometimes sleep? That's where we'll go. It's very dark, and I'll keep the curtains drawn. With the bandages on your head, you'll hardly be recognizable anyway, and we'll have only enough light for her to do her work."

I tried to interject, but Sally refused to give way. She knew it was essential for me to understand that all would not unfold in chaos and disorder, that I could depend on her resourcefulness not to leave me exposed and afraid.

"Our story will be that a poor woman staying in the house—a friend of one of the servants, no one really known to us—has been taken before her time and is eager to hide her situation from the world, hence the secrecy. I'll give it out that you're on a course of laudanum following your fall and are not to to be disturbed. I'll lock your room, just to ensure no one goes in to check. But the house is so empty, I don't think we should have any difficulties there."

She paused for a moment to see if I was still conscious, before going on.

"Now, you know my aunt, Mrs. Norris, our laundry maid? I've told her all this, and she's agreed to help this unfortunate woman in her time of need. When the moment comes, she will fetch the midwife and bring her to the maid's room, making sure no one sees her. Then, when everything is over, she'll take the baby and carry it to my room, where she'll look after it until the time is right to get the little creature to Putney."

"Oh, Sally—what can I say? I couldn't do this without you."

"I know it isn't what you'd hoped for, but we must work with what we have."

"Perhaps—if I'm lucky—perhaps Farquhar will arrive?"

I trembled at the thought of being left without a doctor, forced to depend on the uncertain skills of the old midwife.

"I hope and pray that he will, but if not, the midwife is reckoned to be good of her kind, clean and experienced, if not very learned.

And remember, I'll be there with you, as I've been before. I know what to do and how to help."

It was true, she'd been with me when both Caro and William were born. But then I'd also had a doctor and the apothecary—as well as Georgiana to hold my hand, and my mother to comfort me. My heart shrank, but I saw there was nothing to be done. The pains were coming faster now, and all that was left to me was to trust in Sally and resign myself to what was to come.

There's always a moment in any lying-in when your body recalls exactly what it must go through, and the memory of it flashes brutally into your mind. You'd do anything to escape it, but you can't. That's when you must call upon all the strength at your command, every shred of courage you possess, to support you in your struggles. I'd reached that moment now. There was no choice but to go on.

46

It seemed at first as though the baby was eager to be born, but I wasn't so lucky. Hour after hour went past, and I was no nearer delivery. Soon I felt myself slipping into that netherworld, so horribly familiar to any woman who has experienced a long and difficult labor, where there is no time, where you're conscious of nothing but your pain and the little creature struggling to be born.

I suffered very much from having only Sally and the midwife to attend me, for they had enough to do, and there was no one to hold my feet, which is a great relief when labor goes on for so long. I was obliged to bear the pain unaided, which sapped my strength very much, especially as the first day ran into the second, and I seemed no further on. By noon, I began to fear I was too tired to continue; but I begged Sally to fetch me the drawing of Granville, which I kept in a drawer beside my bed. I held it my hands, kissed it, and repeated his name over and over again, like some magic charm, to give me the spirit to go on. The old midwife asked Sally whether I was a Catholic: she'd seen popish women in my situation pray to saints before. When Sally made no reply, she shook her head resignedly.

"I suppose it's the father, then? It's a pity he can't be here now and see for himself what he's brought this poor woman to."

As I grasped Granville's image in my damp hands, I began to fear that nothing would bring this to an end, and that I would die in this airless dark place. Over and again, they told me this next pain would be my last if only I'd exert myself and push, but try as I might, my strength always failed before I could fulfill its purpose. After almost thirty hours of this, the midwife grew anxious and wanted to summon a doctor. The idea terrified me so much that I believe it gave me the power to make one final effort—and at seven in the morning, after nearly three days' agony, my baby was born at last, a fine and healthy little girl.

I held her in my arms before they took her from me to wash and tidy her. She seemed very small and a little thin—was she really a seven-months' child, just as I had dreaded? I was seized by a terrible fear that she'd be too weak to survive, that I should lose her after having struggled so long and so hard to bring her into the world. But later, when I put her to the breast, she fed well, which is a great sign of health in such a tiny baby, and I began to be reassured. As I watched her greedily at work, I was overwhelmed with such a fierce love for her that I felt the hot tears flow. Here she was, this child Granville and I had made, the living, breathing proof of our love. Whatever might happen in the future—whatever might befall me—I should always have her. Poor little creature—the world wasn't always kind to those born into her situation. I thought of Granville's little son, of Georgiana's Eliza—and my heart clenched with apprehension for her. But at the same time, I knew I should do everything in my power to protect her and keep her safe. She was mine, and that would be my mission and and my joy. Battered and exhausted as I was, as I gazed at her blind, indifferent little face, I knew all my suffering had been worthwhile.

As soon as I could hold a pen, I scribbled a few lines to Granville, to tell him of his daughter's arrival. I was too weak to say much, other than that she had blue eyes and that I hoped he would love her as I did.

———⚉———

*J*t was only then, when all was over, that Farquhar finally arrived, full of apologies and concern. The midwife had long gone, carrying with her all evidence of the birth except the baby herself, for prevention of any suspicion. He looked me over, and I saw he was not entirely satisfied with what he found.

"I don't like to see you losing so much blood. It is not uncommon after such a harsh delivery, and I hope it'll cure itself in a few days; but you're to let me know if it still troubles you after that."

He didn't like me feeding my little girl, thinking it might weaken me further, but I begged so hard to be allowed to continue that reluctantly he agreed. It's impossible to convey what a pleasure this was to me—perhaps because I knew it couldn't long continue. I was allowed only two days to nurse her. It was a terrible moment when Mrs. Norris carried my tiny daughter under her cloak to a carriage waiting in the lane behind the house, on the first step of the journey to the apothecary at Putney who was to care for her. I knew it was for the best and had every reason to believe she'd be well looked after, but it very nearly broke my heart. I thought of Georgiana, and how she must have suffered exactly as I was doing, which only made me even more distressed.

A week after the birth, I finally received the letter I'd longed for from Granville, replying to the news of the little creature's arrival. His palpable relief at knowing both the baby and I were safely through our ordeal made me cry with joy to read it; but it also made me more desperate than ever to see him. I knew it was quite impossible. I could hardly rise from my bed, and there could be no question at all of his coming to Roehampton.

We often imagine, when our labor is over, that we're out of danger; but I have heard it said that far more women die after their baby is born than in the midst of giving birth. I had not rallied from my sufferings. I was terribly weak. I could hardly raise my head, and any attempt to move brought on sickness and a giddy feeling in my head. Worse than that, the bleeding continued unabated, and I grew weaker day by day. Farquhar looked grave—and the anxiety I saw in the expressions of everybody around me only confirmed my fears. I began to believe myself not far from death.

Strangely, I didn't panic, but set to work, writing in secret a great bundle of letters, which I handed to Sally to be dispatched if I didn't survive. Perhaps the most important was to Granville's mother, asking her to take care of her little granddaughter. Lady Stafford knew her attempts to prise her son away from me had failed, and I doubted she thought of me with much goodwill; but I'd always heard she was an affectionate, good-hearted woman. She was so devoted to Granville that I felt sure she would look kindly on the plight of his child; I hoped she would take pity on me too and keep the secret from my own mother and sister, who, I begged, should never know of her existence.

I wasn't wrong to take such steps, as I grew far worse over the next week. I was quite alone, for Lord B was still at the Priory and all my children away. In my sad, reduced state, I wrote a letter, telling Granville how much I longed to see him; and I think Sally must have communicated to him the peril of my situation, for I was conscious one morning of his being in my room, taking my hand and leaning over me. I thought it must be a dream, but if so, it was a very pleasant one, which I didn't want to end. I remember his beautiful face close to mine—I think I touched his lips—and I was sure he spoke to me.

"I love you, Harriet. Don't slip away from me like this."

Then I think he kissed me—but afterward I couldn't be sure

whether I had imagined it, whether it was only an apparition I conjured up in my fever. It was only when Sally assured me it was no illusion that I allowed myself to believe it. I don't know how she contrived it, but somehow, she had spirited Granville into my room. When I realized the truth of what she told me, I could only berate myself for having wasted such an opportunity to take him in my arms. He'd been here—and I had been too weak to take advantage of it. I confess I shed some tears at that thought.

I also had some hazy recollection that I'd asked him, in the course of our dreamlike encounter, what I was to call his daughter. If I needed any further proof that it had indeed taken place, his letter a few days later provided that. She was to be named Harriet, and given the surname of Arundel, which belonged to his family. When Sally read this out to me—for I still was too feeble to hold a letter—I was suffused with joy at the thought that he had bestowed it upon her. I only hoped I might survive to see her baptized with it.

47

It wasn't until the end of September, some six weeks after my lying-in, that the true cause of my illness was at last discovered. Everything had been tried to cure me—my hair was cut off, and leeches were applied to my poor head—but to no avail. I was in a terribly reduced state; the very life seemed to be ebbing out of me. I could barely stand before succumbing to dizziness, so that I thought yet again that death could not be far away. Acting on Farquhar's advice, I consulted another medical man, a Mr. Maldon, who was particularly skilled in managing female complaints. I confessed I'd recently suffered a miscarriage, which I particularly wished no one should know about; and that I feared it had resulted in some internal injury. I allowed myself to be examined, and it was discovered that the old midwife had allowed to remain within me something that should have been expelled at the birth. Farquhar and Maldon gave me remedies that in time acted to remove what nature had not; and from that day onward, finally, I began to improve. It was only some months later that Farquhar told me very few women recover from this complaint and how lucky I was to have escaped death.

Now I was no longer bleeding and could move around once more, I had only one thought in mind—that I should be able to see my little Harriet again and hold her in my arms. During the worst of my illness, I'd been terribly distressed by the thought that I might die without the chance to love and protect her as she deserved. She'd been settled for the time being in the household of the apothecary in Putney, with a wet nurse to feed and look after her. Farquhar had been of great service to me then, visiting her often and encouraging me with accounts of how she thrived, her little cheeks quite plump now, with a fine and healthy color.

"She's really the sweetest child," he told me one afternoon as he took my pulse. "Very much like you. And with a great look of her father about her too."

I was extremely taken aback. This was the first time he'd made any reference to Granville, whom I had never mentioned. I wasn't surprised that he knew, but it would have been in better taste not to have acknowledged it, and it was indiscretions such as this that made me uneasy about my dependence upon him. However, much as I disliked it, I knew there was nothing to be done. It was just another of the many humiliations that a woman in my position was required to bear.

But really, as I told myself, it counted very little when weighed against all the much greater services Farquhar had rendered me. He'd seen me through my pregnancy, just as he'd promised he would, providing a credible explanation for my state, and would have been with me at its end too, if I'd only accepted his opinion concerning my due date, rather than persevere in my own. And it was he who took it upon himself to explain to Lord B the recent change to both my shape and general health, telling him he believed they were partly attributable to the fall I'd taken down the stairs. The shock to my system, though attended with much danger for a while, had in the end proved beneficial; and when combined with the good effects of the lengthy period of rest he'd prescribed, had resulted in a very great improvement to my well-being. Lord B nodded and seemed convinced. What I would have done without Farquhar's endless consideration and guile, his smooth readiness with an easy and credible lie, I really do not know.

48

*W*hen Farquhar finally announced he thought me well enough to see my daughter, I was beside myself with excitement. I was taken in a carriage—not our own, for fear of recognition—to her obscure Putney hideaway. Farquhar had ensured no one should be present but him and myself—and there I spent one of the happiest afternoons of my life.

Everything about my little Harriet delighted me. She was amazingly grown since her troubled birth—now she was a rosy, fat little thing, with a cheerful, beguiling disposition that melted my heart. When she grasped my hand with her little fingers—when she gazed at me with the intent state all tiny babies possess—I honestly thought I'd expire with love for her. She was my own angel, no more, no less, and I couldn't stop looking at her, or stroking her downy head.

Parting with her was agony. As I handed her back to the nurse, it struck me that even now little Harriet must feel more for this other woman than for me, since it was she who held her to her breast every few hours while I was nothing but a stranger; and moreover, that the older she grew, the more this must be the case, for what was I to her? This made me cry as I walked down the stairs to leave her, and I was almost beside myself when Farquhar joined me in the carriage. He watched me as I sobbed; and when I could cry no more, he handed me a handkerchief to dry my tears.

"This is a terrible moment—leaving behind the little object that you've brought into the world with such difficulty must break your heart—and I'm exceedingly sorry for you. But I'm going to give you a little advice, and I very much hope you'll take it in the spirit in which it's intended, for it won't be easy for you to hear."

I looked up, apprehensive, trying to imagine what he meant to say.

"When a lady finds herself expecting a child that can't be acknowledged, her first concern is a simple one—what must I do to keep myself from ruin and my child safe?"

"Yes," I agreed in a small voice, "that was certainly so for me."

"If she's fortunate, and both she and her baby come through the ordeal unscathed, it might seem the worst is over—she can breathe a little easier, even relax her guard. But I'm afraid that's the very worst thing she could do."

He reached over and took my hand.

"If she's of an affectionate disposition, the hardest part of her task is still to come. She'll have all a mother's feelings for the baby to which she's given birth—but she can never express them as openly as she'd wish. Instead, she must find ways to love her child that will never reveal the true nature of their connection. You think what you've just endured was hard enough—months of deceptions, stratagems, and lies—well, that's nothing compared to what's to come. If you love that little creature and wish to remain a presence in her world, you've a lifetime before you of secrecy and evasion. I have seen it often enough to know."

"Why are you saying such dreadful things to me?" I cried, truly distressed now. "What possible reason can you have for tormenting me in this way?"

"Because I believe it's better to know what dangers face us, so that we can prepare ourselves to meet them. I wouldn't use such language to a weaker person, but, for all your melting airs, I believe you possess great reserves of courage and determination, which will serve you very well in managing what's to come. I don't for a minute doubt that you'll fight like a tiger to protect young Harriet; but I wish you to grasp very clearly that this is a struggle which begins from this very moment and will continue until she's quite grown up."

He sat back heavily.

"Tears are all very well, but you don't have the luxury of indulging in them. You'll need to be strong, my dear—strong enough for both of you. Now you've brought her into the world, you must scheme and plan to give her a tolerable life in it."

I wiped my eyes and composed my face. I knew everything he said was right. We didn't speak again on the journey back, but when we arrived at Roehampton, I thanked him for what he'd said.

"It's put a little steel into me, which I'm sure I was very much in need of."

His face softened. "Oh, but you have it, never fear that you don't. Just don't wait too long to exercise it. Decide what you want for your child and begin arranging it as soon as you possibly can."

I thought of little else but Harriet's future over the next few days. Most women in my situation send their babies away, to be hidden somewhere in the country and cared for by strangers. I can't say I liked this prospect, although Lady Elizabeth argued strongly in its favor.

"For us, it's been the best solution. If you seek out kind people to look after them, and pay them properly, it answers quite well. I know my babies are safe, and there is no real risk of discovery."

"But can you see them?" I asked plaintively. "Is it possible you can watch them as they grow, get to know their little ways?"

"I get down to Somerset whenever I can. Once a month in good times, longer when it can't be contrived. I do what I can."

I saw my questions made her uncomfortable, so I didn't pursue the subject; but I hated the thought of being so far away from my little Harriet, of becoming such a stranger to her. And if I'd required any further proof that this was an arrangement I could never countenance, it was my sister who convinced me I must find another answer.

We had begun to see each other again, now that I was recovered from what Farquhar had described to her as very serious and debilitating illness. I certainly looked as if I'd been unwell. My hair had been cut short during the worst of my sufferings, and on the rare occasions when I looked in a mirror, my reflection gazed back at me with a wan and listless stare. Georgiana sometimes commented that I was extremely white and thin, but asked me no questions beyond that, which was exactly as I wished it.

My sister came to see me one afternoon, heavy-eyed with sadness. As soon as we were alone, she confessed the source of her misery—Eliza, who was around nine years old now. She lived mostly with Grey's parents in far-off Northumberland. Neither they nor her father showed the poor child much affection, which was extremely painful to Georgiana, especially as she was forbidden to show the girl any tenderness herself, for fear of arousing suspicion about the true nature of their relationship. Instead she posed as a friendly godmother, who wrote her loving letters and showered her with little gifts. To my knowledge, Eliza was never asked to Devonshire House or Chatsworth; I imagined the Duke had forbidden it.

Lately, however, Eliza had been sent to school, which, far from improving her situation, seemed to have made it much worse. Certain little girls had noticed no one visited her, and as a result had begun to bully her cruelly. Poor Eliza had confessed all to my sister, on one of the rare occasions she was allowed to see her daughter, and the whole nasty story had distressed her beyond measure.

"There is one particular girl who makes it her business to torment her," Georgiana told me, all the while twisting her hands in anguish, "laughing at her, asking where her parents are, and calling her the tinker's child."

She looked up at me, her face contorted with pain. "She tells my Eliza that other girls have mothers and fathers, who bring them toys, but she has no one."

I thought my heart would break as I heard all this. I took my sister tightly in my arms while she railed bitterly at the injustice of it all. "There's nothing I can do," she cried. "Eliza is tormented, and there's nothing I can do."

After Georgiana departed, I was left with a dull ache in my heart. I swore there and then that I'd never put my child in such a lonely, friendless situation. Harriet should not be sent far away from me, where I could neither see her nor protect her from the miseries of her situation. I might never be able to own to her the truth of who I was, but that needn't prevent me from playing some important part in her life. Whether as friend, godmother, or kind patroness—whatever identity I was called upon to assume, it really didn't matter. My first and most important duty to my little daughter was to keep her as close by me as was humanly possible, and never to deviate from that resolve.

I didn't know how it was to be achieved, but I shouldn't rest until I'd arranged it. If this was the steel in the soul to which Farquhar had alluded, I felt myself fully in possession of it now.

49

From her earliest days, I loved my tiny Harriet with an intensity I don't remember feeling with my other babies. I've always been an affectionate mother, but the strength of my attachment to her was a shock even to me. I believe now that I thought her special because she was the result of the great love of my life, that my bond with her reflected in some way the power of the passion I felt for her father. As I'd discovered, it was perfectly possible to feel no desire at all for one's husband, but still adore the children you had with him; but oh, how different it was when your child was conceived in love! How proudly and with what transforming satisfaction you gazed at the little creature you'd created together! I also discovered that the attachment I felt for her only magnified my desire for her father. I wouldn't have thought anything could strengthen my love for Granville—wasn't it already remarkable enough?—but the arrival of little Harriet did exactly that. She'd forged a link between us that could never be broken, whatever the future might hold.

Whenever I could, I went down to Putney to see her. I liked to have her on my lap, sometimes for an hour at a time. I know all mothers think their child perfection, but honestly, she was so fat and fair and beautiful and her little ways were so charming—she was truly the best-humored little creature I'd ever known, as well as being extremely clever and forward for her age. I was soon convinced she recognized me, and that she had a special smile she produced for me alone, which pierced me to the heart when I saw it.

At the same time, I was only too aware of the precariousness of her future. Despite all our difficulties, my children by Lord B would always be comfortably situated; and if anything were to happen to me, there were many relatives and friends who could be depended upon to help them. Little Harriet would never enjoy that security, and this knowledge made me fiercely possessive, poised and ready to do all I could to keep her from harm, but also, desperate to lavish upon her all the unconditional affection she couldn't depend on receiving from anyone else.

For all these reasons, I couldn't bear to be parted from her, and this drove me to take more risks than I should have done. I brought her to Roehampton once, when everyone was away, and played with her there for a whole afternoon. When this passed off successfully, I did it again and again. Granville urged me to be more prudent—but I thought I was safe enough. My sister and I had often spent time with many of the needy children we'd taken in over the years; it was nothing unusual to find me entertaining in the garden some tiny object for whose welfare I was now responsible. Why, I told myself, should Harriet's occasional presence attract any special notice?

But there were times, I admit, when I was very nearly caught out. I recall one morning when Sally burst into my bedroom, swept up Little H, for that is what I called her now, who was gurgling happily beside me, and carried her away moments before my mother arrived. This brush with danger sobered me, and I understood I couldn't long put off finding a safe place for my darling to be lodged. I was determined, however, that she should be placed nearby, close enough for me to see her every day if I wished. But where was I to find such a convenient refuge? And even if the place itself seemed suitable, how could I be sure I was handing her over to people who'd treat her kindly? It made my heart freeze to imagine her slighted or ignored, as poor Eliza had been. And even if I was lucky enough to find such a home—how on earth was I to pay for it? Anything likely to satisfy my high standards would cost a great deal of money, and I had nothing at all of my own.

To any poorer person looking at me, this must have seemed ridiculous. I lived in great houses, was decked out in elegant clothes, had servants at my beck and call—surely, I had income enough at my command? But the truth was that as a woman, I possessed hardly anything that was truly mine. I had nothing, other than the sum specifically named in my marriage agreement—and I had long ago frittered that away. I could hardly ask my husband to assist me. There was only one person to whom I could look for help, and that was Granville.

The thought of approaching him filled me with unease—I was desperate that neither Harriet nor I should become a burden to him—but to my great joy, he volunteered what I had hesitated to ask for. He wrote me, unprompted, a wonderful letter, telling me he considered Harriet as his child, that he would never abandon her and intended to pay for the costs of her upkeep.

I almost collapsed with relief. A huge weight was lifted from my shoulders, and indeed, there was a part of me which rather relished being Granville's dependent, managing our daughter's affairs like some busy housewife. It made me feel as if we were almost a little family.

But in every other respect, I was painfully embarrassed by my reliance upon him. I knew his own resources were slender, consisting mainly of the sums he won gambling at Brooks's. It seemed a terrible hypocrisy to take his winnings when I complained so bitterly of his playing at all; but what was I to do? Granville told me not to concern myself, but I dreaded the thought of Little H becoming a drag upon him. If he didn't resent it now, he might feel very differently at some future time, when he had other calls on his money. By this, I meant, of course, that a wife might not feel as generously inclined toward his illegitimate child as he did himself; but when I mentioned this fear, he brushed it away and asked me to draw up a list of expenses, so that he could know how much to put aside.

My first and most pressing task remained that of finding a more settled home for Little H, and trustworthy people to staff it. Try as I might, I couldn't think of any place that might suit, nor of anyone I thought good enough to care for her. I had begun to despair of finding a solution when Sally came to me with a suggestion. Her father, a tradesman in a small way, lived alone in Chelsea but dined every night with her at Cavendish Square. Sally had long been keen he should move closer to us, but, hitherto, he'd refused to consider it.

"It was the expense that made him reluctant at first—but I think I've found an answer to that," Sally said. "You remember John Gale, who was servant to Master William for a while?"

"Yes, a good steady man, very honest."

"It turns out he too wants to take a house in town. So if he were to join with my father, I think something could be found that would suit them all."

"I imagine that would put your mind at rest."

"Yes," Sally answered briskly, "but I think it might be of assistance to Little Harriet too."

I sat up now, all alert.

"Mr. Gale has a sister, who plans to join them, if everything goes ahead. She's between places just now and has no desire to return to service. She'd much prefer to take on the care of some small child, as she's used to being around babies. She hopes for some steady, long-term arrangement, where she could get to know her charge properly.

She'd expect to be paid decently for her work, but her terms would be fair."

"And what's she like, this Miss Gale?"

"She's a kind and affectionate woman, by all accounts. I've met her a few times and liked her. We know her brother is as calm and sensible as the day is long; and my father loves having small children about him—he says they keep him young. So if it could be contrived, they could all share a house together—I think it might be made into a very comfortable home for Little H."

I was all excitement now. "Do you think she would do it?"

"I think she might. And I have an idea as to how it all might be arranged, without your being required to expose yourself at all."

Every Sunday afternoon, Sally explained, she, her husband, and her father liked to take a stroll together near the Chelsea Hospital. Imagine, she said, if they were to one day meet with Little Harriet being walked toward them from the other direction. And what if Sally should be so taken by the child that she couldn't resist stopping the servant who had charge of it and asking who she was? What a further coincidence, when it emerged that the little girl's mother was dead and her father far away at the wars, and that her friends were even now seeking a new nurse to care for her. If that were to happen—if it could be arranged—then Sally would tell Miss Gale immediately, and if she was interested, would send her to me, as the friend who had taken responsibility for finding the child a home. Then, if we liked each other, it would be easy to come to terms—and everyone would be happy. What did I think?

I leaped at the idea, declaring I'd do anything required of me to ensure such a happy outcome. Under her deft management, all passed just as Sally had planned; when I met Miss Gale, I found her just as agreeable as Sally had said and engaged her on the spot. I couldn't quite believe it—I was beside myself with joy—at last my Little H was to be placed just as I could have wished. It was agreed she should stay where she was until a suitable house could be found for them all, but in the meantime, I had no objection to her making friends with those who were to be her companions. Sally often took her down to Chelsea to visit her father, and soon she was such a favorite that he carried her about in his arms, telling her she was his little pet.

There have been many, many occasions over the years when I've had reason to thank Sally with all my heart for the many services she's rendered me. But when I understood my little girl was to be comfortably settled among decent people who cared for her, that I should visit her with ease whenever I wished and see for myself she was safe and well—I can honestly say I've never felt more in her debt than I did at that moment.

50

Once I saw my child settled, I allowed my thoughts to turn in a more selfish direction. I very much wished to go to Chatsworth, to join the house party my sister was accustomed to hold there each autumn. Granville had already been invited; Georgiana had often been in his company while I was cooped up alone, hiding my pregnancy. He'd set out to charm her, thinking her goodwill could only be helpful to us; and, of course, he'd succeeded, to such a degree that he was now frequently added to her guest lists.

It pained me a little to think she'd probably seen more of him than I had myself, for family and constituency business had kept him in Staffordshire for almost the whole of the summer. I hadn't set eyes on him since I was so ill just after Little H's birth, in that strange dreamlike moment when he appeared at my bedside—but as I'd hardly been conscious of his presence, I felt that didn't count. I longed for him now as some parched and thirsty person craves a cool drink, and resolved that I shouldn't be denied what I considered my reward for all the suffering I had endured over the last months.

I wasn't, however, to be allowed my heart's desire without a fight.

My health was still far from good. I suffered still from the quantity of blood I'd lost during and after my terrible labor; and Farquhar insisted I was to go nowhere until I received his express permission, frightening Lord B into sharing his similar opinion. To my enormous frustration, I was forced to wait helplessly in London, when all I wished was to be on the road to Derbyshire, so that I might take Granville in my arms once more.

I was permitted a rare visit out to see my sister shortly before she left for Chatsworth. We hadn't been together much since Little Harriet's birth, and I felt very self-conscious as she inquired how I did. As usual, I blamed all my woes on the bad effects of my fall. I couldn't tell how far she believed me. One of the worst symptoms of guilt is that it turns all innocent expressions of concern into imagined interrogations. I smiled and joked and brazened it out; but at the same time, I sought to communicate without words, as only sisters can, that I would much prefer it if she asked me no more. She understood, and delicately obliged. And there we left the whole question of what exactly had befallen me, a wisp of suspicion that was neither confirmed nor denied, hanging in the air like smoke until more general conversation wafted it away.

"I suppose I'm breaking no great confidence," Georgiana declared, "to tell you there's a secret purpose behind our gathering at Chatsworth this year."

I looked up, intrigued. I could never resist the prospect of being let in upon a secret.

"I'm hoping it will encourage one of Little G's suitors to declare himself. It's time to discover whether any of them intends to make an offer for her, and whom she will accept if he does."

Little G was my sister's eldest daughter, a Georgiana like herself, but never referred to without her diminutive title. She was just eighteen, a sweet and serious girl, diffident, anxious, determined always to do the right thing. She'd come out into society earlier in the summer, but I'd been too occupied with my own affairs to have heard much about her prospects since then.

"So who are the contenders?"

"For a while I thought the Duke of Bedford was the likeliest prospect. He seems interested and hovers about her, but has not, as yet, come to the point."

The Duke was around my age, and had once been very fond of me, though matters had never progressed beyond a little gentle flirting. Now he was thought of as a possible husband to my niece. How quickly the world turned.

"There'd be twenty years between them," I mused. "What does Little G think of that? And how do you feel about it?"

"I don't mind at all. She's very nervous, and a steady, older man like Bedford might give her some confidence. But she's so reserved on all matters pertaining to liking and disliking that it's impossible to tell what she feels. I believe her real preference is for Morpeth, who's certainly far closer to her in age."

"Morpeth? You mean George Howard, Lord Carlisle's son?"

"Yes, of course. Who else could I mean? He seems really very keen on her, much more so than Bedford."

"I was surprised, I suppose, given his entanglements. You know he was Lady Anne's lover until earlier this year? That he put an end to their affair in the most callous and unfeeling way?"

"Yes—I heard all was over between them. I'm sorry to hear it was badly done."

For a moment Georgiana looked chastened, her excitement on Little G's behalf briefly quashed. She knew only too well the misery of rejection at the hands of a man who could not exert himself to be kind.

"From what I've seen of him, Morpeth always seems a man of few words, and I don't imagine he used many of them in giving poor Anne her dismissal." She sighed, as if to acknowledge the casual cruelty of all young men in a hurry. "And now she has Lord Abercorn, though why she'd want him I can't imagine—security I suppose, and the title. Most people would say she hasn't done too badly."

"Such people might have thought differently if they'd seen her in tears in my drawing room not so long ago. Do you think Little G knows about Anne? They were together for a long time."

"I imagine she does. It was no great secret—and in our circles everyone knows everything eventually. She can't really be surprised. A rich young man like Morpeth is bound to have a history of some kind; they all do. The real question is whether they persevere in it after they're married."

"Little G wouldn't like that."

"No. And Morpeth has no religion at all, which is a great worry to me. He has nothing to guide his conduct except his own ideas of right and wrong. But—if she wants him, she will have him. And despite all the drawbacks that come with the married state, I do believe Little G will be happier as a wife than otherwise."

"From all I hear, Morpeth is ready now to adopt a more regular life—he certainly gave Anne to understand that was his chief motive in wanting to be married."

"Perhaps they all come to that in the end," replied Georgiana. "A settled home and their family around them."

"Well, I only hope I'll be there in person to see it all unfold. I'm determined to travel, but Farquhar looks grim and forbidding whenever it is mentioned."

"You're still very pale. I quite see why Farquhar doesn't like the journey for you."

"With a few weeks of rest, I shall soon be my old self. Then nothing will stop me from coming to you."

"Don't push yourself too hard to come. There will be other times."

"No, I've made up my mind, and shall be there to witness Little G's triumph, you may depend upon it."

But for all my confidence, I began to doubt whether I'd ever be granted my wish. Farquhar fussed about my health, while Lord B grew increasingly occupied with the eternal business of the trust that the Duke had set up help us repay our immense debts. Doctors on the one hand, lawyers on the other, both were advanced as reasons for not leaving London. When Granville arrived at Chatsworth and began to write asking when I was expected, I had no answer to give and was driven almost beside myself with frustration.

To occupy myself I spent a great deal of time with Lady Elizabeth, who was badly in need of a friend. She was pregnant yet again by Boringdon, and her spirits were low. She thought she perceived a great change in his behavior, that he was nowhere near as fond and attentive as he had been during her previous confinement. She feared he was tiring of her, just as his friend Morpeth had tired of poor Lady Anne.

I really liked Lord Boringdon, who had often been kind to me, and who would never be deliberately cruel; but there's something irredeemably inconsiderate about all the male sex. They simply can't imagine what it's like to be anyone but themselves; and they're certainly incapable of putting themselves into the mind of a poor unhappy woman, pained in mind and body, full of anguish and fear at what is to befall her.

Lady Elizabeth strove not to give in to despair, attempting to be as stoic as she'd said she would be in the face of her lover's cooling ardor. I did my best to brace up her spirits and encourage her. But I felt a cold breath of alarm settle on me too. First Morpeth and now Boringdon—how long before the third young man in their tight group of friends took a long hard look at his older mistress, and decided their affair, too, had run its natural course?

Finally, after so many delays and denials, I found myself on the road to Chatsworth. Farquhar had reluctantly permitted my release. He insisted I was to make the journey slowly, but I didn't care—I was so elated at the prospect of seeing Granville once more that I would have gone north on a donkey if that had been the only way of getting there.

But once I was on my way, I began to grow apprehensive about how I'd appear to him. My various illnesses hadn't been kind to me. After my fall, the doctors had cut off my hair and placed leeches on my head. It was bad enough to have lost the dark tresses of which I had been so proud, but that wasn't the worst of my misfortunes. More alarming was the increase in my size. From being very thin, immediately after my lying-in, I'd grown steadily larger and was now a plump, well-covered sort of person. I'd never been one of those slender women, like Bess Foster, who hold on to their girlish figure long into middle age; but I'd comforted myself with the thought that I was merely voluptuous. Now I wasn't sure what to think.

When I asked Lady Elizabeth her opinion, she insisted loyally that she hadn't noticed, but I wasn't convinced. I'd never considered myself a beauty, but now, when I looked in the mirror, I could scarcely believe the face that looked back at me. Sometimes, when I was in particularly low spirits, I'd stare at my reflection and tell myself over and over how old I looked—old enough to be Granville's mother.

I was not quite forty at this time, so this was hardly credible, but my mind tormented me endlessly with the idea that he'd find me unpleasing. I wanted nothing more in the whole world than that he should look at me with pleasure, and yes, with desire too, when we met—but I'd never felt less confident that that would be the case.

I'd hoped on my arrival to find some means by which Granville and I should be alone for our first meeting; but this proved impossible, and I was obliged to speak my first words to the father of my child surrounded by a great crowd of my sister's guests. He smiled and made a little bow.

"Lady Bessborough."

I'd imagined this moment for months and months. It was this thought that sustained me during some of my darkest hours. Now all I longed for was for him to hold me tight and soothe away the horrors of what I'd endured. But instead I politely returned his smile and held out my hand for him to kiss.

"Lord Granville, I'm very happy to see you."

He led to me to a sofa and there we sat, attempting to look as if we were no more than good friends. I can't remember exactly what we said, except that we agreed to proceed with the utmost caution until we became too familiar and uninteresting to attract anyone's attention. Thus, for a while, we carefully rationed the time we spent with each other, resisting the temptation to seek out places where we could be alone—although on one occasion, I permitted Granville to walk with me in the grounds while I sat upon—"rode" is too energetic a word for my slow and measured progress—a very gentle, well-mannered pony. It was then I told him in detail everything that had passed, how much I'd suffered and how only the knowledge of his loving me had brought me through.

"But I'd do it all again gladly if I knew your feelings were unchanged. Please tell me," I asked, shifting uneasily in the saddle, "if that's still so. If it isn't, I'd much rather know now."

"My feelings are exactly what they were." His gloved hand rested for a moment on mine. "You may depend on it."

"I'm not grown too ugly for you, then?"

He laughed. "You may depend upon that too."

A great wave of happiness swept over me, but I knew I must give no sign of it. A smile was all that I ventured to communicate my pleasure—but that was enough for me.

Once Lord B joined us at Chatsworth, his London legal business now concluded, I applied myself diligently to suppressing any sign of my joy. I fought back my desire to gaze at Granville and forbade him to stand too close to me, to speak to me too often, or to approach me at all when other people were around. Because I found it so hard, I thought I'd succeeded, and even congratulated myself on my self-discipline; but I was deceiving myself. I must have been far more transparent than I ever imagined, for a few days after our ride, Georgiana sought me out to upbraid me.

"I know this is a subject on which we both prefer not to speak," she began, "but I beg you to be more guarded in your behavior to Lord Granville."

"Has someone said something unkind?"

"Our mother has asked me about your friendship, as she put it; she's remarked upon it several times. Bess always looks very knowing when Granville's name and yours are mentioned together. Even the Duke frowns. And I've seen others look askance at the little contrivances you make to be around one another."

"I'm very sorry you've been embarrassed."

"It isn't that—" I saw she was exasperated. She took a deep

breath. "I understand there are questions I don't ask, because I'm afraid to know the truth—and I'm equally aware there are things you don't tell me, because you fear the effect they might have upon me."

I didn't attempt to argue with her; everything she said was absolutely right, and we both knew it.

"But if we're to preserve this state of affairs, I must ask you to be more careful. No more pony rides alone. No more early-morning walks in the park, no more chance meetings in quiet corners."

I'd thought we'd been so careful; but even these rare encounters had been noticed. We had permitted ourselves so little, and still it had been remarked upon.

"We are allowed to play at chess now and then, I hope? Only in company, of course?"

"Chess is quite forbidden, I'm afraid. Or at least, as you and he play the game. You make your moves as if you were dancing, each more knowing and more intimate than the last."

She sighed.

"I hate having to speak in this way—but I can't bear to think of you talked about, especially by the men here—there is a kind of leering glee in their manner when they think they have found some poor woman out because she is guilty of some misplaced tenderness. I have felt it myself and it is horrible. I beg of you, don't give them that same power over you."

When I related all this to Granville, he gave a philosophical shrug.

"Circumstances will soon take care of all that. I find I'm obliged to go back to London as soon as possible—some financial matters demand my immediate attention. I have no choice but to leave."

"Gambling," I thought. "He has debts to settle." I decided it was best not to press him on this; besides, all I could think of was that we were to part.

"But when do you go?" I cried. "We've been together for such a very short time."

"In a few days' time."

"As soon as that?"

"I'll try to come back if can," he murmured. "I really will do my best—though I can't promise it."

I was terribly upset. I'd waited so long to be with Granville. And now I was to be denied the reward I'd dreamed of—the supreme pleasure of a few stolen hours together. I felt frustrated anger sweep over me. Why shouldn't I have what I'd desired for so long? No—I simply refused to be thwarted. I would have what I'd promised myself, regardless of the risks involved in achieving it. I felt the spirit of opposition rise up within me and grasped it boldly before it ebbed away.

"I can't let you go without seeing you alone. Properly alone, just you and me."

"I don't see how that can be done, much as I'd like it."

"Come to my room." There, I'd said it. "If you arrive very late, when no one is about, we ought to be safe."

"Are you sure, Harriet? Is this really what you want?"

"More than anything else in the world. But I must tell you that the state of my health will not allow—that is to say, it's impossible for me to receive you on the most intimate terms. Will it be enough for you to hold me in your arms?"

"More than enough, I promise."

So it was that Granville slid silently into my room in the dead of a cold winter's night. When he held me close to his heart, cradled my head on his shoulder, and told me how well I had done, how proud he was of my courage—I was so overcome with happiness, I thought I might cry. In many ways his loving-kindness touched me more deeply even than his passion, for he was not particularly given to those small acts and words of affection that mean so much more to a woman than to a man. I stored them up in my mind, like some provident squirrel with her nuts, ready to feast upon them when we were apart once more.

For a while, we did no more than sit side by side, my hand in his; but that was pleasure enough. I couldn't remember when I'd felt closer to him. We dared not extend our stolen time together for too long, but as he readied to leave me, I scrabbled beneath my pillow for a little bag I'd hidden before he arrived.

"I have something for you, but to obtain it, you must close your eyes and hold out your left arm."

He looked a little unwilling—I believe he thought there was something demeaning about surprises—but I insisted.

"I promise it won't take away from your manly authority if you do as I ask. I offer it up with all due obedience."

He didn't like it when I teased him on this vexed subject, but he complied. I took from the bag a slender bracelet, made from leather and gilt, linked together by a braid of hair. I slipped it onto his wrist; it was a perfect fit.

"You may look now."

I leaned my head closer to his, to explain it to him.

"The braid is made from Little Harriet's hair, mixed in with some of mine. Those tiny fair flecks you can see—those are hers."

He brought the candlestick toward it and turned his arm this way and that.

"I like it very much."

"I hope you'll like her, too, when I have the pleasure of presenting her to you. Indeed, I think you must, for she is such a very lovable little thing."

"Quite like her mother, then," he said, as he leaned his head toward mine. It was on the tip of my tongue to reply that if I had ever been little, no one could possibly call me so now—but I thought it would spoil the moment, and instead, closed my eyes and held up my mouth for a final kiss.

52

For a few days, I was perfectly happy. I'd obtained what I had most ardently wished for and was satisfied. I still regretted Granville's imminent departure, but nowhere nearly so much as I should have done if we hadn't enjoyed a brief moment together before he went.

I tried not to appear downcast at the prospect of his leaving, but instead sought to throw myself into the society of my sister's guests with more enthusiasm than before. Sometimes after supper there was a little dancing, when a few couples stood up while an unclaimed lady played the piano. No one could have called it a grand affair— but it was a cheerful occupation, as much for those who watched as for those who danced. On the night before Granville was to leave, I came in between dances to find my mother chatting cheerfully with my younger niece. Georgiana's second daughter was properly named Harriet, but was always known as Harryo, to distinguish her from me. She must have been about fifteen then, a little plump like me, with bright, intelligent eyes and a slightly sardonic air that made her seem older than her years.

"Harryo was telling me," began my mother as I sat down, "that she's just received a compliment from one of the gentlemen in the billiards room. Go on, my dear," she continued, looking lovingly at her granddaughter, of whom she was very fond, "tell us both what he said."

"Well, to be sure," Harryo began, "he started by telling me I was the very image of my mother, which anybody would be glad to hear."

"There," said my mother, approvingly.

"But though it began as a compliment," Harryo continued, "I'm not sure it ended as one. He spoiled it all by adding, 'But a very bad copy, though.'"

"You didn't tell me that part!" My mother was aghast, but Harryo merely smiled.

"Oh, how very cruel and unfeeling of him," I cried. "Who was this most ungentlemanly gentleman? Tell me, so I can go and upbraid him on your behalf!"

"I think he was drunk," added Harryo, with an amused laugh. "And anyway, I'm used to it. If you're the plain daughter of the most beautiful woman in England, people have a habit of letting you feel their disappointment when they meet you."

"Don't speak of yourself in that manner; you're certainly not plain," declared my mother angrily. "Georgiana herself was nothing very particular until she was sixteen or so. You'll grow into your looks, my dear, never fear."

"Bess Foster thinks I should take more exercise and eat less," Harryo replied. "I've told her it's hopeless. I'll never be ridden, walked, or starved into beauty. She doesn't believe it, of course."

"I'm sure we need not concern ourselves with *her* opinion," remarked my mother, taking Harryo's hand in hers.

"Shall we take a turn about the room?" I asked Harryo brightly, hoping to divert her thoughts from the insult she'd received. "Or go and seek out something warm to drink?"

"Thank you, Aunt, but I think I'll go and find my sister."

She was politeness itself, but I couldn't help feeling I had been dismissed. I didn't think she liked me much.

"Poor Harryo," said my mother, watching her as she went. "She has a great deal to bear. Her father pays her no attention at all—he much prefers Little G, and of course Hart is the heir, so he comes first in all things. It can't be easy to be the middle child—neither fish nor fowl nor good red herring."

As the second child of three, I'd often, when young, been conscious of my own lack of distinction, convinced I was passed over in favor of my more striking siblings. I glanced searchingly at my mother—was this some acknowledgment of failure on her part? It wasn't, of course; she was quite oblivious of any personal application in her words.

We chatted for a while, until she announced she was too tired to stay any longer and said her good nights. I sat alone, musing, until the dancers returned, clamoring for music and forming up into sets once more. They had just begun to whirl about the floor when Granville slid into the seat beside me.

"Don't tell me to go away. I shan't insist upon your standing up with me—and it is perfectly proper for us to have some casual conversation as we watch the dance."

I smiled a cool smile for the consumption of anyone who might have their eyes upon us and turned back to watch the couples. In their midst, Lord Morpeth swung Little G around with every appearance of enjoyment; and she looked into his eyes with such delight that there could be little doubt of their engagement being very speedily announced.

"You might have told me about Morpeth's designs on Little G," I remarked, as I watched them gallop about. "I hadn't the first idea of it until my sister mentioned it."

"I didn't know his intentions myself until very recently. And nothing could be said until he'd settled matters with Lady Anne."

"You make it sound as if there was a discussion, whereas the way I heard it, it was more in the manner of a dismissal."

He inclined his head and said nothing.

"Does he love her, do you think?" I looked thoughtfully at Little G, who suddenly seemed to me very young and very vulnerable. "She is a gentle, unworldly girl, and I'd be sorry to see her hurt."

"That's not a question I could ask him. But I think he sincerely wants to be married, and her good qualities are the very ones he looks for in a wife."

All this talk of wives and husbands unnerved me, and I felt dread settle in the pit of my stomach. If I'd been wise, I'd have left off there, but when was I ever wise?

"I suppose he thinks he's old enough now to become a husband. The same age as you, to the very year. Do you feel it too, this desire to settle down?"

Granville stared into the dancers, as if looking for an answer that wouldn't result in my breaking down in tears before everyone.

"My mother feels it on my behalf. She often tells me I should marry."

I swallowed hard. "It's a natural enough wish. One cannot blame her for it."

"No, I suppose not. Though I don't encourage her to act upon it, much as I know she longs to. She's constantly describing to me perfect young women of her acquaintance she thinks would suit me."

I took a deep breath and fixed my eyes on the floor so that neither he nor anyone else should see the effort it cost to say what I knew I must.

"You should understand that if you were to find some young woman you felt you could like—someone you could imagine as your wife—I would never oppose it."

"I haven't met such a person, so the question doesn't arise."

"I could never stand in the way of whatever might be for your happiness." I felt myself falter, and tears sprang into my eyes. "Even though the thought of it is terrible to me."

"Let us not think of it, then," he said lightly. "No one will push a wife upon me until I'm ready. And I'm not ready yet."

I knew his words were meant to reassure me, and to some degree I suppose they did. So it was not to happen immediately—not next week, not next month, maybe not the month after that, perhaps not even next year. But that chilling little word "yet"—with its clear implication that one day the dreaded moment would arrive—pierced me to the heart. What should I do, what would I say, how should I go on when he came to me with the news that must be fatal to my happiness? I knew I must think of something else before I exposed myself before all my sister's guests. So I fixed my expression into one of brittle cheerfulness, and chatted away to him as if we'd been talking of nothing more serious than whether it'd be dry enough tomorrow for the gentlemen to go out with the guns.

Alone in my bed that night, I told myself that for the sake of my own sanity, I could not, must not brood on the implications of that "yet." If I allowed it into my head, it would undo me. It would be only too easy to dwell in terror upon the moment when Granville would leave me—to rehearse in my mind how I should feel when he found some likely woman to be the wife to him I could never be—how I should be obliged to watch as their family grew, one by one by one, the sun shining on them all, while Little H and I stood in the shadows, ignored. No. That was enough. No more. It was impossible to allow these thoughts to multiply in my mind. What use would I be to Little H if I allowed myself to sink under the weight of my despair?

For her sake alone, I must exert control over my emotions—I couldn't permit myself to be consumed by fear of a future that must be uncertain, but instead must discipline myself into living in the present, trying not to think too far ahead and accepting with gratitude whatever small pleasures and everyday satisfactions the here and now delivered me. Put like that, it does not sound like much of a philosophy. But it was all I had to keep me from despair. I vowed to myself that once Granville was gone, I'd spend the rest of my time at Chatsworth doing all I could to cultivate this attitude of mind, while allowing my poor exhausted body to recuperate. I planned to live as quietly as possible, seeking no one's attention, in the hope that I might be left alone to train my unruly feelings into calm resignation as best I could. So I intended, but it didn't turn out like that at all.

53

*F*or all my good resolutions, I was devastated when Granville finally left. I took to my bed for two whole days to prevent anyone seeing my haggard, tearstained face. Shortly afterward, Lord B announced that he too was compelled to go back to London, to attend the House of Lords. We'd seen very little of each other during his stay—Georgiana always gave us separate rooms, and during the day he'd usually been occupied; whether he'd deliberately kept his distance from me, or simply preferred tramping through the mud with a gun, I couldn't tell—but once he was gone, I was quickly made to feel his absence. I became aware that with the departure of both my lover and my husband, I'd lost both my protectors— and without them, I was exposed, even in my sister's house, to the unwelcome attentions of men who regarded me as what is vulgarly described as fair game. I suppose they reasoned, at least those who had heard of my connection to Granville, that as I'd already strayed from the path of fidelity with one man, it wouldn't be too hard to persuade me to do so again.

For most of them, this amounted to little more than heavy-handed flirting. I'd been dealing with such clumsy overtures for over two decades and had no trouble in dispatching them now. I was far more put out by the behavior of Mr. Hare, one of the Duke's best friends. He was a dry, sardonic character, who regarded the world and everything in it with a jaundiced bitterness he liked to pass off as humor.

Now that I was alone, I found myself the principal target of his incessant teasing, all of which revolved around my passion for Granville. I supposed he'd heard of it via gossip, innuendo, and supposition; it was too disturbing for me to imagine that the Duke himself might have spoken to him about it. When I asked him directly why he was so certain of what he thought he knew, he laughed out loud, saying it was the worst-kept secret in the world: my eyes lit up so brightly at the very mention of Granville's name that there could be no mistaking the truth of my feelings.

However he'd discovered it, he was clearly delighted with his knowledge, and never passed up an opportunity to taunt me. When I looked miserable, he told me it was my duty to remain beautiful for my lover: Didn't I know nothing aged a woman so much as sadness? When I ventured a smile, he berated me sternly, remarking that I could not be very much in love if I could be so gleeful in Granville's absence. On and on it went, a never-ending stream of little pokes and gibes. When this joke palled, he took to handing me things to read— poems, extracts from books, translations from the Italian—all of which, when I examined them, contained references to adulterous love. He watched me beadily, studying my expression as I realized what they contained, desperate, I think, to provoke some reaction from me, which I always refused to gratify.

It excited him, I believe, to tiptoe up to the boundaries of genuine accusation and hover there, like some angry buzzing insect, to see what I would do or say; but I was never truly afraid of him. He was a strange man, with a heartless streak, but I never thought he meant me any real harm. We'd known each other for twenty years, and I sensed he hid a genuine liking for me beneath his goading ways. For all his provocations, I knew he would never venture beyond a certain point. He posed no real danger to me. That came from another quarter entirely.

⊸∽∘∽⊸

J hadn't been pleased when my sister told me Lord John Townshend was to be among the guests at Chatsworth. Indeed, if I hadn't had the promise of Granville to lure me there, Townshend's presence alone would have been enough to make me refuse her invitation. Some fifteen years before, when I was very young and very unhappy, I'd most unfortunately allowed myself to be persuaded into a brief dalliance with him. It was the first time I'd strayed from the path of absolute fidelity; really, when I think of it now, it was as much an act of desperation as of any desire on my part. It didn't last long, and I soon regretted it extremely; but I've paid a heavy price for my foolishness ever since. He had married one of my many cousins, which meant I was sometimes obliged to be in his company; and whenever that happened, he seized every possible opportunity to abuse and harangue me.

He was a volatile man, with a capricious temper and a most unforgiving nature. He'd convinced himself, over the years, that he still loved me, and he blamed me most bitterly for, as he saw it, heartlessly rejecting his affections. This made him in turn either abject or angry in his conduct toward me. Sometimes he sought to throw himself at my feet, declaring there was nothing he wouldn't do to win me back; on other occasions, he was furiously angry at what he called my betrayal, threatening me with every kind of humiliation if I would not accept his advances.

I wasn't the only woman to suffer from his cruelties. He treated his poor wife very harshly, never attempting to disguise his affairs—for his alleged grand passion for me never interfered with his frenzied

pursuit of other women—and indeed, the hapless targets of his interest were just as unfortunate in their own way, for once he'd fixed his
eye upon them, there was nothing they could do to shake him off,
and he'd stop at nothing until he had worn down their resistance,
either by cajolery or menace.

There was another side to him, of course. No man could have
continued long in polite society if his behavior had been only what I
have just described; and when not in the grip of one of his manias—
for I honestly believe that is what they were—Lord John was quite
another being, polished, cultured, with a sharp wit that entertained anyone who heard it. But his moods were mercurial—he
was happy and laughing one moment, beside himself with fury the
next. He could turn on a sixpence into the darkest version of himself,
and there was no predicting what he might do or say. There were
times when I truly thought him quite mad.

Was it any wonder I regarded him warily? He knew about my
affair with Granville, and I saw very quickly that this had driven his
obsession with me to even greater heights. He frightened me; but I
told myself I must stay calm and not provoke him. For a while, this
seemed to answer well enough. Lord John's thoughts were concentrated upon another of my sister's guests, an unfortunate Mrs. Spencer, and I largely escaped his attention. But that all changed when
Granville and then Lord B left Chatsworth, and I was left exposed
to the full rigor of his malice.

The attacks upon me began almost at once. He followed me about,
muttering darkly about my many cruelties to him. He'd loved me, he
declared, since I was fourteen, but I'd treated him with nothing but
scorn. Sometimes he described himself as my slave; on other occasions, his fury with me was so palpable that I could hardly credit
it. I tried to avoid him; but he was always watching for me, placing
himself about me, fixing me with the same cold and angry glare. One
evening, as I took my leave from the party, I saw with horror that

Lord John was following me. When we arrived at my bedroom door, I was at a loss to know what to do. Then he began to harangue me.

"I must speak to you, Harriet. All I ask is the chance to make you understand how I feel."

I said nothing, hoping he'd go away; but instead, he pushed his way into my room, where he was soon pacing about, clenching and unclenching his fists.

"I've loved you since the first time I saw you, but you've always scorned and rejected me. What have I done to deserve such treatment?"

I did not reply, not wishing to provoke him into a greater fury.

"Instead you've given yourself to a man who'll never care for you as I do, whose only possible attraction must be his looks."

Still I said nothing.

"Have you really nothing to say to me? After I've loved you so long and so faithfully?"

"I must take your protestations of fidelity with a pinch of salt, given the number of ladies with whom you've indulged yourself over the years."

This enraged him to such an extent that he grew violent—banging his head against the wall, swearing he loved me. I was so distressed that I ran immediately into Sally's room—which, thank God, was next to mine—hurriedly locked the door, and waited there till I heard him go away, complaining and cursing as he went.

After this, I did everything in my power to avoid him when he was in such a state—but he persecuted me with the fanatical absorption of a lunatic. I was reluctant to complain to Georgiana about his behavior, as it would have concentrated her mind once more on the tender subject of my relations with Granville, but as Lord John's conduct grew worse and worse, I'd almost decided to do so when I was approached by Mrs. Spencer.

"I can't say how sorry I am to see you harassed in this way," she began. "I know better than anyone how intolerable it is—and how badly you, like me, would welcome seeing Lord John brought to heel. But you should think very seriously before taking any step that might antagonize him."

She saw that I seemed unconvinced and went on.

"Unless there are no secrets in your life you wouldn't dread to have revealed, I'd urge you not to provoke him. When I refused him, he tried to put all manner of strange ideas into my husband's head, and it was only because I could prove them untrue that I escaped unscathed. Unless you can do the same, it's far better to conciliate him if you can."

She touched my arm with a resigned sigh.

"It's terrible we should be obliged to humor a liar and a bully like John Townshend, but the alternative is far worse."

Her words confirmed my worst fears. If I begged Georgiana's protection, Lord John would retaliate by running straight to Lord B to tell him everything he knew about Granville and me, and a little more besides. I knew I was vulnerable and regretfully abandoned any further thoughts of speaking to my sister.

Instead, I swallowed my fears and did all I could to conciliate my persecutor. For a time, this seemed to work. He moved from aggression to extreme flattery, praising me with as much warmth as he had previously abused me. I knew his character well enough by now to understand that these apparently very different emotions were two sides of the same coin, evidence of an extremity of feeling toward me that was quite irrational and increasingly beyond his control. The pains he took to please me were no more to be trusted than the insults he had so enjoyed hurling at me before.

But if I had to choose between violent abuse and ludicrous compliments, I knew which I'd prefer; and there were occasions, I confess, when, despite all I knew of him, Lord John's deranged praise was not entirely unwelcome. At a time when I was so uncertain of my looks, so unsure of my continued powers of attraction, his insistent flattery encouraged me to believe there must be something left in me to admire—that I hadn't yet lost everything necessary to please a man. At a moment when I'd been brought to feel so painfully the hard reality of my age, with all the dreadful consequences attendant on that fact—the truth was, that even when it came from such a quarter as Lord John, I took some tiny degree of comfort from his accolades.

I must add, however, that these small gratifications were known only to myself. I never allowed the slightest hint that they were in any way welcome to appear in any of my words, acts, or expressions. On the contrary—beyond the politeness necessary to all social encounters, and the soothing manner I cultivated to try to keep him calm—I never gave Lord John the slightest encouragement to persist in his advances. Gradually, I think, it dawned upon him that he had nothing to expect from me; and immediately, his mood turned darker and his angry temper returned. I took the greatest care never to be alone with him. But one evening, when I least expected it, all my precautions failed me.

I'd gone upstairs early, as I felt unwell and had decided to retreat to my bed. Sally helped me undress before rushing off to find her supper, assuring me she'd be back in half an hour. I was sitting quite comfortably before the fire, clad only in my dressing gown, when I heard the door open. I thought it was she, and looked up with a smile, only to find Lord John standing mute before me. I jumped up in horror at the sight of him, and, in as calm a voice as possible, I asked him to leave. When he didn't reply, I reached for the bell, which sat on a nearby table. He took it from me and silently closed the door. I felt fear begin to rise within me but was determined not to show it.

"You must leave this instant, Lord John. If you don't, I shan't hesitate to cry out. I'm not afraid to make a fuss."

"It would be to no purpose, as there's no one to hear you."

The extreme calmness of his manner, so unnatural to him, terrified me.

"You have nothing to fear, Harriet. All I ask is a fair hearing. The chance to tell you what I feel. Surely, you'll allow me that?"

I nodded blankly—what else could I do?—and he began again upon the same old story, the depth of his love for me and my inexplicable preference for Granville.

"You receive him in your bed, but you won't have me. I've loved you for years, truly and faithfully, but for all that, he's the one preferred to me."

He began to stalk angrily about the room. I sat as still as possible, desperate not to provoke him.

"My love will last forever. I'll still want you when you're sixty—do you think he can say the same?"

I clasped my hands together to keep them from shaking. I was very frightened now.

He sat down on the arm of my chair.

"All I ask is to kiss your cheek—that will be enough for me."

He leaned toward me, and instinctively I turned away. He must have seen the horror on my face, for he threw himself instantly upon the floor and began beating his head against the table.

"You hate me!" he shouted, quite unhinged now. "I see it in your eyes! You'll never love me. There's nothing left for me but death. I should kill myself, and then perhaps you'll be sorry."

I was so agitated, I tried to stand up—he pushed me back, and I honestly believe he intended to take from me by force that which I wouldn't allow him by choice—but I was determined he shouldn't do so without a struggle.

To my surprise, from somewhere deep inside me, I found a strength I didn't know I possessed—and I grappled and beat at him with all my might. This extraordinary fury was, I am convinced, the product of all the anger and hate stored up within me—hate for all the men who had bullied and betrayed and threatened me—a burning, boiling resentment I could no longer suppress—but which exploded now, rising up like steam from a boiling kettle—and would not be denied—until I was a stranger to myself, a raging angry being whose only desire was to crush this man's body, to do it harm before it could commit some outrage upon me, without my permission, without my say, just because it thought itself entitled to do so.

I can't say exactly what happened next—it may have lasted only a minute, though it felt like an hour—but suddenly, as quickly as it had begun, everything was over—he crumpled up—lay crouched on the floor like a child—and was crying hysterically, begging for forgiveness and swearing he'd never do it again. I seized my chance, picked myself up, and ran as fast as I could into Sally's adjoining room, where I locked myself in, wedged a chair under the door handle, and sat on the floor, my heart racing.

I was still there when Sally arrived a few minutes later. Once I was sure it was she, I opened the door and fell sobbing into her arms. She cried out in horror, and I wasn't surprised, for I looked very beaten about—the wounds made by the leeches that had been applied to my head had opened up, and blood had coursed into my eyes. It was some minutes before I could convince her I'd suffered no serious injury.

She guessed immediately what had happened.

"The dirty, disgusting beast. Where is he now?"

"I think he's still next door. I heard him groaning a little while ago."

She picked up the poker from the grate and went to see for herself. She returned with an expression of even greater contempt fixed upon her face.

"Yes, he's there. Lying on the floor, tears rolling down his face, saying how sorry he is. Nasty, nasty beast. I gave him something to remember me by before I left him."

"What do you mean? Did you do him some harm?"

"Not as much as I'd have liked. I gave him a jab in the ribs with my foot—a little more than a tap, a little less than a kick. He'll feel it tomorrow, that's for sure. I couldn't resist it."

I felt a laugh rise within me, but stifled it, afraid it would turn into hysteria.

"We must get rid of him. It would be terrible for him to be found in my room; how would I ever explain it?"

Sally went into my room once more, but it appeared he wouldn't go until I agreed to forgive him. I resisted this most strenuously, for forgiveness was the last thing he deserved from me, but when it became clear he would remain where he was unless I agreed, I was obliged to consent. I was persuaded to extend my hand to him through Sally's barely open door while she stood next to me with the poker, though I would on no account look at him or speak a single word.

When it was done, I heard him shuffle off down the corridor, to offer who knows what explanation to his long-suffering wife. Sally brought hot water and bathed my poor bleeding head, then put me at once into a warm bed. I was so wrung out with the drama of it all that I fell asleep almost immediately. It was not until morning that I felt the cost of what I had endured—I was bruised all over and stiff with unfamiliar exertion. I didn't appear for breakfast and slept and rested for the remainder of the day, but stirred myself that evening to go down to dinner. When I took my chair, I saw him, seated with his wife, at the far end of the table. She waved at me cheerfully.

"Don't be shocked by poor Jack's face. He took a fall on the stairs last night—hit himself on the banister—and it has all but destroyed his manly beauty. Show her, Jack; she'll never believe it."

With an ill grace, he lifted his head to display a huge black eye.

"How very unfortunate." I observed mildly. "You evidently met your match with that banister. I should take great pains to avoid it in future. It clearly means you no good."

He said nothing at all but lowered his face again, unwilling to meet my unflinching stare.

Across the table, Mrs. Spencer arrived, just in time to see Jack's great black bruise. She turned toward me, her gaze a mute inquiry. I returned her look, eventually allowing myself the faintest hint of an acknowledging smile. It was enough. We both understood there'd been a struggle, and I had emerged victorious. She raised a glass of wine to me, and I raised mine back. After all I'd suffered in the last few years, triumph was an unfamiliar emotion. But there was no mistaking its pulse within me. Usually, I should have spoiled the moment by worrying about the future, agonizing about what came next. But this time I confined my thoughts firmly to the here and now, and as I caught another glimpse of Lord John's black eye, I felt very good indeed.

54

*I*n accordance with the wishes of our trustees, Lord B and I spent most of the winter up in Derbyshire, with the intention of living quietly and saving money. We settled ourselves in Hardwick Hall, not always in the greatest comfort. It was very remote, with an ancient and solitary air that often made us feel as if we were exiled from our old life as much in time as by distance; but even there, the events of the outside world pressed upon us. In February of 1801, Mr. Pitt resigned, having been unable to persuade the King to agree to measures relieving Catholics from some of the many disabilities under which they still labored. His departure was immediate and of the greatest consequence. He'd been Prime Minister for seventeen years, and his abrupt renunciation of his post instantly turned the political world upside down.

There was no chance, sadly, of my own political friends coming into office; instead, Mr. Pitt was replaced by Mr. Addington, another Tory, and in every possible way a less impressive figure than his predecessor. In my eyes, this was a disaster for us all, as public affairs were bound to suffer by the change; but for Granville, it was a personal setback of the greatest magnitude. He had long been regarded as a protégé of Mr. Pitt, and knowing he could expect no preferment from the new administration, unhesitatingly followed his fallen patron into the political wilderness. While I admired his loyalty, I saw immediately that the repercussions of his fidelity went far beyond the political. Now that he was no longer obliged to wait upon Mr. Pitt and advance his interest there, he found himself with nothing much to do all day—and what else was there to fill these empty hours but gambling? He wasted not a minute before rushing to the card tables, where he proceeded to gamble, night and day, to the very brink of ruin.

His losses were enormous—thousands and thousands of pounds. I knew only too well what debts of this immensity had done to me, to Lord B, to Georgiana—all of us had suffered terribly from the consequences of our recklessness. But Granville was in a far worse position than any of us, for he had no extensive properties to mortgage, no great name upon which to raise loans, no art collection to sell. He was a second son with no obvious prospects, and his situation was precarious in the extreme.

When in the spring I finally returned to London, I hoped to be of some practical use to him. If I couldn't persuade him to abandon the tables—and nothing I said or did gave me the slightest hope of that—perhaps I might at least keep him from absolute ruin. For the rest of that unhappy year, I took upon myself the miserable task of trying to raise loans on his behalf, discreetly writing to anyone I supposed might be persuaded to extend Granville some credit. I had trodden this sorry road on my own behalf before, so I understood exactly what was required of me. At the same time, I acted as his accountant, keeping a running total of exactly what he owed, together with a note of when payments on what he'd borrowed were due—"remember, there is £50 to be found by the 2nd"; "Coutts must receive so much on such a day," etc. I knew from my own difficulties how to juggle and feint in this way—it was a dismal kind of knowledge, of which I was not at all proud, but for his sake, I was glad to make use of it.

The truth is, however, that I actually took pleasure in being of service to him. It heartened me to think that in helping him as I did, I was important to him, an indispensable part of his life. And it was a source of great joy to me that after so many difficulties and long delays, I was finally able to introduce Granville to his baby daughter. Little H was now over a year old, a lively, loving little creature, full of smiles and laughter. I had missed her terribly while I was up in Derbyshire and had her with me at Cavendish Square as often as I dared. She and her small household were established not far away, so that I was always in reach if needed.

I arranged for Granville to come on a day when the house was empty except for Sally and me. When I heard the knock on the door, followed by his familiar step climbing the stairs, I was so nervous that when he entered the room, I could find at first no sensible words to say.

He strode briskly across the small room and smiled down on Little H from his great height.

"Good morning to you, young Harriet."

Little H looked at this tall figure, turned her head away, and began to wail, which she continued to do for what seemed like an hour. Bemused, Granville sat down in a chair and watched as I walked about with her, trying to soothe her.

"I suppose they do this quite often?"

"She doesn't know you; that's why she's upset."

Eventually, I quieted her and sat her on my lap, from where she regarded him with a wary stare.

"I am so happy she has your blue eyes, not brown like mine."

Now that she was quiet, he came to sit beside me. He held out his finger, which she stubbornly refused to grasp.

"She looks very well."

"My feelings for her are so strong that sometimes I can't quite believe them." I gazed at my Little H with pride, before turning to him. "What about you? Can you love her, do you think?"

He smiled. "How could I not? Considering she is yours?"

I could hardly believe it—the three of us on the sofa, Granville, me, and our child. I had never imagined such happiness was possible. I didn't want to speak: that would have ruined the communion I felt between us. All I wanted was to live in this moment for as long as I could, and then save it forever in my memory.

55

*W*hen Granville asked me very particularly if I could find some quiet place where we could talk without disturbance, I could think of nowhere except Little H's home. So it was there, in the very room where I had recently been so happy, that the blow I'd feared for so long finally fell.

I'd taken the trouble to ensure that everyone was out for the afternoon when he arrived, which was just as well, for once he began upon what he had come to say, I could not keep my composure. I saw from the first that he was uneasy, and when he gestured for me to sit down, without even a kiss to my cheek, I became extremely apprehensive.

"I'm not sure how to speak to you on this subject," he began, "and have asked myself many times in the last few days if it's even necessary for me to do so. But ever since we were first together, you've always urged upon me the importance of our being honest with each other in all things. I've tried to obey your wishes in that respect— and intend to do so now, even though I know what I have to say will be painful to us both."

My mouth was dry; my hands began to tremble, and I sat upon them to still them.

"A while ago at Chatsworth, you asked me whether I wished to marry. I replied truthfully then that I had no plans to do so; but if you were to ask the same question now, my answer would be different."

He took a deep breath, as if to steady himself.

"I shall be thirty quite soon. Everywhere I look, I see men my age settling down. Morpeth will be a father next year."

"You're already a father yourself—to the loveliest child in the world!"

This was unfair, and I knew it; but the pain of thinking Little H ignored tormented me terribly.

"I know, and I am proud to be so. But it isn't the same, Harriet. You know it can never be the same."

I closed my eyes tightly and would have stopped my ears if I could. I wasn't sure I could bear to hear what I knew was coming.

"I have no real home, nowhere that's properly mine. There are times when I can't see you, when you aren't free to come to me. It's a lonely existence when I compare it to what others have. I didn't mind it when I was younger, but I feel it now. I can't go on as I am."

"No," I answered, dully. "You ought to have a regular, established life. With a wife you can own to the world and children everyone can acknowledge."

I took a shuddering, painful breath. "You should have all these things—and I can't give you them. I wanted to be all in all to you— but I know—I believe I always knew—that's impossible."

I began to cry then, with horrible halting sobs. He sat down beside me and took me in his arms.

"Please don't," he said. "I can't bear to see you like this. I am truly sorry, but what would you have me do? I can't live as I do forever."

"I know—and I'll never oppose what you want so badly. I've often told you nobody ever loved a man as passionately as I love you. Now you'll see the proof of it—I'll give you up to another—and I'll do so without complaint, without resentment, if it's for your happiness. But oh, my G, I can't do it without despair—without the bitterest regrets. You can't expect that of me."

He had no answer for this—indeed, what could he have said? Instead, we sat silently for a while until I found the courage to ask the question I dreaded.

"Have you already some lady in mind?"

"No, not yet. I've spoken now to give you time to prepare your mind for when that moment may arrive." He ran his hands through his hair, and I saw that he too was distressed. "This is to let you know my general intention—not to give you notice of some imminent event."

"So I may count myself as yours for a little longer?" I managed a wan smile.

"Part of me will always be yours." He reached down to kiss me— but I would not allow it. If I was to learn to live without him, I must begin to refuse what I most desired, and now was as good a time as any.

I didn't allow him to stay much longer. All I wished to do was to howl and cry with the pain I felt, and I didn't want him to see me in such a terrible abandoned state. The only person allowed near me was Sally—and it was into her sympathetic arms that I flung myself, weeping on her shoulder until I could cry no more. She settled me in bed, giving out that I was ill and not to be disturbed. I remained closeted in my room for two days, trying to come to terms with Granville's announcement, fighting against the lurching sensation of horror that overwhelmed me whenever I rehearsed his words in my mind.

I remember very little of anything I did that damp and gloomy autumn. I sleepwalked through the whole Season, until it was time to go north once more to join my sister's party at Chatsworth. I began to wake up a little once I was there. It comforted me to be among other people, to be part of a lively, informed, and witty gathering, with my sister presiding effortlessly and brilliantly over all. I am at heart a social being; and surrounded by warmth and stimulation, I felt myself begin to thaw. By the time Granville arrived, I was almost human once more.

That, such as it is, can be the only excuse for what happened next. While the smallest spark of vitality remained within me, it was impossible that I should not be drawn toward Granville with a desire I simply could not resist. I had every possible reason for caution—not least that I'd noticed every time his name was mentioned, Lord B made a little grimace of displeasure, which ought to have put me on my guard. But he said nothing directly to me, and the reward of time alone with Granville was too potent a temptation for me to resist. With a terrible inevitability, I found myself in bed with him once more. There—I say that as though it was the pure product of chance, as if neither he nor I had any part in its coming about—as if he did not make his way to my room, down those long, freezing corridors in the dead of night—or—as if I had not, on one rare occasion, headed to him in the same way, remembering when I returned, before the maids rose to light the fires and black the grates, to muddle up my sheets and blankets, so no one should see I hadn't slept there.

Each time it happened, I swore it shouldn't do so again—but I couldn't refuse him—not when I couldn't say how long I should be entitled to hold him and kiss him as I did—for who knew when the ghost wife who hovered behind my every waking thought might take on the form and name of a real, living woman and exile me from these pleasures forever?

After Granville took his leave, my spirits failed me once more. We were to stay on at Chatsworth for a least a month when I should have no chance of seeing him. I felt our separation with a new and bitter poignancy. If enduring a few weeks without him cut me so deeply, however should I survive when we said goodbye forever? The day after he left, a great fall of snow confined us all to the house; had it arrived a few hours earlier, he should have been forced to remain, and I would have enjoyed a week more of his company. I angrily resented the tardiness of that snowfall, which had denied me the only thing I really wanted—more time in Granville's arms. But I knew it could not be so—not now, and not ever—and when I looked through the great windows at the bleak frozen vistas beyond, what I saw reflected the temperature of my heart—no warmth, no life, no comfort, nothing but cold, uncaring indifference as far as the eye could see.

56

When the snow finally thawed, we made our way back to London. It was there, some three or four weeks later, that I realized I was once again pregnant with Granville's child. This discovery weighed heavily upon me. Assuming I carried the little creature to term, it would be my sixth confinement.

I was in a very sober frame of mind when I told Granville my news. With Little H, from the moment I knew my situation, despite all my fears, I'd nevertheless been conscious of a wild elation at the prospect of bearing Granville's child. This time it was different. The knowledge that it was only a matter of time before someone took my place in its father's heart severely depressed my spirits. I wondered whether I should have the strength, in either body or mind, to get through all that was to come. Granville was concerned by my despair, but I was too cast down to respond to his attempts at sympathy.

"I hate to see you so low, Harriet. I know this is a great hardship for you. Tell me what I may do, that might put you in a better state of mind."

Was there ever so stupid a question? I wanted to scream my

answer at him: "Why, give up this idea of marriage, devote the rest of your life to me, to Little H, and to this little unborn babe, if we both survive. That and that alone will wipe out all my fears and put a little courage into me!" But of course, I said none of this.

"It can't be a good thing, either for you or for the child, to remain as wretchedly unhappy as you are now," he continued, holding my hand. "For the baby's sake, if not for your own, can you not attempt to rally a little?"

I was so bitter and so angry that I almost laughed out loud.

"Believe me, what you see now is nothing compared to what I really feel, for I've done everything in my power to conceal the true extent of my misery from you. If you could see me at night or when I'm alone, you wouldn't believe how deep my sorrow goes."

He took my hand to his lips and kissed it—but I was not to be consoled.

"And besides all that—yes, I admit I'm very much afraid. I tell myself I can do it—that I've managed it once, why shouldn't I do so again?—and I hope and pray to be proved right. But oh, my G—to bear all this in the knowledge that you'll soon be lost to me—is it any wonder I shrink from what the future holds?"

He sighed. I believe he understood my fears and felt for me, as far as any man could; but I saw only too clearly that the words I longed to hear—"Very well, I shall not do it. I'll live alone and solitary all my life and think of no one but you"—weren't to be uttered, not now, not ever.

I sensed, too, that as he had no answer to my misery, he would, like all men, soon begin to be bored by the too frequent encountering of it—and it would be but a short step from boredom to frustration, and finally to resentment—that thus I might hurry on the very event I feared. He might conclude that if he were to marry, it would be best to do it soon and put a swift end to a situation that was insupportable to us both.

This thought sobered me. I understood I must reach for a more conciliatory tone if his pity was not to turn sour.

"I'm sorry to be so sad, and I'll do what I can to combat it. But dearest G, you must see that my sadness is a measure of my love for you. I could be cheerful enough if I loved you less. And however fearful I may be for what is to come, I can never truly regret that I've been yours. If I'm spared, if the child survives—I'll always treasure it, come what may, because it ties me closer to you."

Tears welled into my eyes, for every syllable of what I said was true.

Although I felt so fragile in spirits, I couldn't afford to be careless in concealing my state from the world. So I draped myself in shawls and cloaks and bound my figure to appear less huge. I told Lord B I was suffering from a return of the sickness that had plagued me before, which he seemed to accept.

I'd decided not to put myself under Farquhar's care on this occasion. I'd seen him a few times since Little H's birth, and he'd made rather too many veiled allusions to her handsome father. I should always be grateful to him for everything he'd done for me, but I was afraid that attending me for a third time might only increase a familiarity that already made me uneasy. One quiet afternoon, I was musing on what other doctor I might call upon, when to my surprise, Lady Melbourne was announced at the door. It was all I could do to arrange my various coverings about me before she came into the drawing room. It was a while since we'd seen each other, but I could tell immediately she was not remotely fooled by my disguise.

"Well," she said, unblinking. "It seems you are with child."

I went cold with fright, but forced myself to laugh, brushing away the accusation with all the breezy confidence I could muster.

"Nothing of the kind, I assure you."

"Well, if you aren't pregnant, your health must be very bad to look as swelled up as you do."

"It's true I've been somewhat indisposed, but the worst is over now, except that, yes, I've become extremely large."

"Very large indeed," she replied, looking me up and down. "And yet there's nothing in your face that suggests illness. No one looks as well as you do with a shape such as this—unless they're with child."

Before I could say anything, the servant came in with the tea, with my daughter Caro following on behind, which put an end to any more questions. Lady Melbourne stared at me pointedly throughout her visit and stayed only the shortest time before taking her leave with a great air of affront.

"Whatever's the matter with her?" demanded Caro. "She looks for all the world as though she's been shortchanged by her cheesemonger. Something's offended her, that's for sure."

"I really can't say," I replied, attempting to suggest I neither knew nor cared what had produced Lady Melbourne's indignation. "She's very subject to moods."

"Someone has put her nose out of joint. How she produced a model of perfection like William I've no idea. He is all consideration and kindness. Whereas his mother—" and here she conjured up an expression so very like that of Lady Melbourne's outraged sense of entitlement that I couldn't help but smile.

Caro, who was then around seventeen years old, had lately enjoyed a weekend of flirtation with William Lamb, Lady Melbourne's son, while on a visit to their country house at Brocket. I disliked extremely the excited passion this brief encounter had produced in my daughter but knew that I'd only encourage it if I expressed disapproval, so I made no comment.

"Caro, my head is hurting, so I'm going to close my eyes for a while. Will you let down the blinds as you go?"

Once I was alone, I lay quite still in the darkened room, every so often feeling a kick from the child within me. What should I do? I knew Lady Melbourne expected me to share the fact of my pregnancy with her; and indeed, in many ways, it would have been the sensible thing to do. In this respect at least, she was utterly loyal. Once she was "in the know," as the saying goes, I had no doubt she'd work tirelessly on my behalf to prevent anyone else discovering it and would faithfully and directly contradict any rumors that might arise.

Nothing gratified her more than the act of confession, the knowledge that she alone had been trusted with your deepest secrets. Then she would do anything to help you. But there was a price to be paid for her allegiance—once she had your story safely in her possession, you'd be forever in her debt, owned by her in a way you couldn't quite describe, but of which you were always conscious. My sister confided in her once, many years ago, and, even now, she feels the weight of her admission hanging between them, never to be erased.

After much deliberation, I decided to say nothing. I knew that snubbing her in this way was a risk. Though she would have been a demanding confidante, that was perhaps preferable to turning her into a piqued and resentful enemy. Perhaps I'd been too hasty in brushing her off as I did. It made me wonder, too, whether I'd been right not to ask Farquhar to attend me, preferring instead to put myself in the hands of Mr. Maldon, who had been of such service to me before. As the day of my confinement approached, I grew increasingly aware that I had no steady strong-minded supporter on whom I could rely, and I began to feel my isolation and helplessness closing in upon me.

I felt the first pains come upon me while we were still in London, and I hoped I might be delivered there; but at the very last moment, Lord B decided he wished to go down to Roehampton and wouldn't be denied. I sent him on ahead, with the excuse that I'd follow as soon as I'd completed a course of medicine on which I'd just embarked. I was only postponing the inevitable, however; I knew I'd have no choice but to make the journey eventually, even as the pains increased with threatening regularity.

Even now, the recollection of what followed fills me with horror. During my labor, I was compelled to get into a carriage and travel for hours and hours, all the while suffering the most dreadful pains. On arrival, Sally announced to Lord B that my illness had taken a turn for the worse while I was traveling, that I must be put to bed immediately and given laudanum to calm me. He asked no questions and left to dine with friends. She also warned the servants to keep away from my room, as I was on no account to be disturbed; and I prepared myself, as far as was in my power, for what was to come. I approached the prospect with much less courage than I had when confined with my Little H.

My spirits were so low and my body still so weak from the horrors of my last delivery that I feared I might be incapable of doing what was required of me. I seriously thought I would die. While I was still able to write, I sent Granville a most desperate letter, begging that if I didn't survive, he would never forsake Little H and the babe yet unborn, but instead confess all to his mother and entrust them both to her care. Above all, I entreated him not to love me any the less for the burdens I'd brought upon him, to think of me kindly, and never to forget me.

At six the next morning, I gave birth to a son. He was an immense baby, but thin, from coming, like his sister, a little before his time. For all my apprehensions, I was not as ill as I'd been before; this time, I was spared the terrible complaint that had nearly killed me after Little H's birth.

58

Afterward, I was well prepared in all respects, having everything in place to receive my baby boy. He was taken from me even more quickly than had been the case with his sister, and I was distraught when I was forced to part with him—but this time I had the comfort of knowing he was going to the same people who'd cared for his sister in the first few months of her life. I hoped that when he was old enough he might join Little H in the household I'd established for her and where she was thriving. The certainty of his being well looked after in both places, combined with an easier delivery, meant that I recovered my health more quickly than before.

There'd been no chance this time of Granville coming secretly to see me. He'd been far away in Staffordshire, attending to family business and standing once more for election. As soon as I could, I wrote to announce the arrival of his son. He replied very kindly, for which I was grateful, but I knew I wouldn't be completely satisfied until I heard from his own lips that he was happy with me and was pleased to welcome the newest addition to our little family, for such I now considered it—and that he would do all in his power to love the little creature.

It was some weeks before that was possible, but when Granville finally returned to London, I lost no time in arranging a rendezvous for us in our old place of retreat, Lady Anne's apartments. And oh, what a meeting it was! It was everything I could have wished for. From the very moment he entered the room, Granville was all affection, taking me in his arms, kissing me exactly in the way I liked—and questioning me about our son.

"Tell me all about him. Is he large or small? Hair or no hair? Handsome or plain?"

"He is very long, which makes me think he will be tall, as you are. And he has your bright blue eyes. He's a very striking child."

"I'm glad to hear it. And what have you called him?"

"I thought that should be your choice. What name should you like for him?"

"Let him be George." He smiled: it was his own second name. "And for a middle name, he should take Granville. George Granville. I think that sounds well."

I was delighted he'd chosen to bestow upon our boy names that were so closely associated with his family. And when he went on to tell me how very proud he was of me—that he'd missed me terribly— and looked as if he meant it—well, those few heady moments washed away a great deal of unhappiness. I think I fell in love with him all over again that extraordinary afternoon. By the time we parted, I was once more firmly in the grasp of that same overwhelming, dis-tracted passion that had bound me to him for so long.

I can't help but feel some sympathy for the deliriously happy woman I was during that short time. Sometimes I've asked myself if it might have been better if Granville hadn't been so full of loving-kindness that day, if he hadn't showed to such powerful advantage the best and most caring side of himself, in a way that could only magnify my feelings for him. Was it better to fall precipitously from a great height of happiness? Or to tip just a little distance from sadness into misery? Well, I wasn't given any choice in the matter. Happy or sad, bad news was coming for me, and much sooner than I thought.

Some weeks later, when Granville asked to meet me as soon as it was in my power, I was immediately apprehensive. In search of privacy, we were obliged to resort to our old refuge from prying eyes and engage a hackney cab in the park. From the minute Granville climbed into the carriage, I saw he was uncomfortable; I grew steadily more nervous, imagining all manner of horrors, until I could stand it no longer.

"Something is clearly troubling you. I beg you to tell me what it is."

He was silent for a moment, as if considering how to begin.

"It's probably best if I go straight to the point. We talked a while ago about the possibility of my marrying—and I said then that I had no particular lady in mind. I have to tell you that's no longer the case. There is someone—someone whom I'm considering."

My heart froze within me, but I managed to get out the crucial question.

"Who is she?"

"It's Sarah Fane. Daughter of the Earl of Westmoreland."

"And the heir to the Child banking fortune."

He had the grace to look a little shamefaced.

"Yes, that's the lady. She's of an age to marry now, and I intend to pay court to her."

"You and many others. Her money must make her a very desirable prize. Have you any other reason for thinking of her?"

"I know her a little, through my sister. She is a very unaffected, straightforward girl."

Of course I began to cry. I don't even recall what I said next—nothing he wanted to hear, I'm sure. Eventually, he grew exasperated, for what could he do or say in the face of my grief?

"Harriet, it's not a settled thing," he insisted. "It might come to nothing—but you asked me for honesty, and I'm trying my best to obey you. You would hate to hear from someone else that I was pursuing her."

"I can't quarrel with your candor. It's the fact of the thing I can't bear—that I'm to lose you, and there's nothing I can do to stop it."

"So I'm to remain alone forever? To have no wife, no home, no settled life—is that what you want for me? You who say you would do anything to see me happy?"

Around and around the argument went—neither of us had anything to say that we hadn't said before, and soon we were both reduced to a miserable silence. It was Granville who spoke first.

"So what am I to do? Tell me, for I no longer know what you want from me."

"I want what I've always wanted—your happiness—even though I know it must be the death of mine." I grasped his hand and held it to my cheek. "I understand, truly I do. And I'll do everything in my power to summon up the courage to let you go. But I can't pretend it isn't terrible to me—you must allow me that—and who am I to cry to, if not you?"

In the weeks that followed, all I could hang on to, to prevent myself from tumbling into the abyss, were Granville's own words— "It's not a settled thing." A thousand small eventualities might combine to prevent it. On such slender chances, my future, and that of my children, depended. If I was to have any hope of surviving what lay before me, I knew I mustn't anticipate disaster, or present to him so very melancholy an aspect that he would break with me simply to have it over. Lady Elizabeth said to me once that men have no patience with women's unhappiness because it reminds them that they are almost always the cause of it. If I wished to keep him near me, I must hold up my head, fix my gaze straight ahead, and present as untroubled a picture to the world as lay in my power. Self-control must be my watchword now.

59

In September, we took a house at Ramsgate, joining my sister and her family and several friends and acquaintances. Everyone I knew in London seemed to be there, walking on the sands or riding out on the cliffs. I was trying to rest and keep myself as quiet as I could, hoping to bother no one and be unbothered in my turn; but that proved more difficult than I expected.

My eldest son, John, known to all as Duncannon, had some time ago begun a kind of extended flirtation with his cousin Harryo. Their characters could not have been more different, for he was a flighty being, his mind and interests never fixed for a minute, still quite young for his years; whereas Harryo, though still in her teens, seemed by far the elder of the two. I've already remarked on her cleverness, and it was plain to me that in this respect she was very much Duncannon's superior and knew it. They weren't remotely suited, always falling out over slights and offenses, not speaking to each other for weeks at a time, then making up only to repeat the whole tiresome cycle once more. I'll be honest and say I hoped whatever subsisted between them would soon run its course. I'll even admit that I don't think I'd have been entirely happy with Harryo as my daughter-in-law. I'd always flinched from her cool, assessing gaze and was more than a little afraid of her sharp satiric wit. I couldn't help but wonder how often I'd been the object of it, for I often feared she wasn't very fond of me.

Nonetheless, I warned Duncannon not to trifle with her if he didn't mean to take matters further. He brushed away my concerns, declaring no commitment had been made or expected; but I didn't like it, and worried endlessly about what would happen between them. In such circumstances, it was difficult to remain as determinedly calm as I'd hoped; and any further attempts to do so were thoroughly knocked on the head by the arrival of Lady Melbourne and her family.

I knew she was still angry with me, so I endeavored, whenever we met, to keep our conversations well away from subjects that might trespass upon her suspicions—but one afternoon, as we sat on a little wooden bench overlooking the sea, I made a sad blunder, complaining that I could no longer walk about with the same energy I'd enjoyed when I was younger.

"My feet ache and my ankles swell—it takes all the pleasure from a stroll such as this."

"Of course, it's a very common complaint after a confinement," she remarked evenly. "Everyone knows that."

That was the moment when I could have confessed—I could have told her everything, there and then—I could tell she still hoped for it—but for all the reasons I've explained before, I couldn't bring myself to do so.

"I suppose it is." I attempted a smile. "Really, mine are such distant history now that I've quite forgotten them."

She turned and looked at me directly. She fixed her eyes upon me for a great while before launching her attack upon me with a single ironical comment.

"Really?"

I decided not to reply, and she didn't hold back.

"I suppose there are some people who may be so easily deceived, but not me. I always know when a woman's carrying a child, or when she's not long ago been confined. So I advise all Farquhar's little circle of anonymous ladies—you know, I suppose, how he boasts of them?—to avoid me if they wish to keep their secrets.

"I'm sure that's good advice for those who need it," I replied mildly.

"I can always tell."

I didn't rise to her bait, and a little afterward, we parted, not on the best terms. I made my way home, asking myself once more if I wouldn't have done better simply to tell her what she wanted to know.

Later that week, I was invited to a great dinner, which was truthfully the very last thing I would have chosen to attend in my present frame of mind. Lord B, however, insisted, declaring that all our friends were to be present—my sister and her husband; Lord and Lady Melbourne; even my favorite Dr. Farquhar, who'd taken a house a little farther up the coast—everyone, in fact, who knew something to my discredit.

At first, things went well enough, but just as the principal courses were brought in, the conversation turned in a direction I did not much like. The poor health of Granville's sister Lady Georgiana Elliot was raised as a subject of concern, with Farquhar declaring that removing her from Mr. Elliot's presence would be the best remedy, as having so many children so quickly was always injurious to health. Someone then remarked that many of the women in Granville's family had produced large families, which prompted Miss Lloyd, an elderly lady with a gift for saying the wrong thing, to add her artless pronouncement to the discussion.

"I suppose Lord Granville will be next, for he hasn't any children yet."

"Are you sure?" replied the Duke of Devonshire. "It's not unknown for people to have offspring they don't talk about. Surely, it's a very common thing."

He may, of course, have been alluding to his own situation, of which everyone at the table, except for the unworldly Miss Lloyd, was quite aware; but I froze, appalled at where this discussion might end. I don't know what would have happened if, at that crucial moment, Lady Melbourne hadn't, seemingly by accident, knocked a glass of wine off the table. By the time a servant had been summoned, the damage mopped up, the state of the carpet assessed—with everyone except Lady Melbourne herself offering an opinion on whether or not it would stain—the subject of Lord Granville's children was entirely forgotten. It was a while, however, before I stopped trembling. When everyone finally left the table, Lady Melbourne came and sat by my side. She brought with her a bottle of sweet white wine, which she poured into my glass before handing it to me.

"Don't drop it," she said.

I couldn't help but smile. "I can't thank you enough," I began. "You've been a better friend to me than I have to you. It's only fair I should be honest with you now—"

But just as I was about to tell her everything she'd longed to know—surely, she deserved it after rescuing me from my peril at the dinner table—she put her finger to my lips.

"No, not now. There's nothing to say that I can't deduce for myself. And a forced confidence is really not worth having. The only ones that mean anything at all are those that are freely given."

If that was all I was to receive in terms of a rebuke, I thought it fair enough. I raised my glass to her.

"To friendship."

We both took a sip of our wine.

"And to courage," she replied. "You need a bit of that, Harriet, if you're not to stumble and fall. I've told you before, but you won't listen. I recommend a little less indulgence in fine feelings on your part. You allow yourself to be blown hither and thither like a boat in a storm. Harden your heart a little. You'll be amazed how much easier it makes things. Men like it, too. They enjoy being bossed about."

"Surely that rather depends on the man."

"Believe me, they're all the same," she declared, indicating a young man on the other side of the room.

"Look at Adair there—twelve years my junior and half my size, and the worse I treat him, the more he says he loves me. He tells me he crossed Europe to try and forget me, but it didn't work. 'Pooh,' I reply, 'what's that to me?' And he only swoons all the more."

We both knew I was incapable of acting on her advice, but I was grateful to her, nonetheless. And her words didn't fall entirely on stony ground. I decided I should not see Granville for a while. I was utterly exhausted, tired in the very depths of my being, and I honestly thought I'd collapse entirely if I didn't absent myself temporarily from both him and the world. And so for a short time I did. I went down to Roehampton, where I sat in the garden and saw no one except Sally and my Little H. I think it did me good, so when Granville wrote asking if we could meet in London, I felt better prepared for whatever was to come.

60

O ur rendezvous was at Charlton Street, where I had established Little H and young George in a small but very comfortable house. I went with the avowed intention of treating him with the reserve Lady Melbourne recommended, but the minute we met, we were in each other's arms. I couldn't help myself and returned his kisses as ardently as ever; but once the first excitement passed, I grew ashamed and drew away from him. How was it possible I could behave in such a way, when I knew he wanted to marry someone else? How much easier my life would have been, had I been able to get my desire for him under control, so that I could adjust its heat to the circumstances, like a cook dousing a flame to prevent a pot boiling over. But in his presence, to my shame, I was never properly mistress of myself.

"Was this the only reason you wished to see me? Or do you have some news to communicate?"

I smoothed down my dress, angry at my weakness. He had the grace to look a little ashamed.

"I know it isn't fair. I told myself I shouldn't come, but I had to see you. Whenever we're apart, I'm reminded how very much you mean to me."

I glowed, for this was exactly what I longed to hear. But then I remembered Sarah Fane and was angry.

"Is it fair, do you think, to torment me in this way? To continue pursuing me, even as you plan to marry another?"

He moved toward me, as if to take me in his arms, but I pushed him away.

"Why are you here?" I cried. "Wouldn't it be kinder to leave me alone?"

"I long for you, Harriet. I can't help it, but I do."

Then he kissed me, and we were soon beyond the point of no return, giving in to the desire that still drew us together, just as every other consideration forced us apart.

I was furious with myself afterward. Continued intimacies of this kind with Granville were the very worst thing, as they awakened all my warmest feelings, bringing me the greatest pleasure while at the same time plunging me into the deepest despair. I suffered terribly whenever I thought of how I should be thrown off by him when he married Lady Sarah, and when did I not think of it? When I thought of Little H, I couldn't help but recall the miseries I'd gone through in giving birth to her—they seemed nothing to me now, compared to the wretched unhappiness I endured every day, waiting for the news of my dismissal.

I remained for months in this state of anxious expectation; but gradually I began to wonder if Granville's courtship would indeed end in success. Lady Sarah had been keenly pursued by a number of suitors, but most had fallen by the wayside, one by one, until now only Granville and Lord Villiers remained. This was thus the crucial moment; but if I'm frank, I wasn't convinced he'd triumph over his rival. The contrast in their situations was very stark—Villiers was the son of an earl, very rich and with great expectations, while Granville had neither title nor wealth to offer.

His greatest asset in the contest for her hand was himself—his attractions of person and manner, that had acted so powerfully upon many other ladies, not excluding myself; but, as far as I could tell, Lady Sarah seemed indifferent to them. She was never rude, but nothing in her manner suggested she was particularly excited by his attentions. Her treatment of Granville was always cool and measured, as though she considered him some mildly diverting trinket, which she might, or might not, decide to purchase.

In public, he put on a brave face, smilingly attempting to draw her into conversation at assemblies, or to hand her into her carriage when she left, sitting beside her at the theater, while Lord Villiers was placed on her other side, all the time wearing a look of serene contentment, as if everything was going exactly as he'd planned. I wasn't there to witness it myself—I absented myself from scenes that were bound to be painful to me, as well as humiliating to him, and, besides, he made it plain that my presence at such times made him uncomfortable— but I received many accounts from those who were, nearly all of them, skeptical of his chances.

I tried my best to prepare Granville for how I thought it would end, but he wouldn't listen; and after a while, I decided to say nothing. To be candid, I think he knew in his heart she'd never have him, but I honestly believe it was the first time he'd ever encountered so severe a rejection; thus, he couldn't recognize it for what it was, still hoping until the very last minute that she would see the light and say yes.

He was to be sadly disappointed. Shortly afterward, the long-anticipated news of Lady Fane's engagement to Lord Villiers was finally announced, and all Granville's hopes were at an end.

61

*H*ester Stanhope. When did I first hear her name linked with Granville's? It must have been quite soon after his rejection by Lady Sarah. Granville strove to be magnanimous in defeat, presenting no more than an air of mild disappointment to the world; but I knew his pride, if not his heart, had been deeply wounded by his failure.

I always thought there was some connection between his dismissal by one lady and his taking up so quickly with another, as if to demonstrate to himself that his powers of attraction were undiminished. And he couldn't have chosen a more different woman to console him for his loss. Where Lady Sarah had been opaque, diffident, and unmoved by Granville's appeal, Lady Hester was quite the opposite. She was bold, confident, and transparent as a pane of glass, never making the slightest secret of her attraction to him, and wholly expecting her passion to be returned.

She was—and indeed, she remains—a very extraordinary character and is really quite unlike any other woman of my acquaintance. I didn't know her at all when she was very young. She's of Granville's generation rather than my own, which put a distance between us;

and politics, as well as age, worked to keep us apart, for on her mother's side at least, her family were Tories, and very well-connected ones at that—Mr. Pitt was her uncle, and as soon as Hester had any choice in the matter, she moved almost entirely in his circle.

When I first got to know her, Hester had argued with her family—she was never one to shy away from a row—and had gone to live with Mr. Pitt at Walmer on the Kent coast, where he had retreated after leaving office. She acted as hostess, housekeeper, and even, as she was keen to make known, as an occasional advisor to her uncle on the most serious political matters. There may have been some truth in this, for Hester was very clever, and Pitt thought highly of her.

Hester was queen of Pitt's little household, presiding over his table with a positively regal assurance. The other guests were always men—politicians, naval and army officers mostly—I certainly never heard of a single lady's being invited. This was very much to Hester's taste, as she was always happiest in male company. Indeed, I never heard of her having a proper female friend, and think she had a low opinion of women in general.

Perhaps it was from being so much with men that she became so forthright in her attitudes and language. There was nothing she wouldn't say. I heard that once she gazed pointedly at the large behind of some unfortunate visitor and then announced to the company that "he would never do for a hussar." On another occasion, when a man greeted her with an obsequious and very low bow, she declared with a laugh that "one would think he was looking under the bed for the great business." Only Hester would have thought it amusing to make a public joke about chamber pots—but Pitt never checked her, confining himself to observing mildly, "You are too bad, Hester."

Uncle and niece could not have been more different. Her blunt temperament was quite alien to his cautious, closed-in nature, and I think he rather enjoyed it when she shocked him. He was clearly very fond of her; but there was never anything amorous between them. Pitt was quite incapable, I believe, of loving any woman in that way, and was now so burdened with the worries of office that all he wanted was to be entertained, amused, and well looked after. Hester understood this very well, and in return for the safe harbor he offered, she cared for him with the utmost solicitude, bringing life, warmth, and comfort into an existence that was otherwise devoid of all three.

Others, however, were not so monastic in their tastes, and Lady Hester attracted a great deal of male attention. At this time, she was in her late twenties, tall and slim, with dark hair and a commanding expression. She was not exactly handsome, but men liked her—there was such an air of energy and excitement about her that being in her company was like waiting for a firework to go off. She was always in motion, talking, doing, planning. She occupied more space, somehow, than most other women; and like her or hate her—for it was impossible to be merely lukewarm in one's response—she was impossible to ignore.

She wasn't the kind of woman to attract a timid man, or someone whose taste ran to the quiet and submissive. Five minutes in her company was enough to understand that nothing to do with Hester would ever be easy. But for a man confident in his dealings with women, who admired wit and cleverness, who liked to talk as well as to make love, who was impervious to drama and completely secure in the knowledge of his own attractions—in short, for a man like Granville—Hester was an enticing prospect indeed.

Granville was often invited to Walmer, and he attended a series of dinners there during the time Pitt was out of office. He always received the most encouraging welcome from Hester. She made it clear from the beginning, in her frank, open way, that she liked him; and soon they were meeting in London. They walked in the park, rode up to Hampstead Hill, and wandered together over the Heath. Soon Hester was passionately in love with him—and, as she later told me, had no doubt her feelings were fully returned.

Granville called on her, wrote to her, and escorted her about—in short, he paid her the most marked attentions. As Hester had not the first notion of discretion, she made no secret of the warmth of her feelings, declaring to anyone who asked her—and several people did, as they were so often seen together—that in every possible way, she found Granville "perfection."

After the third or fourth time this description was recounted to me, I decided to speak directly to Granville about her. It was far from the first occasion I'd taxed him with his pursuit of other women—God knows, there's enough of them over the years, but as most were married, the worst I had to fear was rivalry for his affections rather the total separation I'd dreaded if his courtship of Lady Sarah had succeeded. I don't mean to minimize the misery these liaisons caused me. We had, over many years, attempted to stay true to the spirit of our agreement that he would always be candid about his other dalliances, as long as I promised never to be jealous. In fact, neither of us managed entirely to keep our respective parts of the bargain, for he never told me everything, and I was always jealous; but I still preferred to hear the story, even if in a severely edited form, from him rather than via some eager gossiping "friend" with malice in her heart.

When I charged him with the stories I'd heard, at first he was nonchalant, attempting to dismiss my concerns.

"It's a flirtation—nothing more."

"And Lady Hester—does she see it like that?"

"I think she understands the nature of these things. She's twenty-eight and worldly, not some green little girl who fancies herself head over heels in love."

"My own example proves that, sadly, age is no protection where falling in love is concerned."

He smiled but made no reply.

"I suppose it's just as well Lady Sarah is out of the picture. She wouldn't have cared much for this 'flirtation.'"

"I doubt it would've made any difference. I think I was fated never to please in that quarter."

"So Hester is by way of a consolation prize in your eyes?"

Granville frowned. I think this struck too close to home for his liking.

"If you make it so unpleasant for me to make these confessions, I shall begin to ask myself why I go on doing so."

"For love of me, of course. That and the discharging of your conscience."

He wasn't pleased, and left shortly after, exuding an air of injured dignity. I didn't like any of this conversation. Granville was, I thought, evasive and dangerously unconcerned with the possible consequences of his actions. I didn't think Hester anywhere near as experienced as he supposed her to be. She may have seemed so, with her indelicate language, her forthright character, and her refusal to act the part of the ingenue—but beneath the tough exterior of which she was so proud, I sensed a very different young woman, one who was as defenseless as the most innocent young romantic convinced she's met her one true love.

I believe Granville entirely misunderstood who she really was; but then men tend to take women at the estimation ascribed to them by the world. Women will devote a colossal amount of time and energy attempting to discover a man's true self, even ascribing to him all manner of motives, thoughts, and considerations that would be quite alien to him if he were to be informed of them; believe me, I speak as someone who has done this only too often myself. Men, however, rarely trouble themselves to discover if quite another being hides beneath the superficial character we women all present to the world.

I have often asked myself how matters might have turned out if I had exerted myself more forcefully that day, insisting Granville give Hester up before things went too far. But I had other concerns that spring.

I was horrified to discover, in the spring of 1804, that I was pregnant yet again. I was forty-three years old and had, I suppose, trusted to my age to protect me from the consequences of my foolishness. Nothing, it seemed, was powerful enough to keep Granville and me apart—not the prospect of his marriage, not my age nor the danger to my health, not the ever present risk of exposure—and though I always told myself this time would be the last, I was never strong enough to keep that resolution. Somehow, we always found a way to be together; and this was my reward for my weakness.

The thought of enduring yet another confinement was truly terrible to me; and the symptoms usual in those early days wore me out so that I really hadn't the energy to think about anything but my own misfortune. Sick and burdened in body and mind, I took Granville at his word. I consigned Hester to the long inventory of other female favorites who'd caught his eye and occupied his attentions for a while. It wasn't until the summer, when I started to feel myself again and began to pay attention to the world once more, that I discovered how serious the situation had become in my absence.

It was Granville's mother, of all people, who alerted me to the true state of things. I liked Lady Stafford and had worked hard to win her goodwill. It had taken me years to get to where we were now. I'd been the instigator of our rapprochement, beginning by writing to her occasionally, always in the politest and most supplicating manner. When I saw her in company, I was charm itself. And gradually, step by careful step, I wore down her resistance until at last we were on tolerably good terms. She now acknowledged my place in Granville's life without ever entirely softening her disapproval of it. She blamed me for his failure to marry and constantly urged him to find a decent young wife. But I knew she had a good heart; she wouldn't fail in compassion where it was most needed.

It was a tribute to my belief in this essential goodness that during my confinements, when I was terrified I might die, she was the person to whom I bequeathed the lifelong care of Little H and George, confident that family feeling would conquer any remaining scruples, and that she would raise them with the most conscientious kindness. It was my habit to call upon her from time to time, bringing any little titbits of political news which I thought might not have reached her. Although our opinions couldn't have been further apart, she enjoyed hearing anything that came from inside the beating heart of politics, to which I was still connected, through my sister, my devotion to Mr. Fox, and even via my brother George, who had, until Mr. Pitt's resignation, been a most active and energetic First Lord of the Admiralty. Thus, I usually had enough interesting matter to carry us well through an afternoon of tea and cakes and leave her feeling satisfied and, I hoped, a little pleased with me.

It was after one such call, when I was just about to leave, that she asked me to stay a little longer.

"I have a question to ask, which I hope won't offend you—but I'm very troubled by certain things I've heard—and wondered if you'd any knowledge of how far I'm to credit them."

"But of course—if I can relieve your mind in any way, don't hesitate to ask."

"Is it true that Granville is to be married to Lady Hester? Her closest friends assure me it's about to happen—and whenever I see her, she seems bursting with barely suppressed excitement. Can it be so, do you think? Granville never mentioned such an idea to me at all."

I was obliged to sit down before I could answer.

"Nor to me either." I attempted a smile. "Which I think he would have done, if he was seriously contemplating such a match."

"Then it's just as I thought," she replied. "I'm sorry to say I believe it's Hester herself who's encouraging the rumors. She's very much in love with him; you can see it in her eyes when she speaks to him. And I'm told by those who've seen it that she places her hand on his arm with such an air of possession that you'd think they'd already been married for a good six months.

"I realize," she went on, "that situated as you are, this is a great deal to ask of you—but is it possible you could beg him to take care? I'm very much afraid he's heading for disaster with Hester—he may have raised her expectations to a point where it would be impossible for him to withdraw. And I don't think she's at all the kind of wife calculated to make him happy." She sighed. "He'll never listen to his mother on such a subject. But he might pay attention to his—his—to you, Lady Bessborough, if you could bring yourself to raise it with him."

I sat appalled on my drive home, horrified to realize that Granville had entangled himself so deeply and so dangerously. My first thought, I admit, was a selfish one—pity for myself. Here I was, pregnant yet again with his child, and required once more to suffer all the torments of jealousy that must overwhelm me whenever I was obliged to imagine him seriously connected to another woman. The mere idea of Granville and Hester together made my blood boil— and when I imagined the endearments he used with her—were they the same ones he spoke to me? I shook my head to drive such imaginings from my mind. Would there ever be an end to the pain and humiliation my ridiculous passion brought down upon my head?

But I was also genuinely alarmed on Granville's behalf. Lady Stafford's fears seemed entirely credible. The more I considered it, the more likely it seemed that Granville had rushed headlong into an affair with no thought at all of where it might lead. Hester's boldness meant she'd have no qualms in freely declaring her liking for him—and frank unqualified admiration is a great encouragement to a man's affections.

I thought it very probable she'd already received him in her bed—Lady Stafford's telling detail of Hester's hand on Granville's arm was particularly persuasive in this respect—and I didn't doubt Granville had been only too ready to take her there. If I was right—and I was increasingly convinced that I was—this promised a world of trouble. It was one thing for a man to amuse himself with a series of compliant, restive, or unhappy wives; but to do so with an unmarried woman, and to take their connection to the most intimate degree—this was courting disaster. Hester's reputation would be tarnished to such an extent that no man of any standing was likely to marry her; and if she was to complain that Granville had led her on, with the expectation of her becoming his wife—then he'd have no choice but to propose to her himself.

I put my head in my hands at the thought of this. From what I knew of them both, there seemed no chance at all they'd be happy. Granville's love of authority would sit very ill with Hester's proud spirit; as a lover, he found her willfulness alluring, but it would be very different once they were man and wife. Those little variations in character that add piquancy to an affair are frequently the very same qualities that ruin a marriage. And while I hoped one day to arrive at a state in which I could welcome resigning him to another, I could only do this if I felt it would result in his happiness. I couldn't bear to see him locked into a miserable union, even if it was his own foolishness that had brought it about.

There was nothing for it—I should have to speak to him again, and this time even more severely than I had ventured concerning any of his other dalliances. Someone, I thought, must bring him to his senses, and no one could do so but me. Before I ventured upon it, however, I thought it best to be as well informed as possible of what was being said about the two of them and decided to inquire from Lady Melbourne, that great possessor of everyone else's secrets, exactly what she had heard.

"Do you really want to know? It won't be much to your taste."

Yes, I insisted, I knew much of it already and merely wished to have it confirmed—and confirm it she did, in the most unambiguous terms. Hester, she assured me, was ardently, passionately attached to Granville—Lady Melbourne, too, thought it likely they were lovers—and didn't hesitate to flaunt her feelings, always hinting they were fully reciprocated. She didn't go so far as to actually pronounce the word "marriage"; but it hung in the air, so that there couldn't be any doubt it was what she expected.

"Granville has acted very much against his own interests in all of this," she observed. "I can't imagine he means to marry her. She has no money at all, and his pursuit of Lady Sarah suggests he's looking for a wife with very different prospects. I don't believe they would suit each other, though you would be a better judge of that than I."

I inclined my head, determined to say as little as possible in a conversation that was bound to be uncomfortable.

"If that's indeed the case," Lady Melbourne went on, "he couldn't have chosen a worse person to disappoint. She'll take it very badly and won't scruple to make a great drama of it—she's not the type to suffer in silence, you can be sure of that. And to involve himself in such a manner with the beloved niece of his patron—to insult the man who holds his career in his hands, who can advance or crush his ambitions with a stroke of a pen—well, honestly, it beggars belief. How could he have been so careless of his own prospects?"

I had no answer to that. Everything she said struck home with the force of truth, especially as it concerned Mr. Pitt. He'd recently returned to office following the fall of Addington's government, the result of its woeful incapacity to effectively manage the war against France; but becoming Prime Minister hadn't distanced him in the least from Hester. On the contrary: she had followed him to Downing Street and now presided there with the same authority she'd previously enjoyed at Walmer.

"Do you think Mr. Pitt knows?"

"If he and Hester are as close as everyone says, I don't see how he can be ignorant of what's happening. She will have told him herself, I'm sure of it. You know what she's like. He'll have been obliged to listen to a recitation of Granville's virtues while weighing the fate of Europe in his hands."

She shook her head, marveling at the short-sighted stupidity of men.

"You should warn him he's playing with fire. He really should know better than to amuse himself with a young unmarried girl. It always ends in tears. If he wants an affair, find a willing married woman. Doesn't he know by now that that's what we're for?"

I did my best. I gathered up my courage, for I knew he wouldn't like it, and spoke to Granville in the strongest terms, telling him all I'd heard—that their attachment was everywhere spoken of, that Lady Hester freely declared the strength of her feelings for him and her conviction that his intentions toward her were serious. At first, he refused to listen at all.

"This is all bosh, Harriet, and I can't believe you credit it."

"This isn't some light fancy on my part—I only wish it was. I know you hate it when I speak in this way—but I only do so because I'm afraid for you and refuse to stand by and allow you to ruin yourself."

Finally his expression softened a little. "If you must know, I've been a little alarmed myself at the strength of Hester's feelings. I've tried to pull back a little, but she responds with such horror to what she calls my *withdrawal*—that I haven't the heart to be as clear in my determination as I know I should be." He took a deep breath. "I'm fond of her, and I don't like to see her cry."

This pierced me like a knife, for it opened up a whole hitherto unconsidered universe of pain. Was it possible Granville did in fact harbor real affection for Hester? That she was not wholly deceived in thinking he felt warmly toward her? I shivered—the thought was awful to me—but smothered my fears and pressed on.

"You cannot continue as you do merely because you don't like to hurt her: that's only postponing a reckoning which must come at some time or another—unless of course you do intend to marry her?"

He said nothing, which I chose to interpret as suggesting that was not his intention.

"Your silence speaks volumes. Hester would be dreadfully distressed to hear it—but if that's really what you think, it's very wrong of you to let her believe otherwise. You owe it to her to be truthful—and to yourself as well. If you don't find a way to withdraw, as Hester puts it, very soon, you're likely to find yourself in a very difficult place. One from which you'll find it extremely hard to escape with any honor."

Once more he did not reply, and I pushed home my advantage.

"I hear she has mentioned it to Mr. Pitt. How do you think he'll like it?"

His face fell. "I think I'm about to find out. He has asked to see me. Tomorrow, as it happens."

"Oh, Granville." There was nothing else I could say. I went to sit beside him and took his hand. "How could you have been so stupid?"

Without a word, he disengaged his hand. I felt the baby move inside me, but this wasn't the moment to draw his attention to that. We sat there in silence, neither properly together nor absolutely apart, waiting for whatever must come next.

63

I don't know what I expected from Granville's interview with Mr. Pitt. I thought he might be given some terrible ultimatum: "Marry Hester or resign yourself to exclusion from public life, so long as preferment lies in my hands." But nothing in my wildest imagination prepared me for the truth.

"I'm appointed ambassador to St. Petersburg, charged with persuading the Tsar to join the coalition of our allies against Napoleon."

Granville himself spoke as if he could scarcely believe it. "I went in expecting a whipping and came out with what most people would regard as a plum. I was never so surprised in my life."

I couldn't speak. I honestly thought I must faint, so great was the shock.

"When must you go? And how long will you be away?" It was all I could think to ask, for "I'm leaving you" was all I heard in his words.

He took me in his arms and held me very close. "I won't go if you don't wish it. Tell me to stay and I will."

Every fiber of my being cried out, "Don't go; don't abandon me in this sad state. I cannot endure it." But I knew I couldn't ask that.

I saw immediately, as Granville must have done too, that this was Pitt's way of removing him from a scene that must soon have become intolerable for everyone concerned, but particularly so for the person Pitt loved most in the world.

Even if I were to beg and plead, and Granville refused to leave me—what did I think would be the result of that? Nothing good. No, bad as it was, this was the cleaner, better way. Granville would be thousands of miles removed, not just from me but from Hester. Distance would do what resolution could not, putting an end to an intimacy that might otherwise explode into the most bitter scandal and recrimination. So I did what I knew I must, and gave him the only possible answer.

"You must go. Oh, Granville, it will all but kill me—but I must harden my heart and you must make up your mind to go."

For a few days, he protested; but eventually, with a heavy heart, he accepted Mr. Pitt's offer. I think he was genuinely unhappy at the prospect of leaving. When I tried to encourage him by reminding him of the good it must do his career—for it was a remarkable step up for a man of his age and experience—he was unmoved.

"You can't imagine I'd make that a consideration, when it means I must leave you in your current state, exposed to all the risks that come with it. I shan't be here when the baby's born, for Mr. Pitt thinks I shall be away for at least a year."

"I hope and pray that I shall get through it. But it would be of the utmost comfort to me to know that before you leave, you'll have a serious conversation with Hester. You must either break with her or ask her to marry you. You cannot go on as you are."

He agreed and nodded and swore that he would—but the weeks crept by, and still he hadn't spoken to her. He was always undertaking most sincerely to do so—but somehow, he never did. The result was that, in the diminishing time left to us before his departure, he spent almost as much time with Hester as he did with me.

When I cried and complained of his faithlessness, he would hang his head and confess that it was largely pity that prevented him from breaking with her.

"I think she hasn't the slightest idea that I might put an end to things between us. It'll come as a terrible blow to her."

"I wish, I wish you hadn't encouraged her as you did."

He bridled a little. "It's very hard I should bear all the blame when her passions were so strong and so willingly offered. I agree I was guilty in accepting them so readily; but honestly, Harriet, I wonder if any man would have had the strength to say no in such circumstances."

"That's a shameful way of thinking. How could you encourage a passion you didn't seriously mean to return?"

"You must understand that what passes between Hester and me—it's nothing at all compared to my feelings for you."

If he'd thought this would please me, he was much mistaken.

"I think that makes it worse, for it suggests a coarse and hardened sensibility that I wouldn't have believed from you. How could these most intimate demonstrations of affection amount to nothing at all?"

But through all these arguments and recriminations, I felt the constant ticking of the clock, counting away the minutes until Granville was to go. It was this which destroyed me. I would sit and shake with fear when I contemplated the appalling possibilities his departure would create. I might never see him again. He might die. I might die. He might forget me. He might meet and marry some other woman in St. Petersburg, of whose existence I was utterly unaware. These ideas went around and around in my mind until I sometimes thought I should to mad.

I couldn't imagine how my life would go on without him. I should feel terribly alone; my older children had far less need of me now. John, the eldest, was studying at Oxford, while Frederick, who'd long wished to join the army, was now a captain of dragoons, eager to be sent abroad, which I was very much afraid would be the case if the war continued for much longer. William, the youngest and shyest of the brothers, was also to leave me; but that had been at my own behest. I'd begged Granville to take him to Russia as one of his junior secretaries. He was an anxious young man, inclined to be silent, and greatly in need of some excitement and occupation to bring forth his hidden talents. Granville agreed to my request and promised to take good care of him. I thought it would be good for William, but we'd always been close, and I knew I'd miss him terribly. I couldn't rely on Caro to replace him. She was too tied up with her feelings for William Lamb, determined she would one day be married to him. The force of her passions sometimes alarmed me, perhaps because I feared she'd inherited them from me. If so, it was a very malign legacy, which I should have done anything to prevent; but I was powerless to change her nature now.

As to Lord B—he made no comment on Granville's mission, once he'd agreed to William's accompanying him. I simply did not know how much he knew about our connection; I occasionally caught some bat squeak of suspicion or displeasure in his demeanor; but he made no more threats and issued no further ultimatums. I think that, like my sister, he'd decided not to ask questions when he knew the answers must be distasteful to him. We lived largely separate lives. He was often away, at shooting parties or staying with friends. In London, he spent most of his time at Brooks's club, watching others gamble, as he could no longer afford to do so himself. I still accompanied him on excursions to the coast, which I knew he much enjoyed; and sometimes we were together at Chatsworth. Even then, it felt as if we were in truth two solitary beings, linked only by proximity, for all the connection there was between us. I was terribly ashamed of the wrong I'd done him, and was never really at ease in his company, though I tried my best to please him, as if to make some amends for my betrayal.

Perhaps the only pleasure left to me, once Granville was gone, would be that which I took in Little H and George. They were the sole rays of sunshine in the gloom closing around me. Little H had grown from an entrancing baby into the most captivating little girl. Her bright, lively intelligence, together with the unforced, genuine sweetness of her character, was a never-ending delight to me. I arranged music and dancing lessons for her, as well as hiring a lady to teach her French; I was determined the accident of her birth should never stifle the talents I was sure she possessed. Baby George was a quieter, more reserved child, but so loving and affectionate that I never regretted he had not a greater share of Little H's energy. But even in their company, I couldn't help but feel sad. Their father would be away for at least a year, perhaps more. At their young age, I supposed it was inevitable, at least until his return, that they'd forget him. I only hoped that nothing, or more particularly no other love, should intervene while he was away, to make him forget them.

I expected Granville to be impatient with my misery, for hopeless unhappiness has a way of frustrating those who can do nothing to alleviate it; but in fact, he showed me nothing but kindness. When I wept, he stroked my hair; when I told him I thought we should never see each other again, he denied it, saying ties of affection like ours were far too strong to be torn asunder by such a little thing as absence. Didn't I know it made the heart grow fonder? I honestly think that on the night he left, I loved him as much—and possibly even more—than I'd ever done.

He was almost as agitated as I was at our last meeting. Both of us wept, he just a little while I cried a great deal. I can't deny it warmed my heart to see him suffer in parting from me. I don't think I could have borne it if he hadn't been touched at all. Our last kiss was terrible to us both; neither wished to be the first to pull away. Then he was gone, and there was nothing to do but wait, month after empty month, for him to come back.

64

J was aware so much distress and anxiety must have a very low-ering effect on my health. My confinement was approaching fast, and once again I'd begun to fear I shouldn't have the strength to go through with it. But we poor women have no choice in the matter—there is no escape—and I was brought to bed in November, low-spirited, abject, and full of misgivings.

This was my fourth secret lying-in, and Sally and I had become expert in the best means of deception. I was delivered at Cavendish Square, with Farquhar attending me, as I was so worried about my health. It was a long labor, but I thought I had my reward for my sufferings when I gave birth to a little girl. I saw her, just for a few minutes—but I was so ill that she was taken from me, and I never held her again. She died not an hour after taking her first breath. When I asked Farquhar what had gone wrong, he could not say with certainty, but thought my constant agitation and worry might have contributed to her death. If anything had been wanting to add to my unhappiness, this cruel judgment completed my misery.

For two days I was so delirious that I don't know what I said or did. When I came around, all I could think of was my poor dead child, and the pain was so great I wished myself unconscious once more. Her loss would've been a bitter sorrow at any time, but in my reduced state, it seemed to represent a further act of separation between Granville and me. Had I now been caring for our little girl, her very existence would have strengthened the bond between us, as it did when Little H and George were born, reminding Granville, far away as he was, of the ties that kept us together. Instead, I'd lost his child—and how long would it be before I might be obliged to bid farewell to her father as well? In this melancholy state, I asked Sally to cut a little of the baby's hair for me. I folded it into a slip of paper and enclosed it in a letter to Granville, with instructions not to lose it as he opened the envelope, thinking it of no account. It was all I had left of her to give—and I couldn't bear that her existence, brief as it was, should go unremembered by him.

65

Chief among the many aggravations I believed had contributed to the loss of my child was Hester Stanhope. Just before he left, Granville had shown me a letter he'd received from her, which had greatly disturbed me. She was bitterly disappointed that he hadn't asked her to accompany him to Russia and made it very plain she'd expected him to marry her. I pitied her, knowing well how such misery felt—but I couldn't approve of the angry threat with which she signed off her note—"You shall see what I shall do."

Quite what she meant wasn't entirely clear, but none of the possibilities were good. I wondered at first if she intended to risk all and follow Granville to Russia, where she would throw herself upon his protection and compel him, by the fact of her presence and sheer force of will, to marry her there. She was quite bold and reckless enough to carry out such an undertaking if she'd thought it had any chance of success; but there was another, darker construction that could be put upon her words. From other hints she dropped in her letter, it wasn't impossible to suppose she intended to kill herself.

This occurred to me at the time, although, on reflection, I thought it unlikely. I suspected that her emotions, though strongly felt, did not run very deep. With her love of drama and propensity for grandiose gestures, I hoped her threats were like a summer storm, which brings with it a great deal of thunder and lightning but passes over quickly, to no great effect. I couldn't have been more wrong. Several months later, I learned that shortly after Granville left, Hester dosed herself with laudanum and some other poison, with the clear desire of destroying herself. I'd often told Granville that I'd gladly die for him, if my sacrifice would bring him happiness; but Hester had really attempted to do what I had only threatened.

Thank God it didn't prove fatal—though she was grievously ill for many weeks—but what a terrible act to undertake. How desperate, how hopeless she must have felt to embark upon it. It was impossible not to feel terribly sorry for any wretched soul driven to such straits.

There is of course another purpose for which laudanum is sometimes used—to put an end to a pregnancy. I couldn't say whether this was Hester's true intention, and I preferred to believe that terrible necessity had not compelled her to resort to such a remedy—but she wouldn't have been the first woman to consider it. God knows, I'd suffered enough when I found myself in such a grim dilemma; but I had the protection, fragile as it was, afforded to a married woman in such cases. As a single woman, Hester was infinitely more exposed, so that if she did indeed make such a difficult choice, there's all the more reason to excuse her.

When Hester finally returned to society after a long convalescence, she was not at all subdued by her experience. She was openly resentful of Granville's treatment of her, declaring angrily to anyone who'd listen that he'd abandoned her; inevitably, this resulted in a great deal of gossip. I was very nervous, fearing some serious scandal would erupt if she continued to speak in so unguarded a manner. I avoided her company, in order not to provoke her by my presence; and she in turn kept her distance from me. So I was surprised one evening, when she arrived at Cavendish Square among a large and cheerful party of people who'd come, as they said, to entertain me.

From the outset, she seemed in a very fragile state, laughing too loudly and arguing about politics. I thought it best not to put myself in her way; and was astonished when she hung back as the others left, asking me very civilly if she might speak to me privately, as she had something of the utmost importance to tell me. Of course, my mind jumped to the most alarming conclusions—but I conjured up a mild, friendly smile, and asked her to sit down.

"I hope you won't mind if I speak of Lord Granville," she began, "but I've come to a conclusion I'd like to share with someone, and naturally I thought of you."

I was taken aback by the idea that she thought me in any way a suitable confidante but was determined to remain calm.

"I'm happy to listen, if you think it'll ease your mind."

She was very agitated, clasping and unclasping her hands, tapping her fingers on the chair arm, never for a moment at rest.

"I'm resolved to avoid everything that reminds me of him— people, places, any sight or sound that brings him to my thoughts."

"That's an admirable ambition, if you think you can hold to it."

"I shall never mention him, never inquire about him, never write to him. And eventually, I hope—I most fervently hope—that I'll never think of him more."

"You wish to forget him, then?"

"I cannot say I wish it—my feelings are still too strong for that— but I know it must be done."

"In my experience, it's one thing to recognize which is the right path to follow, and quite another to find the courage to go down it. I hope you'll prove braver than I've been."

"Oh, I have a will of iron when I've decided upon a course of conduct. This, for example, will be the very last time I'll speak to you of him. I'll never do so again."

"Of course, I entirely understand."

"You've been so kind in listening to me—I'm grateful for your indulgence—but now I've something more difficult to say. I only hope you won't blame me for what I'm about to tell you."

"It's nothing too bad, I hope."

"I'm obliged to tell you I can't visit you anymore."

I confess I was puzzled; we'd never been great friends and had been studiously wary of each other ever since she began her affair with Granville.

"But never, never, dearest Lady B, never think that any coldness on my part arises from my own choice. It's out of my hands."

"I'm not sure I understand." I was perplexed now. "You may come as often or as little as suits you."

"I think I may not. I've been advised—or, perhaps I should say ordered—to break off all acquaintance with you."

"I see." I was grave—but also rather offended. I'm not often guilty of hauteur, but I felt it was justified in this situation. "Then you'd better follow your directions, lest you displease the person who issued them. Am I to know who it is that deems my company so unsuitable?"

"I'm afraid it was the Queen—she and some other ill-natured persons who were quick to follow in her wake."

I suppose I shouldn't have been surprised. Queen Charlotte had disliked both my sister and me for more than twenty years, owing to our long association with Opposition politics, and as allies of their eldest son, the Prince Regent, with whom she and the King were on very bad terms. Had I been younger and in better spirits, I might have laughed at such a low expression of petty spite; but I was miserable and exhausted and had neither the energy nor the will to throw off the blow.

"I shan't ask what has prompted Her Majesty to speak to you about me in such unkind terms," I replied coolly. "But if you believe

I'm insufficiently respectable to entertain an unmarried woman such as yourself, you'd best act upon it."

"Please—I beg you, don't impute such an opinion to me," Hester cried, "but what am I to do when I'm given such instructions—"

I'd heard enough.

"I see why you feel you must comply. But I confess I'm surprised to learn your opinions are so readily swayed. I understood you prided yourself on your independence of mind."

She tried to implore my forgiveness, but when she saw it was in vain, she kissed me on both cheeks, made her goodbyes, and left. It was the last time I ever spoke to her.

For a while, I sat quite still in my chair, thinking over what had just happened. I admit that for all my attempts to disguise it, I was shocked at what Hester had told me. One must must have a thicker skin than I do, not to be hurt by the knowledge that another person wishes you such ill. Of course, that was exactly what Hester had intended me to feel. The whole little charade had been orchestrated with only one purpose in mind—to leave me as upset and miserable as she felt herself.

This may seem a very unfair and perhaps partial interpretation of Hester's motives; and at first, I fought against it, attempting to pity rather than blame her. I knew she resented me as a rival for Granville's affections; and having a jealous disposition myself, I knew only too well how envy eats away at all your better intentions. But even now, I cannot quite forgive her for what she did. She'd wanted to make me ashamed and humiliated, and she succeeded, pushing me into a very dark place indeed. All I could think of in the days that followed was how very much people must despise and condemn me. If this was the general opinion formed of my character, how could I bear to show myself among such harsh critics? I'd never been much affected by the disapproval of those to whom I was indifferent; but now I began to fear that even my friends secretly thought ill of me.

Everyone who I imagined cared for me, who'd shown me nothing but kindness—behind my back, did they too roll their eyes and lament with each other over my many transgressions?

Coming on top of Granville's absence and the loss of my child, this unpleasant episode hit me very hard indeed. For a long time, I could barely get out of bed, let alone bring myself to go out. I saw no one and never ventured from home. I longed to flee from everyone and take refuge somewhere I wouldn't be found, where I could lick my wounds and try to recover a little of my self-worth. Hester had hit me in a very tender place and cast me down into a great depression of mind, so that I was in the very worst state to deal with the next blow that was to fall upon me.

66

The first letter was sent to my daughter, Caro. She read only the first few lines before understanding there was something very wrong about it and flew to give it to me. Thank God she did so, for as soon as I looked at it, I saw it was filled with gross, disgusting indecencies, accompanied by the most lewd caricatures. It was worse than anything I'd ever seen, and to be sent to a young girl like my Caro—I couldn't believe it. I soon began to suspect, however, that the true target was not my innocent daughter but her unworthy mother.

My foreboding was quickly proved right. Over the next few days, I too received several letters, all full of badly drawn horrors and degrading insinuations. Others were sent to my sister and to Harryo. All were bad, but those directed at me were much the worst. They dwelt cruelly upon my affair with Granville, declaring he'd never loved me, that he laughed with his friends about my passion for him, talked with the greatest indifference of the children I'd borne him, and had recently found himself a younger, prettier mistress. They were full of details that could have been familiar only to someone within our circle, who knew both my family and me very well; and soon I was certain that their author was none other than Richard Sheridan.

Sheridan had been a thorn in my side for years. When I put an end to our affair, he convinced himself he'd been unjustly dismissed; and like Townshend, another angry man, he'd vacillated ever since between declaring fervently that he still loved me, and cruelly abusing me for my heartlessness in refusing to return his feelings. In both men, jealousy and cruelty went hand in hand; and Sheridan was relentless in his attacks upon me. He was one of the first to sniff out the rumors that linked my name to Granville's; and from that moment, he was unceasing in his attacks upon me. I have no doubt now that those first indecent drawings I received were from him. Wherever I went, I found him hovering about, eager to poke and stab at me with his nasty gibes. Wild animals scent weakness in their own kind and can always tell when one among them is injured. Sheridan, with his savage, instinctual nature, had something of that skill. With his unerring ability to fix upon the merest hint of vulnerability, he took every opportunity to hurt me without mercy. I suppose it was his writer's knowledge of human nature that gave him the power to strike so effectively. I can only say I suffered very greatly from it.

I couldn't prove at first that the letters came from him, for he disguised his writing and posted them from many different places. I took what precautions I could, tearing up any post I didn't recognize, but still some got through, upsetting me anew with the wickedness they contained. It was several months before they finally stopped coming, but by then, they'd left their mark. It was terrible to imagine they'd been concocted by a man who had once—indeed, still—professed to love me. Who could say what else he might have in mind to humiliate me? I was already low-spirited enough; now I was afraid even to leave the house, lest I find myself subjected to some new and more public insult.

So when Lord Morpeth offered to act as my protector, I was more

grateful than I could say. As Lord B was so often absent, and anyway disliked going much into society, Morpeth undertook to accompany me whenever I went out, indeed to place himself at my entire
disposal. He couldn't have been kinder, and I didn't hesitate to put
myself entirely in his hands. He was Granville's closest friend, knew
exactly what we were to each other, and was therefore one of the very
few people to whom I could speak freely of him. We'd known each
other since those far-off days in Italy, and I considered him almost
as a brother. He was married to my niece and seemed entirely happy
in his situation. And if that wasn't enough to give me confidence in
the disinterestedness of his care, there was also his friendship with
Granville. Wasn't there a kind of honor between men that forbade
any transgressions in such a case?

I was soon disabused of my naive illusions. One afternoon, as we
were talking of Granville, I was overcome with sadness and began
to cry. Morpeth sat down beside me to offer, as I thought, some
comfort—instead, I felt his hand upon me, in so unexpected a manner, that I thought I must have been mistaken. But no—he took me
in his arms in a most determined embrace. I struggled, begging him
to stop, but he wouldn't be dissuaded.

"I can't dissemble any longer—I'm most strongly attracted—
have been so for years—surely you must have perceived it?"

He then attempted to convey exactly what he meant, by his actions
as much as his words. I was more appalled than I could say. My agony
was so unmistakable that it shocked him out of his passion. With
some effort, he composed himself, immediately desisted, and began to
beg my forgiveness.

"I'm so very sorry. I've acted appallingly—my feelings overwhelmed me. I promise on my honor I'll never do so again."

On and on he went, abusing himself without end, but the damage
was done. Was there no man anywhere in whom a poor, unhappy
woman could place her trust? I'd truly loved Lord Morpeth, but in

the way one loves a brother. I'd never given him the slightest encouragement to think of me in any other way. Did he really imagine that because I'd received Granville in my bed, I'd allow him the same favors while his friend was away? It shocked me horribly to think the innocent affection I'd shown him might have been regarded as inviting his attentions.

Most of all, I was bitterly disappointed. I'd trusted Morpeth, and he'd betrayed me. I'd given him that most precious thing, my confidence—and in return, he'd revealed himself to be just another predatory man, with the same base intentions as all the others. A woman must be perpetually watchful, always on her guard. I'd learned to my cost that where men are concerned, there are no exceptions to this rule. Townshend, Sheridan, or Morpeth, there wasn't a hairsbreadth of difference between them. How stupid I'd been to think otherwise.

When Granville's letters had at last begun to arrive, I'd hoped they might offer me some consolation for all the difficulties that had engulfed me since his departure. I'd told myself, however, not to expect too much. He'd never been a natural correspondent. For him, as for most men I've known, writing was principally a means of communicating information—to convey anything more expressive did not come easily to him, which was why I treasured those rare lines written when he was moved to put down on paper exactly what he felt for me. This hadn't mattered so much when he was still in England—although we were often parted, I could always look forward to our meeting at some time in the future; but now I had no idea when or even if I should see him again. Nor, having no experience of Russia, could I conjure up for myself the circumstances in which he now lived. I encouraged him to include in his letters all the little details of his new existence, which would allow me to imagine the world in which he now moved; I even asked him to consider writing a journal, describing what he did and whom he saw each day, but he disliked this idea extremely, and for all my urgings, never adopted it. I scolded him that I learned more from William than I did from him. But I will say that even if his letters were not as evocative and descriptive as I might have wished, he was, by his own standards, a conscientious correspondent.

It was almost impossible to know when I should expect to hear from him. The route by which his letters were obliged to travel, from St. Petersburg to London, involved all manner of difficulties. The couriers who brought them were required to skirt battlefields and to brave the most inclement weather as well as uncertain sea crossings. Sometimes Granville included his letters to me in the diplomatic bag that carried his dispatches home. As this arrived at the Foreign Office, I soon became a regular visitor there, politely asking the clerks if anything had arrived for me, carrying away with delight even the shortest note, tossed off in a hurry "as the courier is this minute arrived at the door." All were proof I hadn't been forgotten.

I discovered from what he wrote that Granville didn't much care for his posting. The task before him was a very great one—the Tsar wasn't persuaded that an alliance with England was the best way of securing Russia's position against Napoleon, and the burden of his mission weighed heavily on Granville's mind. Nor did he find his surroundings congenial. He hated court life and all the formalities that went with his ambassador's rank, complaining bitterly of the boredom and weariness of his role, which obliged him to meet the same people over and over, making empty conversation while never allowing an unguarded word to slip through. He was cheated at every turn, paying out huge sums of his own money for a freezing house full of broken furniture, while spied upon all the while. He was uncomfortable and low-spirited, and he wanted nothing so much as to discharge his duty to the best of his abilities and hurry back home. But all that changed when he met the "Little Barbarian."

Her real name was Princess Serge Galitzin; I don't remember

now where her nickname came from, but it conveys something of her lively, independent character. She'd been separated from her husband for many years, but no breath of scandal had ever tarnished her reputation. As she was also a very great beauty who lived alone with only a female companion, this spoke very highly of either her morals or her skill in concealment; but it must have been the former, as everyone who knew her testified so strongly to her virtue. As soon as they met, Granville was captivated. She was exactly the kind of woman he liked best—worldly, handsome, witty; a brilliant talker on any subject from politics to scandal. I think she was around twenty-five at this time.

From the moment I first saw her name in his hand, I was afraid. I'd always known he'd find someone to console him in St. Petersburg; nothing could prevent that—you might as well ask the sun to stop shining as beg Granville not to flirt. He'd always reveled in the company of women, and throughout our long connection, he'd never been immune to the prospect of some charming dalliance, if it should chance to come his way. I cannot say I liked this, but I felt I could hardly complain, situated as I was. I tried not to let such passing amours affect me, and on the whole I succeeded. It was only when I sensed the presence of something more serious, as had been the case with Hester, that my jealous nature asserted itself.

Now I began to feel the same misgivings about the Barbarian. She occupied far too prominent a place in his letters for me to feel entirely easy about their relations. I reminded Granville of the promise he'd made me, to disclose with absolute candor the truth of any significant romantic entanglement he pursued. He willingly complied with my wish—but everything he told me about her sent chills right through me.

In one respect, I was grateful for his frankness, as it suggested he hadn't yet sundered those ties of complete honesty that I believed helped keep us together. But oh, what pain it caused me to read, in his own words, the progress of their affair! He began by admitting that something of flirtation was mixed into their conversations, although he thought it improbable it would go very far. Then I was told he spent every night at the Barbarian's house, often till two or three in the morning, but so far, nothing improper had occurred. Next, he informed me that she'd allowed him to speak playfully, even affectionately to her, although, for all her seeming encouragement, she hadn't yet permitted him to attempt anything approaching an embrace or a kiss.

It was inexpressibly painful for me to feel that Granville was slowly but surely drifting into a serious affair—that little by little, everyone else was being banished from his mind, as he became more and more absorbed in his pursuit of the Barbarian. Of course he denied it, insisting he wasn't in love with her—on the contrary, he was eager to return to England, the very thought of it was enough to make him happy—but, in a phrase that wiped away any relief I might have felt at his avowal, he added a fatal postscript, confessing that for all of that, he couldn't deny that she'd nevertheless seriously piqued his interest.

This single phrase was enough to drive me into a state of the greatest agitation. It wouldn't be long, I told myself, before Granville and the Barbarian were upon the most intimate terms—even her celebrated resistance must surely crumble under the power of his appeal—and what would happen then? He'd never come home. He'd stay in Russia with her, and what would become of me? Of Little H and George? Day and night I thought of nothing else. So I was already extremely uneasy when one afternoon Lady Elizabeth Monck called upon me. She'd hardly been seated five minutes before she began upon the subject which had clearly prompted her visit.

"You hear often from Granville, I imagine?"

"When his work and the weather permit, which isn't as frequently as I'd like."

"And what's your opinion of the Barbarian? Do you think it's as serious as people say?"

I hesitated before replying, taken aback at hearing her name linked with Granville's.

"Oh, please tell me I'm not the one to enlighten you?" Lady Elizabeth looked mortified. "That would be too bad."

"Yes, I know about her. May I ask how you do?"

"A friend of mine knows a Prince B, who lives in Petersburg. He wrote to her about it, and she told me."

"What a world we live in, where Russian gossip can be sped to London in a matter of weeks and do as much harm here as it's already done in Petersburg."

"I'm afraid I don't believe it is gossip. It was told to me as the truth."

"Gossip always is. It never goes about under its own name, but always masquerades as gospel."

"Perhaps I shouldn't— But there's more, if you want to hear it."

"Will it make me happy if I do?"

"I'm afraid it won't—but perhaps you should know what's being said. I'm not sure ignorance is always the best policy in these matters."

I turned away. If I'd been stronger, I'd have changed the subject or rung the bell and asked her to leave; but I was weak and couldn't bear not knowing.

"If I don't tell you, someone else will only do so."

"Very well. So what's this story everyone knows but me?"

"Lord G's connection to the Barbarian is spoken of everywhere in Petersburg. He's said to have succeeded with her in every possible way, so that their attachment is now pretty much declared. They go about everywhere together, and he stays at her house till the early hours. Her husband has heard of it and isn't pleased—with the result that her divorce is likely to be brought forward with the greatest haste."

"And do the well-informed people who spread such stories say what will happen then?"

"That when Lord Granville returns to England, she'll accompany him, with the intention of their marrying here."

This made me catch my breath. I fixed my gaze on the floor, so Lady Elizabeth shouldn't see the ridiculous, stupid tears that filled my eyes.

"I'm sorry, Harriet. Has Granville said nothing about this?"

"Some of it he's told me. As for the rest—I can't allow myself to give it credit until I hear it from him myself. Then—and only then—will I consider it the truth."

I knew Lady Elizabeth cared for me and didn't mean to be cruel. I understood she truly believed she was doing me a service by telling me what she'd heard. But I believe that, like most unimaginative people, she hadn't considered what I was to do with her news, once she'd ensured I was in full possession of it. Write to Granville immediately, I suppose, passing on what was being said and demanding to know the facts? Of course I'd do that. But it would be ages before I could expect an answer. And if Granville was faced with such a stark question from me—"Is it your intention to marry the Barbarian?"— who knew, for all his protestations of candor, how frank he would be in his reply? All I could do was to worry and torment myself even more than before, which did me no good. Meanwhile, Lady Elizabeth could preen herself on her honesty in having informed me of what "I really ought to know," which only made my sufferings worse.

It wasn't often I allowed myself to feel anything like anger toward Granville, but as I stared blankly from our drawing room into Cavendish Square, I felt a rare wave of indignation. He'd already had everything from me a woman could give. Hester too had sacrificed her hopes, contentment, and peace of mind to him. And thousands of miles away in Russia, another poor victim was about to fall under his spell. How many unhappy lovers did he need? Would there ever come a time when enough was enough? I closed my eyes and clenched my fists as tightly as I could until the resentment eventually subsided.

67

Meanwhile, there was no doubt Hester remained in a distressed and volatile state of mind. I heard news of her from William Hill, a mutual friend, who'd once hoped to marry her himself. Mr. Hill was a bluff, sensible man who referred to himself without bitterness as always destined to play second fiddle to other luckier suitors; but he really cared for Hester, and supported her loyally through all her trials. In my opinion, she could have done a great deal worse than marry him, but when did any desperate woman make such a sensible choice? It was from Mr. Hill that I learned the true reason for Hester's cutting me so completely. He couldn't say whether the Queen had in fact advised her to avoid me, for she had never mentioned that to him. In his view, the real reason was her conviction that I was responsible for ruining her chances of marrying Granville.

"She says you knew Lord Granville wished to marry, and you'd therefore looked about to find him a wife who might not object to your remaining his mistress even after marriage—'living in common,' as she called it."

"And she seriously believes I picked her out as a possible candidate for this role?"

"Yes, and for a while, you thought Hester seemed so infatuated with Lord Granville that she wouldn't object to any terms that would join her to him. But then it became clear you'd miscalculated, that Granville loved Hester more than you—and that she would never be as tractable as you supposed."

"Who could ever describe Hester as tractable? No one who knows her, that's for sure."

Mr. Hill smiled at this, and went on:

"So, as Hester tells it—from having supported the marriage, you now did everything in your power to oppose it, abusing her to Lord Granville until he was persuaded not to proceed."

"So his declining to marry her is to be laid at my door. Can she seriously believe Lord Granville simply did as I told him, that he's entirely subject to my will in all this?"

"Not entirely. Hester doesn't completely excuse him, complaining that he acted very badly, in the light of all he said and wrote, and his encouraging her to believe he meant to propose."

"But that was as nothing compared to my wiles?"

"I'm afraid so. In Hester's eyes, Lord Granville's withdrawal was principally at your behest. He wouldn't have done so if you hadn't insisted upon it."

It upset me terribly to hear myself described in these odious terms—could Hester really believe I was capable of behaving in such a way? It was such a ridiculous story. At the same time, I understood these weren't rational thoughts, but the furious flailing accusations of a bitterly disappointed woman, deadening her own pain by inflicting injuries on another. I can't pretend I wasn't angry with her, but my resentment was tempered by a kind of pity. And from everything I heard through that spring and summer, she was so wretched that only the hardest-hearted witness could have been unmoved by her state.

It was rumored everywhere that she was carrying Granville's

child, which every circumstance seemed to confirm. She hardly ever went out, and every report spoke of her as being very ill—pale and out of spirits—confined to her bed—very much indisposed. I'd long feared she might be pregnant; and it was soon generally believed in London society this was the case. Even my sister hinted at it, telling me Hester had been seen at a small party, where she was so languid and weak that she'd fainted. I replied that I'd heard nothing definite to suggest she was in such a condition, and hoped it might not be so. To others who sought my opinion, I said much the same, refusing to be drawn into speculation that could only be harmful to Hester.

In truth, however, I'm afraid I thought it only too likely that Hester was indeed pregnant, especially as I could get no definitive answer when I pressed Granville upon the subject. I passed on to him all my misgivings, together with detailed accounts of what was being said, hoping to provoke either a confession or a denial from him; but he was evasive, and never either directly confirmed or refuted my fears. By the time summer arrived, Hester must have been confined, if she was indeed with child; but I never discovered, either then or since, whether such an event took place. By the end of August, I knew only that Hester was said to be living with Granville's friend Mr. Canning, and there was no more news about her, other than that she still thought me responsible for all her woes.

I did my best to keep up my spirits in the face of so many lowering trials. Perhaps the only dependable joy in these difficult, lonely days was that which I derived from Little H and George. I saw as much of them as I could, perhaps a little more than was truly consistent with safety, but I could never resist the pleasure of spending time in their company. Little H was just now beginning to be curious about the world and her place in it. I loved to see her looking about her, as it were, with that eager interest little children start to display at that age. There was one question, though, that I dreaded to hear from her. I don't know how I should have answered if she'd asked me directly whether I was her mother; I was profoundly grateful she never did. She knew me simply as "Lady," which she used as affectionately toward me as if it had been the dearest name in the world. She thought of me as her guardian, her protector, the kindly, loving source of toys and treats, hugs and kisses—and for the time being, that would have to suffice. I hoped that one day, when she was old enough to understand, it might be possible to confess to her the truth of our relationship; but I knew, to my sorrow, it couldn't happen yet.

My older children, meanwhile, were passing swiftly into adulthood, and occupied my mind in a very different way. In the spring of 1805, William Lamb, Lady Melbourne's son, finally proposed to my Caro. They'd long wished to marry and seemed very much in love, so that neither of our families had the heart to forbid it. I can't say I was entirely happy with the match. Caro's lively mind required a clever man to satisfy her, and no one could deny that in that respect, she and William were perfectly suited. But in my opinion, her volatile nature also necessitated a husband possessed of enough force, direction, and energy to keep her steady; and in all these qualities, William was sadly lacking. I didn't doubt he cared for her, but his was a cool, languid temperament, disinclined to exert itself in offering either guidance or love; and I feared he would be incapable of demonstrating his affection as often and as extravagantly as Caro would expect.

More selfishly, I was wary of the closer connection the marriage would forge between myself and Lady Melbourne. There was much about her that I truly loved, and God knows I had many reasons to be grateful to her. But her acts of kindness didn't blind me to the streak of ruthlessness in her character. She too thought William and Caro a bad match and told me she very much hoped the daughter would turn out better than the mother. It was said as a joke, but I knew she was in earnest. She was formidable when crossed, especially in anything concerning her children; I dreaded any clash between her iron will and Caroline's mercurial character. But I did my best to put these anxieties aside and celebrated the wedding with every appearance of joy. Caro supported the demands of the day itself without displaying too much of that nervousness that so often afflicts her; but the night that followed was a very different matter.

The newlyweds went down to Brocket, the Melbournes' country house, for a brief honeymoon. Four days later, Caro wrote, asking me urgently to come and see her. When I arrived, I was disturbed to see she was nervous and restless, pacing about the room. William, having made me a slightly shamefaced greeting, soon made himself scarce, leaving me alone with my daughter. It did not take her long to get to the point.

"Married life—one aspect of it at least—has come as a great shock to me."

My heart sank. This was exactly what I'd feared for her. I'd tried to enlighten her about what she must expect. I was afraid of making her unnecessarily fearful, but she was so blithely unconcerned that she didn't really attend. I could only hope her first experience had not been as unpleasant as my own.

"William was not ungentlemanly, I hope? I imagined he would be kind."

"And so he was at first. I admit I was exceedingly anxious about what was to come. When I came into the bedroom—and thought, 'Well, we must share a bed together'—it made me very uneasy. But I was so exhausted after the wedding that I immediately fell asleep."

"And William was content with that?"

"For a while. But then he woke me up—and what followed was not so pleasant."

"I'm afraid no one likes it much at first."

"I was appalled. I was so shocked it took some time to recover. I'm not myself, even now."

She began to cry. "I had no idea of—what it would really be like."

I took her in my arms, and she sobbed on my shoulder. I whispered into her ears all the comfort I could offer—that the hurt grows less and less, and once it's gone, she may even find enjoyment creeps in—but she wouldn't be consoled. I asked myself if I was to blame, if I should have spoken more plainly, done more to disabuse her of the romantic ideas she'd conceived about the married state? I suppose I'd resisted saying more because, for all her worldly airs, her indifference to what could and could not be said, her extraordinary frankness of manner and behavior, she was still such an innocent. And I confess, I was rather proud of that, telling myself that though I was a sinner, Caro was at least the very model of purity.

And anyway, would it really have helped if she'd known what awaited her? Might it not simply have increased her fear, without changing in any way what she was obliged to endure? The truth is that marriage is a great trial to a young girl—and a very unfair one. As on all occasions, men get all the pleasure, while all the pain, both of mind and body, is kept for us. It is a harsh awakening when a woman understands for the first time that this is the way of the world. I wondered somberly how my Caro would respond to this knowledge once she'd fully absorbed it. I hoped for the best, for she seemed genuinely in love with William, and perhaps this would carry her through; but when I thought of her temperament—excitable, skittish, given to extremes in all things—I trembled for her.

My eldest son, Duncannon, was married in September, but not to Harryo, as we'd all expected. They'd gone on for the better part of a year quarreling and making up, without ever arriving at a decision about their future. Duncannon, I'm afraid, was not faithful, entangling himself with a number of other women, which Harryo couldn't bear. When the question was raised between them as to whether they liked each other enough to marry, she insisted he must give up all his flirtations before she could consider taking such a step. Duncannon responded very badly, declaring he wouldn't have rules laid down for him by any woman living, that no wife of his should ever attempt to govern him—and as Harryo found this insupportable, their long dalliance came all at once to an end. It took Duncannon hardly any time at all to fix on someone he thought more amenable to his views. By September, he was married to Lady Maria Fane—the younger sister of that Sarah whom Granville had unsuccessfully pursued. Maria was everything Duncannon wanted in a wife—sweet-natured, docile, enraptured by him—and they soon seemed entirely happy with each other, always in each other's company, he loudly dispensing hearty affection, while she laughed at all his jokes.

I felt sorry for Harryo, who, with all her sharp edges, was in every way more interesting than the pliant Maria. If she was disappointed, she didn't show it, as I fear I'd have done. She kept her feelings hidden from everyone—although my sister told me Little G was her great confidante, the only person to whom she truly opened her heart. To the rest of the world, she presented a façade of studied unconcern, exclaiming how much she liked Lady Maria and listening with a fixed smile as the newly engaged couple tactlessly discussed all their domestic arrangements before her. Her discipline never faltered; the only pointed words I ever heard escape her came as an aside: one heard from them, Harryo said, more about their furniture than their love.

My sister worried that being slighted in this way would be a disadvantage to poor Harryo, and I didn't disagree. She'd already met with several other mortifications, when men for whom she'd shown a liking married someone else. She was only twenty, but I sensed she'd begun to feel failure creeping up on her and would be relieved to find some suitor she could admire in the not too distant future. It's very hard for a young woman in such a situation, for there's very little she can do to help herself except wait and hope that fate will throw someone in her way who will want her as much she does him.

The marriages of my children gave me pleasure and occupied my mind when some distraction was very necessary to me; but nothing, I will confess, made up for Granville's long absence. The Barbarian was constantly in my mind—as she was in his letters, in which he chronicled with the most exacting detail the advances and withdrawals that characterized their relations. He had not, I believed, entirely succeeded with her yet—but there was no sign that his failure to do so had dampened in the least his feelings for her.

So when, in September, he wrote to tell me he hoped to be back in

England in just six weeks, I was both elated and apprehensive at the news. I was terrified when I thought he might not come alone—but as the time for his departure came nearer, and he didn't suggest the Barbarian would be accompanying him, I allowed myself to think this was unlikely. I understood it didn't rule out the possibility of her arriving in England at some later date; but by then, I should have had the opportunity to speak to Granville in person, to hear from him directly what he intended regarding her. I therefore did all in my power to put aside my worries, and fixed my mind instead upon the simple fact that I should see Granville again very soon. I began to count the days, eagerly expecting another letter to give me further details of his plans. But I waited and waited—and nothing arrived. It wasn't until the end of December that I received the disappointment I had dreaded. His return was delayed—he did not expect to be home for at least five months.

This wreck of all my hopes devastated me. All the feelings I'd tried so hard to repress burst out to torment me—longing, jealousy, fear, desire, a simple need to hear his voice once more—they battered me around the head until I could no longer think clearly.

In the end, of course, there was nothing I could do but try to resign myself to what I could not change. In an attempt to console me, Granville urged me to consider that five months was only one hundred and fifty days. He said he intended to get a stick and make a notch upon it every night, as evidence of how quickly the weeks went by. He suggested I should think of some similar device that would make the time pass more quickly for me. He meant it kindly—but I could never have done the same. The sight of so much uncut space remaining, row after row of empty days still to go, would have been more than I could stand.

69

I've said before that it's as well we cannot know what lies before us, for we could never deal with the awful knowledge that accompanies such foresight. Never was that truer than in the dreadful year of 1806. From its earliest days, it announced itself a year of death. In January, Mr. Pitt died—worn out, it was said, by the burdens of office, his constitution destroyed by the unceasing press of business. I couldn't honestly regret him as a politician, for our ideas were so very different; but to lose a man of such experience in wartime couldn't be counted as anything but a misfortune. I felt, too, some private sympathy for him. Granville respected and admired him, which naturally disposed me a little in his favor; and I knew he'd tried, as far as his limitations allowed, to assist Hester, whom I believe he really loved.

My sister, who had no such personal associations to soften her opinion, was more pragmatic. She quickly closed down anything in my conversation that savored of regret.

"Yes, Mr. Fox is right to say his departure leaves a great chasm in the world," she declared. "He's been in power for twenty years. It's impossible he should not be missed. But now," she concluded, "I think at long last we shall see some changes."

I hadn't seen Georgiana so exercised by politics for years. It was as if a part of her being, so long subdued and repressed, had roared back into life. As she'd anticipated, it proved impossible for the Tories, divided among themselves after Pitt's death, to form an administration. Instead, exactly as she'd hoped, our political friends came back in power, with the addition of a few amenable Tories to sweeten the deal. The new government was quickly dubbed "the Ministry of All the Talents," but in truth most of the talent was Whig, with Mr. Fox at the Foreign Office and my brother George as Home Secretary. Even Sheridan found a place as Treasurer of the Navy, though how he was to look after public money when his handling of his own was so disastrous was never explained to me.

Once the new ministry was officially in place, Georgiana took up her position once more as the reigning queen of the Whigs. She held a great celebration, to which every one of our newly appointed ministers was invited, over which she presided with all her old exuberant charm. I stood beside her as we surveyed the supper room, lit up in all its grandeur, alive with excited conversation and barely suppressed glee. The Prince of Wales was there, sitting alongside Mr. Fox, who had smartened himself up with a new wig. Georgiana gazed over the crowd with profound satisfaction, looking happier than I'd seen her for years.

"Now we may truly say," she cried, taking my hand in hers, "'we, the administration,' for that is true again at last."

That first dinner was only the beginning. Night after night, guests flocked to Devonshire House, which had become again what it was always meant to be, the acknowledged headquarters of Whig political life—and there, at the glorious center of it all, was Georgiana, restored to her element, happy, full of life, and delighted to be a busy, useful part of the political world.

Then, in the midst of her triumph, she fell ill. She hadn't been really well for some time. Her poor eye, which had never really recovered from that terrible inflammation of several years ago, still caused her great discomfort. She was subject to kidney stones, which were excruciatingly painful until they were passed, as well as numerous bilious attacks and low fevers. When she took to her bed in the middle of March, her doctors thought at first it was yet another stone, and that her symptoms would disappear once it was expelled. But she didn't improve; and when I saw how low and reduced she'd become, I went to stay at Devonshire House to nurse her, thinking no one could care for her more tenderly than myself.

Thus began the worst week of my life. I saw at once her sickness was something quite different from the stones. She had a high fever and terrible fits of shivering, which sometimes lasted for hours. The doctors had no answers when I asked them their opinion and disagreed among themselves about the seriousness of her condition. Not one of their remedies made the slightest difference. They gave her powders to drink—shaved her head—put blister plasters on her poor skin, which only increased her pain without diminishing in the least whatever caused her suffering.

Even now I cannot bear to recall the horror of what followed. As she grew worse and worse with every hour that passed, I understood in a frenzy of panicked desperation that Georgiana was dying. I wish I could say she went gently, but that wasn't so. Anything so distressing as the three days' agony she endured at the end I've never witnessed. And through it all, there was nothing I could do to ease her suffering—except hold her in my arms through all her struggles—kiss her as she drew her last painful breaths—and press her lifeless body to my heart when she was finally released.

When they led me from her bed, I was stupefied, dumbstruck with shock. Georgiana was gone, and yet I was still alive—I couldn't comprehend how this could be. We'd always thought and felt as one. Why had my life not ended with hers? It was only later I understood that in a way it did, for a part of me died with her in that ghastly sickroom. You cannot share a soul with another being, as I did with Georgiana, and not feel something of yourself perish with their loss. Even now, there are moments when I yearn for her so desperately that I wish with all my heart I could have followed her. But I hadn't the courage to do it myself, and my grief, terrible as it was, proved not enough to do it for me.

So I have gone doggedly on since her loss, one foot before the other, for what choice do I have? It is said time is the great healer, but I cannot say I have observed that myself. My sister has been dead six years, and the wound inflicted by her loss is still as raw as ever. But I wouldn't have it any other way. My pain is a measure of how much I loved her, and I could never wish to see that fade from my mind.

70

When later that same year, Mr. Fox died too, I thought the shock would be almost too much for me to bear. In a matter of months, I'd lost two of the people I loved best in the world; I had never felt so alone. For a long time, I was so crushed and destroyed that I could hardly speak. I was utterly broken, indifferent to everything around me, mute with a misery I thought I should never throw off. Amid my grief, I longed for Granville, yearning desperately for the comfort of his presence. Writing to him did me no good. I was so sunk in despair that I couldn't find the language to tell him how I felt. For the first time in my life, words failed me. All I I wanted was the silent consolation that he and only he could bring me.

I could scarcely credit it when I received a letter from him telling me he was to return. His mission had made no progress, and he was called home. For a long time, I refused to allow myself the pleasure, the extraordinary relief of believing this to be true; only when he was considerably advanced on his long journey did I permit myself to count the days remaining before I should see him again.

He wrote to me from his ship the instant it arrived, asking where he could see me. I arranged, with my usual contrivance, to find a safe place for us to meet—as I could no longer call upon Lady Anne's generosity, we were obliged to rendezvous at our children's house, which I had beforehand ensured was empty enough to receive us. As was always the case when we'd been parted for so long, I was terrified he wouldn't like what he saw when we met. The terrible loss I'd suffered had left its mark on my looks; I was forty-five and felt every year weighing heavily upon me. I tried to tell myself that, if this proved to be so, perhaps it was just as well, for it would prevent us from falling back into our old intimacy, that my haggard features would persuade him, as none of my earlier entreaties had done, that the time had come to live chastely, as a loving brother and sister might.

But I was delighted—no, triumphant even—to discover I was quite wrong. We were immediately in each other's arms; and all my resolutions to resist him—even if just for the shortest time, to prove to us both that I wasn't entirely his to command—were quite useless. Afterward, I stroked his hair, always one of my greatest pleasures, scarcely able to believe we were together once more.

"You know," I said to him, "the power you have over me is extraordinary. The only way to have prevented what just happened would've been for me never to see you—and I couldn't have borne that—never to have looked into your eyes—which would have been impossible; I've gazed away my whole existence in them—or for you never to have touched me, for then I always crumble. I try to be better than I am— and in your presence, I always fail."

"You say that as though you regret. I'm not sure I really believe you. I've been imagining this moment for a very long time. It would have been a great pity to cast a shadow over it with a reluctance you don't really feel. I'm not sorry at all that you show me what you feel so readily."

I blushed at that; but I couldn't deny it.

We had four days in which we were able to meet alone, which passed for me in a fever dream of pleasure. I don't mean by that solely the physical intimacy we enjoyed. There was also a sad kind of comfort in consoling each other for those we had lost, for Granville's mother had died while he'd been in Russia, a source of great remorse to him, as he was a very loving son. I drew some melancholy comfort in confessing to him the magnitude of my own anguish—the sense that my very life had been torn asunder by Georgiana's death—knowing he would understand and feel my pain. I think we were of some help to one another. Then we were obliged to part—he to visit friends and relations, me to retreat to Roehampton. As soon as he was gone, my happiness leaked away, and all I could think of was when I should see him next.

We were in each other's company again, in various places—at the seaside, at Roehampton, in London—but we were hardly ever alone. Granville's return to our society made him a great subject of conversation, some of which, when recounted to me, was not much to my taste. I heard a great deal about his involvement with the Barbarian, which was everywhere talked of; the universal opinion, which was even more distressing to me, was that he was very sorry to have left her and missed her very much. I knew she wrote to him; and I had begun to suspect they'd discussed the prospect of marriage, which Granville, when taxed upon it, didn't entirely deny.

"I think she loves me," he admitted. "I wasn't sure before, but when I was called back to England, she was very distressed."

"And what do you intend to do about it?"

"I cannot exactly say, as her intentions are not always plain to me."

He wouldn't be drawn further, but I saw she was much on his mind.

This prospect of his proposing to her was so awful to me that I did everything in my power to push it from my thoughts. I reminded myself of the thousands of miles that stood between them, of the likelihood of whatever feelings they had for each other being gradually extinguished, not just by distance, but also by the impossibility of their ever meeting again.

I think I was mostly successful in hiding my anxiety from the small society in which I moved. At Devonshire House, where I was a frequent guest, I gave no hint of my apprehensions, either to Bess Foster, or to my niece Harryo. Granville often joined us there, and I watched, with indulgent composure, as he and Harryo played chess together. His presence always seemed to cheer her, and I liked to see her happy. Her situation was very uncomfortable since Georgiana's death, living in the same household as her father and his mistress, without her mother's benign presence to blur the true nature of their connection. I understood that at some point Harryo's plight would have to be resolved; but I thought I'd time enough to come to her aid, that I could address her happiness when my own was more secure.

But as I was to discover, the very opposite was true. Granville had been back in England for barely eight months when he was asked to return to Russia, to persuade the Tsar to accept substantial British subsidies in return for continuing to fight the French. I thought I'd die when I heard he'd agreed to take the post, especially when he confessed to me the true motive for his determination to go.

"I must find out how I stand with the Barbarian, if she's prepared to renew our old—our intimate and confidential intercourse. If I don't take this opportunity, I'll never discover what she truly thinks."

"Then you intend to ask her to marry you?"

Somehow, I got out the words, though I thought it'd destroy me to say them.

"I'll know better when I can see and speak to her myself."

I began to cry. I'd sworn to myself I wouldn't, but I couldn't bear the thought of it. He reached out his hand to me, but I shrank away.

"I understand why you must do this. I understand it's inevitable—but I cannot pretend not to suffer at it."

I saw him flinch and felt his distress.

"Harriet, if you really want me to do so, I'll tell her it's over. Is that what you wish?"

Of course I said no. How could I say otherwise? I loved him too much for that.

And then, in barely any time at all, he was gone, back to the east. I could almost have laughed at the cruelty of fate. Only a few months before, I'd believed he was truly returned to me. Now I was alone again, and likely to remain so. I was in such despair, so low in body and mind, that I honestly wished to die—but death doesn't come by invitation, and anyway, what would've become of Little H and George if I had? So instead, I clung stubbornly, if not with much gratitude, to a life that seemed to offer me a little in the way of either hope or happiness.

71

*A*t last, I emerged from the miserable lassitude into which Granville's departure had plunged me, and I turned my head to the problem of Harryo. No young woman could be expected to relish such a difficult situation, but it was made far worse by Harryo's unconquerable hostility to Bess. She'd always regarded her as an interloper, who'd betrayed Georgiana during her lifetime and usurped her position now she was dead. She never spoke so plainly to me, for she knew that despite everything, I truly loved Bess. I was never blind to her faults, which were many, and there was perhaps a grain of truth in Harryo's accusations—no one could say Bess wasn't aware of where her advantage lay. But my sister had loved her dearly, and I'm always inclined to think the best of anyone precious to those I adore.

However, even I could see that Bess hadn't given much consideration to Harryo's tender feelings. As Harryo was the only daughter remaining at home, many of her mother's duties should have fallen to her—presiding at the table, ordering meals, managing all the domestic details that are the concern of the lady of the house. Instead, Bess claimed all these for herself, acting in every way as if she'd inherited by default all Georgiana's privileges; and implying too that it was only a matter of time before she became legally entitled to them as well, making it as plain as possible that after some decent interval, she fully expected the Duke to marry her eventually. It's impossible to exaggerate the horror this prospect induced in my family, and Harryo, exposed to it as she was, felt it more bitterly than anyone else.

The Duke, who might have felt some sympathy for his daughter's discomfort, did nothing at all to protect her. He'd never really cared for Harryo. She once told me, in an unguarded moment, how thrilled she'd been when, for the first time in her life, he'd shown her real affection, shaking her by the hand and kissing her twice. She was then twenty-three years old. Usually, she came a poor second to the Duke's dogs, on whom he lavished all the attention he denied to his unfortunate daughter, laughing fondly at their antics, while Harryo tried her best to join in.

I did what I could. I carried Harryo off to Roehampton, promising her the warmest room in the house and every small domestic pleasure in my power. As, I believe, she'd never come first in anyone's calculations, this pleased her, and she thanked me with real gratitude. I hoped very much that this would mark an improvement in relations between us, for we'd never been close before. For the following six months, Harryo spent a great deal of time with me, both in London and in the country, with every appearance of pleasure. But we both knew this was no permanent solution to her discontent, for in the end, she was always obliged to go home to Bess and the Duke.

Her best method of escape would have been marriage; but no serious contender for her hand had emerged since Duncannon had rejected her a year ago. I think it was my brother who suggested she should stay for a while with his family at Althorp. There was a great deal of talk about the benefits of fresh air and a change of scene, but everyone understood, no one more than Harryo herself, that this was an obvious attempt to find her a husband. The candidate was my brother's eldest son, Jack—in theory an excellent match, heir to the Spencer earldom, not ill looking, and near her own age. Pressed by everyone around her to put herself in his way, and seeing no alternative to going, Harryo duly plucked up her courage, subdued her pride, and went off obediently to see and be seen.

The visit was a disaster, bad enough that she opened her heart to confess to me something of its horrors. Jack Spencer, it appeared, was a man obsessed with a single pursuit—hunting.

"He's never really alive unless he's on horseback. Nothing else means anything to him. He doesn't care whether he's amused or bored, happy or sad, awake or asleep—if he's not in pursuit of some poor wild creature, it's all one as far as he's concerned."

"Is it really that bad? What does he do in the evening? Or when the weather's against him? He must have some other occupations, surely?"

"Yes, he'll listen to music, play at cards sometimes. But he's merely passing the time until he can be out with the hounds again. He's present in body, but his mind is elsewhere—following the fox, I suppose."

"So you felt nothing for him, then?"

She laughed. "On hunting days, he's so excited, so desperate to be out and away, that it's like watching some great Newfoundland dog let off the leash and bounding joyfully into the distance—you can't help but smile at so much eager, innocent pleasure. But while those are amiable traits in a pet, they're scarcely the qualities one hopes for in a husband."

Her mood changed after this disappointment. I think she felt Althorp had been her last chance, and now that it had failed her, she had nothing to look forward to. She seemed to turn in on herself; I certainly felt her pull away from me. She returned to her old manner—polite but reticent, grateful for any attention but holding me at a distance. I wondered sometimes whether there was some untold, unrequited object of her desire, whom she cherished in secret but regarded as utterly beyond her reach. Perhaps that might account for her air of frustrated unhappiness? I put this one night to Bess Foster. She didn't care much for Harryo—it's hard to like someone who makes their disapproval of you so evident—but as she lived with her so closely, I thought she might have noticed signs I had not.

"There is indeed someone she likes. And I believe I know exactly who it is—although you won't like the answer."

"You must tell me now. Who is it?"

Bess laughed. "Lord Granville, of course. I can't believe you've never noticed it. Didn't you see how she acted when he was here in the autumn?"

This was the very last name I had expected. I was completely astounded.

"Are you sure? I'd never have imagined she liked him. She always talks very slightingly of his pride and thinks he's very pleased with himself."

"Like and dislike are often at war when you're attracted to a man of whom you don't entirely approve."

"What makes you think she cares for him?"

"Before he went away, she talked of him constantly—what he was doing—whom he was seeing—whether he'd call here—how long he might stay. And there's an expression she has when he's around—you won't have seen it, because you have eyes only for him—but she has a little of the same look, as if she'd like to eat him all up. It's unmistakable, once you've noticed it."

"Have you ever asked her about it?"

"She irritates me sometimes with her holier-than-thou manner, and once I teased her with liking him. She denied it, of course—and regards it as just another example of my vulgar indelicacy. But I assure you, she cares for him. I've no doubt about it at all."

I was so surprised at the strength of Bess's opinion that it took me a little while to decide what I thought of it. On reflection, I was forced to agree that there were indeed instances that suggested Harryo wasn't indifferent to Granville. A look that lingered for a moment too long. His name on her lips more than was usual for someone who professed to find him aloof and disdainful. Yes, I decided, Bess was right on all these counts.

But even if that were so, what did Harryo imagine could result from her fondness? I thought it extremely probable she knew of our affair. Her sister must have been told by Lord Morpeth the terms we were on, and I didn't doubt she'd shared that knowledge with Harryo.

This wouldn't encourage her to think well of Granville as a marital prospect. Harryo was a moral little creature; she had no patience with adultery, having experienced for herself the malign consequences wreaked on those innocents caught in its turbulent wake. As a child, she'd very much resented her mother's long absence abroad, the years she spent in exile after giving birth to Grey's child. I couldn't say how much Harryo now understood about the true reason for her mother's apparent abandonment of her children; but even if she knew all, I doubted it would have made her any more sympathetic to Georgiana's plight. The great passions that had disrupted my sister's life and mine were, as Harryo saw them, no more than selfish indulgences, which should have been resisted in the interest of the children. Her impatience with my son Duncannon over his "flirtations" demonstrated how deeply this distaste was fixed in her character; and if, as I suspected, she was fully aware of the long connection between Granville and me, I didn't think it would be much of a recommendation to her in considering him as a potential husband.

I didn't doubt that for all her misgivings, Harryo might still harbor a strong physical attraction to Granville—who wouldn't find him as beautiful and as irresistible as I did? But I was sure nothing could ever come of it, that her liking was no more than a passing fancy, a phantom passion which would evaporate as soon as some solid, real-life suitor presented himself. And anyway, she wasn't at all the kind of woman Granville preferred. His taste was for a certain worldly experience, for a particular kind of handsome assurance, none of which Harryo possessed. She cheerfully admitted she had no pretensions at all to either beauty or elegance and was often awkward in company she didn't know well. It was true she was clever, which was important to Granville, but hers was a biting, satiric wit, which I doubted would be much to his liking.

So all things considered, even my jealous nature wasn't roused by what Bess told me. Instead, it encouraged me to redouble my efforts on Harryo's behalf, to find her a real husband to replace the fantasy she'd conjured up around Granville. I swallowed hard, for I didn't find her the easiest companion, but I dutifully took Harryo under my wing, sweeping her into society as often as I could, in the hope that she might finally meet someone who interested her.

I did my best, but I can't say I enjoyed it. I no longer took much pleasure in great routs and parties, and the obligations of a chaperone removed the remotest possibility of my meeting with any amusement of my own. Harryo would not stir three steps without me, which meant that if she was speaking to anyone, I dared not move even though I saw some old friend nearby, for what if my departure should interrupt some promising conversation? And if I was by chance engaged with someone myself, I often felt a tug on my sleeve, accompanied by a plaintive request that we "go into the next room now, Aunt," for there was no one worth talking to here.

Yet, for all my efforts, which were sincere, I don't think she was any more comfortable with me than I was with her. Somehow we contrived to irritate each other, and I felt as though I trod on eggshells during every outing. But I wished to see to her settled and happy, so I persevered, hoping that, in time, the right man would finally appear.

72

*A*lthough I did my best to put on an agreeable face when I was out in the world, I suffered very much behind my affable mask. Granville's second absence was to me a particularly bleak and hopeless time, for it seemed I had little to look forward to but news of his impending marriage to the Barbarian. As if to confirm my worst fears, he wrote to ask how I thought the Barbarian might be received in England, if she divorced her husband and arrived here as his wife. His meaning couldn't have been clearer—if the circumstances allowed, he'd resolved to marry her.

He added that he'd also confided in his remaining sisters, to whom he was very close, seeking their advice as to the probable reception of the Princess; but, he told me, it was my opinion for which he waited most eagerly. He relied on our long intimacy, on the absolute candor and sincerity that subsisted between us, for me to give him an honest and considered reply.

I had the greatest possible respect for Granville's sisters, especially the Duchess of Beaufort. Untouched by scandal themselves, they'd shown me nothing but kindness once they understood the strength of the ties between Granville and me. They'd even been introduced to Little H and George, and no hint of recrimination for the circumstances of their birth ever escaped their lips. Their own behavior was always scrupulously correct, but they never allowed their morals to compromise the natural generosity and affection of their characters. In light of all this, I was anxious to know how they'd respond to their brother's request, so one afternoon I went to visit the Duchess in the hope of finding out.

"Of course, it's impossible to say for certain in these matters," she began, "for so much depends on the manner of the Princess herself—whether she's proud and defiant, or capable of a little sober, modest reserve. But honestly, I'm inclined to think all would be well in the end—and my sister agrees with me."

I was very surprised; I'd expected her to deliver a much more severe judgment.

"Do you think she'd be received at court? The Queen takes a harsh view of any who trespass against the strictest rules of behavior."

"Perhaps not, although again I think previous good character does a great deal to sway Her Majesty's judgment. And if it should go against the Princess—well, perhaps exclusion from those dusty royal precincts mightn't be the worst proscription in the world."

She must have seen my face fall, for she held out her hand and took mine.

"I can only imagine how hard this must be for you; but rest assured, whatever happens, my sister and I wish always to remain your friends."

When I arrived home, I sat for a long time at my desk, pen in hand, paper poised, deciding what I should say. It was some time before I reached a conclusion. I began by telling Granville he should rely far more on his sisters' opinions than mine. Their protection alone, once extended to the Barbarian, would do a great deal of good in itself.

But while I respected everything they said, I regretted to tell him that I couldn't agree with their view. I thought they were far too sanguine as to the manner in which a divorcée—even a princess—would be treated by general society. She'd never be admitted to the most exclusive circles, and her divorced state would incur the disapproval of many less-elevated persons. She would need to cultivate a thick skin. Perhaps, I concluded, my pessimism might be entirely unfounded, and the combination of his charm and her good looks would be enough to disarm the harsher critics—but he'd asked for my honesty, and I could not but tell him what I truly believed.

It was only much later that I heard Granville had told the Barbarian that divorced women were not well received in England, and that she was very much offended as a result. I don't know how much this contributed to the slow fizzling out of their affair. Certainly, there were other reasons for their growing apart—the Princess loved her independence and was reluctant to leave her own country; she had also been informed by kind friends of the other women with whom Granville had been involved at home, including, presumably, myself, which did not please her.

Granville was puzzled at first by the apparent contradictions of her feelings for him. Her words, he told me, suggested that she'd decided to give him up; but, for all that, there remained a certain kindness in her manner, which suggested otherwise. He was at a loss to explain it; what did I think? I replied that I thought her conduct was difficult to interpret—I thought very well of her in many ways—but, nevertheless, there was perhaps an element of caprice in her character that would not be desired in a wife.

A few months later, he informed me he'd given up all thoughts of marrying the Barbarian, as her sentiments had altered so much that it seemed she no longer wished to belong to him, as she once had. He was very low in spirits, cursing his decision to accept this second mission. Everything, in both his private and public affairs, was as disagreeable as possible. The Barbarian had disappointed him; and at the same time everything he'd worked so hard to achieve in the diplomatic sphere had collapsed. The treaty he'd negotiated at St.

Petersburg was rendered meaningless when the Russian army was defeated by the French in so complete a victory that the Tsar felt obliged to change his allegiance and ally himself with Napoleon. All Granville's efforts had come to nothing; the French were now masters of Europe, with no serious challenge to their supremacy.

When Granville was at last summoned home, in November 1807, in matters of war and politics, all was therefore as black and gloomy as could be imagined. I, however, was sustained by a single glimmer of hope—that he was returning as a single man. I could not be sure, for he was still very much in thrall to the Barbarian, and everything might alter if she changed her mind. But if she was resolved not to have him, he would come back alone. How much of that was due to my influence, I preferred not to consider.

It would be two months before he was finally back, and I diligently ticked off every day in my mind, just as if I'd had in my possession the marked tally stick he'd once recommended to me. I called as often as I dared at the Foreign Office to discover if there was any news of him, until the clerks ran away when they saw me; and every storm or great wind plunged me into terror at what he must endure, crossing the North Sea at such an unseasonable time of year.

I couldn't help but fear how he would behave when we were reunited. The disappointment of losing the Barbarian would, I knew, weigh heavily upon him. And any triumph, any relief I might feel at her withdrawal could be only temporary. Sooner or later, there would be another candidate for his hand. I'd known this for years—and yet my own feelings were unchanged. I'd tried, while he was away, to tailor my affections to what I knew they ought to be—but no struggle, no resolution had made the least difference. I knew I'd greet him with the same desire as ever. Before I loved him, I'd never suspected I was capable of such passions; and even though I understood I must in some way or another ready myself to lose him, they remained obstinately alive, despite all my attempts to repress them.

A few days after Granville arrived back in London, I arranged for him what I hoped would be a most affecting scene. We went together to the house where our children lived, and watched as they performed a little concert to celebrate his return. Little H, now seven years old, played at the piano and sang a short song—she had been rehearsing it for weeks—and at the end, young George, now quite a little boy, came on and made an excellent bow. We clapped, the children looked pleased, toys were handed out, and pleasure ensued—but of course they didn't know Granville and were stiff and formal in their manner. It would take some time, I reassured him, before they were properly used to him and could be utterly at ease in his presence.

I confess I felt a little the same myself. We'd been apart for so long that some of our old familiarity had worn away, and at first I was self-conscious in his presence. Only when we were finally alone did that lingering sense of reserve disappear, as I surrendered myself to him with as much pleasure as I ever felt in my life. Afterward, I lay in his arms, happier than I had been for years.

"You don't find me entirely unappealing, then? I still have some attractions left to entice you?"

"You'll always be beautiful to me."

"And you to me. Oh, G, if you only knew what I feel for you, how much I love you, body and soul."

I reached out for him once more; but he gently moved away from my embrace.

"Harriet, I've something to tell you that I know you won't like to hear. But it must be said."

A chill crept over me. I knew something dreadful was coming.

"You must believe me when I say our intimacy has given me the greatest pleasure over the years. You can't ever have doubted how much I've enjoyed it. But I think—I'm afraid—I feel this must be the last time we allow ourselves to indulge in it."

I threw my hands to my mouth and bit my knuckle to stop myself crying out.

"You hate me. I am repulsive to you."

He bent over me and laid his hand on my cheek. "No, that will never happen. But you must understand, I still wish to marry as soon as I can. Matters didn't end well with the Barbarian, but that's only made me more determined to find someone else. And in those circumstances, I can't allow us to go on as we have. You asked me once before why, if that was my intent, I persisted in approaching you, implying it was grossly unfair of me to do so. I've come to think you were right. It would be dishonorable on my part to continue. I'd despise myself for it, and after a while, you'd come to hate me too."

I wanted to cry no, no, that could never be true. I would bear anything in order to lie in bed with him like this forever, but I knew it was hopeless and gave way to the most bitter tears. He let me sob, holding my hand until I could cry no more.

"Does that mean I shan't see you anymore? That everything between us is over?"

He shook his head and kissed me.

"Of course not. I shall still rely utterly on your friendship—on those affections that bind us more tightly than anything we do in bed. When we first met—when you were determined not to receive me as I wished, you tried to persuade me that *amitié*—that was the word you used—was worth more than passion, for it far outlasted physical love, surviving unto death. That is how I propose we live in future—attached to each other by the strongest possible bonds of *amitié*."

It was particularly painful to hear my own words used against me—but what could I say to contradict them? Of course I consented to his wishes, for honestly, what choice did I have? While he insisted he still cared for me, I would have agreed to anything to remain in his company.

"Tell me what you want from me, and I'll be anything you wish—as long as it secures me some place in your heart."

"You know you'll always have that."

I took his beautiful body in my arms, kissing it furiously, trying to keep the touch and feel of it in my mind, for this was the last time I should have the freedom to do so. He would never be completely mine again. Then I dressed myself and slipped away. I understood with a cold, clear certainty that that part of my life was over now forever.

In the weeks that followed, it gave me some comfort to see that Granville had meant everything he said, and that he continued to treat me with all the affection, candor, and sincerity he'd shown before. I was profoundly grateful that he meant to keep his promise, and that this aspect of our love would go on as before. But I cannot pretend I didn't regret the end of the intimate pleasures we'd shared for so long, and which were unlike anything I'd known before. If it's possible to grieve the loss of something as insubstantial and eva-nescent as physical passion, then I've mourned it very often since it passed from me. Indeed, I regret its loss even now and think of it still, always with a sense of longing nothing can relieve.

Granville wasted no time at all before fixing upon a possible bride. He was thirty-five now, and even more impatient to get on with the business of a man's life. He had distinguished himself as a diplomat who could expect further opportunities in the public sphere, if he wished for them. All that was wanting was a parallel sense of achievement in his private life—legitimate children, a home of his own—both of which required a wife.

I'd known for some time that this was his plan. But I think the somewhat frenzied energy he now devoted to obtaining the chief of these objects had its origins in another quarter. We rarely spoke of the Barbarian—but I was convinced he'd been deeply humiliated by her rejection. It was Sarah Fane all over again, but, in truth, he never cared enough to be seriously hurt by his failure there. The Barbarian, however, was a very different matter: his feelings for her ran far deeper than he liked to admit, and the pain of her refusal wounded him in a very tender place. His throwing himself with such desperate eagerness into the pursuit of another lady was, I believe, intended to erase all that had passed in Russia with the quick and easy win of a suitable marriage to a woman of stature and means. That would show the Princess what a chance she'd missed.

No one could say he did not aim high, for the lady he fixed upon was Susanna Beckford, daughter of one of the richest men in England. Most of William Beckford's huge wealth came from that darkest of trades, sugar; produced by the thousands of slaves that it was his great shame to call his own. He was a strange, eccentric man who spent his time and money amassing a vast collection of art and building extravagant follies; but there was still enough of it left to make his daughter the object of many ambitious suitors. He'd played little part in raising his children, as scandal had driven him abroad for many years—his fondness for men once being discovered, he'd had no choice but to flee. Susanna had been brought up among her cousins, and it was generally supposed they'd move heaven and earth to marry her to one of their own. Lady Abercorn—my old friend Lady Anne—informed me blithely that "Granville has *no* chance at all," and I don't think it was jealousy that made me agree with her.

Miss Beckford was a silent young woman, surrounded at all times by a gaggle of protective relations, and it hurt me extremely to see Granville once more the supplicant, rebuffed on all sides. I couldn't believe he'd any real feelings for her—they hardly knew each other. All she had in her favor was her tainted fortune—and it distressed me more than I can say to watch Granville pursuing it so avidly.

For that reason, I was glad when Lord B announced his plans to visit our estates in Ireland. He'd often talked of such a visit, but somehow it had never come about, so that, to my shame, I'd never visited the place that was the source of so much of our income—had never seen the house and village that bore the Bessborough name, never seen the farms and fields and woods that produced the rents we depended upon.

"I think we might make a trip of it," Lord B suggested. "Go north first, perhaps even to Scotland—I think you'd enjoy seeing Edinburgh—I know I'd very much like to see the Highlands—and then across the sea to Ireland."

I readily agreed, for I was happy to be removed from a spectacle I had no desire to see unfold. Granville wrote regularly while I was on my travels, seeking advice and reassurance, but really, I had nothing of any use to offer. I felt myself drifting further and further away from him, and not only because of the steadily increasing miles between us. When he addressed one of his letters with formal salutations to *Lady B*—no endearments, just a name and title he hadn't used for years—it struck a terrible chill through me. Was this all we were to one another now?

It's always been my nature to plunge easily into the blackest of moods, a propensity of mind that has increased upon me since I lost my beloved sister. While she was still alive, I took refuge in the thought that if Granville left me, I should still have her love to rely upon. But now that that horrible event seemed imminent, who could I depend upon to support me once he belonged to someone else? Sometimes I was so lonely that I thought it would have been better for me if I'd followed her into death. My misery was such that when I heard of a young woman of my acquaintance who was sick and likely to die, her situation seemed almost like a blessing to me. She would never know the wretchedness of outliving all that was worthwhile in life, and for that I almost envied her. I tried to tell myself I owed it to all those I loved never to think in such a way. But as we jolted along on terrible roads, ate at dreadful inns, and slept in grubby beds, I began to ask myself who'd really care if I died? Granville, I knew, would feel it—though perhaps not as deeply as might once have been the case—and anyway, he'd soon have a family of his own to absorb him. Little H and G would be safe under the protection of his sisters—and they were so young that I'd soon be little more than a memory to them, though hopefully a fond one.

My other children would mourn me—but they had their own lives now, ties that rightly meant more to them than I did. It occurred to me, as I ran through this gloomy list, that the person who'd suffer most from my passing would be the man sitting calmly beside me in our carriage, examining the drawings he'd made in Derbyshire. Lord B's life alone would be emptier for my absence. He'd regret me more than anyone else.

Do I mean to suggest that he loved me? In truth, I think we were beyond all that. He felt me watching him and returned my gaze with a mild smile before turning back to his sketches. We managed well enough; indeed, perhaps to our mutual surprise, in the last few months we had drifted back somewhat into each other's company, doing those things together that occupied people at our stage in life—excursions like the one we were currently embarked upon, visits to friends and to see our children. We were calmer, easier with each other. For my part, I did all I could to make him happy and contented. When he was ill—he suffered terribly from gout—I nursed him tenderly; and when he was well, I made sure everything in our household was arranged just as he liked it. Some of this, I know, arose from guilt, was a manifestation of the shamefaced gratitude I'd for so long felt I owed him. But I think there was some affection there too—the kindness and understanding born of long familiarity, which, while it never transports you to extremes of passion, shields you somewhat against the vicissitudes of life and loss.

In return, he was friendly and indulgent to me, all anger and jealousy seemingly exhausted. When he treated me so fondly, it was impossible not to ask myself how much he really knew about what had passed between Granville and me. Certainly he never mentioned it. I believe now that he had long been aware of our continuing connection but for his own reasons had chosen not to confront me about it. The only explanation I can suggest for his behavior is the one I've advanced before—that he simply turned his head away, preferring to ignore my guilt rather than compel me to admit a truth he didn't want to hear. Perhaps he felt himself unequal to the scandal that would result from my exposure; perhaps he wished to spare our children the horror of seeing me thus condemned; perhaps he no longer had the energy or vengefulness to exult in the spectacle of my ruin; or perhaps he simply preferred a quiet life, and the pursuit of his own small pleasures, to pursuing me through the divorce courts. All of these considerations, I believe, contributed to his passivity.

But I like to think that there was a little more to it than that. I genuinely believe, that in his own strange way, he would have missed me very much if I'd been forced to leave him; and, despite all my transgressions, he couldn't face the prospect of life without me. He was a lonely man at heart, with no really strong connections other than with his children, whom he really loved—and, as I came to understand, with me. He needed me—and I confess this knowledge gave me some comfort in my dull despair, little though I deserved it, for it made me feel that despite everything, he at least preferred to keep me with him than to set me aside.

We never ventured to speak openly of such things. I think we both understood that each of us had sinned against the other—his cruel behavior to me—my many betrayals of him—in ways that could never be talked, reasoned, or argued away, so that there was nothing to be gained by raising them again. Neither of us, then or since, has ever shown the slightest desire to discuss what cannot be changed. This unspoken pact has been the basis of any comfort we've found in each other, and I think we both value it enough not to disturb it.

We were away far longer than we'd expected, as we found a great deal to occupy us in Ireland. I was delighted to see for the first time the Bessborough properties from which Lord B derived both his name and his income. His tenants greeted us with great enthusiasm, and we resolved to visit more frequently. It was plain to me that absentee landlords like ourselves bore some responsibility for the very unsettled state of the country, which had been much embittered by the failure to relieve Catholics from the many disabilities under which they labored. I should like to say we carried out this good intention, but as yet, I must admit, we've had neither the time nor the opportunity to do so.

Throughout our travels, Granville had written regularly, describing the progress of his courtship of Miss Beckford. It wasn't going well. Her relations seemed desperate to exclude him from her society, and the lady herself made no protest at this. He was forced to conclude that she was indifferent to him, and when at last we arrived back in London, I saw for myself that his gloomy prognostications were entirely justified. She paid him not the slightest attention. He suspected he'd been outmaneuvered, and he was right. Soon it was announced she was to marry one of her cousins, as her family had always intended.

Granville didn't take this snub well. It was his third disappointment—a great blow to a man who'd rarely been denied anything he really wanted. He was utterly disconsolate and resisted all my attempts to raise his spirits.

"I'm never to marry, it seems. No one will have me," he complained.

"I hardly think that's the case." I tried to be brisk. "You've been unlucky, that's all."

"One refusal is bad luck. Two might be unfortunate. Three suggests a pattern."

"Perhaps," I ventured, "you should set your sights a little more realistically. Choose someone other than a great heiress. The competition for them is bound to be immense."

"I don't think that's the problem."

"What's your explanation, then?"

"I can tell you my view, but you won't like it."

I frowned at this, for I thought it couldn't bode well, but I'd gone too far not to pursue it.

"After such a warning, you have to tell me what you mean—or I'll imagine every kind of horror."

"None of these women would marry me because they all knew about you. About the two of us—the terms we are on, the long connection between us."

He spoke quite calmly, as if he didn't want the truth to hurt me, although he knew it must. I shivered a little.

"I'm sorry to hear that. But who will these ladies marry if they take that line? I can't think of any gentleman of your acquaintance who wasn't connected with someone else before he married. Think of Morpeth—think of Boringdon. Why should you be any different?"

"It's the nature of our affair that makes them hesitate. It's widely believed that you govern me—and that you fully expect to carry on doing so long after the wedding has taken place."

All unbidden, Hester's voice made itself heard in my mind, for this was her argument exactly. It sounded just as ridiculous coming from him as it had from her. The idea that Granville, with his love of authority and insistence upon obedience, should allow any woman to rule him was so preposterous I couldn't help but smile.

"No one who really knows you—or indeed, me—could possibly imagine that to be true!"

"There are more ways than one of bending someone to your will than by issuing commands. There are softer, more subtle means— tears may work as well as orders and threats."

"Don't forget your own methods: coldness and disdain. You've always found those effective in bringing me to heel."

"Let's not argue. I'm trying to be frank—isn't that what you always ask of me?"

"It's what we ask of each other, I believe. I understand the charge against me, ridiculous though it is. But are you saying there's some justice in it?"

"The word 'govern' isn't at all what I mean—'influence' is more like. That's how it was with the Barbarian. My sisters offered me one opinion, you put forward another—and I didn't hesitate to accept yours above theirs. She asked me about it, you know—was it your view, which I passed on to her, which made her decide not to come? She didn't like it when I told her it was."

"Would you have preferred it if I'd lied about what I thought?"

"No. But perhaps I shouldn't have asked at all. Maybe it's time I relied on my own judgment in matters that touch me so closely, and which must be so painful when I ask you about them."

"So I'm to say nothing on a subject of such great importance to you?"

"I'll always want to hear your views when they're practical and to the point. So, yes, I agree when you say I've aimed too high, pursuing ladies unlikely to welcome a husband with no title and very little money. I must give up the pursuit of heiresses, it seems."

"I think that would be wise."

"I think so too. Next time, I intend to look for someone already well disposed toward me—already inclined, perhaps, to like me. Liking is a great incentive to accept a marriage proposal, I believe?"

"I've certainly heard that's the case."

"It must also contribute to the happiness of the match—a disposition to be pleased is a great encouragement to marital satisfaction, I imagine?"

"I'm not best placed to answer that."

He was so engrossed in his thoughts that I'm not sure he even heard me.

"So—someone who knows me, someone who likes me—and someone with whom I think I could be happy. Whoever I think of next must suggest herself to me on all these counts, if I am to have any chance of success."

"And when you find her—and she asks about me—what will you tell her?"

He was silent for a moment, as he considered how to frame what he wished to say.

"I must be able to tell her that our connection is no longer what it was—that I'll always want you as a close and confidential friend—but that I make my own choices as to whom I marry, influenced by no one—and that you'd never dream of coming between us, once we're husband and wife."

He paused for a moment, thinking. "And I must be able to say all this in the knowledge that both of us understand it and believe it to be true."

I'd always known this must be so, eventually—but to hear it spelled out so clearly and calmly—to know it drew a final, immutable line between what had been and what was to come—that these were the rules by which my future existence would be governed—this was almost too much for me to bear, but I assured him I'd never stand in the way of what he wanted, which was only reasonable and right. He held my hand, and eventually I was calm enough to say my last words on the subject.

"I'll make every effort to accept what must happen—if I know it's for your happiness, I'm sure I can do it. But if I'm to make this sacrifice, to sever absolutely all those ties of frankness and confidence that have sustained us for so long—then I must be sure the one who replaces me is truly someone you think you could love. It will be the greatest pain for me to know it. But I couldn't do it for anything less."

75

I suppose it's human nature, when faced with the prospect of some distressing event, to think, "Well, it may not happen for some time, and when it does, I'll have prepared myself for it." I tried my hardest to think in this way, but it was quite impossible. I'd used up all my resources of distraction, prevarication, and pretense. None of them worked anymore. I simply withdrew into myself and waited. To outward appearance, my life went on—I played with George and Little H, consoled Caro when she complained of her husband's shortcomings—why, she wailed, was marriage so different from court-ship; did all men's passion cool as quickly as William's had?—and even went out into the world on occasion—but inside, I was full of dread.

In the event, it wasn't long before I discovered my fate. One sum-mer morning, Granville asked to meet me at our children's house. I knew what it must concern. He was already there when I arrived. The rooms were silent, the children having been taken out to allow us some privacy, and the place had a melancholy feel, even before he began to speak.

"I've fixed upon someone who I think would suit me excellently as a wife. I intend to begin courting her as soon as possible, but I wanted to tell you first. I've discussed this with no one, not even the lady herself. You're the very first to know."

So this was it at last. The announcement I'd feared for so long.

"Who is she?"

"I think you'll be surprised. I doubt very much you'll have thought of her in this respect. I didn't do so myself until very recently."

"I ask again, who is she?"

"You may want to sit down—"

"Tell me who she is!"

"It is Harryo. Georgiana's daughter."

So Bess Foster had been right. It'd been there before my eyes, and I'd seen nothing at all. I still couldn't quite believe it.

"Harryo? You want to marry my niece?"

"Yes. I've thought it over long and hard, and I believe we'd do very well together."

I shook my head, a little dazed. It was not difficult to understand why Harryo cherished a secret liking for Granville—but what was it he saw in her?

"Then you must tell me what attracts you, for I admit she wouldn't have been my first thought for you."

"She's very clever and I like that. I could never be happy with anyone dull and stupid. You've taught me the value of a good mind in a woman, and I couldn't give up on that now. It's the same with conversation—having been so long in your company, I must have someone who talks wittily and well. And she does both."

"I doubt her temper is as yielding as mine."

"Marriage might soften her. I think she's extremely unhappy. And she has a very good heart"—he looked at me almost beseechingly— "you must have seen that for yourself. I feel she has a great capacity for love."

"She has a great capacity for sharp judgment," I thought, "which I doubt you'll like," but I said nothing.

"And I don't mean to sound presumptuous," he continued, "but I believe she likes me. I've thought so for some time."

"What makes you think so?"

"Little signs, little gestures. Certain looks. A man nearly always knows, sometimes even before the woman does herself."

All those hints Bess had noticed—which I had also seen, once she pointed them out—he had been aware of too.

"You know she won't have any money? The Duke is unlikely to be generous to her. She's never been his favorite child—and her hatred of Bess is well known to him."

"I've resigned myself to not marrying a fortune. I'd rather be happy than rich."

"And you truly believe that marrying Harryo will make you so?"

"Who can say for certain? But I honestly think I've as good a chance of finding contentment with her as with anyone else."

"And what about us? I believe she's aware of our connection."

"You'd know more about that than I do. But if that's so, at least she'll be used to the idea. And once she understands we are on different terms now . . ."

"You'll tell her that?"

"If it comes to it, how can I not?"

I put my head in my hands, consumed by shame.

"No, I suppose it must arise. And George and Little H? What of them?"

"We must take this a step at a time, Harriet. I don't even know if she'll have me yet."

How was it possible she wouldn't? Yes, the heiresses had refused him, but they hadn't known him, had never been exposed to the full force of his appeal. Harryo had been in Granville's company for years. Of course she liked him. Of course she'd have him. There was no doubt in my mind about that.

76

In the days that followed, I tried hard to absorb the implications of what I'd been told. Granville would be married—and to my niece. The first idea was a familiar source of horror. I'd lived with the threat of it for years, hoping that time would reconcile me to the prospect, that age would bring me better sense along with gray hair and lines around my eyes. I only wish I'd been so lucky. Nothing, regrettably, had changed for me—the thought of losing him wounded me as deeply now as it had ever done before.

The second prospect—that it'd be Harryo who supplanted me—was harder for me to unravel. At first, it was almost impossible to contemplate. My mind shied away from it; it was easier to imagine him married to a stranger than to my niece. But gradually, it dawned on me that if I must resign him to another, it might be better for me if she were a relation. If Granville had married outside our intimate circle, our separation must have been immediate and complete. I should hardly ever have seen him if he'd married Sarah Fane. There were no real ties between her family and my own—no excuses for there to be any continued sociability between Granville and me, and any attempt to remain on friendly terms would have been immediately remarked upon. Whereas, if he married Harryo, he'd always be among us on the most legitimate and unimpeachable terms. I could still talk to him—we'd never be lovers again, I knew that, but the rupture between us wouldn't be absolute. I wouldn't be denied the chance to look upon him now and then, to take pleasure in his happiness, even if it had been bought at the cost of my own.

I wasn't blind, however, to the darker side of our proximity. Yes, I'd see him more often than if he'd married away from us—but how should I like watching at such close quarters as he gave himself up to another? Wouldn't it torment me to watch Harryo occupy the place I'd once considered my own? And was it likely she'd welcome me about them when the mere fact of my presence must remind her of Granville's long connection to me?

These weren't small matters, and I didn't attempt to diminish their importance. But eventually I concluded that a match with Harryo had more to recommend it than not. I'd prefer to be occasionally in Granville's company, even with all the associated disadvantages, than to be exiled from him forever. I persuaded myself that Harryo and I would find a way to manage any embarrassment that might arise between us; that once she understood she'd nothing to fear from me, in time she'd accept me in their society. And there was one further reason, perhaps the most important of all in my mind, which made me prefer her to any other possible wife—if I were to die, I believed she would be kind to Little H and George.

I didn't imagine Granville would ever abandon them—but it's very hard for a man to care for two illegitimate children in the face of the indifference or dislike of his wife. His sisters would have helped him, I was sure of that, but how much easier Little H and George's lives would be if their stepmother didn't hate them. Harryo could never be guilty of such an act—she had a good heart and would never fail in generosity toward a pair of innocents, who were, after all, her relations as well as Granville's. It was this consideration,

I admit, that tipped the scale for me in deciding that if Granville were to marry anyone, Harryo was by far the best option. I'd still be unhappy, of course; but less so than if he'd married Sarah Fane. And it was my destiny to be unhappy. My own foolish unconquerable passion had long ago ensured the truth of that.

Once I'd come to this conclusion, I persuaded myself it was somehow my responsibility to move matters forward as quickly as possible. I thought Harryo might need careful handling. I was certain now that she'd indeed harbored a secret attraction to Granville, perhaps for many years—but I wondered how far she'd ever properly acknowledged those feelings, even to herself. Her awareness of his long intimacy with me must have been a great discouragement to doing so, and, for the same reason, it would surely come as a considerable shock when Granville began to pay her very marked attentions. Once she understood all was over between us, I hoped she'd admit to herself the strength of her attraction to him and give in to a fondness I truly believed she felt. But it was a very delicate situation and must be managed with the greatest care.

I knew Harryo well enough to be sure she'd dislike anything in the nature of a public courtship. She was proud and prickly, very sensitive to her single state, and desperate not to be humiliated again. Granville would need to act with the greatest consideration in navigating so many tender emotions; and it seemed to me that this would be most easily achieved in a place where Harryo felt comfortable, surrounded by friends, and not exposed to the merciless gaze of curious onlookers. A house party seemed to me by far the best solution, so I suggested that Granville ask his sister the Duchess to arrange a gathering of intimate friends and family at her Badminton house. She readily agreed—Harryo accepted her invitation—and everything was soon in place, exactly as I had hoped.

Of course, I didn't attend myself. But I imagined I'd hear from Granville about everything that passed between them. This had aways been our rule—he held nothing back from me, ensuring I could rely utterly on his candor, even when what he told me caused me pain. I expected he'd do the same now, and it consoled me somewhat to think this link between us hadn't yet been broken. I was tearful on the night before he left, and he was extremely kind to me, so I thought nothing had really changed between us, in that respect at least—until I asked my usual question.

"And you'll let me know all that's said and done? You'll write every day with anything of importance? Exactly as it happened?"

"I'm not sure I want to do that. I don't think I'd be comfortable consigning such things to a letter."

I was utterly taken aback.

"But you've always done so before. Frankness has aways been our watchword."

"I can tell you everything when I return."

"But it's not the same as hearing from you in the moment—for then I understand completely how you feel—it's almost as though I'm there with you."

"That, I believe, is part of the problem."

He saw my look of astonished horror—but didn't waver.

"Harriet, you must understand this isn't a matter on which I wish to send regular reports. It isn't fair to Harryo—or indeed, to me."

"So all our honesty is at end, then? You're to have secrets now, confidences which'll be kept from me?"

"I've no intention of deceiving you. I promise I'll hide nothing when I'm ready to talk of it—but I must be allowed to manage this in the way I wish, on my own terms."

And so we went on, me pleading and him resisting, until neither of us had any more to say.

It was a sad parting—I was miserable, and he was angry. He left without a kiss or any loving gesture, with nothing to fall back upon but a sense of my exclusion. I wasn't to be his confidante, at least not in the intimate manner I'd been before. I was to be informed but not consulted. It was a blunt reminder that if this marriage happened, I'd soon be made to feel the change in our circumstances. I'd accepted that we were no longer lovers—now I must learn to surrender every other tie that bound us together, watch them severed one by one, till nothing remained but my useless, unwanted adoration.

Once he'd arrived at Badminton, Granville wrote exactly as he said he would, neither as often nor as candidly as I wished; but I was only too well informed by other means. Georgiana Morpeth, Harryo's sister, was one of the guests; she wrote to Bess Foster's daughter Caroline, who wrote to Bess—and Bess could never resist sharing what she knew. So in the end, there was very little I didn't hear about the progress of Granville's courtship, including a great deal I should've much preferred not to know.

From Granville, I discovered that his courtship proceeded very slowly. As I suspected, Harryo had been taken aback by his approaches, and her response to them confused him. Sometimes she seemed agreeable to his overtures, but on other occasions was wary and subdued, as if she'd made up her mind to resist him. He was puzzled by this—and being uncertain how to proceed, withdrew a little, so as not to embarrass her, should his intentions not be welcome. This didn't help, as Harryo treated his delicacy as evidence he wasn't sincere in his pursuit of her; then she seemed, if anything, even less receptive to his attempts to please her.

I wasn't entirely surprised by Harryo's reticence. There were a thousand reasons why she might respond uncertainly to Granville's interest in her. But I was astonished when I learned from Bess the true reason for her caution.

"I'm afraid she's convinced herself that Granville isn't really free to marry her."

"If she's thinking of our connection, she must know that's over for him—that he means to begin afresh with her."

"I believe she thinks *he* would like to do so—but fears you stand in his way. That you don't like the match, and that while you appear to smile upon it, in private you do all you can to prevent it."

Harryo, so Bess told me, had persuaded herself I controlled Granville and had extracted from him a promise that he'd take no step or make her any offer until I had been consulted. She detected my hand in every action she mistakenly believed suggested uncertainty on Granville's part—and attributed his apparent hesitancy solely to my malign influence, and to the many flaws she'd so often observed in my character—my affectation and lack of principle—my jealousy and self-regard—my reckless indulgence of my passions, which had deadened my sense of right and wrong.

This wasn't the first time I'd heard such an argument deployed against me; it had been used by both Hester Stanhope and the Barbarian. But they did not know me and could thus put any construction that suited them on my character. The same could not be said of Harryo. She'd been brought up all her life in the closest proximity to me, and I'd always endeavored to treat her with the greatest kindness. And yet she honestly believed me capable of behaving in so cruel and dishonorable a manner.

I cannot say how wounded I was when I discovered this, especially as I'd so readily stood aside on her behalf when Granville had asked me to do so. God knows, that had required enough from me, but to discover I was exerting myself to please someone who despised me was almost enough to plunge me into total despair.

77

With the benefit of time and distance, I can now look back upon Harryo's accusations with a little more understanding. I see they were the result of her conflicted feelings and of the distress that overwhelmed her when she was unable to reconcile them. Granville's pursuit left her bitterly divided, her heart urging her all the time toward this man whom she had so long desired, while her head told her it was the height of folly even to consider becoming his wife. How could she possibly accept him when she knew he'd been my lover for so many years—and when she believed he might remain under my influence even after they were married? Granville wasn't at all the upright, moral character she had always promised herself she'd choose for a husband—and yet she was irresistibly drawn to him. Harryo was caught between what she wanted and what she feared, and her inability to decide what to do was a torment.

It was this turmoil in her heart, I believe, that led her to think so ill of me. For all her complaints of Granville's conduct, she couldn't bring herself to blame him for her present situation; whatever she might say, in truth, her affections were already too engaged for that. Instead, I was appointed the villain of the piece. I, and I alone, with my selfish reluctance to let Granville go, stood in the way of her happiness. I begged Granville to allow me to write to her, explaining the truth of our situation to soothe her fears—but he was adamant it'd do no good, and that he wanted no long explanations until he was sure of her.

He'd expected to be at Badminton for a week or two, but such were the complications of his courtship that it was a month before the party finally broke up. In retrospect, I think he played his hand very well. He made no proposal, fearing too much haste might hurry her into a refusal; but instead, worked gently, day by day, week by week, to convince her of the sincerity of his intentions, and the different manner of life he envisaged as a married man.

Slowly, slowly, he broke down her resistance, and he returned to London hopeful of his eventual success. I wasn't surprised—no one knew better than I how persuasive Granville could be when determined to obtain his desire—but I can't say I greeted the news with any pleasure. I was in the very same state as Harryo—divided between what my heart longed for and what I knew was for the best.

When Granville came to see me on his return, I did my best to conceal my sadness, although my red eyes gave away the truth of my feelings. While he described all that had happened, I kept my unhappiness tolerably in order—but when he announced he intended to propose while Harryo was staying at Chiswick—Bess Foster had convened a second agreeable little party there in the hope of bringing matters to a successful conclusion—my spirits failed me, and I began to cry.

He was very kind, held my hand, tried to soothe me—but had no comfort to offer me.

"I can't tell you these things if they make you so upset." He wiped a tear away from my cheek. "But you always say you want to know."

"Do you think I'd be happier if I were ignorant of your plans?"

"No—but it's very hard to see how it distresses you."

"I'm sorry if my misery is inconvenient to you. It must be a terrible burden to bear."

"I know you don't believe me, but I do feel it. You can't think I like to see you so dejected."

"Then it seems we must both become more hard-hearted. I must learn not to care that I'm losing you, and you must teach yourself indifference to my distress."

"I'll never be indifferent to your distress, Harriet. But I cannot sacrifice every prospect of future happiness to it. I thought we both understood that."

"I don't deny it—I know it must be—but try as I might, as the day of reckoning approaches—that you must and will abandon me—I cannot pretend it makes me anything but utterly desolate."

"Well, who knows? Perhaps she'll refuse me."

"Of course she won't—but Granville, dearest Granville—tell me you'll write as soon as you know. Don't keep me waiting, I beg you."

This time he made no objection, but agreed, gently kissed me once more, and left.

On the day he had fixed to propose, I vowed to have no communication with him at all, but to wait calmly for his news in silence. It was a good intention, but I couldn't keep it. I drove myself instead into a state of terrible agitation. Was this truly the day on which we were to part forever? My wretchedness was overwhelming; I didn't know how to how to bear it. It was like a great weight pressing down me, forcing the very existence out of me. I clung to the idea that this was all for his good. I'd often told him I'd give my own life to secure his happiness. It was my determination to prove the truth of my promise that alone prevented me from sinking into complete despair.

A few days later, Bess gave a great dinner to mark the occasion. All our family was invited, alongside our closest friends, and I didn't think I could bear to sit among them, a false smile pasted to my face. But when I declined her invitation, Bess arrived immediately at my door to persuade me to reconsider.

"I understand how difficult it'll be for you, but I urge you with all my heart to gather up your courage and come."

"Such courage as I had is all used up. There's nothing left, nothing to draw upon."

"You'll be surprised at your own powers if you try." She leaned toward me, earnest and determined. "I know this seems impossible, but you must find the strength to attend. Your behavior now will set the pattern for everything that comes after. If you refuse to be in their company, everyone will think that's how you intend to behave forever after."

"Surely I'm allowed a little time—a little time to accustom myself—" Unable to continue, I put my head in my hands.

"Delay will only make matters worse. The prospect of meeting them will become an obstacle in your mind you'll never overcome. It's far, far better to do it now."

"And what about Harryo? Will she want me there? The ghost at the feast, as it were?"

"She told me she'd like you to come. She wishes everything to be as unremarkable as possible—and your absence would be noted, you must see that."

"If I do, how will I be received? Is she still angry with me?"

"No. I think, having made her decision, she's so perfectly happy with her choice that she sees everything *en rose*. When she thought as she did, it was because she was tormented and miserable. She feels quite differently now, I'm sure of it."

"Yes," I thought, "she has no reason to be jealous of me now. She can afford to be generous."

In the end, I was persuaded to do as Bess wished. I put on my best clothes, applied a little rouge, had Sally dress my hair. When she'd done, I looked into the mirror and tried to smile, but that was beyond me; I almost began crying again.

"Don't ask too much of yourself," Sally whispered to me. "Composed and calm. That'll be enough."

All the way to Chiswick, I kept those words in my mind— composed and calm, composed and calm. I don't know what I expected, but in the event, I was treated with nothing but delicacy by those who understood my situation. Georgiana Morpeth spoke to me fondly. Lady Melbourne squeezed my hand. And then— inevitably—I found myself standing before Harryo. I didn't know what to say, so I gently kissed her cheek.

"I wish you joy, truly I do. All the happiness in the world."

"Thank you. I'm very happy and very grateful. I couldn't have believed I'd ever feel so joyful. It's not a feeling I'm used to."

Her delight was so transparent, her pleasure in her new situation written so clearly on her face, that even I felt the force of it.

"Perhaps you might come and see me after the wedding?" I ventured. "I'd be sad if we became strangers."

She readily agreed—although I believe she'd have assented to anything at that moment, so buoyed up was she by her excitement. But, as we parted, I breathed a small sigh of relief—our first encounter was over, and we'd both conducted ourselves as well as we possibly could.

I didn't speak to Granville until just before we were called to the table.

"I'm very proud of you," he said. "You've behaved in every respect exactly as I could've wished."

My stupid heart swelled with pride, as it always did when he praised me. The habit was so deeply ingrained—I couldn't help it.

"I hope you understand what it's cost me."

"More than anyone, believe me."

"I can't promise always to be so rational. You cannot expect that. The task of giving you up is not to be achieved so easily. You must expect me to grieve for what I've lost."

The very thought was almost too much for me—I felt the hot tears about to spring into my eyes, but I fought against it—I wouldn't expose myself, wouldn't give in to misery where everyone could see.

"I'll come and see you, either tomorrow or the next day. Sometime very soon."

He smiled at me, with an expression that mingled warmth and sympathy, and left me, to take his place at the head of the table, to give and receive the toasts that celebrated their union. I longed with all my being to follow him—but I knew I couldn't—and for a moment, I didn't know what to do, standing there alone, dumb with misery. That was when I came closest to collapse—but before I could give in to my despair, I felt a strong arm on my shoulder and heard a familiar voice in my ear.

"A little wine at a time like this does no harm and might do a great deal of good." Lady Melbourne pushed a glass into my hand. "Just a few sips, no more." Then she spoke to me sternly—I'd been through worse—this was nothing, I could bear it—I owed it to him—to

Harryo—to my family—and most of all to myself. She spoke to me with so much quiet vehemence that slowly, slowly, I began to recover myself.

"Now—we'll go in together," she declared, "and you'll smile and look about you as if nothing untoward at all had happened."

I'm not sure I managed that. But I did my best; and when, as I left, Granville came to wish me goodbye, I whispered a single question to him.

"I conducted myself pretty well tonight, I hope? At least, I thought so."

"You did indeed. And I thank you for it."

I was grateful for any tender words he had to offer—and his kindness was a great comfort to me, as it suggested there would be no sudden rupture between us, no immediate shift into chilliness and distance, which I don't think I could have borne. But I didn't deceive myself that these were words of love—or not love as we'd once understood it. This was something different—it was compassion and warmth, affection, if you like—but stripped of all desire, of all passion. That would be the most I could expect from now on. Granville had slipped quickly and easily into this new state of being—he already seemed quite at ease with it, practiced in the language and manner that showed he still cared for me, but in a profoundly different way.

How I longed to be capable of doing the same—of adjusting my emotions as easily as he'd altered his—but my obstinate heart rebuffed all my efforts to teach it discipline. There was nothing to do but suffer it out, accustoming myself day by day, hour by hour, minute by minute, to the thought that he was no longer mine.

In the weeks that led up to Granville's wedding, I saw him only rarely. He was very much occupied with all the business that precedes a marriage—and I'd promised him repeatedly I wouldn't trespass on his time or cause him any annoyance—but there was one question to which I desperately wanted an answer. I wished very much to know exactly what he'd told Harryo about us, for it couldn't help but govern all my future relations with her. To his credit, he didn't brush me off with false reassurances and lies but explained very plainly what he'd said.

"I told her that for a great many years I'd been on terms of such intimacy with you that there was scarcely a thought of mine that I didn't share with you; and that I'd always considered you a most delightful and valuable person."

He saw me flinch at that description—but went on.

"I explained that I'd spoken to you of my liking for her as soon as I felt the strength of it—that, with your customary generosity, you'd expressed the highest opinion of her. I added that you'd always encouraged my intention of marrying her."

As I made no comment, he continued.

"I hoped, I said, that eventually she would find it in herself to think as generously of you, as you had done of her. At that, she said she really loved you, and how much happier she'd felt since seeing you at Chiswick."

I considered for a moment. It was both more and less than I had expected him to say.

"It's the truth, as far as it goes—but hardly the whole story."

"I believe she knows full well what terms we were on. I didn't think it necessary to spell it out—especially without consulting you first."

"And the children? You didn't mention them?"

"There will be plenty of time for that when we've been married for a while."

I was silent for a moment. I could feel the agitation rising in me as I reflected on his words.

"This is quite wrong, Granville. You can't begin your married life with a deception."

"In what way have I deceived her?"

"By not telling her everything. She's owed that, you know."

I thought of Harryo saying that she loved me—and I knew then what I must do.

"I'll tell her. It would be better coming from me. It takes away the need for you to say the words. If she's angry or resentful, she can fix upon me as the one at fault."

"Do you really believe this is necessary?"

"I do. She must be told about Little H and George. She may know already, I cannot say. But there's no room here for doubt."

"I'll speak to her. If you really feel it must be done so quickly, I'll do it."

"No—it has to be me. Nothing can make amends for the lies and betrayals my love for you has driven me to—I've acted wrongly over the years toward everyone I care for—but I won't be guilty of deceiving Harryo as well. I must be honest with her, or I couldn't live with myself."

We argued for what felt like hours before he finally agreed to my proposal. I would write Harryo a letter explaining everything that had passed between us. He would give it to her immediately after they were married, leaving the decision to her whether she wished never to see me again, or could find in herself some forgiveness for all my transgressions.

The next day I sat down and wrote Harryo such a letter as I'd never done before. I held nothing back. I owned all my guilt. I confessed I'd loved Granville passionately, almost beyond reason, and willingly surrendered to him every proof of love it was in my power to offer. The result was the existence of two unfortunate little creatures, who, much as I adored them, could never be acknowledged as I'd wish. They'd been raised in secret, to save my family and everyone I cared for, from the truth of my disgrace. I knew I must have shocked her and that I fully deserved any repugnance she must feel at my confessions; but I begged her to believe it was impossible she should think worse of me than I did myself. If she decided to have no further dealings with me, I should understand her decision and respect it. I only begged that she wouldn't betray me and that she might find in her heart some sympathy for my weakness and pity for my children. There was more, much, much more—but this was the heart of it. The story of my life told in a few desperate lines. I sealed it up so that I could change nothing in it—and gave it immediately to Granville.

Confession is said to be good for the soul. I cannot say I felt better for what I'd written. I asked myself many times whether there was even a kind of selfishness in what I'd done—was I unburdening my own soul at the cost of Harryo's happiness? I truly thought not. I'd lived with secrets for so long that no one understood better than I how they corroded all sincerity and were the enemy of all comfort and contentment. And if what I'd told her was too much to forgive— well, then I'd be the one sacrificed to her righteous anger. Nothing should stand between her and Granville—she should have him as I never could—and in such a situation, how could she fail to be the happiest woman alive? Whatever she decided in regard to me, the bright sunshine of her good fortune would soon make up for any brief pain my sad admissions caused.

79

I didn't go to the wedding ceremony. I'd intended to—but I simply couldn't do it. Even if my will had been strong enough to
drive me there, my body flatly refused. I felt so tired— and battered
too, as if I'd been through some great physical ordeal. I sent Granville
a gold toothpick in the prettiest little case as a present—something
small enough to be unremarkable, but that he'd have in his hand
every day—alongside a last request. What I most wished for was a
single line from him—written on his wedding day—to know that,
in the midst of that most important moment, I hadn't been entirely
driven from his mind. A simple "God bless you" would be enough.
I wouldn't expect to receive it immediately, but the knowledge that
it'd been written on the day of days would be enough for me.

I see now that this was the greatest favor I could have asked of
him—to have me in his remembrance at so profound a moment—and
even now, I'm a little surprised that he obeyed. It was no more than
a hurried scrawl to say I was in his thoughts. But it was enough. I
held it all that day, most of which I spent in bed, speechless with
misery. Sally sat beside me, knowing better than to offer any false
consolation. In the evening I roused myself, called the servants

together, and drank to Granville's and Harriet's health with a bowl of very strong punch. Afterward I went back to bed, sending even Sally away. I lay looking into the darkness, with Granville's picture in one hand and his note in the other, wishing him happiness with all my broken heart.

80

*A*fter her marriage, Harryo wrote me the kindest possible reply to my anguished confession, insisting all was understood and forgiven, and wishing we might meet next as friends. I cannot say how this relieved me—I'd dreaded the very worst—imagined her conceiving a great dislike of me. But her generosity so relieved me that I could breathe and think once more. When Granville wrote to tell me how glad he was at having made this confidence, I knew I'd acted rightly; but when he seconded my praise of Harryo, and added his own appreciation to mine, I admit it hit me hard. Part of me was glad to hear he already thought her "a perfect angel"—what was my sacrifice for, if he'd concluded otherwise?—but try as I might, my jealous nature undermined my best intentions, and I was eaten up with envy at his loving words.

As far as it lay within his power, Granville treated me with considerable sympathy in the early days of his marriage. While he and Harryo traveled about the country all that spring, he wrote to me as often as I could reasonably expect. I'd been so accustomed to set down on paper to him every idea and impression that it would have been dreadful to have such a long habit of mutual confidence ripped suddenly away from me. I no longer addressed him as "my G"—I wasn't entitled to that familiarity anymore—reverting instead to "Lord G," a term I hadn't used for more years than I could recall. I tried not to bury him in letters but waited for him to write first—and when he did, tried to take what pleasure I could in the scenes of quiet domestic contentment he described. Their married life was a stately round of visits, staying in the houses of family and friends, walking in the daytime, spending the evenings playing chess and reading. It was exactly the existence I would have chosen for us myself, if we'd been able to live together as man and wife.

So the months went past; and by the time summer arrived, I'd discovered a sad truth about loss. There is a kind of drama in parting that in a curious way sustains the spirits for some time after the actual moment of separation. Terrible emotions are accompanied by an awful energy that absorbs all thoughts even as it plunges you into grief. It is only when all this subsides that the true pain begins. Nothing hurts as much as the dawning realization that this is all there is—all there will ever be.

This bleak understanding crept upon me step by step, seeping into my being no matter how hard I tried to resist it. In July, I learned that Harryo was to have a baby. I knew I must be pleased for them—and the better part of my nature did indeed rejoice; but when I thought how this child would be feted and admired—and of the very different circumstances of poor Little H's and George's births—of the contrast in prosperity that must await this child, compared to their uncertain prospects—how could the comparison not cause me pain?

It was very clear that the arrival of a child was all that was required to complete their happiness. Everyone who saw them was struck by the pleasure they took in each other, by the easy affection that already bound them. Once, when I was at Devonshire House, I heard Georgiana Morpeth reading to her husband, in a low, confiding voice, a few lines from a letter she had just received from Harryo. They thought me too far away, too old and deaf to hear, I suppose; but that was not the case. I caught only a few words—but that was enough. "His splendid blue eyes . . . his many thoughtful kindnesses . . . he's a vision of beauty even while eating a breakfast roll."

Oh, how it pierced me to the soul. I knew only too well how it felt—to look upon that face and think it was yours! Well, it was mine no longer. All this joy, all this excitement was theirs now. They were everything to each other; there was no room for a third. They were sailing away from me, disappearing on a great tide of happiness into the distance, as steadily and remorselessly as the ocean itself. All that was left to me was to wave from the shore, hoping for an occasional acknowledgment of my existence. It was only then I really understood all I'd lost, only then that I felt truly bereft.

I used to think one could die from unhappiness. Certainly, it happens often enough in novels; and perhaps there are occasions in real life when it's been known. There have certainly been times when I thought I would welcome death. But then I remembered Little H and George, Caro and all her marital woes, and knew I couldn't leave them. I did the best I could. I got up in the morning, went to bed at night, and in between, occasionally ventured out. I saw my friends and my family; I read a great number of books, played many a game of chess, and worked hard at my drawing. I looked, I imagine, as if I was tolerably content. I hope so, for I put a great deal of effort into seeming so. But the ache within me never really eased. Always at the back of my mind was the sense of something gone, something ripped from me, a loss from which I could never recover.

It dulled my senses, numbed my feelings, so that I think in truth I have been only half alive since that summer.

81

*A*nd there, I suppose, my story stops.

Years and years of letters. A month or so of reading. And now I'm at the end. I sit for a moment, silent, listening to the sound of my own breathing.

There's no reason to look at anything further. I'm only too familiar with the muted half-life, the shadowy existence in which I've dwelt since losing him. No, the letters have nothing left to tell me. I'm quite finished. I fold up the remaining packets and place them carefully in the cedarwood box, closing the lid. I draw from my pocket the ribbon to which the key is attached and lock it.

I lie on my bed thinking for some time—long enough for dusk to fall—before finally I rise, make my way over to a chair, and ring for Sally.

"This can be put away now."

"You've finished, then?"

"I have."

"And was it any use, all that reading?"

"I can't tell for certain yet. But I doubt it."

She frowns, as if to say, "I told you it wouldn't answer," but wisely keeps this to herself. "I'll have it put away directly."

I nod, as if I've hardly heard her. I'm too dazed by everything I've read to think clearly. Instead, I rise stiffly from my chair, close the curtains, and ask for candles to be brought in. A little later, I take off my clothes, unpin my hair, and dose myself with as much laudanum as I hope will send me soundly to sleep for a night and a day.

When I emerge from my stupor, I summon Sally to dress me. She helps me into my dressing gown, seats me at my dressing table, and stands there, brush and comb in hand, waiting to begin upon my hair. My reflection stares back at me, and I can't say I like what I see. I was fifty-one recently, and what woman of my age stares into a glass with any pleasure? Well, I'm used to that daily disappointment. But today something strikes me beyond the familiar lines and gray hair—there's a defeated expression about me that I don't care for. It suggests only too clearly the depression of spirits that has descended upon me since I finished the letters. I observe the concern in Sally's expression and know she's seen it too. I doubt she'll waste much time before asking me about it.

I count three, or perhaps four, brisk strokes of her brush before she speaks.

"I can see you're unhappy. It's exactly as I feared. The letters have upset you."

"Yes, I should have listened to your advice. There's something very melancholy in contemplating them."

"They brought you no comfort, then?"

"Not of the kind I'd hoped for. So many thousands of words—but no one thing I could fix upon to settle my mind. No telling paragraph, no single line that'd allow me to say to myself, 'Ah, that's what he truly felt.' No great declaration to help me understand what it all meant. Nothing like that at all."

"Did you really expect to find anything of that nature? I warned you not to rely upon it."

"I know. I suppose I suspected you were right, but I hoped against hope there might be something. Well, I was wrong. The letters had nothing to tell me except what I already knew. I loved, I lost, I suffered."

"And you endured. You mustn't leave that out."

"And really," I continue, "what do they amount to in the end? Nothing more than the sad story of one woman's life."

"You say that as though it's a small thing."

"I'd certainly hoped for something more significant."

Sally puts down her brush.

"Then perhaps you should think again. Not many of us are offered the opportunity to see our lives in full, as it were. We don't have the time for reflection. We go on from day to day and leave no trace behind us of what we thought or felt. But those letters—they offer you the chance to see everything in the whole. And that's no small thing."

"I don't see how that will be of any service to me."

"You said when you began upon all this that you hoped for understanding. I think you'll only arrive at that, not by dismissing what you've read—but by turning it over in your thoughts, taking it to your heart, and reflecting upon it. If you give it time, a shape will emerge—it will come to mean something—and when it does, hold on to it in your mind—for that, I think, is your best hope of finding peace."

She picks up her pins and begins to put up my hair.

"After all," she goes on, "it's only by telling our story to ourselves that we finally make it our own. Or so it's often seemed to me. How often have you heard someone give an account of some matter in which you were both involved, and said to yourself, 'No, that's not how it was,' and longed to set down the truth as you saw it? Well, I suppose that's what I'm urging upon you. The chance to make sense of what happened as you saw and felt it."

I've known Sally for so long that I'm no longer surprised by the sharpness of her mind or the acuteness of her perceptions; and the more I consider her words, the better sense they make. Over the next few days, I allow her advice to mature in my mind, considering it this way and that until I'm persuaded that I understand what's required. I let my thoughts develop at their own pace, drawing on everything I've read in the letters, and little by little, something slowly begins to emerge.

Sally would have called it a story. I prefer to think of it as a series of reflections, but however it's named, I know immediately what it represents—nothing less than my attempt to understand the defining experience of my life—my long affair with Granville. It's as close a reckoning with my past as anything else I'm likely to arrive at. And here it is, for what's it's worth—here is the story I tell myself when I ask once again what it all meant.

From my earliest days, my affections were always very strong—and I believed, largely unrequited. I felt I came first with no one—not with my parents, not with my husband—not even with Georgiana once she met Bess Foster. I longed for a connection with another soul so powerful that it'd erase those memories forever, joining us together with such passionate intensity that I'd never need to ask again what true love looked like. In Granville, I thought I'd finally found it—and the intensity of my response to that discovery turned my life upside down. I wrote once that I loved him to distraction—and I see now this was perhaps the best description I ever found of what my passion did to me. It picked me up, shook me about, and turned me inside out until I hardly knew myself. I turned my back on all the better qualities I admired—loyalty, duty, honesty—replacing them with a burden of guilt and shame I carry to this day.

I surrendered many other things, too—not least a spirit of independence, which I once thought central to my character—and did so with only passing regret, because I believed my obedience brought me closer to him, made me more his own. Did I give up too much? Perhaps so. I was never proud of my abject professions of submission, but some dark part of myself saw desire in his demands that I submit to his authority, and I never could resist the prospect of making him love me more. For seventeen years, he was everything and all to me, as necessary to life and happiness as food, drink, and sunshine. I was only truly happy in his presence. His smile made me bloom with joy, like a flower on a warm day. His slightest touch turned me to water. Yes, I loved him to distraction—that's exactly how it was.

And what did he feel for me? Did he ever return my passion in equal measure? At the beginning, I think he did, when he was very young and before I was conquered and abject in his arms—then his feelings were just as powerful as my own. Later—well, I'm not so sure. He was never a man much given to endearments—the language of love was not often to be heard on his lips. He either couldn't or wouldn't shower upon me the affectionate words and loving declarations I longed for—does he, I wonder, find it easier to favor Harryo with them? But he used to say, 'You should judge what I feel not from what I say but by how I behave'—and by that measure, I felt more confident of his commitment. I knew of course that there were other women—but none was ever serious enough to make him give me up. There were so many occasions on which he might have put an end to things—not least on his many sojourns abroad—but he never did. He always came back to me, in a way that was not usual in our world. When we began, there were several secret affairs in our circle, but none of them endured as ours did. Our affair lasted longer than many marriages. Something kept him tied to me for so long a time, even if he was reluctant or unable to give it a name.

And as to the way we parted—well, his letters reminded me only too clearly that I'd always known, right from the very beginning, how it would end. My situation and my age conspired against any other conclusion. It was impossible that our relations could ever have been put upon a more acceptable footing. While the years that stood between us were no disincentive to our being lovers, it would have been very different if we'd ever married. As Granville's worldly and experienced mistress, I was a prize to be celebrated—as his much older wife, I should have been ridiculed and despised. I'm proud now that I held out against his insistent demands that I should leave Lord B and marry him. Think how angry he'd be now to find himself still shackled to me. I knew the rules of the game, and so I understood that there could be no happy ending for me.

So why, with all that I knew, did I not call a halt to an entanglement that could only make me suffer? God knows I tried—the letters bear painful witness to the efforts I made to conquer my desires, and to the misery that overwhelmed me when I failed. I simply wasn't strong enough. I wanted him too much to resist. I was only too aware of the risks I took, of how I gambled not only with my own peace of mind but with the happiness of all those I loved—but I went ahead, regardless. Nothing, it seemed, could deter me. Years ago, at Chatsworth, an old friend used to tell me that I was in love with ruin—and I wonder now whether he was right. I think I was seduced by that feeling that sometimes comes upon you when you walk very close to the edge of a cliff—when you look down into the sea below, with the waves crashing upon jagged rocks—you know you should step away to safety, but another voice in your head urges you to throw yourself into the void—and nothing feels more seductive in that moment than to comply. I often sensed in myself that pull to destruction. I think I danced with danger so regularly that it became second nature to me. It was almost as if I abandoned everything sensible, circumspect, and rational when I gave in to my love for Granville.

Well, I've certainly been punished for it. I suffered terribly over the years, in both mind and body, for the choice I made, driven almost mad by jealousy and prostrated by despair. The horrors I endured in giving birth to our children almost killed me.

It's impossible that I'd remember all this without feeling a great deal of remorse and regret; indeed, it's only right I should do so, for I often acted very wrongly. But I can't deny I have other feelings, which don't reflect so well on me. I can never forget the transporting, joyous exhilaration I felt as Granville's lover. I don't mean by this only the intimate pleasures I enjoyed in his arms, revelatory as they were; no, every encounter with him, whether physical, sentimental, or emotional, was touched with delight for me. My adoration of him was absolute; and when I felt my love returned, I existed in a haze of happiness such as I believe few people ever know.

When I ask myself whether I should have preferred a quieter existence, tied to some unexceptional man, with only the mildest attachment to sustain me, I know that would never have been enough for me, that I'd always prefer the extremes of a great passion over the steady dullness of mere liking. That was and, I fear, still is, the ruling conviction of my heart. So if I was asked by some benevolent fairy whether, by a single wave of her wand, I wished to experience all that had passed between Granville and me again—I'd like to think that, knowing what I do now, I'd be sensible enough to refuse her offer. But I'm only too aware that I'd never do so. My darker self, the part of me that craves passion and danger and thrives on the most extreme emotions—she'd be shouting yes, yes, yes, before the fairy had time to change her mind.

This, then, is the story—for perhaps Sally's term is the right one after all—which I've settled upon as mine. I don't doubt that Granville's, were he to tell it, would be very different; but I obeyed Sally's injunction to make mine my own. And just as she predicted, it has, to my surprise, consoled me a little. I cannot say exactly why that is. Perhaps the knowledge that I couldn't ever bring myself entirely to regret our connection has had some bearing on my mood. Whatever the cause, I cannot deny I'm calmer. I wouldn't say I'm happy—but then I never expected that. I am, at the very least, neither so sunk in despair nor so angry—with Granville, with the world, with myself— and that, I tell myself, must suffice for now.

82

Some weeks later, I receive a letter from him. We still correspond—not as often as we did once, and without that intimacy which was once the defining character of everything we wrote. It's no more than a few lines. He'd like to come and see me—can I suggest a time? This is unusual—we rarely meet alone now. Of course I agree. I promise myself I won't be too excited—I'll treat it as I would any other visit; but as the day approaches, my resolve crumbles. I bustle about, hunting down a favorite shawl, my prettiest shoes. I discuss with Sally what I should wear and how she should dress my hair. I cannot bear he should look upon me and be surprised. I'm very gray now, and no thinner than I was, but I think at times I can still conjure up an air of majestic stateliness. Certainly, men still pursue me—old ones, young ones, even long-standing friends such as Lord Holland, who takes every possible opportunity to flirt with me. But I've only ever wished to please one man—and even now, after all that's happened, that hasn't changed. Sally is a reluctant participant in all this primping and doesn't approve of our meeting, any more than she did of my reading his letters.

"I hope he hasn't come to disturb you again, just as you were becoming a little more settled. I shall think very badly of him if that's the case."

I know it's concern that prompts her to speak in this way—she's afraid our encounter will send me back to where I was, speechless with suffering, beside myself with grief. Once, I would have feared that too; but I am truly calmer now. I'm fairly sure I won't disgrace myself or embarrass him; and I'm very curious to discover what he wishes to say. At the same time—yes, I'll admit my heart beats a little faster at the thought of seeing him. I can't help it—but I'm determined not to let it show.

When he walks into the drawing room, however, I'm obliged to breathe a little deeper to steady my nerves. He's still so beautiful. He'll be forty this year—but time has hardly touched him at all. Still the same tall, slim figure, the same thick, curly, dark hair through which I loved to run my fingers when he allowed it. A first hint of gray at the temples, perhaps? Certainly a few lines around those blue eyes—but nothing to dull their extraordinary brightness. It's as hard to stop looking at him as ever it was; but I won't falter.

We're formal and polite to begin with, exchanging small talk. I'm surprised to see that he's no more at ease than I am. Thinking to turn the conversation to a subject close to his heart, I ask after Harryo—her second child is due later this year.

"I hope she's well?"

"Yes, she seems so at the moment. The doctors have told her to rest, which she doesn't much like."

"It can be a tedious time, all that waiting. I remember it well."

His eyes meet mine. He pulls his chair a little closer.

"Harriet, I'm here, in part at least, at her request. She's been turning over in her mind a subject of great importance to us all. Something has occurred to her—she's asked my opinion on it—and I think it a good enough idea that I've agreed to put it to you."

I shiver a little, sit up straighter, and try to remain composed.

"You'd better do so, then."

"Harryo wishes to have Little H to live with us, to be brought up among our family."

I am so shocked I have no words. This was the very last thing I'd expected from him.

"She'd be treated exactly like our other children, with every kindness and consideration. This comes only from the most generous feelings on Harryo's part. She honestly wishes to improve Little H's situation."

"Well. I see."

It's the most I can find to say. I take a deep breath.

"This is quite a surprise to spring upon me."

"Yes—but I thought it best to be direct."

Suddenly, the words tumble from me. "Do you think her current situation so very bad? I've always done my best for her. She's known nothing but love from me, and I've kept her as near to me as I dared—she's never been neglected or ignored. Please don't let me hear you say I've failed her."

He leans toward me, all concern now.

"No, that's not what I mean at all. I know you love her—that you've done everything in your power to care for her—and you've succeeded admirably; no one could have done better. But think a little. You pass her off as the child of a friend who couldn't raise her—one you care for out of charity. And it's worked well enough so far. No one has asked too many questions, though there must be some who suspect the truth. But she's twelve years old this year. How long can she continue as she is, hidden away from the world? How can you send her out into society? Whom will she marry? Once she's a woman, what must become of her?"

I'd imagined, before we met, that there was nothing else he could say that could possibly make me cry, that I'd shed enough tears in front of him to last a lifetime; but I was wrong. He's touched me in a very tender place. Fear of what the future holds for our children is never far from my mind. It stalks my thoughts at night when sleep won't come and haunts my dreams when it does. Once they're grown, how will they be provided for? Who'll protect them, guide them, assist them? George's path will be the less precarious, for young men, even those of similarly uncertain parentage, have more opportunities than their sisters. I've imagined some liberal profession for him, the law, or perhaps the Church, or even the army, if his inclinations go that way. But even then, his prospects can never be as bright as those of his legitimate counterparts, for whom can he rely upon to act as his patron, to whisper in the right ears and pull the proper strings when such assistance is required?

But Little H's position is infinitely worse. A young girl of her background has nothing to look forward to as a means of support but marriage; and as things are, she's unlikely to attract a suitor of any distinction. She has no money; and, as she's kept so much in the shadows, all her pretty ways and sweetness of character are seen by no one but myself. Although Granville continues to support both Little H and George, I am their chief protector, their only real connection with the wider world.

And what would happen if I died? I'd already seen for myself the very worst fate that could await her. When Lord B and I made our great tour to Scotland and Ireland, we'd stopped on our way north at Hawick, the country house of the Grey family. We were introduced to everyone except one poor girl, who remained in the background, neither quite family nor yet a servant, her face a picture of melancholy, her whole demeanor conveying uncertainty and trepidation. I understood immediately that she was Eliza, my sister's illegitimate daughter. Lord B, who knew nothing of her story, later asked me whether she was the governess. It's an image that's haunted me ever since, the outcome I most dread for Little H. I couldn't bear to imagine her, fallen somehow through the cracks once I was gone, exiled to a place where nobody loved her, all her lively affectionate nature snuffed out, her eager innocence crushed by the ambiguity of her position.

"If she comes to us," Granville continued, "she'll live openly among all her relations. Harryo will introduce her to Morpeth's daughters so that she'll have friends and companions of her own kind. Everywhere we go, she'll come with us. She'll be seen and, I hope, appreciated in a way that's impossible now. And sooner or later, she'll be respectably married. With our support, that's not just possible but likely. Family acknowledgment is everything in these matters."

"When you say acknowledged, what do you mean? As your daughter?"

"I imagine that'll be the supposition, but I don't intend to make any great announcement. People may draw their own conclusions by our having her with us and treating her as one of our own."

"And what about me? What part am I to play in her future if all this comes to pass?"

"Well, at present, it is understood that she's my child—and that you, as my greatest friend, raised her out of affection for me—is there any reason to alter that supposition?"

"I suppose I had always hoped a time might come—when she's old enough to understand—when I could tell her the truth about who she is."

He pulls his chair a little closer to mine, very earnest now.

"Harryo is anxious that Little H shouldn't be told you're her mother. As she doesn't know this now, Harryo believes very strongly that it'd be unwise to tell her. It'll only confuse and unsettle her."

"So those are the terms of your offer—that I'm to be thought of merely as her friend and guardian—and not just for now—but evermore?"

"I wouldn't say never. Perhaps there may come a time—but not yet. Harryo honestly believes it's for the best. It'll be easier for Little H to form new connections, to think of herself as belonging more to us in this way."

I laugh. "That's exactly what I fear. If she doesn't know who I really am—if she doesn't feel herself tied to me by the strongest possible bond—what's to stop her drifting away from me, exactly as you've done?"

"No one wants that. Some regular arrangements can surely be made. I promise you, Harriet, this is an offer rooted in kindness, in wanting to do the best for our child. It isn't intended to hurt you."

"But how can it not?" I'm angry now, passionately so. "Don't you see it will break my heart? I've already lost you to Harryo—and now I'm to hand over our daughter into her possession as well? I'm to watch her take my place, raising our daughter, and never be allowed to say a word about what I really am to her?"

He reaches out and takes my hand, holding it tightly in his own.

"I know there's nothing greater that can be asked of you. And I'd never have suggested it if I didn't sincerely believe it's the best way to secure the future happiness of our children—for you should know, we'd take George in too, if Little H settles as we hope, and you're agreeable. And you must know, Harriet, that they'll be loved, valued, and cared for in every way exactly as you'd wish."

"But not by me." I'm sobbing now. "Harryo will be the source of all these advantages—she'll be the one they look to, for comfort and affection, for love. Not me."

"I'll be with them too. You always wanted that, I think. And you'd still see them—in a way not so different than you do today."

"No, Granville, it'd be utterly altered. Now I'm first in their lives. If I agree to what you propose, that'll never be the case again."

"I won't belittle what this requires of you. And I'll won't press you more than I've done already. I leave the decision to you. I understand the scale of the sacrifice—only you can decide if you think it worthwhile."

I stand up, suddenly, a little surprised by own decisiveness.

"I've heard enough. I think you should go now. Come back in an hour. I'll tell you then what I've concluded."

He's surprised but rises obediently and leaves me alone.

Once he's gone, I sink back in my chair and sit there frozen, trying to absorb all he's said. I understand there's no real possibility of my refusing; I knew that from the moment I heard what he proposed. What kind of mother would I be if I put my happiness before that of my children? I don't need an hour's reflection to tell me what I must do. Every rational thought, every intelligent impulse, assures me I am right; there is no other way. But my heart is another matter. For every one of those sixty minutes, I wrestle with my feelings, I fight, with all my strength, against the wicked desire to shout, "No, I cannot do it, I cannot give them up, I cannot bear another renunciation, it is too much, don't ask me to do what you know I cannot refuse!" I let it all wash over me, like a great storm, until gradually, it blows itself out. Then and only then, am I ready to do what I know I must.

I am tolerably calm when Granville returns. For a moment there is silence—then I make haste to speak first, before he can utter a word.

"I will do it. I don't think you'll ever know what it costs me, but my answer is yes."

Then I cry a little, for I cannot help myself, and he sits beside me and holds my hand again, and words tumble out of me, as if they will never stop.

"How could I refuse? I cannot tell you what it means to know they'll be safe—if anything should happen, if I should die, they will be safe. You would never have abandoned them, I'm sure of that, but to know this is done with Harryo's blessing—that she herself suggested it—that they're wanted and will be loved—I cannot tell you how it relieves my mind. To think they'll be brought out of the dark and not live hidden away—however it hurts, whatever pain I feel, how could I possibly deny them the very best gift they could be offered? How could I do that?"

"I knew you wouldn't. I couldn't have lived so close to you for all those years without understanding the true goodness of your heart. It is an excellent thing you do today, Harriet. I'm very proud of you."

How sad it is that after all this time—even in such circumstances—hearing him praise me makes my heart swell with a bitter joy.

"It is the last sacrifice I can make for our love. My last surrender."

"No one knows that better than I."

It's such a long time since we've been together like this, speaking with all our old accustomed intimacy. I fall so quickly into past habits that I find myself talking just as I used to do, as if we are still on our former terms. Perhaps it is this that emboldens me to pluck up my courage and speak frankly to him. I sense this is my last chance to ask anything I truly long to know, that we will never be as close as this again.

"You'll never guess how I've been employing my time. I've been reading your letters. All seventeen years of them."

He smiles. "Whatever could have made you begin upon so thankless a task? You always complained of them. Too stiff, too short, too lacking in life, color, feeling, in everything that made a correspondence worthwhile."

"I wasn't reading them for their style. I was trying to discover if you ever loved me. Really and truly loved me."

"Do you doubt that, then?"

"Yes, sometimes I do. Sometimes I did. It wasn't always easy to tell."

"And what have you concluded?"

"I haven't yet decided. Perhaps you should have the final say?"

"I told you once I owed some of the happiest times in my life to you. I think that still."

"I like to hear you say that. It's something to hold on to. Is there anything else?"

"In all the time we were together, I never had a thought, a worry, an impression of any kind at all—that I didn't confide to you. No one on earth knows me better. I opened myself absolutely to you. I held nothing back. Doesn't that sound like love?"

"Perhaps. Is there any more?"

"And in return, you formed me. Your taste, your judgments, your wit—even when I bridled against them, I learned something. I honestly believe I shouldn't be the man I am if we'd never met, never been together. I know our circumstances are different now, but you left a mark on me I'll carry forever. In that sense at least, you are always with me."

"Is that all?"

"You told me at the beginning of our affair how it would end. I didn't want to believe it at the time, and it took many, many years before I saw you were right. Perhaps I should have listened to your warnings. I might have had what I enjoy now—a settled life, a family, a home—ten years earlier if I'd done so. But I don't regret a single one of our years together, and I don't believe you do either."

I close my eyes, overwhelmed. When I open them again, I see he is standing, ready to go.

"That's really all I can say. Except for one final secret. You have my letters—well, I have yours—every one of them, going right back to Naples days. You needn't fear; they're quite safely locked away. No one knows of them but me. But my having kept them—and I have numbered them too, marked each one so that they'll never be lost or confused—that tells you something of what I feel—what I've always felt—doesn't it?"

He leans down to me just as he used to do and kisses me very softly on my cheek. I sit still, silently watching as he walks to the door.

"You've shown yourself today to be everything I knew you to be. I couldn't think more highly of you than I do at the moment. I'm proud to have been loved by you."

Then the door shuts gently, and I'm left alone.

83

$\mathcal{E}$verything moves quickly in the weeks that follow. When I explain to Little H what's to happen, she's apprehensive at first—but once she absorbs what it means, I see that she's delighted, full of barely contained excitement, eager for a change she understands can only be to her advantage. I can't say it doesn't hurt me as she chatters away, telling me how very much she hopes Granville and Harryo will find her pleasing, how she longs to meet the Morpeth sisters, how keen she is that everyone should like her; but I smile through my pain and assure her she need have no fear, for to know her is to love her, and that I'd never have agreed to send her if I wasn't convinced she'll receive the most affectionate welcome. It'll be terrible when I'm obliged to say goodbye, but the more I watch her, the more I'm sure I've made the right decision. She's been the light of my life since her birth; but I understand I can offer no greater demonstration of the depth of my feelings than to give her up.

It occurs to me, as I watch her writing lists of what she'll take with her on her journey—busily crossing things out, beginning again as new necessities occur to her—that perhaps this is how we may best judge the depth of our affections. The deepest love is never selfish—it will relinquish all that's dear to it if called upon to do so—regardless of what it costs in suffering and grief. If that's indeed the case—if the greatest measure of love lies in its willingness to surrender—I've felt the force of that truth more than most. I've made the greatest sacrifice, not once but twice, and have done so as willingly and courageously as lay within my powers.

Usually, such thoughts would agitate and distress me, but to my surprise, I am quite still and composed. Granville told me he was proud of me—I'd been so touched and grateful for his words—but it strikes me suddenly that they were no more than I'd deserved. I've done everything that was required of me and more. I've stood in no one's way, have cast no shadow over anyone's future happiness. I've caused no embarrassments, staged no dramas. I've hidden my misery, swallowed my pain. I haven't dishonored our love at its ending—and for that I have every right to feel pride.

And with that pride comes a little self-knowledge—and it is this, I think, that will carry me eventually through to some happier, calmer place. I finally understand that there was really no point in agonizing over whose passion was the more profound, or indeed, whether all I had endured was worth it—whether the ecstasies I enjoyed made up for the miseries I suffered. Love isn't a balance sheet, with columns under which debits and credits can be duly entered—with a final figure at the bottom, representing an answer of sorts. Love can't be weighed and judged in such a manner. I was never going to find any relief in attempting such an impossible calculation.

If I genuinely wish to live without regret, I must learn to trust my own heart to tell me what it all meant. I have earned the right to do so, God knows. And as Little H comes bustling toward me, ribbons in hand, asking which one she should take with her, the red or the green—I know exactly what I think. I loved Granville with every fiber of my being, and nothing can diminish that truth. I shall have the remembrance of that love always within me, and celebrate it, for it is not given to many women to enjoy such intensity of feeling as I've done. There was pleasure, and there was suffering, for in my circumstances it wasn't possible to have one without the other, but in time I'll learn to embrace both. I'll do my utmost never to regret what was, nor rue what might have been. And in doing so, I hope in time I'll have it in my power to be happy once more. I ruffle Little H's hair, and she smiles back at me, with Granville's bright blue eyes. I kiss her soft cheek and think no love is wasted that could create such a being as this; and in that moment, at least, I am content.

Afterword

Harriet never left Lord B.

In the years that followed, she was almost entirely absorbed in the lives of her children, especially that of her daughter Caroline, whose explosive affair with Lord Byron was perhaps the greatest scandal of its time. It was a great trial to Harriet, who feared she'd passed on to her daughter her own sad susceptibility to a dangerous passion; but in public she defended her as doughtily as her often fragile health would allow, even if she privately regretted the increasingly outrageous acts to which Caro's misery drove her. The affair brought an end to Harriet's long and sometimes ambivalent relationship with Lady Melbourne, who resented the humiliation of her son William, Caro's husband. When Byron finally rejected Caro, he began a long and flirtatious correspondence with Lady Melbourne, in which he hinted he'd have done much better to have chosen her as a love. Lady Melbourne, thirty-seven years his senior, implied he was probably right.

When not worrying about her daughter, Harriet turned her mind to the safety of her soldier son, Frederick. He'd distinguished himself in the Peninsular War fighting under the Duke of Wellington, had been badly injured, and was with the Duke once more at the battle of Waterloo. Harriet was in Switzerland with her family when she heard that Frederick had been killed. Shortly afterward, new reports suggested he was still alive, but not likely to recover from his wounds. Harriet set off immediately, leaving the others to follow behind. She crossed Europe alone in just seven days, braving every possible danger, before arriving in Brussels to nurse her son back to health. She'd never lacked courage, but this was perhaps the most extraordinary proof of her fearlessness.

In 1821, when she turned sixty, Harriet was traveling in Italy with Lord B, her son William, and William's young family. In Parma, her beloved grandson took a turn and died of fever. Harriet, who'd ministered tirelessly to the little boy, was devastated. By the time the grief-stricken party reached Florence, she was seriously ill herself, with a bowel complaint she was too weak to throw off. She died on November 11, with Lord B and Sally at her bedside. She asked to be buried beside Georgiana in Derbyshire, and it was Sally who accompanied her coffin all the way back to England.

Not long after Sally's return to London, two of Harriet's sons arrived at Cavendish Square. They asked Sally to produce the cedarwood box, which contained so many compromising letters. When she denied knowledge of its whereabouts, another servant admitted she'd seen it in Sally's room. The box was discovered, along with the key; and everything it contained was thrown into the fire and burned.

Lord B was heartbroken by Harriet's death. When she knew she was dying, she'd urged her son William to look after him once she was gone. He settled a generous pension on Sally and her husband and went to live with William and his family, where he stayed for another twenty-two years until his death at the age of eighty-three.

It was William who wrote to Granville from Italy to tell him of Harriet's death. Granville was so grief-stricken that he locked himself away for several weeks and refused any attempts to console him.

Despite this, his marriage to Harryo was a great success. They had four children together and kept their promise to raise Little Harriet and George with all the care and attention they lavished upon Granville's legitimate sons and daughters. As Granville's diplomatic career flourished, the entire blended family accompanied him in every posting—ultimately to Paris, the most prized ambassadorial role of all. Little Harriet was so successfully brought into society that she eventually married the heir to the Duke of Leeds. As a young man, George spent time in India and later acted as his father's secretary. They were said to be very good friends.

After Granville's marriage, Hester Stanhope left England and traveled to Athens, where she met Lord Byron, who described her as "that dangerous thing, a female wit," and complained that she had "a great disregard of received notions, in her conversation." From there, she went on to Istanbul, where she adopted Turkish dress. She had other lovers on her travels, but in 1814 she told a companion that Granville "was above all other men I ever saw." She eventually made her way to Lebanon, where she lived for many years, dying there in 1839.

When the playwright and politician Richard Sheridan lay on his deathbed in 1815, Harriet called upon him to say goodbye. He told her he planned to haunt her after his death; and when she asked how he could speak to her so cruelly, he told her he was determined she should remember him.

Sally Peterson died in 1860, at the age of ninety, in Derbyshire, probably close to where she'd been born.

Janice Hadlow, March 2025

Author's Note

In the years I've spent in Harriet Bessborough's company, I've become extremely fond of her, partly because I feel I know her so well. This is a tribute to her brilliance as a letter writer—she was a tireless correspondent who described everything that happened to her in highly entertaining detail. She tells her own story so engagingly and with so much candor that it's impossible not to enter into all her triumphs and difficulties. She's always a joy to read, writing in an easy, direct style, and endlessly fascinated by her own inner emotional life. A self-confessed romantic, she believed passionately that to experience true love, and know it returned, represented the highest form of human happiness, and her own shifting feelings and those of the people closest to her are the central preoccupation of almost everything she wrote.

I've been inspired by all that I've read, both by Harriet, and about her, but the interpretation in these pages is my own. Though based on real events, *Rules of the Heart* is a work of fiction in which I sometimes allow myself the freedom to imagine what Harriet might have thought and felt. Her extraordinary frankness, however, in describing the great love affair of her life, has offered me very clear paths to follow, and I've always striven to reach conclusions suggested by her own words and actions.

I hope readers encountering her for the first time will have fallen under her spell just as I did.

Anyone wanting to know more about her life should search out Janet Gleeson's *An Aristocratic Affair* (2006), a very readable biography which covers all aspects of Harriet's life. The two volumes of Granville Leveson-Gower's correspondence, published in 1916, include a large number of letters from Harriet, and can sometimes be found on secondhand book sites. Harriet's unpublished letters to Granville Leveson-Gower are held at the British Library in London.

Acknowledgments

I'd like to thank the British Library for so helpfully making available Harriet Bessborough's unpublished letters to Granville Leveson-Gower for me to consult.

I'm also extremely grateful to my editors for all the help they've given me during the writing of this book. I'm very much indebted to Madeleine O'Shea at Macmillan and Serena Jones and Micaela Carr at Henry Holt for all the invaluable advice and encouragement I've received from them. The meticulous work of Gillian Stern and copy editors Marian Reid and Jolanta Benal has also been much appreciated.

My agent Caroline Michel has been tireless in her support and matchless in her kindness, always there for me whenever I've needed her. My friend Claire Powell has been extraordinarily generous with both her time and her judgment, offering me an invaluable reader's perspective on the novel as it evolved. And, finally, a huge thank-you to my husband, Martin Davidson, without whose loving patience this book could not have been written at all.

About the Author

Janice Hadlow worked as a television producer and commissioner for most of her career. She graduated with a first-class degree in history from King's College London and has always been fascinated by the eighteenth century. She is the author of *A Royal Experiment*, a family biography of George III, Queen Charlotte, and their children. *The Other Bennet Sister*, her fiction debut, was named a best book of 2020 by *Library Journal*, NPR, and *The Christian Science Monitor*. It is currently in production as a drama for BBC television.

ALSO BY

JANICE HADLOW

"[A] great achievement." —JO BAKER, *The Guardian*

THE OTHER
BENNET SISTER

A NOVEL

JANICE HADLOW

THE OTHER BENNET SISTER

"Exceptional storytelling and a true delight."
**—Helen Simonson, *New York Times* bestselling
author of *The Summer Before the War***

HOLT